3/10/06

X

Pra___ __ R__ C_____

D0807055

"The hi-jinks of _____ ___ eroine
makes J___ _____

Bestselling Author of The Last Dance, Nan Ryan

"Fast-paced, sizzlingly sexy fun!"
USA Today bestselling author Karyn Monk

"JINXED is a wonderful addition to
any reader's library."
Romance Reviews Today

★★★★
"Ciotta scores in this wonderfully warm, witty and
sexually charged novel."
Romantic Times BOOKclub Magazine

Charmed
Beth Ciotta

Dedication,

For my mother-in-law, Marie Ciotta—a saucy heroine with strong beliefs and a heart of gold—and my father-in-law, Angelo Ciotta—a charming hero, WWII veteran-Iwo Jima survivor . . . and he's still fighting for noble causes. Once a Marine always a Marine!

Published 2004 by Medallion Press, Inc.
225 Seabreeze Ave.
Palm Beach, FL 33480

Copyright © September 2004 by Beth Ciotta

Cover Illustration by Adam Mock

Printed in the United States of America   Library of Congress
Cataloging-in-Publication Data

Ciotta, Beth.
   Charmed / Beth Ciotta.
      p. cm.
   ISBN 1-932815-04-X
   1. Women storytellers--Fiction. 2. Organized crime--Fiction. 3. Bodyguards--Fiction. I. Title.
   PS3603.I58C48 2004
   813'.6--dc22

                              2004023705

Acknowledgments

My thanks to:

Shelly (Michelle) Kutch for her invaluable tips on juggling and for allowing me to weave a couple of her real life antics into this story. You're one of a kind!

Cat Cody for her insight and advice on martial arts.

Mary Stella and Julia Templeton for critiquing my work and keeping me sane.

The specialty entertainers who brightened my life for several magical years during our stint at an Atlantic City casino. I've never laughed so hard in my life! Gwendolyn Crozier-Carole, Brooks Conner, John Crowe, Billy Damon, Carmy Diamond, Michael Dupris, Patricia Durante-Thomas, Sebastian Goldstein, Michael Hinman, Lin Houser, Shelly Kutch, Duane Leeds, Keith Marceski, Wendy Nichols, Jose Rivera, and Dale Varga . . . I'll cherish our friendship forever!

Author's Note:
Although this story takes place in Atlantic City, New Jersey, please note that the Carnevale Casino and Oz, the multi-entertainment facility, are purely fictional.

Charmed

Beth Ciotta

GOLD IMPRINT
MEDALLION PRESS, INC.
FLORIDA, USA

Chapter One

The Princess is in danger. TL4/CT1&3
Bogie

✱ Protection Specialist Colin Murphy memorized the subsequent address. He erased the text message from his cell phone, abandoned his watered-down Scotch, and left Charlie's Pub mulling over the cryptic directive. After a month of babysitting a delusional convenience store mogul followed by two weeks of downtime, life was about to get interesting again.

Stepping outside, he slid on his rimless Ray-Bans and buttoned his black leather blazer. It was sunny, but cold. Uncommonly cold for October. Historic Smithville, a small but trendy village of unique shops and restaurants, was deserted save for a few diehard boutique browsers and a group of bohemian teenagers storming "Java John's." Apparently locals and sightseers had opted for a trip to one of the nearby casinos, or to a mall or movie of their choice. Or maybe they'd decided to spend a lazy afternoon at home. Fireplace raging. TV blaring.

Then there was Murphy. He preferred the raging fireplace and blaring TV of Charlie's Pub with its familiar, informal atmosphere and the company of a bartender who knew when, and when not, to initiate a conversation. Murphy had never been one for small talk—a quality appreciated by ninety percent of his clients, a source of amusement to his select circle of friends.

The closest of those friends, a man he called brother, had just enlisted his help. The manner in which he'd received the request—the obscure lead—was typical Bogie, when Bogie was undercover. The meaning was clear—*watch her back*. The code, helpful, but vague.

Threat Level Four (TL4) indicated the principal was low profile but in possible danger of attack. Category of Threat: one and three (CT1&3) meant that her safety and emotional well-being were at risk. If he had to guess, he'd say he was dealing with a potential kidnapping.

The princess part he'd yet to figure out. What was a royal doing in Margate, New Jersey? Why was the FBI involved? Especially if she was "low profile" (indicating that she was of little international or diplomatic importance). Why didn't the agency trust the princess's own executive protection team? And why had Bogie, and not the SAC, reached out? Typically the Special Agent in Charge, if not an Assistant Director, contacted Murphy for freelance work.

He knew that Bogie would call with details at the first opportunity.

Maybe the principal wasn't a true royal. Maybe she was only indirectly involved in his current case. Maybe she wasn't involved in the case at all, but simply a friend of a friend, or a family member in trouble. With Bogie, a man who'd been obsessed with fighting crime ever since he'd devoured his first *Dick Tracy* comic at age six, anything was possible.

Processing the angles, Murphy fired up his black Jaguar—an excessive gift from an insistent, high-profile client—and pulled onto Route 9. Twenty-five minutes later he was in Margate, the ritzy shore community five minutes south of Atlantic City, the gaming mecca of the eastern seaboard.

The Princess is in danger.

Gambling debts? Loan sharks? Given Bogie's warped sense of humor, "Princess" could be a euphemism for "Rich Bitch." Wouldn't be the first time a pampered wife had taken desperate measures to hide excessive spending from an influential husband. That's *if* the princess had a prince. Or, indeed, a gambling problem.

The possibilities were extensive. All of them, given Bogie's line of work, criminal.

Murphy parked the Jag at the corner of Atlantic Avenue. Beach block. Not exactly the low-rent district. Bogie's address matched a three-story Victorian. Federal blue with pink trim. A colorful oddity wedged in between two rambling, white mansions. Pocketing his keys, Murphy eyed the decorative Halloween wreath on the screened porch door and the smiling jack-o-lantern on the front stoop. The pink Volkswagen Beetle parked in the driveway spoke volumes about the owner. Could the property be any more welcoming?

Expect the unexpected.

Even though he preferred to rely on his martial arts training, standard routine spurred Murphy to retrieve his Glock from a customized compartment beneath his dash. Weapon concealed, he approached the house, noting the obvious lack of security. No barrier walls or fences. No strategically placed closed-circuit television (CCTV) cameras, security lighting, guard dogs, or visible evidence of a protective team.

The curtains of every window were open indicating the residents moved about without fear of being watched.

Again, he wondered if this was personal. Not that it mattered. He'd snuff out the sun for Bogie, no questions asked.

Increasingly intrigued, Murphy scaled four cinder block steps to read the brass nameplates mounted above the mailbox. Luciana Ross, Sofia Marino, and Viviana Marino.

It was relatively safe to assume that all three of the residents were of Italian descent, two of them related. Aside from that he was clueless, and growing more curious by the minute.

No doorbell, so he knocked.

No response.

He twisted the knob expecting it to be locked. It wasn't. The lock was busted. Frowning at the women's lax security, he slipped inside a cramped screened porch. Three bicycles. Two steamer trunks. A mannequin. Easels. Canvases. Boxes brimming with assorted arts and crafts.

He navigated the absurd obstacle course still pondering the princess and Bogie connection.

A plaque reading "There's No Place Like Home" marked the main entrance.

He knocked.

The door swung wide open.

"Hi!"

Even through his sunglasses, her smile was as bright as her neon pink lipstick. Her dimpled cheeks shimmered. Her brown eyes sparkled. Her pixie face, decorated with artfully applied glitter and rhinestones, radiated pure joy and whimsy. A crystal tiara winked at him through an upswept mass of wild, golden curls. She wore a pale pink, floor-length gown—corseted bodice, the skirt a voluminous mass of stiff crinoline. A gown befitting a princess. A fairy-tale version anyway.

"Hello," Murphy said, hoping to hell she didn't expect him to add *Your Highness*.

"I'll be with you in a minute." She waved him inside the foyer and then turned and limped to the far side of what he assumed to be the living room. The only hints—a couch and a nineteen-inch television.

He moved into the obscenely cluttered room, sliding his sunglasses to the top of his head for a clearer look. Scattered stuffed animals. Piles of books, videos, and dog-eared magazines. A Hula Hoop. Pink-wheeled roller skates and a Twister game. Walls of theater posters and cartoon art. Broadway meets Nickelodeon.

To top things off, the place reeked of lemons and bubble gum. Could a man OD on sunshine and lollipops?

He focused on the princess, who was searching for something. Considering the disorganized state of the room, she could be looking forever.

"Where is it?" she mumbled to the underside of a chair, its style and color indistinguishable as it was heaped with bolts of multi-colored, multi-textured fabrics—all of them accented with glitter or sequins or some sort of metallic trim.

He sidestepped an overflowing sewing basket. "Can I help?"

She straightened, red-faced and winded, her tiara askew. "That would be great." She pursed her lips and her gaze darted from one pile to another.

She'd yet to focus on Murphy. Yet to ask him who he was or what he was doing here. He could be a murderer or a rapist, and yet she'd invited him in without hesitation. *No peep hole. No chain lock. No "Who's there?"* Just opened the door and invited him in.

If Bogie was right, if she was in danger, she was oblivious. For the moment, he allowed her the fantasy. "What are we looking for?"

"A glass slipper."

"You're joking."

"Well, it's not really glass. More like acrylic or plastic. Whatever, it's see-through." She hiked the hem of her gown. "Pretty, huh?"

Pretty *sexy*. Murphy admired her naked foot through the transparent pump. She stood lopsided, one shoe on, one shoe lost, her left heel elevated a good three inches above her right. Her toenails painted a frosty shade of pink. Cotton candy came to mind. "Where's your bedroom?"

She pointed to the staircase. "Second floor, third door on the right. But I already looked in there," she shouted after him in her little girl voice.

He did a visual sweep of the adjoining rooms, ascertained she was safe, and then jogged upstairs. He was back a minute later, glass slipper in hand. Navigating her bedroom had been amusing. He'd been particularly intrigued by her queen-sized bed. Or rather the rainbow assortment of underwear piled next to a colorful collection of teddy bears.

Tearing his mind away from her lingerie, he focused on the enigmatic princess. Stretched flat out on the floor, she groped under the sofa for her missing shoe. The hoop beneath her crinoline bowed up, allowing him a full view of her backside. Unfortunately, for him, she was wearing knee-length, ruffled bloomers.

The scene struck him as comical. This woman struck him as comical. Bogie's message did not. "Princess."

She whipped her head around. Though flushed, she looked exactly as she had when she'd greeted him at the door. Adorable. "You found it!" She bounced to her feet and hobbled toward him. "Where was it?"

"Under your bed."

She nabbed the shoe and slipped it on. "I could have sworn I looked there. Oh, well." She threw up her hands and breezed by.

Murphy followed her through a compromised dining room (sewing machine, dress dummy, spools of ribbon and lace) to an immaculate kitchen. Spotless stovetop. Untapped spice rack. A glass pantry stocked with cans of soup and jars of store-bought sauces. The lady's creativity, it would seem, did not extend to cooking.

"I can't thank you enough. Now I won't have to drive like a maniac to get to my gig on time. If Farrah's party hadn't gone overtime, I wouldn't be in this fix. Not that I'm complaining. My fault. I shouldn't have booked a double." She opened the refrigerator, pulled out a Lara Croft–Tomb Raider thermos, and handed it to Murphy. "This is the second time this week Sofie's forgotten her protein shake. Without Viv here to look after us . . . well, you don't want to hear about that."

Which meant "the Princess" was Luciana Ross. *Ah, the wonders of deductive reasoning.*

She prodded him back into the living room. "It was awfully nice of you to drive over here for Sofie. If she'd just eat the employee cafeteria food like the rest of us, but oh no, she thinks she's fat. She's not fat. She's brainwashed." She fluttered a hand toward a stack of fashion and celebrity magazines. "Poison, I tell you."

Murphy agreed, but didn't say so. He was still trying to figure out how in the hell he'd ended up with an action heroine thermos.

She continued to ramble while shrugging into a shaggy, ankle-length fake fur coat. *Grape Kool-Aid purple.* "I, on the other hand, care squat about high fashion."

Obviously, Murphy thought, as she snatched up a pink poodle purse. He watched in fascination as she hooked a Hula Hoop over one shoulder, a patchwork tote bag over the other. "Could you grab my May Pole? Thanks." Then she scrambled out the door.

It didn't surprise him that she hadn't asked him to shut it behind him, or God forbid, lock it. Regardless, he turned the inside lock and closed the front door tight before tackling the porch and its compromised outer door, a five-foot, ribbon-wrapped pole and a video game star thermos in tow. Hotfooting it down the steps, he slid his sunglasses back down. Anonymity was a true blessing on days like this.

Luciana Ross moved pretty fast for a woman in a ball gown and heels. When he reached the driveway she was stuffing herself into the driver's seat of the pink Beetle. Layers of crinoline puffed up and over the steering wheel. She didn't seem to notice. She used her right hand to key the ignition, her left to gesture to the pole in Murphy's hand. "Just slide it in the back."

He did. Along with the thermos. She'd be none the wiser. The back seat of her car was as cluttered as her house. He reached through the open front window, past layers of lacy pink poof, and shut off her car.

"Hey!"

"We need to talk, Ms. Ross."

She winced. "Please don't call me that."

Okay. But he wasn't going to call her "Princess" either. He needed to get her head out of the clouds long enough to explain his presence. "Luciana—"

"Lulu," she said with a smile. "Viv's the only one who calls me Luciana and that's only when I'm in deep doo."

As in shit? What planet did *Lulu* live on anyway? Murphy raised an eyebrow. "As a matter of fact—"

"I'd love to talk, but I'm late. Maybe another time." She reached for her keys.

He closed his hand over hers, conscious of her delicate bones, satin-smooth skin, and the mouthwatering scent of tangy lemons. He had the damnedest desire to flick his tongue over her pulse points. Highly inappropriate given she was the principal. *Translation: Hands off.* "It's important."

She blinked at his possessive grasp. "Listen Mr. . . ."

"Murphy." Sensing he'd alarmed her, *finally*, he released her hand, bent forward, and braced his palms on his thighs, putting himself at eye level with the woman. He hadn't decided yet whether to thank or curse Bogie for sticking him with this clueless ball of energy. Instinct told him she was going to be a handful. The convenience store mogul might have been a pain in his ass, but at least he hadn't triggered any sexual awareness.

"Mr. Murphy—"

"Just Murphy."

The left corner of her mouth quirked up. Flecks of iridescent glitter sparkled on her pronounced cheekbones. "Okay, *Murphy*. Whatever problem you're having with my sister, I can't help. Sofie has a mind of her own when it comes to men and relationships. Nothing I can say or do will give you an edge on any of her other boyfriends."

She shooed him away from her car and revved the engine. "I can tell you one thing. She tires quickly of pushovers. Next time she asks you to run an errand, tell her you're busy."

And with that she stepped on the gas, leaving Murphy in the dust.

Or so she thought.

Chapter Two

✳ When was Sofie going to stop toying with men's affections? Lulu cranked up the car's heater and sighed. One day her sister's outrageous flirting and string of affairs were going to catch up to her. One day she'd meet her match and then she'd be in deep doo. Sofia Marino, the youngest descendent of the famous theatrical Marinos, was hot-blooded, ambitious, and irresistible to the opposite sex. When like met like—BOOM!—beware of fireworks.

Lulu glanced in the Bug's rearview mirror and adjusted her tiara. Speaking of fireworks, she'd experienced a few sparks when Murphy, the poor besotted slob, had touched her hand. She didn't know who was more pathetic: him or her?

No, wait. Definitely her. She'd bet her Austrian crystal jewels Murphy wasn't sexually deprived. He was, after all, dating her sister.

So where was this one from? Philadelphia? New York? With his dark jeans, maroon crewneck, and stylish leather jacket, he had a hip look about him that suggested he was in the business. Sofie usually stayed away from actors as they were stereotypically self-absorbed and Sof, herself, craved enormous attention. Murphy didn't strike her as needy. The man hummed with quiet confidence. Maybe he was the screenwriter her sister had been emailing. Or that cameraman she'd mentioned hooking up with on her last commercial shoot. Although hadn't she raved about his beautiful, long black ponytail? Murphy had a salt and pepper buzz cut à la George Clooney. S-e-x-y. Not that she'd noticed.

Actually, she *had* been oblivious at first. She'd been preoccupied with finding her shoe, memorizing the details of Molly McGuire's personalized fairy tale, and hitting the road on time. She'd rather stick a needle in her eye than to be late for a child's birthday party. You only turn five once. Sofie often joked that the sun could explode and Lulu wouldn't notice if she were "in the zone."

Only she wasn't "in the zone" now, thanks to Murphy. He'd wrapped his warm, strong hand over hers, breaking her concentration and rousing physical desires she'd thought comatose. One heart-jolting touch and she'd been ready to rip off his clothes and tackle him in the driveway. In broad daylight. At least that's the way the racy scenario had played in her brief fantasy.

Rudy and Jean-Pierre would be so proud.

Her meddling friends constantly urged her to explore her sensual side. Rudy Gallow, a man who'd spent the last few months with his nose stuck in a growing library of self-help books, was especially committed to helping her discover the joy of a healthy physical relationship (stress on the word healthy). Even more so than her buttinski sister. *That* was saying a lot.

But Lulu had been so shocked by her burst of sexual interest, that instead of flirting with Murphy, she'd raced away from him as though he were the devil. Which in a sense he was. Tempted by her sister's boyfriend. How wicked was that?

Focus on Molly McGuire's loonytale. Get into character.
Focus.

She merged onto the Garden State Parkway heading north and stepped on the gas. Soon she'd be surrounded by little children and everything that was good in life. *Focus.*

She drummed her fingers on the steering wheel.

Maybe Sofie met Murphy during one of her shifts at the casino. As a scantily-clad greeter-girl she rivaled the poker tables in attracting male gamblers. In the four weeks that she'd been employed at the Carnevale, the exotic, mocha-skinned brunette had racked up an astonishing total of proposals, only half involving marriage.

Given her sister's unique beauty and innate talent, it boggled Lulu's mind that she'd failed in her attempts to secure a major Broadway role. Sure she'd landed supporting roles, several cable infomercials, and had even enjoyed a stint as a QVC spokesperson, but major stardom eluded her. Credible roles had dwindled this past year along with her bank account. Though Sofie would never admit it, Lulu knew the moment the ambitious actress had reached her emotional limit. The phone call in which she had griped, "If I could just lose ten more pounds" had prompted Lulu to take control.

Enough was enough.

She'd immediately guilted her little sister into moving back into their grandmother's home for the winter. "Viv's in Florida for the next several months," she'd said. "It'll be good for both of us. I could use the company and you could use the financial break. You can work part-time at the Carnevale Casino like me, and zip up to Manhattan for prime auditions."

When Sofie balked, Lulu played the sympathy card, crying loneliness and depression. Her ex-husband, Terry Ross, had moved to Chicago with his girlfriend, and their grandmother Viv had temporarily transplanted to Orlando to "reminisce" with an old boyfriend. It wasn't entirely a lie. She *had* been lonely. But mostly she'd been worried that if Sofie didn't get out of Manhattan fast, her insecurities and the competitive acting market would eat her alive.

Funny, Sofie considered Lulu the vulnerable one, but Lulu knew without a doubt that beneath her baby sister's tough exterior beat an ultra-sensitive heart. As restless and driven as her sister was, she also knew Sofie would soon tire of living down at the shore. If she'd just stay long enough to recharge, Lulu would feel a heck of a lot better about her leaving. Surely the attention she was getting at the Carnevale was boosting her confidence. Sofie adored flirtatious men and reveled in witty, sexual banter.

Not Lulu. Although enormously popular in her role as Gemma the Juggler, *she* couldn't wait until the day she could afford to quit the adult playground.

Then stop daydreaming and focus on your real passion. Get into character. Focus!

Miraculously, by the time she hit the cookie-cutter housing development, parked the Bug, and knocked on the McGuire's front door, she was firmly back in the zone.

"Princess Charming!"

Fifteen girls, ranging in age from four to six, stampeded Lulu. Grinning ear to ear, she reveled in the delightful assault. Several hugged her while others stared up in awe. All of the girls "oohed" and "ahhed' over her latest creation—a shimmering pink gown inspired by Glenda the Good Witch from *The Wizard of Oz. Thank you, Jean-Pierre for the sequined trim and daisy appliqués!* Her friend, and costume designer extraordinaire, was right. The extra glitz and whimsy made a definite impression.

Six boys huddled at the opposite end of the McGuire's spacious living room. The younger ones too shy to approach;

the older ones too cool to care. Lulu wasn't worried. She'd win them over with her wizard sticks, her creative answer to the girly magic wand. She hadn't met a boy yet who wasn't a sucker for her wizard stick.

"I'm Molly!" a red-haired girl exclaimed. She was tall for her age, plump with baby fat and cute as a kitten. She wore a frilly white and yellow dress, yellow tights, and white sneakers with (surprise) yellow laces. Her ponytail, held high on her head by a yellow satin scrunchie, drooped to the left.

"It's her birthday," two other girls said.

"Indeed," Lulu said, affecting a British accent. " `Tis why I am here." She bent at the waist, coming eye to eye with Molly. " `Tis a very special day. And you," she winked, "are a very special girl."

"Princess Charming."

This time the voice was adult. Molly's mother. Lulu had never met Mrs. McGuire face-to-face. They'd conducted their business over the phone. But she recognized the voice, not to mention the way she was looking at Molly with motherly pride.

"Go into the family room, kids," she said. "I need to speak to the princess."

The boys hightailed it. The girls didn't budge.

"I'll be along shortly," Lulu promised. "And have I got a surprise for you!"

The girls squealed in delight and skipped after the boys.

Mrs. McGuire smiled. "Molly's been looking forward to this all week. She fell in love with you at Lisa Hadley's party last February. It's such a shame Lisa came down with the flu this morning. She cried buckets when she realized she was going to miss you."

"Please give her my best," Lulu said, scrambling to put a face with the name. This year she'd appeared at nearly a hundred parties. After a while names and faces blurred. Not to mention her memory was less reliable than her seventy-two-year-old grandmother's. Which is why she kept detailed files. Repeat calls and referrals constituted most of her free-lance work.

"I know once you get started I don't stand a chance of getting you alone, so I thought I'd square things with you ahead of time." She handed Lulu a folded check. "Could I bother you for some business cards for the other mothers? It's extraordinary what you do with these children. Getting them involved. Encouraging their imaginations. Teaching morals. And the personal *storybook*!" She squeezed Lulu's hand. "I can't wait to see Molly's."

"I think she'll like it."

"I know she'll love it."

Lulu fidgeted. "Thanks." No matter how often a parent gushed over her loonytales, she still got embarrassed. She'd never been comfortable with compliments, but that didn't mean she didn't appreciate the kind words. They reminded her of why she continued to pursue a stressful, financially unstable career. Making a positive difference in impressionable children's lives was worth the occasional cancellation, bounced check, or obnoxious client.

She stashed the payment in the side pocket of her patch-work prop bag, dug out a handful of business cards, and passed them to Mrs. McGuire. If she was lucky, she'd book three to four future engagements based on this evening's performance.

What she wouldn't give to be able to support herself solely on *Lulu's Loonytales*. Unfortunately, since she refused any sort of financial support from Terry, she now had to supple-ment her freelance business with the part-time job at the Carnevale. In addition to the steady income, she needed the health benefits. Thank goodness she'd inherited her grandfather's talent for circus skills. She'd watched, learned, and practiced at an early age, and therefore, she was proficient at juggling balls, torches, and clubs.

The Carnevale had been thrilled to welcome her into their strolling entertainer program. She'd been there nine *looong* months. It wasn't the job that she resented, but the revealing costumes the specialty performers were required to wear. It was one thing if you were a cast member of Venetian Vogue, the featured variety show in the casino's showroom. There was a big difference between appearing on the main stage, where that imaginary fourth wall separated you from the audience, and performing your act in public areas, where patrons assumed they had unlimited heckling privileges. Day after day she endured catty comments from petty women and the stares of rude men. The worst were the sexual innuendos pertaining to her juggling. If she had a nickel for every time a man had said, "I've got a couple of balls you can handle," she'd be a flipping millionaire!

She blamed Anthony Rivelli. The former casino vice president had set a precedent embracing the not-so-original motto "sex sells." Even though the Casino Control Commission had demanded Anthony's resignation due to a personal scandal, the casino had retained his policies. The current powers-that-be didn't care that juggling required mobility. They didn't care that her boobs almost popped out of her sequined corset at least once daily. They cared that the Carnevale was the highest ranking casino in Atlantic City, largely due to its aggressive, T&A entertainment campaign.

Some days she felt like cheap eye candy instead of a talented performer. Thank goodness she only had to sell out three days a week.

A burst of girlish giggles reclaimed her attention, reminding her that this was not one of those days. Today she was in her element. In her glory. Today was devoted to young minds and pure hearts yet untainted by the cynical world. Focused and energized, she smiled at Mrs. McGuire. "I should probably get in there."

"You go on," the woman said. "I'll slip into the kitchen and let the other mothers know you're about to start. The loonytale takes an hour, right?"

Lulu nodded.

"We'll have cake after. I hope you'll stay."

"I wouldn't miss it." She usually stayed an additional half an hour anyway, free of charge for casual hang time with the kids. More than a gig, this was her contribution to mankind.

Adrenaline pumping, armed with her imagination and a bag full of magic, she hustled into the balloon and streamer filled room. Coming face-to-face with twenty-one expectant, sugar-crazed munchkins would have intimidated a normal grown-up. Lulu beamed. "I'd like you to meet a friend of mine," she said, looking up and to her left. "Dexter the Dragon."

An hour and forty-five minutes later, she said her good-byes.

Or tried to anyway.

Of the six boys who'd started out wary, three now wiggled their wizard sticks at their parents, hoping to turn them into frogs. The other three stood on the lawn, waving farewell to Dexter the Dragon, Princess Charming's invisible sidekick.

She had a devil of a time shaking the girls. They wanted her and Dexter to spend the night. She finally convinced them that Dexter would lose his ability to breathe fire if he didn't return to the Enchanted Forest before nightfall. The girls eyed the setting sun and then hurried the Princess and Dexter on their way.

Halfway to the corner, she experienced the icky sensation of being watched. She'd had a similar feeling a few times over the past few weeks. It was ridiculous really. As a performer she naturally drew attention. If people *didn't* watch her she'd be unemployed. Still, this was different, the creep factor enough to give her the nervous prickles.

"Snap out of it," she grumbled, attributing the paranoia to an overactive imagination and exhaustion. The only thing she was in danger of was falling asleep at the wheel.

Just then a small voice screamed, "Wait!"

Lulu whirled to find Molly McGuire racing down the sidewalk, her cheeks sparkling with pixie dust, her hair braided with the royal ribbons of Loxley Castle. The little girl launched herself at Lulu and hugged tight. "I love you, Princess Charming."

Lulu's eyes misted as a lump the size of a juggling ball welled in her throat. It didn't get better than this. How many times she'd wished she had a child of her own to cherish. "I love you back, Molly." Children were easy to love. Children inspired joy and hope.

If only adults could be so pure of heart.

She pushed the bitter thought aside. No matter what Sofie lectured, she wouldn't blame her ex-husband when it was she who was flawed.

Forcing a smile, she kissed the top of Molly's head and then sent her back to her parents. Once the little girl skipped into the safety of her front yard, she lugged her May Pole and prop bag down the street and around the corner. It wasn't until she was sitting in her Bug that she let out a weary sigh. Mentally and physically drained, she looked forward to getting home, stripping off her costume and makeup, and soaking in an aromatic bubble bath.

She'd been crazy to book two loonytales in one day.

Between the driving, the costume changes, the personalized stories and games . . . This morning she'd been a mermaid, princess of the magic seas. This afternoon a fairy-tale princess of the enchanted forest. The McGuires had booked months ago. The Ditellis just last week. She'd tried to beg off, but Mr. Ditelli had been persuasive, saying that they'd only just heard about her and his little girl was set on an under-the-sea adventure with Princess Charming. How could she break the heart of a four-year-old? She'd convinced herself that, despite the added pressure and two hour round trip out of her way, it was worth the effort if only to see the smile on Farrah's face when she introduced her under-the-sea sidekick, Seymour the Sea Serpent.

Envisioning that bubble bath and a cup of French vanilla coffee, Lulu followed her scribbled directions in reverse and headed back toward the parkway. With today's loonytales behind her, she was finally able to relax. Once she merged onto the divided highway, she cranked up the radio and gunned the accelerator.

She was singing along with an old Cyndi Lauper song and zipping merrily south when she spotted the state trooper car sitting in the median. "Crap!" She took her foot off the accelerator and tried to slow down ever so discreetly, but the trooper had already flicked on his siren and peeled onto the highway. "Rats!"

Wondering how she was going to get out of this one, she turned off the radio (this girl was no longer having fun) and pulled over to the side of the road. She couldn't afford another speeding ticket. Another point on her driver's license and her auto insurance would skyrocket beyond her means.

Pasting on an innocent smile, she rolled down her window and blinked up at the stern-faced trooper. "Good evening, officer."

"Do you know why I pulled you over?" he asked in a deep, bored voice.

Why did they always ask that? Was there some clever answer? If so, she wished someone would clue her in. She twirled a renegade corkscrew curl around her finger. "Um, was I speeding?"

"Yes." Unsmiling, he checked his radar gun. "Seventy-eight in a sixty-five zone."

It was all she could do not to ask how many points that would be. It didn't matter. She couldn't afford even one. "Gosh. Really?" she asked in her best blonde-bimbo voice.

He held out his hand. "Could I have your driver's license, registration, and insurance card, please?"

Crap. "Sure." She dug the plastic coated IDs out of her poodle purse and passed them to him. Drumming her fingers on the steering wheel, she watched in the side mirror as he walked back to his car, climbed in, and conversed with his partner. Wait until they ran her name though the computer and got a load of her driving record. *Double crap.* She tensed when he walked back, leaned down, and returned her ID.

"You have quite a record, Ms. Ross."

She screwed up her face. "Please don't call me that." She'd been trying to revert to her maiden name for months. The legal process was proving painfully slow.

"Okay . . . Your Highness." The left side of his mouth lifted as he gestured to her crown. "Did you just win a beauty pageant or something?"

Yeah, right. At least he was intrigued. Maybe if she distracted him with conversation, he'd forget about the ticket. "Actually," she said, adjusting her tiara, "I'm a princess. A fairy-tale princess," she added before he assumed she was delusional, although she wasn't sure the embellishment helped. "I'm a professional performer."

"That so?" He glanced in her back seat, noted her props, and then thumbed up the brim of his official cap giving her a prime view of a pair of amused blue eyes. "What exactly do you do, Princess?"

"Interactive storytelling is my main gig." He looked unimpressed, so she added, "I also juggle."

His eyebrows rose. "You juggle?"

Bingo!

"What do you juggle?"

"Balls, torches, machetes, clubs. I'm pretty versatile." She had to be to compete with the other tri-state jugglers.

He straightened. "Would you mind stepping out of the car?"

What now? She opened the door and climbed out, resisting the urge to reach back in and grab her coat. Darn, it was cold, but her bulky, ankle-length coat would effectively conceal her pretty gown, and though she hated to stoop so low as to bedevil a cop to avoid a ticket, at this moment she had no pride.

He crooked a finger. "Follow me."

Oh, no. Was he taking her in? For speeding? Did she have more tickets than she realized?

When they reached the patrol car, the other trooper stepped forward. Between the uniforms, the guns, and their superior physiques, she supposed most people would be intimidated, or at the very least impressed. Most of her girl-friends, jeez, even Rudy and Jean-Pierre, went ga-ga for bulked-up crime fighters. Cops, soldiers, secret agents. Men trained in weaponry and hand-to-hand combat. Men who kick butt.

Violence, in Lulu's estimation, had been glamorized by Hollywood. The world would be a better place if people conducted their battles with words. Diplomats were sadly underrated. She smiled at the state troopers, totally unaffected by their macho personas.

Trooper number two braced his hands on his hips. "What do we have here?"

"A princess," his partner said. "Princess . . ." "Blue eyes" looked to her.

"Charming." She fluffed her pink crinoline skirt to keep from rubbing her goose-pimply arms. "But you can call me Lulu."

Both of the men smiled. "Blue eyes" spoke. "Lulu juggles."

"Really," said trooper number two. "Can you juggle something for us?"

Will you forget about the ticket? "I could," she said, "except I don't have any of my equipment with me." She'd stowed her clubs and balls in her locker at the Carnevale. Her rings were at home. "Wait," she said when "blue eyes" frowned. "I can get creative." Creativity was her middle name. She glanced at their utility belts, didn't figure they'd hand over their guns or batons, so she settled on an alternate suggestion. "Do you have three flashlights?"

"Just one."

She wasn't beaten yet. "It has batteries, doesn't it?"

The troopers laughed, and the next thing she knew she was juggling her heart out on the side of the Garden State Parkway and treating them to impromptu banter. "Check out this routine, boys. It's high energy, electrifying. This could really light things up!" Juggling flashlight batteries in a princess gown and a tiara. She had to look like an idiot, so she milked it for all it was worth, ending with a flourish. The things she'd do to avoid a speeding ticket, although this was way better than relying on her feminine wiles. That was Sofie's strength.

When all was said and done, they let her off with a warning. Today was her lucky day.

She stuffed herself into her Bug, waved good-bye, cranked the heater, and drove sixty-five mph the rest of the way home (even when the speed limit dropped to forty-five). Admittedly she had a short attention span, and before long she was thinking about fireworks and temptations instead of sirens and warnings. She was thinking about Murphy, and suddenly the car was racing as fast as her heart.

Chapter Three

❋ Murphy turned the corner in time to see his bubble-headed principal clipping a garbage can as she zipped her car into the driveway. He parked the Jag curbside, one house down. He'd easily tailed her north. The trip back had been more complicated. He'd had to drive past her when the trooper pulled her over for speeding. Luckily, there'd been a rest stop just ahead, and he'd been able to watch the proceedings through a pair of high-powered binoculars. He still couldn't believe it. The woman had juggled three flashlight batteries in a ball gown and heels, visibly charming the pants off two of New Jersey's best. *Un-freaking-believable.*

The princess had a lead foot, great hands, and, apparently, multiple talents.

She *really* had a way with children. He'd observed from a distance, his chest constricting when he'd witnessed an enthusiastic group hug on the front lawn–Luciana the center of attention. The scene had initiated a flashback to a time when he'd experienced a similar show of affection–from starving Somali children. Operation Restore Hope represented the best and worst of his military career. Sometimes even the purest of intentions went amiss.

The princess, however, had hit a home run. Whatever she'd done inside that house, she'd won the hearts and devotion of twenty-some little rug rats. Even the boys. *Impressive.*

She was a performer of some kind, obviously, specializing in children's parties. A character, like a Barney or Elmo, only cuter. "Princess Charming," he'd heard the little red-headed girl call her.

He wondered if she'd been "in character" when he'd met her this afternoon. He knew from experience that certain actors slipped into their roles the moment they donned a costume. That had been the case with the Hollywood diva he'd had the *privilege* of protecting during a controversial film shoot four years ago. Maybe that was the case with Luciana. That's why she'd been so bubbly. Bubbly suited a tiara and puffy pink dress. It also suited her nickname. She was a "lulu" all right.

She burst out of the tiny car, an explosion of pink netting and purple shag, with the stuffed poodle looped over her shoulder. He imagined her in street clothes, because somehow that made the assignment easier. If he was lucky, she smoked, drank, and swore like a hip-hop artist. *That* he could deal with. "Bubbly" was a stretch. He couldn't imagine any woman being that damned cheerful twenty-four hours a day.

Why would anyone want to hurt kiddy-heroine Princess Charming? It didn't make sense. He took off his sunglasses and hooked them over the visor, exploring another theory. Underneath that goody-two-shoes façade lurked a bitch on wheels. A woman who'd somehow pissed off the wrong people. *Wrong people* being Bogie's specialty. Normally, by now, he would've made a few calls. Checked into her background. But not knowing how she tied into Bogie complicated matters. Specifics would help.

For now, Murphy would have to play it by ear.

Dusk loomed, the sky fading from cool blue to dismal gray. Still, he had no trouble making out her form as she wiggled and shimmied, trying to maneuver her overstuffed tote bag out of the backseat. He lost his mind for a second and imagined her wiggling and shimmying out of that gown. Imagined her, of all things, naked.

Get a grip, man. She's a freaking kiddy-heroine. You don't do kids. You don't do women who carry pink poodle purses and live on Mars.

With a squeal she yanked the bulging bag free and shut the door with her hip. When she tried to step away, she faltered. A significant chunk of her skirt had caught in the door. He shook his head as she gingerly worked the fabric. Either she'd locked her keys in the car or she'd jammed the lock. She dropped the patchwork bag and bent down to jiggle the handle. That's when Murphy saw a dented blue Lincoln zip by and slide into a parking place a few doors down from Lulu's house. A squat, bruiser of a man wearing a rumpled suit and a long trench coat emerged with a box tucked under one arm, double-chin lowered, gaze intent on Lulu.

Shit.

Seconds later, Murphy was at her side. "Need some help?"

She yelped and straightened, her hands pressed to her corseted middle. "You scared the daylights out of me!"

Not quite as bubbly as earlier today, he thought, but still pretty damned chipper. Especially for an adult who'd just spent two hours entertaining a large group of little kids. Attention span: zero.

"Sorry." He placed himself between her and the suspicious subject who was now a few feet away.

What in the hell was in that box?

"Did you lock your keys in the car?" he asked, ready to drop the grunt when he finally diddybopped into range.

"No, I . . ."

"Lulu!"

She peeked around Murphy and groaned.

"You know that guy?"

"Sam Marlin. He lives at 111 Lark Street West. We're at 111 Lark Street East. Sometimes the delivery man confuses us."

That would explain the box. Still, Murphy held his position. Marlin was a suitable name, he decided. The man resembled a bloated fish.

Fleshy lips curled down in a bitter pout, rounded shoulders hunched, Marlin grunted and thrust a white cardboard box at Lulu. "Another one."

Murphy intercepted the package. "Thanks."

Lulu shot him a baffled look and then smiled at the Marlin character. "Yes, thank you for bringing it over, Sam." She studied the mailing label while giving her skirt another tug. "Hmm. No name, just *Girl of My Dreams*. No East or West, just 111 Lark. It *could* have been a gift for your mother. You have to admit, this time it wasn't entirely the deliveryman's fault."

"Mother doesn't have any admirers."

"How do you know?"

The man stuffed his hands in the pockets of his coat, once again pricking Murphy's unease. He'd once witnessed an innocuous civilian hauling an AK-47 from behind a billowing *Dishdasha*. Dangerous suspects came in all forms. "What about all the other times?" Sam asked with a sullen huff.

"No one's perfect," she said calmly.

Except maybe you, Murphy thought. *This guy was a prick. Lulu was not only patient, but kind.* There went his bitch theory.

"I called your number several times," Sam complained.

"Sofie and I were out all day."

"You're always out. And I'm always getting your packages."

"Not my packages," Lulu said. "Sofie's. And you're not always getting them. It's just that lately there have been more deliveries than usual, so it seems like a lot."

Sam's hands shot out of his pockets and up into the air. "That doesn't make any sense!"

"Does to me." Murphy pacified him with a bland smile. *Come on, dude. Make a move so I can kick your whiney-ass into the next yard.*

The man squinted his eyes and twisted his chapped lips into a snarl. "Who are you?"

"Sofie's boyfriend," Lulu said.

"Actually—"

"Another one?" Sam snorted in disgust. "Show people."

"Hey," Lulu said, looking devastated. "That's not nice. Just because Sofie wouldn't go out with you—"

"Stuck-up slut." He turned on his rubber soles and stomped toward his car, his drab gray coat billowing behind him.

"Sam Marlin, you take that back!" Fist raised, she lunged after him but her gown was still wedged.

Murphy caught her before she took a header, pointedly ignoring how warm and soft she felt in his arms. Of course, she felt warm and soft. She was cocooned in shaggy fake fur. Big-eyed and cute as hell, it was like holding a freaking stuffed animal. "Easy, killer. I think he was referring to your sister."

"I know." She blinked up at him, while batting away the curls that escaped her haphazard up-do. "Which is why I wanted to throttle him, not that I would have . . . actually. But I would have given him an earful . . . or something." Her voice trailed off as she continued to hold Murphy's gaze. He registered an unmistakable spark of interest in her long-lashed eyes just before she tensed and pushed out of his arms. "Actually, *you* should have handled him," she said, her voice jumping an octave. "*You're* her boyfriend."

"About that—"

"No wonder she wants to dump you," she mumbled, bending over and struggling with her gown. "She's never gone for wimps."

For a moment he forgot about the uncomfortable possibility that they might share a mutual attraction. Murphy *almost* laughed. A former Marine, he'd been called a lot of things, but never a wimp. He would have had no problem decking Sam Marlin if he'd made a threatening move on Lulu. "Where are your car keys?"

"It's not the lock, it's my dress. Somehow it jammed up the workings."

He sensed frustration and an underlying temper. *A glimpse of the real deal? Bring it on. Please, Jesus, insert some reality into this bizarre assignment.* He set the suspect package on the roof of her car and gave her a gentle nudge. "Let me have a look."

She straightened with a pout and folded her arms over her middle. "I can't believe he called her a stuck-up slut. She's not stuck-up."

Murphy raised one eyebrow and kept working.

"She's not loose either," she ranted on, answering his unspoken question. "She's just . . . social."

The lock popped and Murphy freed her gown.

"Thank you."

"You're welcome." He reached down and hauled up her patchwork bag. "Want the May Pole too?"

"No, thank you. I'll get it later," she said, her voice losing its edge.

By the looks of her backseat she'd intended to get quite a few things *later* and had forgotten. Her car was a toy chest on wheels. He shut the door, frowning when she made no move to lock it. Was she that trusting? Or that forgetful?

An old-fashioned yard lamp flickered on, bathing the princess in muted, for chrissake, pink. Her neon lipstick had worn off along with much of her glitter. Yet somehow she still managed to sparkle. The temper tantrum he'd hoped for was history, but he could see her wheels turning. It was as if she'd already forgotten about Sam Marlin and his derogatory comment. Now she was openly contemplating Murphy.

"I guess you took me literally when I said we could talk later," she said, snagging the white box off the car roof. "Don't tell me you waited out here the whole time I was gone."

"I didn't." He looped her burgeoning tote over his right shoulder, thinking she was a helluva lot stronger than she looked, and relieved her of the mystery gift.

"I'm sorry I called you a wimp. It's not that I approve of violence, in fact I teach against it, but I do think you should stand up for people you care about. Since you seemed so intent on picking my brain about Sofie, I just assumed you were head over heels. I can't believe you didn't defend her." She sighed and looked at him as if he were the most pitiful creature on earth. "She's really got you down, doesn't she? All right. Come inside. The least I can do is listen."

He didn't have the faintest idea what she was talking about, but at least he'd gained an invitation to come inside and talk. *Progress.* He wanted her out of that fairy princess costume and into her civvies. He wanted to meet the real Luciana Ross. Maybe then he'd get a clue as to why he was here. He followed her in silence to the door.

She glanced over her shoulder as they maneuvered through the crowded porch. "You're not one for chitchat, are you?"

"Not really." He tempered the answer with a smile, which is probably why she kept talking.

"Sofie should be home in about an hour, so if you don't want her to know you were here—"

"I don't have a problem with that."

"Oh." She scrunched her nose. "You're not going to make a scene or anything, are you?"

"I make it a habit to avoid scenes." Basic PS training had instilled the notion of shielding the principal from altercations, even if it meant ignoring an insult or personal provocation.

"Me too. Although in special instances I have been known to wig out."

He couldn't imagine.

She reached for the knob and twisted. "Crap. It's locked."

As if it shouldn't be. He swallowed a lecture on basic home security.

"Hold on." She rooted through her poodle purse. "It's in here somewhere."

"Isn't it on the ring with your car keys?"

"No," she said, as if he were nuts. "Then I'd get them mixed up. Oh, never mind." She stooped down and retrieved a key from under the welcome mat.

"You're kidding."

"You don't have a spare key hidden somewhere?"

"It wasn't hidden." Murphy took the key out of her hand. "It was under the mat. The first place anyone who wanted to break in would look."

"This is a safe neighborhood. Everyone knows everyone. Mostly," she added as he slid the key in the lock and turned, "everyone's nice."

"As nice as Sam Marlin?" He pushed open the door and stepped in, flicking on a wall switch and conducting a visual sweep before moving aside so that she could enter.

She brushed past him, hung her pink poodle on the coat tree and shrugged out of her wooly mammoth coat. "Haven't you ever heard the saying, 'ladies first'?"

Not when there could be an assailant lurking on the other side of the door. Mumbling a distracted apology, he moved into the living room, flipped on more lights. He peeked into the adjoining rooms.

She schlepped in after him and kicked off her glass slippers. "Stop worrying. I told you, Sofie's still at work. If you talk fast I'm sure you can pour your heart out in less than an hour." She regarded him with a panicked expression as he moved back into the living room. "You can, can't you? I mean this isn't like a cry on my shoulder all-nighter thing, is it?"

He grinned, thinking this Sofie must be one hell of a heart-breaker. Although he couldn't imagine how she could possibly compare to her cute-as-hell sister. "Do Sofie's boyfriends always seek you out for relationship advice?"

"If I had a nickel . . ."

He joined her in the living room, set the box on the cluttered coffee table and her tote bag on the floor next to the couch. He unbuttoned his jacket and rolled back his shoulders. "How many people know about this key?"

She shrugged. "The neighbors on either side and three or four friends."

Jesus. He passed her back the key. "You need to hide this in a less obvious place." He walked back to the front door and turned the deadbolt.

"You're paranoid," she said when he reentered the room.

"Comes with the job."

"Speaking of . . ." She collapsed on the couch and plucked out the hairpins grounding her tiara. "So what are you? A screenwriter? A director?"

He contemplated skirting the issue and then glanced at the mysterious white package and nixed the idea. "I'm a protection specialist." He pushed aside a stuffed purple dragon and sat down beside her. "Executive and personal."

Her movements slowed, and her voice took on a wary quality. "Sounds like a fancy term for bodyguard."

"It is."

She studied him with those beguiling eyes. "You don't look like a bodyguard. Aren't they usually built like football players? Big as a barn and mean-looking. Kind of like a thug? You don't look like a thug."

"That's good."

"Why is that good?" she asked, dumping a handful of hairpins into a fairy-shaped container. "Aren't you supposed to scare people away from whomever you're protecting?"

"I'm supposed to protect the principal, the client," he clarified when she looked at him quizzically, "without drawing attention to him. Believe it or not, I'm actually good at my job." He smiled. "For a wimp."

"Boy, did I have you pegged wrong." She sounded disappointed. "But it makes more sense. I mean I'm sure Sofie considers your profession sexy. Most women would."

"Most women," he repeated, increasingly intrigued. "But not you."

Blushing, she took off her crown and set it on a stack of celebrity magazines, her gaze lingering on the covers. "So you protect movie stars?"

"Celebrities, politicians, corporate executives, diplomats."

"Famous people," she said, removing two decorative rhinestone combs and giving her head a shake.

"And not-so-famous people." White-hot desire shocked his system as her hair tumbled to her shoulders, framing her face in a golden halo of sexy, tousled curls. How was it possible to look like both a mischievous imp and a guileless angel? The combination ignited a firestorm of X-rated images. *Well, hell.* He looked away and pointed to the package. "How do you know that's for Sofie and not you?"

She flopped back on the worn cushions, her thick shoulder-length curls a riot of shining gold and tawny brown against the drab blue upholstery. "Right. Like I'm the girl of someone's dreams. Besides," she said, before he could comment, "Sofie has been receiving a string of deliveries lately. Flowers, chocolates . . ." She lazed forward, snapped up the package and studied it with pursed lips. "Is that what this is about? All the gifts she's been receiving? *Girl of My Dreams.*" She slowly turned toward Murphy, eyes wary. "You're not one of Sofie's boyfriends, are you?"

"No, I'm not."

"This is a professional visit."

She was smarter than she looked. He gently pried the package from her hands. "Yes, it is."

She folded her arms over her middle and regarded him with a combination of worry and disgust. "Did her agent hire you? She told me Chaz is a little overprotective and not too happy about her move back home. Of course, his concern could easily translate into obsession. I wouldn't be surprised if he's smitten with her too. Does he want you to scare away her admirers? Are you here to interrogate me? If you are," she said, jabbing a stern finger in his direction, "I'll have to ask you to leave. I'm not going to provide you with a list of her boyfriends' names so that you can break their legs or whatever."

"You have a hell of an imagination."

"Comes with the job," she said, still frowning.

"I'm not a hired thug," he reminded her. "I'm a protection specialist. I don't care about Sofie's boyfriends. Right now I'm concerned with that package. Mind if I open it?"

Her eyes rounded, and he couldn't help noticing that they weren't just brown. They were pecan-brown. Nutty. Like her. "Why?" she asked, leaning closer and torturing him with a mouthwatering whiff of lemon. "Do you think there's something creepy in there?"

Not liking the way she made his pulse spike, he forced his gaze from hers. "Let's find out." Plucking a multi-tool from his inner jacket pocket, he flipped open a knife, sliced the packaging tape, and carefully opened the small box. Inside, nestled amidst bubble wrap, sat a sterling silver, scallop-shaped box.

"A seashell," she said. "Pretty. Not creepy."

Not yet anyway, Murphy thought. He inspected the decorative gift, noted a small metal crank on the underside. "A music box." He flipped open the lid, and hooked the contents, lifting the strand from the box for their joint inspection. Murphy raised a lone brow at the pearl thong dangling from his fingertips.

Lulu eased back and cleared her throat. "That's not for me."

"How do you know? There's no card."

"I don't get jewelry."

"Technically, it's not jewelry." He passed her the intimate gift. "It's a thong."

"Definitely not for me," she repeated, cheeks flaming. She inspected what little there was of the ornamental lingerie. "This can't be comfortable."

He stifled a grin as he set down the seashell and gave the packaging another look. "I don't think it's meant to be worn for long."

"It's gotta be for Sofie."

"Why not Viviana?"

"Our grandmother?"

"*Viv's* your grandmother?"

"Yes. Why?"

"You call your grandmother by her first name?"

"That's the way she likes it. Grandma makes her feel old."

"Isn't she?"

"Old?" She snorted. "Only chronologically."

He recalled then that Viviana and Sofia shared the same last name. He glanced at Lulu's left hand. No wedding band, but that didn't mean there wasn't a husband. Maybe she was separated or divorced. Maybe the guy had yet to give up. His interest, he told himself, was purely professional. "Present from your significant other, maybe?"

"I'm divorced," she said shyly. "And I'm not seeing anyone. I'm . . ." she cleared her throat, tossed a carefree hand, "busy. Sofie, well, she's . . ."

He glanced from the thong to Lulu. "Social?"

Red-faced, she nabbed the silver seashell, dropped the pearl thong back inside, and snapped the lid shut. "Listen, Murphy, I appreciate your, *Chaz's*, concern, but this is ridiculous. If Sof was having trouble with one of her boyfriends, I mean, if one of them was getting, you know, obnoxious, she would have said something to me." She set the music box on the table, stood, and motioned him to follow. "I don't mean to be rude, but I've had a long day and Sofie's had an exhausting year. I'd appreciate it if you'd leave before she gets home. She has enough on her mind without having to contend with a delusional agent."

If anyone was delusional, Murphy thought, taking in Lulu's pixie face and fairy-tale getup, it was this one. She seemed oblivious to her infectious charm. Incapable of believing there was a chance that *she*, and not her sister, had an admirer, she'd never believe that he'd been sent here to protect *her*, and not the, apparently, goddess-like Sofie. As Bogie's message had been limited, he couldn't even back his reason for being here with substantial facts.

He glanced down at the music box. Maybe she was right. Maybe this gift was for her sister. But what if she was wrong? What if *this* was the Bogie connection? What if the princess had won an ardent stalker from his nefarious neck of the woods? The fact that Bogie hadn't called yet meant that he was in deep. Which complicated matters. Not that Murphy was complaining. The more complex the case, the less time he had to sit around Charlie's fighting an uncharacteristic bout of depression.

Who could be depressed around Miss Sunshine? He studied Lulu with a cocked eyebrow. He'd wanted interesting. She registered off the charts.

He moved toward the door, deciding not to push the situation until he had more to go on. He'd assess the perimeter, monitor the property from his car, and await Bogie's call. "Do me a favor," he said, handing her a business card with his cell phone number. "Keep this handy."

She rolled her eyes, but accepted the card. "Goodnight, Murphy."

He nodded, trying his damnedest to ignore how adorable she looked standing there in her glittering princess gown. Trying not to stare at her pretty, bare feet or her sexy, madcap curls. "Call if you need me. Twenty-four/seven," he added, thinking she was the type who wouldn't want to trouble him in the middle of the night. He forced himself to leave, cursing his fascination with the naïve woman as she shut the door behind him. In the real world, the world he operated in, naïveté got people killed.

He shook off the morbid thought, smiling, when he heard the deadbolt click home.

Maybe there was hope for her yet.

Chapter Four

✳ "What do you mean you're not coming home?" Juggling her cell phone and a bottle of soothing body lotion, Lulu tightened the sash on her pink terrycloth robe and sank down on the edge of her bed. "I really need to talk to you, Sof." After Murphy had left, she'd zipped upstairs to shed her costume and to slip into a steaming therapeutic bath. Two loonytales and one protection specialist had added up to a triple shot of chamomile bath oil to promote tranquility. Unfortunately, even after a thirty-minute soak, she still felt like a stress ball. What had Sofie gotten herself into? "Another gift came today."

"If it's from Chaz, throw it away."

Lulu's lips twisted. She knew Sofie and her agent were on the outs, but she didn't know why. Whenever she asked, Sofie changed the subject. She'd just assumed it was a business tiff. He'd mishandled her career. But what if it wasn't business? What if it was personal? *Seriously* personal? Now wouldn't *that* be interesting? Mind buzzing, she slathered her legs with lemon and eucalyptus lotion. "I don't know who it was from. There wasn't a card."

"Oh." Sofie's voice brightened. "Maybe it's from Reece. You know, the cameraman with the glorious hair. We really hit if off."

Her cheerful tone rang false, causing Lulu to pry. "Were you and Chaz seeing each other . . . socially?"

"He's my agent, period."

"Maybe now. But when you were living in Manhattan, were you . . . did you . . ." She could feel Sofie's tension radiating through the phone. "The package was addressed to *Girl of My Dreams*."

"Trust me," she said coolly, "I am *not* the girl of Chaz Bradley's dreams. Listen, Lu. I've got to run. I'm meeting a friend for cocktails."

"A man friend?"

"Is there any other kind?"

Lulu tossed the lotion aside with a sigh. She wanted to discuss that pearl thong and whatever was going on with Chaz. She wanted to laugh off the fact that a bodyguard, a man who protected people from danger, had shown up on their tranquil doorstep. She *so* did not want to do this over the phone. But she also didn't want to stay awake until three in the morning, which was probably about the time her sister would roll in. "Listen, I met a man today—"

"It's about time."

Her cheeks prickled as she braced herself for a familiar lecture. Next Sofie would remind her that sex doesn't always have to be about procreating. She preached that sermon every time the subject of Lulu's non-existent social life came up. Lulu's response was always, "*But it should be special.*" She believed that heart and soul. Being intimate with Murphy was absurd. She didn't even *know* the man. Never mind that she'd had two or three fleeting fantasies.

That was different. In the land of make-believe, happy endings were a given.

"It's not like that," she said, pressing her hand to her flaming cheeks. "It was business. He wanted to talk about . . ." Hmm. She shoved her fingers through her damp curls, trying to kick-start her stalled brain. He'd found her shoe, freed her gown, criticized the hiding place of her house key, and scrutinized the mystery gift. "Actually, I'm not exactly clear on why he was here, although he did give me his number and—"

"Was he cute?"

He'd certainly made *her* mouth water. "More like quietly handsome, not that that matters."

"No, but it's a definite bonus."

She heard Sofie jostling around, could easily envision her in the Carnevale dressing room reapplying her makeup and slipping into something sexy for her date. Then her sister asked, "Was he nice?"

Lulu shrugged. "He protects people for a living. How *nice* can he be?"

"What, like a bodyguard? A sexy bad boy with a ripped body?" Audibly jazzed, Sofie adopted the tone of a drill sergeant. "Call him. Ask him out. Be adventurous! You've got to get back in the dating game at some point, Lu. You're full of life and love and you're wasting away because of Terry-the-bastard. Fuck him." She banged something loudly. "Strike that. Fuck the bodyguard. All that testosterone. He's probably hot as hell in bed. It's about time you discovered the joy of no expectations sex."

Lulu fell back on the bed, winded and speechless. She wasn't sure which stunned her more—Sofie's language or her suggestion. Not wanting to seem like a prude, she forced a reply. "I can't have sex with a stranger."

"Sure you can. Just make sure he wears a condom and let me or Rudy know where you are."

Lulu rolled her eyes. "Why not Jean-Pierre?" As if she didn't know.

"Because Frenchie, bless his heart, wouldn't know what to do if, God forbid, you needed rescuing."

"But you and Rudy would." *Here it comes.*

Sofie's confidence was evident in her cocky tone. "Let's just say we're excelling in our Tae Kwon Do class."

Lulu sighed. Rudy had enrolled in the martial arts class for spiritual reasons. Sofie had joined out of curiosity. Now it was an obsession. "You really need to ditch this Lara Croft fixation, Sof."

"It's not a fixation. It's a goal. So are you going to do it?"

"Learn Tae Kwon Do?" As if she'd ever purposely strike anyone!

Sofie laughed. "No, silly. Are you going to screw the bodyguard?"

"I wish you wouldn't talk like that."

"Are you?"

A nervous giggle bubbled in her throat. "Okay. I am officially mortified. That is so not me, and you know it."

"That's why I've decided to give you a makeover."

"You're giving me a beauty makeover?"

"Not exactly. We'll talk about it tomorrow. My date's waiting."

Lulu palmed her forehead, trying to reassemble her thoughts. Her baby sister had blown her mind. "Do me a favor and make this guy buy you dinner," she said, needing to reassert herself as the older, wiser sibling. "You left your Thermos at home which probably means you skipped lunch. You have to eat, Sof."

"I'll order a Bloody Mary with a celery stalk."

"I'm serious."

"So am I."

"Sofia—"

"This chick's gotta fly, Mother Hen. Don't wait up."

Lulu frowned at the sound of silence. Disconnected from her sister . . . in more ways than one. She tossed aside the phone, snagged Binky Bear, a childhood gift from her grandmother, and hugged him tight. This was as close to a heart-to-heart as the Marino sisters had had in a long time. It seemed that each of them was always trying to downplay whatever emotional crisis she might be suffering in order to spare the other worry. They were incredibly different—the seductress and the clown—yet intensely the same. Like Lulu, Sofie struggled with insecurities and broken dreams.

Her thoughts drifted toward Terry and his pregnant girlfriend. Her stomach cramped, and she quickly shoved the man from her mind. Brooding about something you had no control over was ridiculous, and she refused to wallow.

She bolted upright, the faded brown bear clutched in her lap. She could either curl up on the sofa and watch a movie, or, like Sofie, meet up with a friend. Except this was Saturday night and most of her friends were performers so they'd be gigging. She could call Jean-Pierre except he'd mentioned something about taking Rudy dancing. She enjoyed dancing, but wasn't crazy about feeling like a third wheel.

Well, crap.

The phone rang and she instantly brightened. Maybe it was a potential client. "Lulu's Loonytales. Lulu speaking."

Silence.

"*Hello*? Is someone there?" *Stupid question. Someone had dialed. So, what? Wrong number? Crank call?* She narrowed her eyes. "Chaz?"

Chirp.

Releasing a shaky breath, she tossed the phone on her pillow. If it was Chaz, he wasn't talking. At least not to her. "That's a first." Sofie's exes *always* wanted to talk to her, assuming she had some sort of influence over her sister. *Sof*, she told each and every one, *has a mind of her own.* Most of the guys gave up pretty easily, which told Lulu they weren't *really* in love with her sister. Maybe Chaz was different.

So why the creepy feeling?

Anxious, she pushed off the bed and padded barefoot to her mirrored-dresser to twist her unruly hair into two funky pigtails. She should have questioned Murphy instead of kicking him out. He probably had the answers she was looking for, or could have at least shed some light. She'd assumed he was working for Chaz, an assumption he hadn't confirmed or denied. Why hadn't she probed? Why had she been so desperate to show him the door?

She braced her hands on the dresser top and stared at her rosy-cheeked, wide-eyed reflection. "Because he threatens your safe world. Because he's hot, and you're . . ." she turned away from the mirror as she shrugged out of her robe, "flawed."

She tugged on a pair of lime-green cotton briefs, a far cry from that pearl thong. A thong that had incited a sexy glimmer in Murphy's smoldering brown eyes. A glimmer that had spurred a naughty fantasy in her normally squeaky-clean mind. But instead of enjoying the graphic daydream and the sensual tingling between her legs, she'd panicked.

After Terry had walked out, she'd shut down sexually. It was safer that way. *She* was safer. But Murphy ignited fierce desires that burned through her personal fire curtain. Every time they touched, she *burned*. She'd never burned for a man. It unsettled her about as much as the gun she'd seen holstered to his belt when he'd pushed off the sofa. Calling him socially was not an option. Even if she did get past her own shyness, she'd never get past that gun.

She wondered if he'd ever killed anyone.

Her stomach flipped. Not because she was intrigued with Murphy and his dangerous career, she rationalized, but because she was starving. Eight o'clock in the evening and, except for a piece of birthday cake, she hadn't eaten since this morning. *Practice what you preach, Lu.* She plucked up the phone and speed dialed Pizza Piazza while searching her room for a pair of comfy jeans and her favorite T-shirt. "Yeah, hi. This is Lulu . . . Ross." *Sigh.*

"Small cheese pie and a can of cola, Princess?"

She used to feel special, the way Franco knew her order. Tonight she felt pathetic. "Yes, please." She pushed aside her tiara in search of her bubblegum lip gloss as Franco rattled off the price and the estimated time of delivery. She probably imagined him muttering, "*Get a life, bella.*" Probably imagined the zap when her fingers connected with the crisp white business card—she had a stellar imagination—but she was restless, and lonely, and okay, a little spooked from that one-sided phone call. "No, wait." She stared at the raised print. The name. The number. "*Call if you need me.*" Her heart pounded. *Be adventurous.*

"Cancel that order, Franco. I'm going out." She signed off, her hands trembling at the thought of a one-nighter with Colin Murphy. *Colin.* Sexy name. Sexy man. Irish.

Falling is easier than rising.

She shook off the disquieting Celtic saying. She'd fallen for Terry in high school and she'd yet to regain her footing.

Sighing, she punched in a series of numbers. Her tense shoulders sagged with relief when a familiar voice answered, *"Oui?"*

"Hi, Jean-Pierre. It's me."

One of these nights I'll get back in the dating game, she thought, while pocketing Murphy's business card.

Just not tonight.

Chapter Five

✳ Murphy glanced down at his cell phone willing it to ring. Six hours since initial contact and he'd yet to hear from Bogie. It wasn't the waiting that chafed—he was well acquainted with the boredom of surveillance—it was the lack of information. The sooner he knew specifics, the sooner he could devise a plan. If he was to maintain covert protection twenty-four/seven he'd need to contact a relief man, someone to sit watch while he grabbed a couple hours of sleep, showered, and changed into fresh clothing. Unfortunately, the core members of his protective team, the four men he trusted most in this world aside from Bogie, were on holiday. After six months on assignment in Washington, DC, and a month with Albert Nibler, the eccentric convenience store mogul, the team had agreed to take a three-week break. Even though he knew they'd come running, Murphy refrained from making that call. Rejuvenation was key for a sharp mind and steady nerves. His team was superior. He aimed to keep it that way. He had another ace up his sleeve, a trusted local. A pain in his ass, but a top-notch professional.

If the threat necessitated one-on-one coverage, he'd have to have a heart-to-heart with Lulu. He'd have to encroach on her lifestyle in a major, personal way. That option, though tricky, held a thrill factor hard to ignore.

He'd participated in countless high-risk operations and met a lot of interesting people, saintly *and* disreputable. But he'd never experienced a phenomenon like Lulu Ross. Fifteen minutes in her company and he was captivated. Part of him wanted to bury himself inside of her, to meld with all that sunshine and goodness. The other part, the logical, cynical part, wanted to give her a full-body shake, a wake-up call to his world. The real world. A chaotic, dismal battlefield overrun by drug dealers, rapists, kidnappers, and assassins.

It was a clichéd shame, but sometimes you had to be cruel to be kind. She'd waded into a pool of deep shit. How in the hell was she going to see her way out wearing rose-colored glasses?

At this point, even with his eyes wide open, he was operating in the dark. Until Bogie called all he had to go on was gut instinct and logical assessment. All signs pointed to his current number one theory: the princess had a dangerous admirer. The question was how dangerous? How far would the stalker go? Was she a fixation to be adored from afar? Or would he make physical contact? Could this escalate into a potential kidnapping with the threat of sexual assault? It wasn't a pretty thought, but Bogie didn't mix with pretty people.

Murphy didn't look forward to having *that* particular discussion with the princess. He could picture her rolling those nut-brown eyes. At least he wouldn't have to worry about her flipping out and falling apart, because she wasn't going to believe him. She struck him as a free-spirit, the type who operated under the illusion that bad things only happen to other people. He could envision her gliding through life on her pink-wheeled roller skates, head in the clouds, oblivious to political, criminal, and world affairs. He'd be surprised if she watched CNN or read the newspaper, although she probably devoured the comics.

Once upon a time he'd been that innocent and carefree. *Yeah. When I was five.* He wasn't sure if he was appalled or envious.

Speak of the devil, or in this case, the angel, Lulu burst through her front door and trotted toward her car wearing . . . could it be? *Yes, thank you Jesus, jeans and sneakers.* She'd thrown on another shaggy coat, only this one was waist-length and either white or pink in color, he couldn't tell. Given that her yard lamp bathed the perimeter in rosy hues, even her madcap curls, now divided into two perky pigtails, looked pink. *No mistaking the color of the poodle purse.*

He shook his head as he fired up the Jag. If Bogie were a prankster he'd begin to suspect this case was an elaborate joke to lighten his dark mood. Except Bogie never joked about work, and Murphy hadn't let on to his friend that he'd been in a funk. Bogie would want to know why. Murphy didn't have an answer. Besides, delving into his psyche was not his idea of fun. He'd get over this . . . restlessness. Distraction was the key. And the mother of distractions had just backed her pink Beetle out of the driveway.

He glanced at his digital clock as he maneuvered the Jag two car lengths behind the Bug. It was 2100 hours on a Saturday night. "Where are we headed, Princess?" In anticipation of Bogie's call, he fit his headset over his right ear while cursing Lulu's driving. The woman drove like a maniac, swerving in and out of heavy traffic as she barreled toward the bright lights of Atlantic City. Disregarding the speed limit, she gunned through multiple yellow lights. Murphy ran two reds in order to keep her in sight. Luckily there weren't too many pink Beetles on the road. On the other hand, she was an easy mark for a stalker.

Another topic of discussion: less obvious transportation.

At first he'd thought she was heading for a casino like the rest of the incoming traffic, but she continued north on Atlantic Avenue toward the Inlet, a section of town presently under reconstruction because of a city-funded renewal project. After making a series of turns and navigating a new single-home subdivision, they came upon a row of Victorian town homes. Lulu zipped her car into a tight space between an SUV and a stretch limo. She hopped out and race-walked for the door marked one-thirty-four.

Murphy parked the Jag across the street, two doors down. He had his night-vision binoculars in hand in time to see her move into the arms of a good-looking, shaggy-haired man. He kissed her on both cheeks, hugged her close, and then pulled her inside and shut the door.

"I'm not seeing anyone."

Then who was Mr. Friendly?

He spent the next hour replaying that affectionate hug, wondering what they were doing inside that townhouse, and fighting off an obnoxious opponent: jealousy. He was beginning to think that he should've taken his teammates' lead and escaped to a tropical isle to refresh. Sucker punched by the green-eyed monster. A freaking mindblower exacerbated by the fact that Lulu was a veritable stranger.

Twenty minutes later, Bogie still hadn't called and Murphy's need for information escalated. His principal exited the townhouse flanked by two men. Mr. Friendly and a hulking guy that could have passed for Sylvester Stallone on steroids. All three climbed into that stretch limo, Sly at the wheel.

Time to go with the ace up his sleeve: the trusted local, Jake Leeds. A private investigator with an agenda Murphy respected. Too bad Jake had a bug up his ass. At one time they'd actually been pretty tight. But that was before Murphy had slept with the man's sister.

He switched on his headlights and followed the limo at a discreet distance while getting the private investigator on the line.

Jake answered on the fourth ring. "If this is about Joni—"

"It's not." Amazing how Caller ID had negated automatic cheerful greetings.

"Because she's happily married."

"To Carson. I know."

"They have a new baby daughter—"

"Kylie. Your niece. I know. I just spoke to Joni last week. Congratulations, Uncle."

The man grunted. "Every time I lament the fact that that sweet baby's father is a musician I remind myself that it could've been worse. It could've been you."

Murphy plowed on, ignoring an increasingly familiar ache in his chest. "Whether you believe it or not, Jake, I really do love your sister and wish her only the best."

"Then stay out of her life."

"Can't do that. Listen, can we move past this?"

"No."

"Great." Murphy blew over the man's hostility, banking on his core ethics. "I need an ID on two men. They just escorted my principal, a woman, out of a townhouse and into a limousine."

"Against her will?"

Jake's swift change of tone came as no surprise. When the safety of women and children was at stake, the man was blind to all else, including ancient grudges. "I don't think so. But I can't be sure. I don't know what I'm dealing with, Jake. I'm acting on a tip that this woman's in danger. I have no specifics."

"Hold on. I'm booting up my laptop. Is she a local?"

"Lives in Margate. Luciana Ross." He dictated her home address. "Might've picked up a stalker. I need your help and I need this to remain between us."

"Got it." No questions asked.

Murphy's tension eased knowing he had a trusted ally on the case. Now if Bogie would just call.

"Let's start with the two men," Jake said. "Determine if she's in immediate danger. What's the address of the town-house?"

Murphy recited the information along with the limo's tag numbers, while negotiating bumper-to-bumper traffic. They were back in the heart of Atlantic City.

Jake sighed. "Is this a joke?"

"Am I laughing?"

"I know that address as well as my own. It's the residence of Rudy Gallow."

"Approximately five foot ten? Mid-twenties? Wavy, shoulder-length hair?"

"That's Jean-Pierre Legrand. Rudy's partner. Rudy's six-three. Short, dark hair. Goatee."

"The one driving the limo. Is he in the business?" *Built like a football player. Big as a barn and mean-looking.* Gallow fit Lulu's stereo-typical description of a bodyguard to a tee.

"No. I know he looks menacing, but he's cool. He's a chauffeur. Runs a limo service."

"How do you know him?"

"He's my wife's best friend."

"No shit." Murphy raised an amused brow. "You're comfortable with that?" Jake was a control-freak. Over-pos-sessive and overprotective of those he loved. No one knew that better than Murphy. And, according to Joni, Jake was head over heels, crazy in love with his new wife, Afia. He couldn't imagine the controlling P.I. embracing a cozy friendship between his wife and another man. Especially when that man had the face and body of a Hollywood action star.

"You can relax," Jake said. "Luciana's in safe company. Although I can't say the same for Rudy and JP, can I?" He swore. "Afia's not going to like this."

"Afia's not going to know."

"Right." He swore again. "How long have you been on the case?"

"Since this afternoon."

"And you have zip on your client?"

"Nickname's Lulu. Stage name's Princess Charming."

"An actress?"

"Works with kids."

"Sounds familiar."

"Cute, bubbly, young. A real Pollyanna. She's got a man-magnet sister and a dotty grandmother. Other than that, I'm clueless," Murphy admitted. "Can you run a background check?"

"Give me an hour. How do I get in touch?"

"My cell. If I don't answer, leave a text message."

"You're flying solo on this?"

"The team's on hiatus."

Jake made a sound in the back of his throat. "Didn't figure I was your first choice."

"You're my only choice in this instance." Murphy reflected on his conversation with Joni. On Jake's domestic bliss and how he and his wife were trying to have a baby. The man deserved to know what he was getting into. "Joe Bogart's involved."

Five seconds of silence followed by a muffled, "Fuck."

Murphy scraped his hand along his jaw. "You want out?"

"Hell, no. What do you take me for?"

"A happily married man. Wouldn't blame you for wanting to play things safe."

"Yeah, well, I wouldn't be happy if something happened to Rudy and JP. They're my friends too. *Afia* would be devastated. Even if they don't figure into this mess, what about the Pollyanna princess? Uh-uh. You called me, I'm in."

"Good."

"Where are you now?" Jake asked, pushing them past awkward niceties.

Murphy stated his location while following the limo down a side street and into a crowded parking lot adjacent to Oz, a recently expanded multi-entertainment facility. Due center: Emerald City, a trendy dinner theater. The Wicked Witch west wing featured Flying Monkeys, a Euro-hip rave for partying twenty-somethings. Over The Rainbow skywalk and to the east stood Ruby Slippers, a popular alternative lifestyle dance club.

"Oh, man," the P.I. said with a smile in his voice. "You going in?"

"If they do," Murphy said, suddenly clear on why Jake wasn't jealous of his wife's relationship with Rudy Gallow.

Jake laughed. "Watch your ass."

"You're a riot, Leeds. Just call me when you have something." Murphy signed off, pocketed his cell, and ditched the headset. His adrenaline pumped as he watched the trio link arms and hustle toward Ruby Slippers. A couple of Auntie Ems and a Lulu. Oh, and her little dog, Toto, the stuffed pink poodle wonder.

This case was quickly progressing into the realm of the bizarre.

He locked away his Glock on the chance the club's bouncers patted down incoming clientele, left the Jag, and crossed the street. Saturday night in the gaming playground of the east. Suspicious characters abounded.

He eyed the drunk propped up against a neighboring building with a brown-bagged liquor bottle tipped to his mouth. The two stiletto-heeled prostitutes cruising Pacific Avenue. A rowdy gang of bandana-headed teens. And, dead ahead, the line of patrons awaiting entrance into Ruby Slippers. The majority, mostly men, looked as though they'd stepped off the cover of *GQ Magazine*—hip hair, chic clothes. Somewhat of a clothing junkie himself, Murphy assumed he'd have no trouble blending in—the objective if he were to keep an eye on Lulu—as long as he didn't insult the first guy who asked him to dance.

To think this morning he'd been hungry for a challenge.

Chapter Six

❋ *There is no hope of joy except in human relations.*
Rudy Gallow blocked out the deafening disco music and
mentally chanted the obscure quote—*Antoine de Saint-
Exupery was it?* He closed his eyes and breathed deep, willing
positive thoughts. Nothing positive would come from reaching
across the table and popping his roommate and current lover
in his interfering pretty-boy nose. Jean-Pierre hadn't known
what a trial it would be for Rudy when he'd volunteered his
chauffeur services to the current entertainment coordinator of
Oz, Anthony Rivelli. Didn't believe Rudy when he'd said
he'd rather endure a business slump than get pulled back into
the club scene.

Or maybe he had, and this was all a test. A test to see if
Rudy, the former King of Quickies, was capable of frequenting
Ruby Slippers on a regular basis without being tempted to
stray and indulge, well, in a quickie.

Or worse, maybe after spending every night of the last four
months with him, maybe Jean-Pierre was bored. Yes, they had
a common love of gourmet low-cal cooking, classic movies,
and Broadway musicals. But Jean-Pierre also liked to party.

Rudy knew that before they'd hooked up, because he used to party himself. He'd never been into drugs, never abused alcohol, but he did like to dance.

And screw around.

Ruby Slippers had been his second home for several years. Being here now brought back a flood of memories—most good, most illicit. He knew at least a quarter of tonight's patrons intimately.

Hell.

He lifted a full glass of cabernet to his mouth and drank deeply.

Oblivious to his troubled thoughts, Jean-Pierre scooted closer and draped his arm across the back of Rudy's chair. "This is nice, no? This working together?"

"No." The man's naturally seductive voice coiled Rudy's stomach into a delicious knot. Until he'd met Jean-Pierre, he'd never thought a French accent all that sexy. Maybe it wasn't the accent as much as the man. *Damn*, he was turning into a sap.

Jean-Pierre eased back, the glow of the table's singular candle illuminating his chiseled features. "No?"

Genuine hurt shone in his partner's long-lashed eyes and Rudy instantly regretted his gruff tone. He set down his glass and dragged a hand down his neatly-trimmed goatee. "We're not working together, Jean-Pierre. I'm chauffeuring specialty entertainers to and from Oz as dictated by Rivelli. You're designing costumes for Flying Monkeys' cage dancers and Ruby Slippers' drag queens. In the two weeks since we started, we've barely crossed paths."

"You misunderstand," the younger man said. He paused, stroked the stem of his own wine glass in a sensual manner. Then again Jean-Pierre could sneeze and Rudy would find that sexy. "I meant that it is nice that we are working together to make our dream come true."

The bed and breakfast lodge in Vermont. Rudy had once mentioned that he wanted more than a toss in the sack; he wanted Christmas in Vermont. A meaningful relationship. Jean-Pierre had taken the notion a step beyond, suggesting they relocate someplace quiet and start their own business. Somehow—amazing since neither possessed the required experience—they'd come up with the idea of opening a bed and breakfast retreat. Of course, at the time they'd been tipsy on sangria and delirious from an all-night movie fest.

Since then Rudy had been struggling to keep his freelance chauffeur business afloat. He'd been ready to drop his Tae Kwon Do class and gym membership when Jean-Pierre had dragged him into a meeting with Anthony Rivelli, the former casino executive who'd established the glitzy wardrobe policy at the Carnevale. The policy that kept Jean-Pierre up to his neck in costume creations and alterations.

"Okay," Rudy conceded, easing his clenched jaw. "Maybe I did need the steady work." Rivelli had put him on Oz's payroll. With the exception of an occasional run to Manhattan, most of his bookings were local. Shame washed over him. Instead of bitching, he should be thanking Jean-Pierre for the cake job. But, dammit, pride and the feeling that it was too good to be true caused him to stumble. "You, however, already work full time at the Carnevale. You're going to run yourself ragged with this second job."

"*Moi?*" Jean-Pierre flashed a cocky grin. "I have the energy of ten men, *mon amour*."

"Tell me about it." Jean-Pierre Legrand had the lasting power of the damned Energizer bunny. The man was tireless on multiple fronts. Rudy felt a familiar stirring south of his belt. And more importantly in his heart. He could envision his best friend, Afia, shaking her finger at him, saying, "*When are you going to get it through your thick head that this is the real thing?*"

Well, damn. "I'm acting like a bitch tonight, aren't I?"

Jean-Pierre smiled. "We'll leave after Virginia Hamm does her set. I promised Anthony I would check out her costumes. He thinks she can do better."

"Meaning you can do better."

The man winked. Modesty was not his strong suit.

Rudy sipped his cabernet, his gaze drifting toward the lively dance floor. Though he and Jean-Pierre were sitting alone, they hadn't come alone. "Virginia doesn't go on until 1:00 a.m. It's not even midnight and we've already been here for two hours." He nodded toward the whirling dervish in the pink high-top sneakers dancing with a couple of Ruby Slippers' regulars. *Been there, done them*, he thought while draining his glass. *Dammit.* "I'm worried about Lulu."

Jean-Pierre nodded, his expression perplexed. "Earlier tonight she was so . . . preoccupied. Now she is most, how do you say, wound up."

On cue, Lulu waggled her fingers at her dance partners and zigzagged through the crowd to get to her friends. "I can't remember the last time I had this much fun!" She kissed Rudy on the cheek and plopped into Jean-Pierre's lap. "Thank you for letting me tag along."

"But of course, *Chaton*." Jean-Pierre smiled at her, and then turned to Rudy and shrugged.

Hmm. If he didn't know better he'd think the mutual friend they'd dubbed "kitten" was hammered. But he knew better, and so did Jean-Pierre, hence, their bewilderment. Lulu didn't drink. She didn't flirt. She didn't date. She certainly didn't bump and grind with half-naked men. Of course, these men were gay, hence, safe, but still.

"No, seriously," she shouted over the blaring music. "You're the best." She pursed glossy pink lips around a straw and noisily slurped the remnants of her soda. Then she poked

Jean-Pierre in the shoulder and sprang to her feet. "Let's dance!"

The Frenchman stared up at her, his brow crinkling with concern. "You have been dancing for one hour straight, *Chaton*. Sit. Catch your breath."

She threw her hands in the air and waved her arms in time with the pulsing rhythm. "But I *love* this song."

A club mix from the *Queer As Folk* soundtrack. "Do you even *know* this song?" Rudy asked, mildly amused.

"No," she said, seemingly entranced by the colorful laser lights bouncing across the mirrored panels of the upper level. "But so what? It has a great beat."

She wiggled her hips seductively, catching the eye of a nearby femme. Not wanting the woman to waste her time, Rudy smiled and waved her off before she made her way over to proposition Lulu. Then he looked to his own partner for help.

Jean-Pierre rose and maneuvered Miss Happy Feet into a chair. "The next song, I promise, I am all yours. Just now I need you to keep Rudy company while I purchase another round of drinks."

"Why don't we all switch to water," Rudy suggested, worried that although she'd downed three sodas, she might be in danger of dehydrating. Her face was flushed, and her cartoon T-shirt was damp with perspiration.

"Whatever," she said, shimmying in her chair while tightening her springy pigtails. She'd been dancing non-stop and still had the energy of a six-year-old, making him feel twice his age and then some.

Jean-Pierre mouthed, "Keep an eye on her," and then reached over and gave Rudy's shoulder an affectionate squeeze before elbowing his way toward the three-person-deep bar.

The heat of the Frenchman's touch lingered, and he found himself staring after his sexy lover, possible soul mate. He *wanted* to believe they were lifetime partners, but Jean-Pierre was several years younger than he, and realistically, they were still in the honeymoon phase of the relationship. He jammed his hand through his spiky hair and sighed. How many self-help books was he going to have to read before he actually got the hang of this commitment thing?

"I know," Lulu said, misinterpreting his befuddled expression. "He's so gorgeous and *soooo* sweet." She clasped her hands together and giggled. "I could just eat him up."

Rudy tapped his fingers on the table, trying to discern if they had a problem. As she was naturally warm and enthusiastic, he wouldn't have given Lulu's blinding vibrancy a second thought, except earlier this evening she brooded about Sofie's mystery admirer. Then when they'd first entered Ruby Slippers, she'd elected to sit at the table sipping her soda while he and Jean-Pierre danced. Now they couldn't keep her off the floor and she was anything *but* reserved. Had someone bought her an alcoholic drink when they hadn't been looking? Had she been too polite to refuse? For a teetotaler, one strong drink was a sure-fire ticket to happy land.

The woman faltered in the face of his silence, her cheeks blooming a deeper shade of red. "Not that I would. Eat him up . . . or anything." She tugged at the hem of her T-shirt. "I mean he's taken. By you. And besides he's not my type, if you catch my drift."

Rudy grinned.

Both elbows on the table, she cupped her chin in her hands and sighed. "Do you know how lucky you are, Rudy?"

He looked around the room, sized up the lonely singles trying to hook up, and acknowledged the swell in his heart.

"Damned lucky. Sometimes it seems too good to be true."

She smiled, but it was a winsome expression, one that compelled him to raise a subject he knew she hated.

He leaned forward and rested a calming hand on her bouncing leg. "So what is your type, honey? What are you waiting for? What are you afraid of? Trust me, I've been around, and they're not all schmucks like Terry. You just have to open your heart. Be willing to take a chance." God knows he was doing that with Jean-Pierre.

"Do you hear that?" she asked, blowing over his questions. "I *love* that song!" A remix of a Bill Medley/Jennifer Warnes tune blared over the state-of-the-art speaker system, and before he knew it she was out of her seat and halfway to the dance floor. "Tell Jean-Pierre I'll be back!"

Rudy groaned, wondering how he was going to keep an eye on her when she'd disappeared into the throng of writhing bodies. Unless he joined those writhing bodies on the dance floor. Those mostly male, mostly shirtless, toned, writhing bodies. The old him would have jumped at the chance to get up close and nasty with a few of those tasty cakes. The new him hustled to the bar in search of Jean-Pierre. This was definitely a team effort.

* * *

Lulu refused to let Rudy dampen her night with his soul-searching questions. She'd almost blurted that Murphy was her type, but that was ludicrous. The man carried a gun. He was so not her type. Okay, he was extremely handsome. And charismatic. And . . . fine, sure, a little . . . a lot sexy, but that didn't mean he was Mr. Right. Mr. Right would have to meet specific requirements, and she was certain Colin Murphy would crap out. He was, after all, Alpha and Irish, and the combination equaled old-fashioned and family driven. Not that that was a bad thing. In fact, under normal circumstances that would be a very good thing. Too bad her circumstances weren't normal.

She palmed her sweaty brow. Why was she even giving that man a second thought? He represented trouble and she wanted no part of it. She shoved him out of her mind and focused on her dance partner, a non-threatening, skinny red-headed guy with kind eyes and great moves. She was foot-loose and fancy-free. She was having the time of her life!

A re-mix of the theme from *Dirty Dancing* roared over the speakers. She loved this song. Loved the movie. Loved the way shy, innocent, Baby's eyes were opened to an exciting world by Johnny Castle, that older, oh-so-sexy dance instructor.

She shut her eyes and a vivid image of Murphy exploded behind her lids. She envisioned his arms around her waist, his thigh wedged between her legs. Imagined them swaying, grinding . . . the heat of him, the scent of him . . . primal, intoxicating . . .

She forced her eyes open to maintain her balance and lost herself in the chaotic lighting, pulsing music, and mingling scents of fragrant hair gels and body colognes. Her senses tingled. Absolutely, she'd never felt this way before. She twirled, gyrated, and bopped. Her partner, a guy named Jim, was here with Harry, but Harry didn't like to fast dance. Jim was gay, which was perfect, because she could dirty dance to her heart's content, and he wouldn't care. He was into dancing, not her body. She wanted to feel sexy, but she didn't want to have sex.

Sofie would call her crazy. But she just wanted to know that part of her, the sensual part, was still working. She didn't need the rejections or the consequences that went along with making love. She just wanted to . . . express herself.

Maybe she *was* crazy. She'd had an extremely long day, performed *two* loonytales. She should be exhausted, yet she felt amazingly energized, almost euphoric. She was acutely aware of the music, the lighting, the nonjudgmental atmosphere. She felt free. Free of past regrets. Free of her inhibitions. Free of fear.

Maybe she was overly tired. That would explain the slight headache and sudden, annoying eye twitch.

The super-fast dance mix segued into a slow, driving version of a song she'd never heard. Jim abandoned her for Harry, and surrounding men latched onto one another making Lulu feel like an outcast. She lifted a hand to her throbbing temple, feeling slightly disoriented. She needed to find Jean-Pierre and Rudy. She needed to sit this one out.

She excused herself, bumping into one couple after another, trying to find her way to the edge of the dance floor. That's when she spotted a dark-haired man coming toward her. He smiled. She smiled back. An automatic reaction, and yet he did look familiar. He was still several feet away when Jean-Pierre caught her eye. He frowned.

Her head throbbed. She definitely needed to sit this one out.

The stranger moved closer. No, not a stranger. She'd seen him before. But where?

Her eye twitched. Her vision blurred. She turned abruptly, panic fluttering in her chest. Jean-Pierre caught her elbow as she hurried by. "What is it, *Chaton*? What is wrong?"

"Nothing." She waved him off. "I'm fine, just hot. I'm going to sit this one out."

"We'll come with you," Rudy said.

"Don't be silly." She massaged her temples and marveled at her dry throat. Hadn't she just polished off another soda? "I just need a drink of water."

"There are three bottles of spring water at our table," Jean-Pierre said, his eyes soft with concern.

"Perfect!" She smiled to ease their worry. "Enjoy the dance." She hurried toward their secluded corner table, only it looked very dark over there. That panicky feeling kicked up a notch. Again her eye twitched, and suddenly a dose of fresh air seemed more inviting than a drink of water.

She switched directions and slammed into a tower of hard muscle. Strong hands clasped her forearms. Absurdly panicked, she lifted her chin to demand her release. The words stuck in her throat when she locked eyes with Colin Murphy. "What are you doing here?" she squeaked.

"Dance with me." He coaxed her back onto the floor.

Her heart thudded against her ribs as he wrapped his arms around her and pulled her flush against the length of him, leaving nothing to her imagination. *Jeez, Louise, Sofie was right.* This man was ripped. Even his muscles had muscles. The kind that came from working hard and eating right. Zero-percent body fat. Enveloped in an aura of raging masculinity, she couldn't think. Couldn't breathe. Had she passed out from exhaustion and overexertion? Was she dreaming?

He dropped his mouth close to her ear. "Do you see him?"

Warm breath fanned her neck, tweaking her already fevered brain. Her eyes rolled back in her head as she breathed in an intoxicating mixture of spicy aftershave and fruity shampoo. *Wow.* "Who?"

"Whoever scared you."

The stranger who wasn't a stranger. "I wasn't scared," she lied, knowing her fear was unfounded. It's not like the man had done anything wrong. He'd just smiled. "I was hot," she said, her throat scratchy and tight. "I wanted some fresh air."

"Uh-huh." Holding her close, he maneuvered her slowly

across the floor with an easy grace that melted her bones. "So do you see him?"

She clasped her hands tightly about his neck for fear her knees would buckle—she felt as boneless as a rag doll—then scanned the crowded room. "No," she said, surprised at the relief in her voice. What in the world was wrong with her? The man had smiled at her, so what?

Her anxiety eased as Murphy stroked his hand down her stiff spine. The throbbing in her head lessened. Euphoria returned in a dizzying burst as the seductive music droned on, and Murphy's hand connected with the bare flesh of her lower back. Her T-shirt had ridden up, but for the life of her she couldn't dredge up her usual modesty. She felt at ease with her sexuality. Safe.

Oh, no. "Are you gay?"

He regarded her with an amused expression. "No."

She sighed. "Oh, good. I mean . . ." *Be adventurous.* "So then what *are* you doing here?" she repeated, slipping her hands beneath his shirt.

Something flashed in his dark eyes. Censure? Pleasure? "Watching you."

The husky declaration zapped her like a lightning bolt, feeding her boldness. She slid her palms higher, marveling at his exquisite physique. His magnificent back muscles tensed beneath her touch, and she almost pulled away. Sofie's words spurred her on. Adventurous meant throwing caution to the wind, to indulge in a fantasy. She wanted to dance dirty. Really dirty. She wanted to cast away her inhibitions and to experience a spontaneous, sensual moment. With Murphy. She closed her eyes and, just like that, she was Baby and he was Johnny Castle—she did have an amazing imagination after all. Her senses tingled as she straddled her partner's thigh and indulged in a slow grind.

Desire, hot and intense, simmered in her belly.

She burned.

Murphy gripped her hips and swore beneath his breath. "You're putting me through the wringer tonight, Princess."

"I am?" Excitement buzzed through her veins. Was it possible? Was he as turned on as she was? She hadn't been this aroused since . . . actually she'd never been this aroused. She felt strangely disconnected, unleashed. She continued to grind against him and risked his gaze. "Have you ever had sex in a coat closet?"

He searched her eyes, groaned. "You need some fresh air." He practically carried her off the floor.

Was that the dating code for "Let's go some place private?" Giddy at the prospect of jumping this man's bones, she tried to remember Sofie's rules for a one-night-stand. Oh, right. "Do you have a condom?"

"Do we know you?" Scowling, Jean-Pierre stepped directly into Murphy's path. Rudy loomed beside him, his bulked-up arms folded over his massive chest. They looked ready to kick some bodyguard butt. Gosh, that was sweet.

"He's gay," she blurted. They wouldn't hassle him if they thought he was a member of their church. They wouldn't see him as a threat.

"He's not gay," Rudy said.

"Bi?" Lulu tried.

Jean-Pierre snorted.

"Fine," she snapped, her headache returning with blinding force. She'd never understood that whole gaydar thing, but obviously Murphy blipped STRAIGHT on her friends' internal screens. "He wandered over from Flying Monkeys and picked me up. If you must know, we were stepping out to have sex."

Her friends gawked.

Her vision blurred. Had that come out of *her* mouth? Her eye twitched madly as she endured a sudden wave of nausea. "Can I take a rain check?" she asked Murphy. "I think I'm coming down with something."

He held her steady, stroked her back like Viv used to do when she had the flu and had her head stuck in the toilet bowl. "Is she hypersensitive to drugs?" he asked Rudy.

"Midol makes her loopy."

"Hell," Murphy grumbled.

And with that she lurched forward and threw up on her fantasy lover's shoes.

Chapter Seven

✳ Murphy had known the moment something was amiss. Lulu had spent the early part of the evening sitting at her table, sipping her soda, leaving once to visit the ladies room. Thirty-minutes later and she was the life of the party. Her excessive energy and provocative dancing had given him a heads-up and a hard-on. No doubt her "admirer" had been equally aroused, the sick bastard.

Given her behavior and the symptomatic side effects, Murphy suspected MDMA otherwise known as Ecstasy. The popular club drug lowered inhibitions and increased awareness and feelings of pleasure. Whoever had slipped her the illegal stimulant had intended to take advantage. A cynical conclusion, but one based on experience and facts. Not to mention his gut.

Fortunately, a few of those side effects—overheating, dehydration, and anxiety—had kicked in, prodding Lulu off the dance floor and into his arms.

*Un*fortunately, she was experiencing an extreme reaction.

He parked the Jag in front of her house, retrieved his Glock. The game was on. He regarded the unwitting target with a frown. She'd maneuvered herself into a tight ball, her thighs clutched to her chest, her forehead resting on her knees. At first he thought she was crying, but then she turned her head and looked at him, dry-eyed. *Thank you, Jesus.* Usually he wasn't bothered by tears. But there wasn't anything "usual" about this woman.

"I'm so sorry," she said for the umpteenth time.

"Stop apologizing." Realizing he sounded curt, he opened his door and stepped outside, cursing the stars as he rounded the car. For chrissakes there were worse things than a woman hurling on a man's boots. The "unfortunate incident," as Jean-Pierre had dubbed it, didn't even make Murphy's Top Ten List. Between his Marine Expeditionary Unit missions and his executive protection assignments, he'd seen some damned disgusting shit. He had a cast iron stomach, nerves of steel, and a closet full of shoes. *Hell, all she'd had in her stomach was cola. Cleaning up had been a cinch.*

Convincing her friends that he would be the one driving her home had been more complicated.

He'd waited until the concerned crowd had dispersed and Jean-Pierre had escorted her into the club's head before sharing a few choice words with Gallow. No wonder Jake got along with the guy. They walked the same walk. Sexual preference aside, they both treated women with a tangible reverence. The term chivalrous came to mind, along with fearless. Lulu's dark-suited champion had proven a pain in the ass even after the phone discussion in which Jake had told him to trust Murphy and to do whatever he advised, no questions asked. Per Jake's request Gallow didn't question, but he'd sure as hell said his piece. He even went into detail about which bones he'd break, and in what order, if Murphy were to harm even one curl on Lulu's head–that's if Sofie didn't kill him first.

He'd listened in earnest. Well, at least he hadn't laughed. No use insulting a man whose intentions were honorable. Even his twinkle-toes boyfriend had grit. Throughout the confrontation, Frenchie had managed to look semi-intimidating even in his tight leather pants and orange paisley shirt. In reality, Murphy could drop the pair without breaking a sweat. Not because they were gay, but because he was good. His team would argue *fuckin' scary*.

As for Sofie . . . A man-magnet with a kiss-ass mentality? He actually looked forward to meeting this woman. Lulu had mentioned she was out with a friend. He didn't think she was home yet. *No car in the drive. No lights in the windows.*

No lights. "Son of a bitch." He opened the passenger door and helped Lulu out, that home security lecture tripping off his tongue. "Leave on a couple of lights when you're out at night," he said as he escorted her toward the porch. "A burglar's less likely to target a house if he thinks someone's home."

"We don't have burglars," she said, shivering beneath her shaggy jacket. "This is a nice neighborhood."

"An affluent neighborhood. And there's always a first time." Actually, he was more concerned about a stalker than a thief, but for some reason he shied away from the subject. A few hours ago he'd been itching to give her a wake-up call. Now he wanted to shield her from the ugly reality that she'd been drugged, possibly by a sexual deviant—a man almost certainly connected to the mob. Maybe it was because she looked so damned young in her pigtails, cartoon T-shirt, and hot-pink high-tops. Or because she smelled like lemons and bubblegum. Or maybe because he was beginning to think that she was the real deal. A chaste soul. She actually thought she'd caught the flu. Wait until she sobered up and remembered that she'd suggested they steal away for a hot slam. His words, not hers.

The hell of it was, he'd been tempted. Bad enough that he'd been turned on *watching* her dance. When she'd practiced those seductive moves on him he'd nearly maxed out. Though petite in stature, she wasn't bone skinny or overly defined. She was soft. Feminine. Possessing the winsome appeal of one of those lush women featured in Renaissance paintings. *Imp and angel. Lethal combination. Much like Madonna and whore. Easy to see how she'd picked up an admirer.* Easy for him anyway.

Convincing Lulu would be a trial. He'd never known a woman less conscious of her sexual appeal.

"I'd invite you in," she said as they breached the busted outer door and weaved through the assorted boxed paraphernalia. "But I don't want you to catch whatever bug I picked up."

"You're not contagious."

She pressed a trembling hand to her damp brow. "How do you know?"

"I've seen this before." *And worse.* Like early in his protection career when a diplomat's son had overdosed on heroine. A standard op turned clusterfuck because the team leader, a man Murphy thereafter disassociated with, hadn't known his ass from a hole in the ground. "I really need to speak with your sister." Since she still thought he was somehow connected to Sofie, he worked that angle. No way was he leaving this woman alone.

She turned and faced him, eyes narrowed in confusion. She pressed the heel of her hand to her forehead and sighed. "Oh, right. The thong."

There was that. He also wanted to know about the other gifts that had been delivered over the past few days. According to Lulu, there'd been quite a few. Had they been specifically addressed to Sofie? Had the cards been signed?

Or, like today, had they been anonymous?

Mostly he wanted an excuse to come inside. This op was no longer covert. He was moving in. He'd tell her tomorrow after the effects of the drug subsided.

She glanced over her shoulder at the darkened door and shivered. "Actually, I have to admit I wouldn't mind the company."

Before she could change her mind, he stooped down and groped under the welcome mat for the key he just knew was there. Sure enough, his fingers touched metal. He checked his annoyance, tripped the lock, and moved inside.

Lulu brushed past him, flipping on lights as she moved from room to room. He stuck close, raising a brow when she turned on the television *and* the radio. What the hell? Then she paused on the landing and wrung her hands. "Have you seen the upstairs?" she asked, staring up into the darkness. "Viv hasn't redecorated in years, but it's really quite interesting. Four bedrooms, a bathroom. Lots of nooks and crannies. Sofie and I grew up here. One of our favorite games was hide and seek." She worried her lower lip. "Lots of places to hide."

Then he got it. *Paranoia. Another side effect.* Or maybe it was a gut feeling. He knew about those. His own gut told him that they were alone. Chances were her admirer had seen her leave the club flanked by three men, and had watched her drive away with one. The creep was probably off fantasizing about their next encounter. Still . . .

Murphy would've told her to wait, but then she might've felt abandoned. Instead, he offered his hand and took the lead. Her grip was cold and clammy. He could feel her tension mounting with every step. *Hell.* He made small talk for her benefit, asking about her childhood, her sister, their similar career choices. When Jake had called earlier he hadn't had much to report yet—other than that Lulu was thirty-one, divorced, childless, and working part-time at the Carnevale Casino as a juggler, in addition to operating a free-lance storytelling business. She'd racked up a helluva lot of speeding tickets, but, other than that, she was clean. The only thing that had surprised him was the fact that she was thirty-one. It made her naïveté all the more shocking. And sweet. *Shake it off, man. You don't do sweet.*

"Entertainment is in our blood," she said in a soft, scratchy voice. "We have a theatrical background that can be traced back for generations. Actors, dancers, variety artists. Various degrees of success and fame."

Her voice trailed off as they hit the top step. He could feel her pulse tripping beneath his touch. He cursed himself for planting the image of a burglar in her mind. Yes, he wanted her to be more cautious, but he hadn't meant to scare her. He knew her reaction was heightened by the mood-elevating drug; but dammit, her fear was real, and it turned something inside of him.

"Where'd you learn to juggle?" He wanted to keep her talking, to occupy her thoughts with something other than bogeymen. Although he sensed no immediate danger, he'd make a show of inspecting every room. Anything to put her at ease.

"How did you know I juggle?"

Because Jake told me. Because I saw you juggling batteries this afternoon when I tailed you. Shit. "Because I saw a juggling magazine downstairs." *True.* "And three neon rings in the living room corner." *Also true.* "Given all the props in the backseat of your car, I just assumed they belonged to you."

"Oh."

He flipped a switch, flooded the hall with light, and then tugged her toward the first room. "So?"

"Oh. I learned from my Grandpa Marino. His circus skills were amazing. He was featured on *The Ed Sullivan Show* a few times."

He glanced over his shoulder and grinned. "No kidding?" She smiled, and his insides twisted. *Well, hell.*

"That's where he met Viv. She started out as a puppeteer. She can do these really funny character voices. Anyway, she was only sixteen at the time, but Grandpa was a goner. Love at first sight. He waited for two years, until she was legal, before he made his play. Can you imagine?"

"If she's anything like you . . ." He stopped cold, stunned at his words. *What the hell?* He broke physical contact, switched on the bathroom light and, after a quick inspection, motioned her inside. "Why don't you freshen up? I'll look in the other rooms. Check out those nooks and crannies."

"Murphy, I . . ." She blinked up at him with those long-lashed, nut-brown eyes. Rocked back and forth on her sneakers. Those freaking pink high tops did him in. "I feel so stupid. I'm never this jumpy. I just . . . you mentioned a burglar and I . . . Tomorrow I'll find a better hiding place for that spare key."

Saints be praised.

She shut the door and he continued his search. Four bedrooms. Lots of hiding places. No bogeyman. The last place he checked was Lulu's closet. He skimmed through the colorful array of costumes, surprised to find that her wardrobe extended well beyond that of a fairy-tale princess. Native-American princess. Celtic-warrior princess. He stopped when his fingers connected with the blue-green sequins of a mermaid tail. He eyed the form-fitting lower-half. The sequined bra-like top.

He thought about the silver seashell and that pearl thong.

"Is everything okay?"

He turned and dragged a hand down his face. She stood in the doorway, arms wrapped around her middle. Her face was scrubbed bright pink, her hair loose and damp. She'd changed into pale blue, terry cloth sweats and a pair of fuzzy mouse slippers—but he imagined her in that mermaid get up.

"I took a quick shower," she said, shifting self-consciously, probably because he was staring. "I thought it might make me feel better."

"Did it?"

"Not much." She moved to her dresser, slathered her hands with cream and dabbed pink-tinted balm on her lips.

Mermaid. Ocean. Shells. Pearls.

Thong.

She'd mentioned pulling a double today. He wanted to ask her if she'd been a fairy-tale princess on both jobs. Had she played the mermaid recently? When? Where? Who'd hired her? But that would have to wait until tomorrow. She still looked ready to claw out of her skin. He glanced at his watch. "It's almost one in the morning. Do you want to go to bed? I can hang out downstairs, watch CNN, wait for Sofie."

"I don't think I can sleep right now. I feel . . . I'm not . . ." She lifted a hand to her cheek. "My eye keeps twitching. I'm overly tired, I guess, but I'm not sleepy." She turned to him, eyes brimming with hope. "I thought we could watch a movie. You know, until Sofie gets home."

"Okay."

"Okay."

She didn't move, so he took her hand and led her back downstairs.

"My collection is pretty extensive, but I'm in the mood for something light. Something," she shivered, "uplifting."

"Okay."

"Okay." She led him over to her video and DVD collection.

He hated to break it to her but all of her movies, from the Doris Day classics to the Meg Ryan comedies, were light and uplifting. No twisted or tormented endings for this woman. The Disney movies alone took up two shelves. "How about this one?"

"*The Little Mermaid?*" She beamed up at him. "I just watched this one last night for inspiration. But I don't mind watching it again. It's one of my favorites." She handed him the DVD. "You put it in and get it started. I'll get us something to drink. We don't have any hard liquor. Sofie has some wine—"

"Water's fine."

"Okay. Good." She hurried toward the kitchen.

Murphy shut off the radio and loaded the DVD player. He closed the living room curtains and flicked off the majority of the lights. On the off chance the stalker *was* out there, he didn't want him pulling a Peeping Tom.

He shrugged out of his leather blazer, draped it over the arm of the couch and sat down. Checked his cell phone to make sure Bogie hadn't left a text message—he hadn't—then snatched up that silver seashell. He flipped open the lid, inspected the thong.

Girl of My Dreams.

He was about to turn the musical dial when Lulu returned carrying two glasses of sparkling water. Her cheeks flushed a deeper shade when she spied the sexy gift. "I meant to put that in Sofie's room."

I don't think it's for your sister, honey. He contained that thought for now, setting the shell aside.

She set the glasses on top of the magazine-covered coffee table, and then plopped down at the opposite end of the couch.

Murphy hit play on the remote control.

He made it through the opening scene and credits before

stealing another glance at the princess. She'd wedged herself into the corner, curled up tight, her knees clutched to her chest. She looked vulnerable, a far cry from this afternoon's bubbly sprite.

Maintain professional distance. Distance is key. Distance equals . . . Hell. "Lulu."

Her gaze flicked to his. "Yes?"

"Come here."

She swallowed. "Where's your gun?"

"In my jacket."

"I don't like guns."

He draped the blazer over the sewing basket, on the floor next to the couch, within his reach, but out of her sight.

Satisfied, she crawled over and burrowed in next to him, sighing when he wrapped an arm around her.

Oh, yeah. This little act of kindness was going to bite him in the ass. Even now he could feel the nip of consequence's sharp teeth.

"This is a really good movie," she said just as a pipsqueak seahorse introduced King Triton. "The music's awesome."

Her voice was calm now, but he could feel the coiled energy in her body. An enticing body that had rubbed up against him, intimately, a short while ago. He clicked off the sexy image, the feelings she'd aroused at Oz, and simply held her. He told himself he was offering comfort and nothing more. The effects of Ecstasy usually wore off in three to five hours. She should be crashing any moment now. The way she'd been going all day, he'd be surprised if she made it through the movie without falling asleep.

"Colin?"

Tension settled at the base of his skull. He didn't mind that she'd called him by his first name. He minded that he liked it. "Yeah?"

"Are you sure I'm not contagious?"

"I'm sure." He dragged his gaze from the mer-people and arrogant crab to focus on the living, breathing character in his arms. Big mistake.

She palmed the back of his neck and pulled him down for a kiss.

His mind clouded. His senses buzzed. All that femininity. Those full lips—soft, warm. *Delicious*. She tasted like bubblegum. He savored the sweetness longer than he should have, but damn, she was a helluva kisser. Despite the saccharine-sweet tune chiming in the background, graphic thoughts danced in his head. Blood pooled in his groin. Before she could deepen the kiss, before *he* took advantage, he eased away. "Listen, Princess . . ."

She placed her fingertips over his mouth. "Please don't say anything. I know I'm not your type."

He wasn't so sure.

"And on top of that I guess it's hard to be attracted to someone who threw up on you."

Guess again.

"I just wanted . . . Sofie told me to be adventurous."

"What?"

She broke eye contact, rested her head on his chest, and focused on the screen. "We talked on the phone and I told her about you, and, well, she told me I should call you and ask you out on a date. But I was too shy. And then there you were and I was feeling . . . adventurous. So I asked you about the coat closet, but that didn't work out. So I just . . . I've been dying to kiss you. So I did, and . . . I'm glad. Because it was really . . . nice. You're nice."

Nice?

"But I'm not your type, and you're definitely not my type, so let's just forget about the kiss and the sex thing and watch the movie." Instead of moving away, which would have made sense after that statement, she snuggled closer.

Nice? It took every ounce of his will-power not to haul her up and throw her back on the couch. He wanted to devour her delectable mouth with an open-mouth, no-holds-barred kiss. He wanted to lick every inch of her lemon-scented body. He wanted to bury his cock inside of her and fuck her until the sun came up.

But he was nice.

Bogie, if he ever called, would never believe it. *He* didn't believe it. A beautiful woman was nestled in his arms, a woman high on Ecstasy no less, and instead of messing around they were watching an animated flick. A goofy crab, a skittish fish, and an impetuous mermaid.

Well, hell. At least he wasn't depressed.

Chapter Eight

❋ *Swimming.*

She was pushing through a sea of mer-people. Swimming toward something special.

She heard the excited squeals of children as they crab-walked over the finish line.

Racing. Running. From someone. Toward someone. Music blared. Caribbean music. No, Dirty Dancing. "I've had the time of my life . . ."

Then she saw him. Dark. Dangerous. Shark!

"Call me if you need me. Twenty-four/seven."

She screamed, but nothing came out. Throat dry. Can't breathe.

Drowning.

"Murphy!"

Strong hands gripping her, pulling her toward the surface. "Open your eyes, Princess."

The shark smiled, colorful laser lights glinted off his razor sharp teeth. "Another time."

"Luciana."

Her eyes flew open as she broke the surface and gasped

for air. "Murphy." She sagged against him, her heart thudding against her ribs.

"Shh." He held her close and stroked her hair.

She clung to his body, his strength, and still her pulse raced.

She heard footsteps. Someone running.

"Shark," she rasped, her thoughts hazy with the convoluted dream. "Danger."

"No danger," he said. "I'm here."

"Get your hands off of my sister, you bastard, or I'll cut off your balls."

Lulu grimaced. "Sofie?"

Murphy eased her back against a mountain of feather pillows, glanced over his shoulder. "Gallow warned me about you," he said, a trace of humor in his voice.

A light clicked on.

Lulu blinked to clear her vision. She wasn't in the ocean or Oz, or even her living room. She was lying in her bed. She must've fallen asleep during the movie. She had the fuzzy memory of Murphy carrying her upstairs, of her asking him not to leave. Had he lain down beside her? She couldn't remember. Just now he was sitting on the edge of the bed looking intrigued, wary, and incredibly handsome with his salt and pepper five-o-clock shadow.

Sofie stood in the doorway brandishing a pair of sewing shears. She looked mega-watt lethal in her low-cut sweater, form-fitting skirt, and spiky heels. Like Jennifer Lopez in that movie where she'd played the kick-butt U.S. Marshal. Only instead of a gun she wielded scissors. And instead of coming to wits and blows with George Clooney, she was facing down . . . *Murphy*.

Lulu's pulse slowed to a painful drone. They looked beautiful together. "Sofie, put down those scissors before someone gets hurt. This is the man I told you about."

Sofie cocked one perfectly tweezed brow. "The body-guard?"

Lulu nodded, her head pounding with the effort.

"Colin Murphy." He rose slowly and flashed some sort of ID. "Protection Specialist."

Weapon still in hand, Sofie squinted at the wallet, then glanced at Lulu. "I was coming in the back door when I heard you scream. I thought . . . If he wasn't hurting you, then . . ." She looked from Lulu to Murphy and back. "Oh." She lowered the scissors, let out a noisy sigh. "Damn, Lu, I didn't think you'd actually take my advice. You could have called, warned me."

Lulu flushed from head to toe. Surely, Sofie didn't think . . . They were fully clothed for cripes sake. "It's not like that," she blurted. "I went dancing with Rudy and Jean-Pierre and I got sick. Murphy brought me home."

Sofie glided into the room, placed the scissors on the nightstand, and sank down on the bed. She pressed her hand to Lulu's forehead. "You don't have a fever, but you are sweating."

"She had a nightmare," Murphy said.

"That's why I screamed." She massaged a weird tightness in her chest. "I think I have the flu." Or maybe she was lovesick. Every time she looked at Murphy, a herd of elephants tap-danced on her heart.

Sofie's hand fell away. "That sucks."

Totally. "Don't worry. Murphy said I'm not contagious."

"How does he know?" Sofie smirked over her shoulder. "What, are you trained in medicine too?"

"Certain aspects."

Sofie grunted. "Why didn't Rudy and JP bring her home?"

"Because Murphy needs to talk to you," Lulu said, suddenly wishing they'd both go away. Seeing them together made her feel worse.

"About what?"

She realized that her sister was glaring at the man and that the scissors were still within her reach. "About that gift. The one that came today." She reached out and touched Sofie's arm. "Stop frowning at him. He's nice."

Murphy made a strange sound and then headed for the door. "I'll wait downstairs, put on a pot of coffee." He glanced back at Sofie. "You look like you could use a cup."

When he was gone, the sisters locked gazes. "What did he mean by that crack?" Sofie asked.

"You look upset."

"I thought you were being attacked! What do you expect?"

"No, I mean, your hair's kind of messy and your eyes are bloodshot." Even those imperfections couldn't mar her exotic beauty. Lulu sighed. It wasn't Sofie's fault that she'd been blessed with amazing genes. She pushed herself into a sitting position and took a closer look at her frazzled sister. "Have you been crying?"

"Hell, no." Sofie tossed her long, dark hair over her shoulder and shrugged. "I had a few too many drinks, that's all."

"I hope your *friend* didn't take advantage."

Sofie rolled her eyes. "I swear you were born in the wrong century." Then she grinned and nodded toward the door. "You were right. He's handsome."

You noticed. "You were right. He's ripped."

"How do you know? I mean he looks fit, but it's not like he's shirtless and wearing a Speedo."

"We danced together. Then later we snuggled on the couch and watched *The Little Mermaid*."

Sofie's lip twitched. "You got a man like that to watch a Disney movie?"

"He picked it out."

"That's just weird." She held up a palm. "Wait a minute. You said you went dancing with Rudy and JP. At Ruby Slippers?"

Lulu nodded.

"And Colin was there?"

"He likes to be called Murphy, but yes."

"Ah."

"No, *ah*. He's not gay. I asked."

"Maybe he lied."

"I kissed him. Trust me, he's straight. And if you don't believe me, there's Rudy and Jean-Pierre. He flat-lined on their gaydar."

"*You* kissed *him*?" She whistled. "I'm impressed."

"Don't be." Lulu fell back with a groan. "I wasn't feeling like myself. I think this flu bug made me delirious."

"Hmm." Sofie crossed her arms, cocked her head. "So how do you feel now?"

"Better. Just tired." *And miserable*.

"No wonder. It's almost five in the morning."

"I can't believe you stayed out so late."

"I can't believe you kissed a stranger."

Lulu's body tingled in remembrance. Her insides had melted the moment their lips had touched. She'd wanted more. Much more. But he'd pulled away. She'd bet her tiara he wouldn't have pulled away from Sofie. "You told me to do more than that," she reminded her sister.

"True." Sofie blew out a breath. "I thought I wanted you to be more daring, Lu. To sample life and lust, but I don't think I'm ready for that."

"The way you're talking you'd think *you* were the older sister." Lulu turned into her pillow. It had been a long day, a disappointing night, and she just wanted to escape. "I'm supposed to take care of you."

"Age, as you should know from Viv, is a state of mind. You're a babe in the woods compared to me." She reached for the lamp.

Lulu's heart fluttered. "Wait."

"Oh, right. The nightmare."

It was murky now. Something about mer-people and sharks. Probably inspired by the movie she'd fallen asleep watching. Although she couldn't imagine why it had triggered a nightmare.

"I'll leave the light on. It'll be dawn soon anyhow." Sofie smoothed a maternal hand over Lulu's furrowed brow, and then stood. "I'm going down to talk to Murphy. I hope you feel better when you wake up."

"Thanks, Sof." As long as Murphy was gone—out of sight, out of mind, she thought as her eyes drifted shut—she'd feel just fine.

* * *

Sofie clenched and unclenched her fists as she descended the stairs. *Breathe deep. In and out, in and out.* She tried to center herself, to slow the adrenaline that had surged the moment she'd heard her sister's scream. Fear and rage had engulfed her when she'd seen a stranger's hands on Lulu. *Assess. Assimilate.* If not for the inner voice of her Tae Kwon Do instructor, she would have lunged without warning. She would have stabbed an innocent man.

Jesus. The things you'd do to defend a loved one.

She followed her nose to the kitchen. True to his word Murphy had brewed a pot of coffee. *Cheeky bastard. Make yourself at home.* She grabbed the mug that he handed her and kept walking. She opened the cupboard, reached past the olive oil, baking powder, an unopened five-pound bag of flour, and grabbed Viv's secret stash. She poured whiskey into her coffee and drank deeply.

"Sorry for the scare."

Sofie turned and glared at the stern-faced bodyguard. She wasn't too fond of him just now. These days men in general were scum.

She'd lied to Lulu. She wasn't drunk. She could hold her liquor better than most. She'd spent the night crying on Anthony Rivelli's shoulder. Crying over Chaz. Instead of ending their platonic date after drinks as planned, Anthony had driven her back to his apartment so they could talk at length. This was the second time since they'd met that he'd shirked his business responsibilities to rescue her from a melt-down. It helped that he was going through a similar crisis. He too was hung up on someone who wasn't good for him. Difference was *he* didn't cry at the drop of a hat. Feeling like a total loser, she poured another shot into her coffee before replacing the bottle on the back of the shelf.

Murphy said nothing.

"Take a picture, it'll last longer." She was used to men staring. But this was different. She didn't get a sexual vibe off Murphy. Nope. She felt scrutinized. Worse.

"I was just thinking that you and your sister don't look anything alike. There's a similarity about the eyes. Other than that—"

"Same father, different mothers." She cocked a hip against the counter, took another sip of her spiked coffee, welcoming the stiff burn. "So what's going on? What are you doing here?"

He reached behind him and then set a silver seashell on the counter in front of her.

"The infamous gift?"

"Open it."

She did. A pearl thong. Dread rippled through her as she studied the naughty lingerie. "So?"

"It was addressed to *Girl of My Dreams*. Lulu thinks it's for you. Thinks it's from your agent."

"Ex-agent." Though she schooled her expression, her body hummed with betrayal. She'd been seduced by a handsome face, the "L" word, and the promise of success. She and about ten other actresses on Chaz Bradley's roster. She shrugged off a bout of self-disgust. One of these days she was going to learn *not* to mix pleasure with business. She dropped the thong back in the shell and snapped shut the lid. "It's not from Chaz. He would've signed his name." Would've wanted her thinking about the great sex she was missing. What she *missed* was what she thought she had. A grip on her future.

Murphy cleared his throat. "Lulu mentioned that there've been quite a few gifts lately."

She nodded. "Flowers. Chocolates. Perfume."

"All from Chaz?"

"Some from Chaz. Our relationship . . . our *business* relationship," she clarified when he raised a brow, "ended badly."

"The other gifts?"

She shrugged. "I assumed they were from some of the men that I've met at the Carnevale. High rollers. Executives. Some of them are very persistent."

"You're a striking woman."

She braced herself for a come-on, marveled that it had taken him this long to turn this into something sexual, but instead he topped off his coffee, and leveled her with a look that was all business. "I think this particular gift was intended for your sister."

She tightened her grip on her cup as she rode out another ripple of dread. "People give Lulu teddy bears and homemade cookies, not pearl thongs."

"I'm going to be straight with you, Sofia, because I think you can handle it."

Her pulse hammered. "I can."

"And I might need some help."

"If it has to do with Lulu, I'm there."

He sipped his coffee, gazing over the brim at her, dark eyes intense. "I'm acting on a tip from a trusted source. Your sister's in danger. Seems she's picked up an admirer."

"What, like a stalker?"

He nodded.

Deranged fan obsessed with local celebrity. A scenario ripped out of any one of a dozen bad movies. Her stomach clenched. "I knew it." She set down her coffee cup, shoved her bothersome hair off her face with a weary groan. "I've warned Lulu to keep those oddballs at arm's length, but she's polite to everyone, including the watchers. Claims they're not weird, just eccentric. Trust me. They're weird."

Murphy angled his head. "The watchers?"

"Devoted fans of the casinos' free entertainment— strolling entertainers and lounge bands. People, primarily men, who show up regularly. The lurkers. The leerers. The guys who hover on the fringes and ogle the female performers." She twisted her lips in disgust. "So which one is it? Maurice? Sam? The Clapper? Wait. It has to be Photo-Boy. Sometimes I wonder if he's even got film in that camera."

"Hold up." Clearly intrigued, Murphy abandoned his coffee and folded his arms over his chest. "Sam? As in Sam Marlin?"

She nodded. "Not as creepy as Photo-Boy, but definitely a watcher. As bad luck would have it, he also lives in the neighborhood. Lulu mentioned him?"

"I met him." Murphy glanced at the seashell. "He hand delivered the package. Said it came to his house by mistake."

"Yeah. That's been happening a lot lately." Sofie winced. "I guess Sam was in a mood then."

"You could say that."

"He doesn't like the idea of other men horning in on his women." She snorted. "The man's deluded."

"I wasn't aware that he's hot for Lulu," Murphy said. "I thought he liked you."

"He's hot for anything in fishnet stockings. Although I think I'm the only performer at the Carnevale that he's actually asked out on a date." She smirked. "Lucky me."

Murphy dipped his chin in thought. "When Lulu appears at the Carnevale, does she use the name Princess Charming?"

"No. That's her storybook persona for Lulu's Loonytales. She transforms into the Princess for children's parties. At the casino she's Gemma the Juggler." She frowned. "Why?"

He glanced up. "According to my source, quote, The *Princess* is in danger. Unquote."

"So Sam was at one of Lulu's parties?"

"I'm not convinced that we're talking about Sam."

"I don't know what's more upsetting. The possibility that a sicko was at a children's party, or that said sicko is stalking my sister." Sofie wanted to laugh off this entire conversation, but Murphy's professional demeanor, his aura of grim authenticity, had her swallowing the scenario in one sobering gulp. "I could use some specifics here, Murphy."

"So could I. Unfortunately, I'm working with what I have."

She moistened her lips. "Which is?"

"The tip. The gift. The mermaid costume hanging in Lulu's closet."

Mermaid. Seashells. Pearls. Although she didn't want to, she easily followed his thinking. "Go on."

He flipped over the seashell and turned the crank. Music

tinkled. A lively Caribbean song. A tune from *The Little Mermaid*, one of Lu's favorite movies. Sofie massaged her temple. "She did a mermaid gig yesterday morning." *Damn.* "What else?"

"I don't think she has the flu. I think she was drugged at the club. My money's on Ecstasy. I think her admirer planned on taking advantage."

"But you were there."

"I was there."

Her knees wobbled, but she'd be damned if she'd show weakness. Someone had to champion Lulu, and Viv wasn't here. Terry . . . he wasn't here either, the bastard. "Ecstasy. Jesus. No wonder she came onto you."

"She told you about that?"

"She told me she kissed you." She frowned. "Anything else I should know?"

"I'm not in the habit of taking advantage of vulnerable women."

"Then you are a rare man indeed."

He grinned. "You're a cynical one."

She shrugged. "Call 'em as I see 'em."

"Your sister on the other hand . . ."

"Thinks you're nice."

He shifted, eyed his mug. Obviously, he was uncomfortable with that description. *Probably liked to think of himself as big, bad, and deadly.* He was after all in the business of protection and intimidation.

She smiled, drawing morbid pleasure from his discomfort. "Lulu thinks everyone's nice."

"I've noticed."

They drank in silence for a moment. Her spiked coffee was bracing, the kitchen toasty, but Sofie suffered a bone-deep chill when she glanced over at that seashell.

"You have to trust me, Sofia."

Her gaze flicked to Murphy's. He was asking a lot of her, but this was her sister they were talking about. Something in his eyes urged her to take a leap of faith. "Okay."

"Good."

"But, you can't tell her she was drugged."

"Why not?"

She set down her mug, sighed. "Lulu's not like most people. She's . . . she'll be devastated if you tell her she was rolling."

He raised a brow. "You know the slang."

"I'm not Lulu."

"Meaning?"

"I've been around. Don't tell her she was drugged. She'll think it's the end of the world."

He considered her plea, met her gaze. "No promises."

As if that would matter. She wasn't sure if she'd ever trust a man again. Desperate to numb her raw nerves, Sofie retrieved the whiskey bottle. Only this time instead of spiking her coffee, she poured a straight shot. "So, Mr. Bodyguard," she said, tipping the glass to her lips. "How are you going to protect my sister?"

Chapter Nine

✱ "If you're not out in three minutes, Jean-Pierre, I'm leaving without you." Rudy pounded on the bathroom door, glanced at his watch. "Two minutes and fifty-eight seconds."

The door whipped opened. "Calm down, Bunny. I am ready."

If he weren't so ticked, he would've admired the view. An avid runner, Jean-Pierre had a killer body—buff torso, rock-hard thighs—and a package that belied his average height. Instead of voicing his admiration, he stated the obvious. "You're in your briefs."

"*Oui*." Jean-Pierre breezed past him, into their bedroom.

Rudy smirked. "But you're ready."

"*Oui. Une minute*."

The doorbell rang. Rudy threw up his hands. He'd wanted to leave an hour ago, but Jean-Pierre had stalled saying it was rude to show up uninvited at someone's house before dawn. Rudy wasn't feeling polite. He certainly didn't think of Colin Murphy as *polite*. He wanted to drive over to check on Lulu and Sofie in person. He trudged down the stairs of the two-story townhouse, as bristly as a nylon brush. Sleeping had been impossible last night. He opened the door, narrowed his eyes. "I want to talk to you."

"Ditto." Jake Leeds walked past him and jogged up the stairs.

Rudy followed, admiring his best friend's husband's attire. The man was a walking Gap store. Faded denim jacket pulled over a classic navy T-shirt. Blue baseball cap. Work boots. The jeans—low rise, slim fit—were especially nice.

"You better not be checking out my ass, Gallow."

"Get over yourself," Rudy said, although he'd been doing just that. If Afia were here she would have been ogling right along with him. They both agreed her husband had the butt of a Greek God. The rest of him deserved equal worship. Short blond hair. Killer green eyes. Jean-Pierre once commented he had the lips of Brad Pitt. True. No wonder kissing had become Afia's favorite past time.

"Where's JP?" "Golden-boy" asked as he crested the stairs.

"Getting dressed."

"What's for breakfast?"

Rudy rolled his eyes. "You don't have food at home?"

"I didn't want to bang around in the kitchen. Afia was sleeping."

"So what?" Earlier this year, after the IRS had confiscated her house, and before she'd met Jake, Afia had spent a month as Rudy's houseguest. Too polite to take his room, she'd crashed on the sofa. "Afia sleeps like the dead."

"Not lately." Jake pushed up the brim of his baseball cap and headed toward the kitchen. "I thought she was insatiable before, but now that we're trying to have a baby . . . She's killing me, man. Every time I turn around she wants to have sex."

"My heart bleeds for you." Rudy knew the P.I. was as hot

for Afia as she was for him, and it wasn't just about baby-making. No matter what the future held, no matter if they had zero or ten kids, they'd always be together, in love and in lust even after they'd turned old and grey. He smoothed a hand over his thick, choppy locks, wondering if Jean-Pierre would be as attracted to him when his hair thinned and his muscles shriveled.

And vice versa.

"Cereal." Jake smiled when he spied the box on the counter. "Excellent." He swung open the refrigerator door nabbed the skim milk. "Got any fruit?"

"Blueberries. Second shelf." Jean-Pierre sauntered into the living room zipping up his favorite Ralph Laurens. "*Bon jour*, Jake."

"Morning, JP."

Rudy braced his hands on his hips, flabbergasted at his partner's state of undress. Although he'd poured himself into the brown and tan floral print jeans, he was still barefoot and shirtless. "You take longer to get ready than a woman."

"Doubt it." Jake nabbed a bowl and a spoon. "Ever been around when Afia's trying to pick out something to wear?"

"Yes," they both answered.

Jake chuckled. "Right. Sometimes I forget."

"Who's this Murphy character," Rudy asked, trying to swing the conversation back to the source of his foul mood.

Jake brushed past him armed with the breakfast of champions. "A protection specialist."

"I got that much last night," Rudy said, following him into the dining room. "Who is he to you, and what's he doing with Lulu?"

"He's an associate, and he's doing his job."

Jean-Pierre carried in a carafe and three cups. "*Café?*"

Jake released an orgasmic sigh. "God, yes."

"Ah, *oui, café* is life." The Frenchman grinned and poured. "I could use another cup myself. *Someone* has ants in his pants this morning. Keeps rushing me."

Rudy grunted. "I happen to be concerned about a friend. I don't know this Murphy."

"I do." Jake pointed to Rudy with his spoon. "Take a load off. Have some bean-juice."

"But—"

"Sit."

Talk about controlling. Rudy frowned. "I don't know how Afia puts up with you."

Jake grinned. "That makes two of us."

"If you say this Murphy is trustworthy, then of course we believe you," Jean-Pierre said. "We simply wish to look in on Lulu, to make sure that she is feeling better. Also, we need to return her car."

"The pink Beetle parked out front? I wondered about that." Jake shook his head, sipped his coffee. "Who the hell drives a pink car?"

"If you knew Lulu," Rudy said, "you'd understand."

"This is so." Jean-Pierre smiled, nabbed his steaming cup. *"M'excusez, s'il vous plaît.* I am going to finish dressing."

"It's about time," Rudy grumbled.

"Love you too, Bunny." Jean-Pierre planted a chaste kiss on his frowning mouth, and then hustled toward the bedroom, cup in hand.

Jake groaned. "I hate it when you guys do that."

"Screw you."

"You wish." Jake waggled his brows, and then spooned wheat flakes into his mouth.

Rudy laughed. He couldn't help it. *That* was why Afia loved the guy. There wasn't a judgmental bone in his body. Not really. "All right. So what did you want to talk to me about?"

His hetero friend sobered. "Lulu and Murphy." He met Rudy's gaze. "And Afia."

Dread warred with curiosity, causing Rudy to lean forward. "What about Afia?"

"She can't know about any of this."

"Any of what?"

Jake toyed with his cereal. "Late last night I remembered where I'd heard the name Princess Charming. Lulu performed for the kids at the Sea Serpent, didn't she?"

The daycare center where Afia volunteered. "Yeah. She did a show there last month," Rudy said. "So what?"

"So Afia knows her."

"Casually."

"And likes her."

"Everyone likes Lulu." Rudy crossed his arms over his chest so as not to bang his fist on the table, or worse, into his friend's nose. "You're irritating the hell out of me, Jake. What's going on?"

"Golden-boy" pushed his bowl aside and leaned forward. "Afia would want to help the woman if she thought she was in trouble."

Rudy's pulse quickened. "*Is* Lulu in trouble?"

"It would seem so."

"Why didn't she say something last night?"

"She's not aware of the situation. Yet." Jake shrugged, repositioned his ball cap. "It's complicated. And it's about to become more so, because I'm dragging you and JP into it. Murphy's not happy about that, which personally floats my boat, but I told him you were already invested and wouldn't be easily dismissed."

"You got that right." He dragged a hand over his goatee in exasperation. "So are you going to fill me in before the first snow?"

Jake angled his head, his emerald eyes glittering with determination. "As soon as you agree that Afia's out of the loop."

Rudy's expression was just as adamant. "You know what happened the last time we kept her in the dark." She didn't speak to Rudy for days, and broke up with Jake for months.

"We'll just have to risk it."

Which meant the danger level was in the red zone. Rudy jolted his senses with two gulps of cinnamon-laced caffeine. "Agreed. Now spill."

* * *

Sundays were Lulu's favorite day of the week. Old-fashioned to the bone, she rarely worked on the seventh day. It was a sacred day. Not that she attended church regularly, but that was only because she found it hard to accept one specific faith as the true faith. She supposed she was more spiritual than religious. She had Viv to thank for that. Her grandmother was a loving, tolerant soul and the finest example of a human being that Lulu had ever known.

No, Sunday wasn't so much a day to attend church as a day to attend one's soul. To reflect upon one's life and family. To kick back and enjoy. A day to count one's blessings.

Even when things had been at their worst–when Terry had been so terribly distant because, yet again, she'd failed to conceive–she'd managed to count her blessings. He was healthy. She was healthy, relatively. They had each other. That was enough. Or so she'd stupidly thought.

As of late, Sundays were a depressing reminder that she was a failure as a wife. Considering her bungled attempts to seduce Colin Murphy, she supposed that made her a failure as a woman, period. Talk about depressing.

Okay. On second thought, she hated Sundays.

Forget that she'd slept until noon and had enjoyed a leisurely shower. She still felt distracted as she towel-dried her wet curls and moisturized her dry skin. She couldn't stop thinking about yesterday. It was like one long, blurry dream. The back-to-back loonytales, Murphy's visit, her escapades on the dance floor. She cringed when she thought about the way she'd rubbed up against all those men, *especially* Murphy. Her only excuse was that she'd been delirious from exhaustion, lack of food, and that stupid flu bug.

Asking Murphy to have sex in a coat closet had been the topper. *No*, puking on his shoes had been the topper, or rather the downer of the evening. Kissing him . . . she scraped her teeth over her lower lip and sighed . . . Kissing him had been bliss. She'd told him it had been "nice," but in truth she'd seen stars. Orbited the moon. Who would've thought one's soul could soar because of a kiss?

Of course, if she had claimed an out-of-body experience, he would've thought her juvenile or daft. Obviously, she hadn't set any of his body parts afire or a-flight. He'd pulled back, clearly uncomfortable. At the time she'd eased the sting of her humiliation by telling herself that he was being a gentleman. She should feel blessed instead of disappointed. He so totally could've taken advantage.

Which only made her want him all the more.

This man was considerate to the bone. She reflected on how he'd carried in her prop bag and nagged her about home security. The way he'd been there for her at Oz and later at home when she'd felt spooked. How he'd carried her upstairs when she'd fallen asleep and comforted her when she'd awakened in a panic.

For a few brief hours Colin Murphy had been her true life hero, her very own Prince Charming. She'd felt cherished and protected. *Special*.

Then Sofie had come home and broken the spell.

Groaning, Lulu jerked on her black cargo pants, a long-sleeved white oxford, and her Converse All-Stars. Her mind buzzed. She assumed Murphy and her drop-dead gorgeous sister had met downstairs to discuss that pearl thong. Imagined they'd exchanged heated looks and sexy banter. They were probably really good at that. She knew Sofie was. She wondered if they'd succumbed to temptation. Did Sofie model that thong? If she did then Murphy probably ravaged her. She imagined them kissing. They were probably really good at that too. She knew Murphy was.

By the time she was through—she had a heck of an imagination—Murphy had morphed from Prince Charming into Casanova. Her stomach churned, the tips of her ears burned, and it wasn't due to that dratted bug.

Fists clenched, she tiptoed down the hall to Sofie's room and peeked in. Her sister was conked out, sprawled across the bed, face down. Good thing Murphy had gone home, at least she assumed he had since he wasn't in Sofie's bed, because she would've given him an earful for taking advantage of her sister when she'd been so upset. Although Sofie had attributed her bleary eyes to alcohol, Lulu didn't believe it. She'd never seen Sofie drunk. Nope, she'd been upset about something, but instead of spilling her guts to Lulu, she'd smothered the hurt with sex. Maybe not with Murphy, she thought rationally, but most probably with her mystery date.

"Oh, Sof," she whispered. "What am I going to do with you?" Wishing Viv were there to make them both feel better, Lulu trudged down the stairs muttering, "I hate Sundays."

She hit the bottom step and smelled cinnamon rolls and coffee. She inhaled deeply, allowing the dreamy aroma to soothe her grumpy mood. Cinnamon was Jean-Pierre's favorite spice. Hopeful, she peeked out the front window.

Yup, her Bug was in the drive and Rudy's motorcycle was parked behind. If anyone could cheer her up it was Rudy and Jean-Pierre. They'd tease and gossip and make her forget all about the quietly-charged bodyguard who'd shocked her comatose sexuality to life.

She wasn't ready for this . . . attraction. Along with desire came longing, frustration, and a gazillion insecurities. Numbness had been preferable.

She moved effortlessly through the living room and dining room, marveling that she didn't have to hop over or sidestep a single item. The guys had been busy. They'd put away the bolts of fabric and scattered sewing supplies. Shelved and alphabetized her videos and DVDs. They'd even organized her games and props, and Sofie's magazines.

She sauntered into the kitchen and smiled at the domestic, perfectly suited couple. Rudy stood at the stove, hovering over a skillet. Jean-Pierre whistled a happy tune while drizzling icing on a tray of cinnamon rolls. "Jeez, not only do you bake and cook, but you clean. How much would you guys charge to come in once a week?"

Jean-Pierre stopped whistling. "Clean? We did not—"

"Morning, sleepyhead," Rudy broke in. He noted her casual togs, winked. "You look cute."

"She always looks cute." Jean-Pierre shook off his perplexed expression, strolled over and kissed her on both cheeks. "*Bon jour, Chaton.* You are feeling better, no?"

She nodded, slid her hands into her back pockets. "Must've been a twelve-hour bug." Whatever had ailed her was history. No headache, eye twitching, or dizziness this morning. As long as she didn't think about Murphy, she felt perfectly fine. "I'm really sorry about last night. I hope I didn't gross you out."

"Of course not, honey. You couldn't help being sick," Rudy said.

"Well, it was totally embarrassing. Even more than the way I behaved on the dance floor. I don't know what got into me."

The men traded a quick look then concentrated back on their tasks.

Lulu shifted her weight. "What?"

Jean-Pierre shrugged, smiled. "It was good to see you have fun."

Her cheeks flushed with the knowledge that she'd actually had a blast. Well, except for the part where she'd thrown up.

Rudy tipped the skillet and slid a fluffy omelet onto a plate. "Hungry?"

"Starving." She schlepped over to examine his culinary creation. Knowing him, he'd forgone the best parts, specifically ham and cheddar cheese. "What's that green and red stuff?"

Rudy lifted a brow. "They're called vegetables."

"Asparagus and bell peppers," Jean-Pierre said, concentrating on his rolls. "Very tasty."

"And healthy," Rudy added as he sprinkled some sort of herb on top.

Lulu scrunched up her nose. "I know you didn't find asparagus in our refrigerator."

"Your fridge looks like a wasteland for take-out leftovers, and your freezer rivals the frozen section of a grocery." Rudy carried her plate and utensils over to the breakfast nook. "I've never seen so many microwavable dinners."

"They're the healthy kind. Sort of." She sat, sipped her orange juice, and then peered up at her friends. "Aren't you having anything?"

"We already had breakfast," Jean-Pierre said. "We wanted to check in on you and return your car. We figured we would make a day of it. Treat you and Sofie to brunch and a movie-fest. We brought along three Cary Grant classics. Sound good?"

"Sure." She dug into her omelet and eyed Rudy as he poured himself a mug of coffee. Something was up. If she breathed too deep she'd choke on the tension. She wondered if he and Jean-Pierre had quarreled. She'd heard them bicker countless times, but never seriously. Maybe the newness of their relationship was beginning to wear off. *This is where the real work begins*, she was tempted to say. *When the going gets tough, the tough get going. Or like Terry . . . get gone.* Instead, she quietly chewed her vegetable omelet thinking it wasn't half bad.

Jean-Pierre flitted around the kitchen cleaning up. Rudy returned to the table, sat, and studied her as he sipped his coffee.

She fidgeted. "What?"

"How is it possible that you and Sofie are half-Italian and neither one of you cooks?"

"I cook."

"Nuking ready made soups and TV dinners doesn't count." Rudy shook his head. "You eat poorly. Sofie doesn't eat at all."

She purposely laid down her fork so as not to clang it against her plate. "Are you saying I'm fat?"

Jean-Pierre made a strangled sound. "Dangerous territory, *mon amour*."

Rudy waved him off. "No, I'm not saying you're fat. Why do women always go there? Good nutrition isn't always about losing weight. It's about maintaining good health."

"I'm fit." She downed the rest of the orange juice. At least she was chock full of vitamin C.

He snorted. "You're a cream puff. I'm thinking you should follow Sofie's example."

"And starve myself?"

"*No*, smarty pants. Join our Tae Kwon Do class. Exercise your mind and body and learn how to defend yourself in the process."

She didn't like where this conversation was going. "I can take care of myself."

"What would you do if someone attacked you?"

"I don't know. Scream, I guess."

"That would be my first reaction," Jean-Pierre said.

Rudy glowered.

"Someone told me once that you should scream, *Fire*! Even if it's a mugging or attempted rape. They said people are more likely to run to your rescue if they think it's a fire." She cast Jean-Pierre a befuddled look. "Isn't that horrible?"

"Shocking."

Rudy frowned, closed his eyes as if counting to three, and then focused on Lulu. "This is unacceptable. If you don't want to come to class, I'll give you self-defense pointers myself."

"What's this sudden concern about my being attacked?" Then it dawned on her. She narrowed her eyes, drummed her fingers on the table. "You've been talking to Murphy. Mr. I-don't-like-where-you-hide-your-house-key. Well, he's just totally paranoid."

"He has good reason to be concerned," Rudy said.

She sat back and crossed her arms over her chest. "Okay. Let's hear it."

Jean-Pierre cleared his throat. "We have been sworn to secrecy."

She crinkled her brow. "By who? Murphy?"

"Jake."

Lulu gritted her teeth as her temper began a slow burn. "Jake who?"

"Jake Leeds," Rudy said, sliding an exasperated glance at

his partner. "Afia's husband."

Rudy's best friend. The sweet young woman she'd met at the daycare center. "Isn't he, like, a private investigator?"

"Exactly so," said Jean-Pierre.

Her leg bounced with nervous energy. "What's he got to do with anything?"

"He's a friend of Murphy's."

"Yes, but . . ." she hopped up out of her chair and began to pace. "Oh, my, God. What's Sofie gotten herself into?"

Again she caught the two men trading looks.

"What? *What*?" She stopped in her tracks and threw up her hands. "Stop doing that. Whatever it is, whatever you know—just *tell* me."

Rudy rose with a sigh. "Calm down, honey." He gripped her shoulders and guided her back into a kitchen chair. "Just sit for a minute. Take a breath."

"Have a cinnamon roll," Jean-Pierre said, setting the entire tray in front of her.

"I don't want a cinnamon roll. I want to know what's going on."

Rudy frowned and squeezed the bridge of his nose. "When Murphy gets back—"

"He's coming back?" she squeaked.

"He's moving in for a while." Jean-Pierre dropped into the chair next to her. "Sofie invited him—"

"Oh, no. Uh-uh. No way." She rose stiffly and backed toward the kitchen door. "If Sof's in so much trouble that she needs a bodyguard, we'll just go to the police." How was she supposed to function in close quarters with a man who made her soul soar? A man who made her do idiot things like suggesting sex in a closet? *Oh, no. No no no!*

Rudy got to his feet, frowned down at Jean-Pierre. "You suck at this undercover stuff."

"You are the one who lost his cool and brought up the attacker," Jean-Pierre countered.

"What are you, Starsky and Hutch? *What attacker?*" Lulu threw up her hands and stormed out of the kitchen. Her heart thundered in her ears. She wanted answers and she wanted them now. She marched to the base of the steps and yelled up at her sister just as she'd done countless times when they were kids. "Sofie! Wake up! Get your butt down here!"

She swiveled to find Rudy and Jean-Pierre standing directly behind her. "Where's Murphy?"

"We don't know." Rudy held up his hands in self-defense. "Swear."

She planted her hands on her hips. "Would Jake know?" She yelled up the stairs again. "Sofia Chiquita Marino!"

"Probably."

Jeez, it was like pulling teeth. "Well, where the heck is he?"

Jean-Pierre cocked a head toward the front of the house. "Outside. Making sure no bad guys get in."

"Oh, for . . . I suppose he's wearing a trench coat and hiding in the bushes."

Rudy smirked. "No. He's wearing a cute denim ensemble and sitting in his Mustang. Now will you please come back into the kitchen and—"

"Does he have a gun?"

The two men looked at each other.

Blood pounded in her ears. "It's a sunny Sunday morning, and this house sits one block from the boardwalk and beach. Do you have any idea how many children ride their bikes up and down this street? And your friend's out there with a gun, ready to shoot it out with the bad guys?"

Rudy jammed a hand through his hair. "Well, I don't think—"

"Obviously!"

Sofie skidded down the stairs in a skimpy satin robe, hair mussed, eyes wide. "What is it? What's wrong?"

Lulu glared at her sister. "This is all your fault!" she shouted and then flew out the door with the force of a tornado.

Chapter Ten

The calm before the storm. Murphy acknowledged the familiar sensation, his muscles knotted with anticipation as he stepped into the Jacuzzi shower. *Charged air. Eerie quiet. Unstable conditions ripe with the threat of disaster.*

He braced his hands on the granite wall and lowered his head. Four pulsing jet sprays pounded the hell out of his tense body. Even though he'd achieved REM sleep, his power nap had been a bust. He'd dreamt, vividly, of Lulu. A fairy-tale princess who tasted like bubblegum. An adventurous mermaid hunted by a voracious predator. "*Shark,*" she'd whispered.

He'd jerked awake in a clammy sweat.

Preying on an innocent. Someone who dedicated her life to children. A woman who carried a poodle purse and said words like "jeez" and "crap." He knew this was a sick world. He'd learned that when he was ten years old and his Ma and Da had died in a fire. And all because Charlie Murphy had stood up to "the bad guys."

Senseless violence.

Murphy lifted his face to the shower spray, willing it to wash away the shitty feeling of helplessness. If Bogie hadn't invited him along on a family camping trip that fateful week-end, he would've died that night too. He'd dealt with the guilt long ago by making a personal commitment to protect the innocent. Bogie had made the same commitment, two weepy, snotty-nosed, ten-year-old boys signing a pact in blood.

But his friend had chosen a different path. A path that con-sistently steered him into Mafia waters. Only this time Murphy feared he was in over his head. Bogie *still* hadn't called. Which meant he couldn't call. Not without blowing his cover.

Somehow, someway, Lulu had crossed paths with Bogie and an underworld slime ball.

"Don't tell her she was drugged. She'll think it's the end of the world."

Sofie had verified his suspicions that Lulu was a poster girl for sugar and spice and everything nice. *Untainted. Untouched by the cynical world. Talk about a rarity.* And all he could think about was corrupting her. Getting in her ruffled bloomers and driving her to orgasm . . . again and again.

Murphy swore under his breath as he scratched shampoo through his hair and soaped his thrumming body parts. This op was a personal nightmare. Being sexually attracted to the principal was a major pain in the ass, unprofessional, and risky. Maintaining emotional distance was essential to clear thinking.

He tossed the soap in the caddy. "I'm screwed."

In addition to Lulu, Bogie was involved. He'd pondered the dilemma after Sofie had gone to bed, her words ringing in his ears. *"How are you going to protect my sister?"* The answer was simple. *By moving in. By shadowing her every move.* Although, without his team, the actual execution would be slightly more complicated.

Never one to shirk a challenge, Murphy had placed a call to Jake and then hauled ass home, an isolated four-bedroom Tudor nestled in the Pine Barrens, to regroup and pack a suitcase.

The suitcase was packed. Regrouping was another matter.

His normally buried emotions were abnormally floating near the surface. Although he'd effectively protected Lulu for a few hours by entrusting her to Jake and the dynamic duo, he could do nothing to shield his childhood friend and surrogate brother. Special Agent Joseph Bogart was fearless. He also had a heart as vast and deep as the Atlantic, and that, Murphy had always sworn, would be his lethal downfall.

He told himself to trust in Bogie's superior judgment and abilities. He adjusted the faucet for a frigid blast of cold and ordered himself to get a grip.

By the time he'd rinsed off and dressed in fresh jeans and a knit pullover, he had it together. *Calm, rational, and objective. Mr. Cool.*

Until his cell phone rang and Jake said, "Cute and bubbly? She's a freaking nut! She threatened to call the cops unless I drove away or came inside the house."

Murphy reached back and massaged a twinge in his neck. "Where are you now?"

"Hiding out in her bathroom. Mark my words, this *will* be the longest leak of my life. She accused me of endangering children!"

"She likes kids. *A lot.*"

"Well, so do I. I also like my Glock. I can't believe I let her talk me into handing it over."

Neither could Murphy. Then again, she *had* juggled her way out of a speeding ticket. *Innocent, but enterprising.* He smiled. The tension in his shoulders eased. "You'll get it back."

"I better."

Jake relayed the details of the confrontation. Murphy nabbed his suitcase and exited the organized sanctity of the master bedroom. His gaze skated over the spacious living area as he whizzed through the downstairs conducting an habitual security check. Everything in its place, not that he owned anything outside of essentials. There was a certain comfort level in living simply. Though he was certain the packrat Marinos would disagree. Only someone who'd lost everything would understand. "I need to swing by the pub and take care of some business. I'll be there in forty minutes."

"Handle business over the phone and make it thirty. I think Gallow's about to crack. Your Pollyanna princess almost made JP cry. She's brutal, man."

"What about her sister?"

"Tough on the ego. Easy on the eyes."

"Easy on the eyes?" Murphy shrugged into his leather jacket, and moved toward the front door. "You *are* happily married." Sofia Marino was a walking, talking centerfold. Not that he'd been affected by her blatant sexuality. Still he appreciated the package.

"Deliriously in love. So shoot me. I'd shoot myself," Jake snarled into the phone, "but I don't have my *fucking gun*!"

Smiling, Murphy initialized the house's security system. "I'll be there in twenty."

* * *

Lulu rarely wigged out. But when she did, it was ugly. She'd pace, rant, lecture, and go for the jugular. Certain things pushed her buttons. Cruelty to humans and animals. Someone threatening a friend or family member. Violence.

She'd imagined a renegade bullet hitting an innocent child, and she'd seen red.

Jake Leeds had endured the brunt of her rage. He'd talked a cool game, but trying to reason with her only made her angrier. "How can you justify hurting someone?" she'd shouted. It wasn't until she'd threatened to call the police that he'd relinquished his gun. Begrudgingly.

She'd taken it. Begrudgingly.

She'd felt nauseous, as she'd wrapped her fingers around an implement of death. What kind of person aimed and shot at another person? Did the shooter experience pangs of remorse when he hit his target? She supposed soldiers and police officers felt justified, and rationally she understood that, but did they feel remorse? How did someone kill and live with it? Self-preservation, she imagined, would entail hardening one's heart. Developing a tough hide.

Jake Leeds, she'd decided after five minutes in his company, was definitely tough. Talking him out of his weapon had been a cinch compared to obtaining information. He'd answered all of her questions with a dry, "Ask Murphy."

Frustrated, she'd laid into Sofie, who'd stonewalled her with a grumpy, "I haven't had my coffee yet." So she'd turned on Rudy and Jean-Pierre. She couldn't remember half of what she'd spewed, but it must've been pretty rough. Jean-Pierre had clammed up. Jake had fled for the bathroom. Rudy had shot a scathing look, saying, "We're on a need-to-know basis, Lulu. We *know* that you're in danger."

"You mean Sofie's in danger," she'd corrected.

Her sister had shoved her bed-mussed hair off her face, saying, "Rudy had it right. Now stop badgering everyone and . . ." She sniffed the air. "Well, *that* smells decadent." She gave a wistful sigh, and regarded Lulu with a sympathetic smile. "Indulge in a cinnamon roll, hon. God knows I can't.

I'm going to get dressed. Murphy should be back soon. He'll explain."

And with that the red haze of anger transformed into a purple swirl of confusion. She wanted to ask Sofie for details, but her sister was already halfway up the stairs. She wanted to ask Rudy and Jean-Pierre, but they escaped into the living room. Jake was MIA.

Her boiling rage cooled. Sofie wasn't in danger!

Count your blessings.

Relief flooded through her, making her joints swishy. She dragged herself into the living room and sank down in Viv's chair. Fear had robbed her of her usual calm. Fear that someone wanted to hurt Sofie. Fear that Jake might accidentally shoot a child. Mind-blowing anxiety combined with the panic of having to deal with her attraction to Murphy.

She'd flipped.

Cheeks burning, she glanced over at Rudy and Jean-Pierre. They sat side by side on the couch in stony-faced silence. They'd never seen that side of her. Sofie had been unfazed, then again Sofie knew that soon after Lulu blew her cork, she fizzled out and quite often regretted her harsh words.

Well, she'd blown, fizzled, and now she was regretting big time.

"I'm sorry, guys. I freaked."

Rudy grunted. "I'll say. In addition to Tae Kwon Do, you might want to consider anger management classes."

Shell-shocked, Jean-Pierre blinked and scratched his forehead. "*Merde.*"

Contrite, Lulu stared at the toes of her sneakers. When Jean-Pierre had repeated his "sworn to secrecy" plea, she'd railed, "*What kind of a friend are you?*" In truth, he was the best of friends, and she knew her jab had cut deeply. "I didn't mean what I said, Jean-Pierre."

"I know." He cleared his throat. "Do not fret, *Chaton*. All is well."

Rudy interlaced his fingers with Jean-Pierre's, clearly worried his partner was still upset. "Where the hell is Murphy?"

"On his way." Jake Leeds walked in and dropped into the rocker recliner.

Regret continued to sing through Lulu's veins. She'd not only hurt Jean-Pierre. She'd ticked off Rudy.

"You're not yelling," Jake noted.

She glanced up, her voice thick with embarrassment. "I overreacted."

He met her gaze, a hopeful glint in his eyes. "Can I have my gun?"

"Are you leaving?"

"No."

"Then, no." She regretted a lot of things, confiscating his gun was not one of them.

Sofie strode into the living room wearing funky-heeled, pointy-toed boots, slim-fitting black pants, and a bright red form-fitting T-shirt. Her subtle make-up and upswept ponytail suggested she was going for casual. She'd achieved stunning.

Lulu glanced over to see if Jake's tongue was hanging out of his mouth. It wasn't. Then again, he'd seen Sofie in a skimpy robe and had done little more than raise a brow. He must really love his wife, she thought with a pang. Rudy was right. Not all men were schmucks.

A knock on the door caused Sofie to spin on her heels and Lulu to sit ramrod straight.

Murphy.

Anxiety bubbled. She would have preferred hostility. Anger was preferable to confusion. Certainly preferable to excitement. The man had introduced chaos and guns into her safe, calm world. How was it possible that she was actually looking forward to seeing him?

She sprang to her feet as Sofie led the infamous bodyguard into the living room. He looked freshly showered and shaved, and to-die-for handsome in his casual, yet hip, attire. Again she noted how he and Sofie complemented one another. Dark hair. Dark eyes. They'd make beautiful babies.

She massaged an ache in her chest, her pulse quickening when she realized she was the object of Murphy's sole attention.

"We need to talk, Princess." His tone, like his expression, was eerily calm, as if to say, "*Don't panic. It'll be all right.*"

Viv had taken a similar approach when she'd sat the sisters down to relay the news that their dad and Sof's mom had perished in a car accident. Lulu had been only seven at the time, but she well remembered the creepy suspense. Presently, her entire body buzzed with similar dread. She didn't want to hear whatever Murphy had to say, but rather than running from the room, she balled her clammy hands into fists and stood her ground. "Where's your gun?"

"Locked in my car."

"At least you know where yours is," Jake said. He pushed up the brim of his ball cap. "Okay. Where do you want to do this?"

"Why don't we sit around the dining room table?" Jean-Pierre suggested. "This calls for *café* and sweets."

"Sounds good," Sofie said. "The coffee part anyway."

Rudy, Jean-Pierre, and Jake rose simultaneously. Lulu's heart constricted. Sofie took a step toward her, and her anxiety tripled. "Why do I feel like I'm being ganged up on?"

"Because you are." Sofie looped her arm through Lulu's. "This is an intervention."

Perplexed, she eyeballed each person in the room.

Friends, family, and two authority figures. "I don't get it. Doesn't that pertain to substance abusers?"

Murphy closed the distance between them. He stared down at her with those intense eyes, and the ground shifted beneath her feet. "It pertains to an endangered person in denial."

"I'm not in denial. I'm not in danger." The words came out in a breathy croak. Rudy said something wise, something he'd probably read in one of his self-help books, but she couldn't focus on his words. She'd been struck stupid by Murphy's physical nearness. He didn't touch her, but she felt his strength and compassion all the same. Her heart bumped its way into her throat.

"That thong was for you, Princess," he said. "You've snagged an obsessive fan."

She blinked up at him. That was it? *That* was the bad news?

"An unsavory character with sexual intentions."

Nervous relief caused her to laugh. "That's ridiculous."

"No, it's not." Sofie gave her arm a squeeze, her eyes soft with concern. "It's dangerous. Some creep wants to get in your pants, and he's not playing nice."

Dumbfounded, Lulu gawked at Rudy and Jean-Pierre. "Do you believe this?"

They nodded. They *did!*

Head spinning, she unconsciously leaned into Sofie. "Even if someone," she paused, rolled her eyes, "has a crush on me. And even if the thong was a totally inappropriate gift, it was addressed to 'Girl of My Dreams.' How is that sinister?"

Sofie and Murphy traded a look.

"That's really getting on my nerves." Exasperated, Lulu pushed off her sister. "It's like you're all keeping a secret from me, tiptoeing around *whatever* because you think I won't be able to handle it." What she couldn't handle was the creepy suspense. "If there's more to this, then darn it, just spit it out!"

Sofie cursed under her breath. "Fine. You didn't have the flu last night."

Murphy grasped her shoulder, his eyes brimming with tenderness. "You were drugged."

Chapter Eleven

✳ *Nothing like being the bearer of bad news.* Murphy wanted to comfort Lulu by hauling her into his arms and kissing the misery from her brow. Instead, he tightened his grasp on her shoulder and allowed her to process. Sofie knew her sister well. The news that she'd been drugged hit hard. He felt her sway, mourned the devastated look on her face.

He cursed himself a bastard for delivering the blow.

Lulu glanced up as though she'd heard the mental chide, and whole-heartedly agreed. "I need some fresh air." Tight-lipped, she shook off his hand and stalked out of the room.

Murphy whistled low, and regarded the ragtag team with arched brows. He'd known this wouldn't be easy. "Give us a moment."

"Better you than me," Jake grumbled.

"I won't be shut out," Sofie said.

Gallow and Jean-Pierre seconded her decree.

Murphy nodded. "Noted." He caught Lulu on the screened porch righting a bicycle she'd knocked over in her wake.

"I don't believe you," she said without turning.

"I know." Rather than trying to calm her, he allowed her to blow through the outer door. First chance he got, he'd safe-proof the chaotic porch and replace the busted lock. The absence of a man in this household was glaring. He followed Lulu down the front steps—nearly tripping over that damned jack-o-lantern—and across the lawn. He fell in beside her as she race-walked toward the beach. "You're angry."

"No, I'm upset. There's a difference."

"I heard you have a hell of a temper." His lip twitched. "Sorry I missed it."

"I'm not." Her pale cheeks flushed pink. "It's not a pretty sight."

He'd lay odds it was a beautiful sight, but he kept that bet to himself. She radiated a natural beauty and a charged innocence that blew him apart like a nuclear missile. Maintaining professionalism in her presence was a trial. This was a definite first.

She continued her purposeful trek up the asphalt sidewalk, gaze fixed on the blue horizon.

He scanned the perimeter.

Upscale houses. Manicured lawns. Luxury cars parked in driveways. A man trimming hedges. Up ahead he saw kids skateboarding on the boardwalk and a yuppie couple rollerblading. Nothing suspicious. Unless you counted the oncoming platinum-haired, elderly woman walking her long-haired, pip-squeak dog. They wore matching yellow sweaters, rhinestone chokers, and flowery hats with rolled brims. Poor dog.

"Lulu!" The woman waved and trotted toward them, her garish red lips curved into a face-splitting smile. The dog trotted, but didn't smile. Probably hated the hat. Who wouldn't?

Lulu lifted her hand in a half-hearted greeting. "Good afternoon, Flora."

The woman pressed a hand to her ample, sagging bosom. "Who's your friend, dear?"

"This is Murphy. Murphy, this is Flora." Lulu reached down and scratched the chin of the snow-white dog. "This is Fluffy."

Flora and Fluffy. Murphy grinned. The princess kept colorful company. But instead of engaging in conversation, Lulu murmured a polite, "Have a nice day," and kept walking.

"Toodles!" Flora smiled and waved.

Murphy waved back. "Neighbor?" he asked Lulu.

"The neighborhood gossip, actually. But she's nice."

Naturally. He held his tongue until they'd scaled the sun-bleached steps of the southern end of the world famous board-walk. Five miles north: the Atlantic City casinos. And Oz. "There *are* some not-so-nice people in this world, Princess. Bad people who do bad things."

"I know that. I just don't . . . I don't mix with bad people." She grasped the wooden railing, stared out at the deserted beach and the white-capped Atlantic, and took a deep breath.

She'd grown up in her grandmother's house, had probably played on this beach as a child. How often had she escaped to this place to clear her head? To seek calm? He itched to know this woman. From her background, to her dreams, to her favorite brand of toothpaste. Getting to know someone, engaging in small talk, had never been more appealing.

Murphy moved in beside her, forced himself not to cover her hand with his own. Touching her, even in comfort, was dangerous. She looked amazing in her button-down shirt, cargo pants, and high-top sneakers. Her golden curls blew wild in the tangy ocean breeze. She was a spirited tomboy. A sexy enigma. And vivid images of last night only exacerbated his misery–the dancing, the kiss . . . *Focus, man.* "I know you don't want to believe that you were drugged, hon, but I'm pretty sure you were."

Her cheeks burned red. He wasn't sure if it was because of the endearment, a careless slip, or because of the subject matter. He pressed on. "Judging from your behavior and the symptomatic side effects, my money is on MDMA. In small doses it's a relatively harmless stimulant. A mood elevator that produces a euphoric state. Enhances sensations. Lowers inhibitions."

She pressed the heel of her hand to her forehead as if trying to push back the memory of her provocative dancing. Transparent as hell, she was reliving and regretting last night's escapades, and he knew it.

He took advantage of her silence. The more she knew, the safer he could make it for her. "MDMA is a tablet, candy-like in appearance. It comes in various colors—blue, yellow, pink—and it's stamped with a logo. Different logos for different brands. Anchors, rabbits, hearts, skulls . . . Sound familiar?"

"No." She gripped the railing tight, rocked back and forth on her sneakers. "Wait. Yes." She glanced sideways at Murphy. "Someone in the bathroom offered me a mint. It had a smiley face on it. I thought it was cute. It tasted awful, but I didn't say anything. I didn't want to make her feel bad. I think she liked me." She blushed. "You know, *liked* me."

Murphy's brow rose. "You mean she was a lesbian."

"I suppose she could have been bi. Or just a really friendly straight person. According to Jean-Pierre, curious women float over from Flying Monkeys once in awhile. Gay, bi, straight. I'm not very good at reading the signs. I guess I don't really care. If a person's nice . . . I *thought* she was nice." She pushed off the rail and began to pace. "I can't believe it. I broke a basic rule. *Never take candy from strangers.*" She thunked her forehead with the heel of her hand, once, twice. "How could I be so stupid?"

"You're not stupid, you're trusting." He smiled to ease her distress. "There's a difference." A subtle difference in his experience, but he kept that thought to himself. "Let's get back to the person who gave you the mint. Is that the same person who approached you later on the dance floor?"

"No. That was a man." She stopped in her tracks as a little kid zoomed by on his bike. She stared after the boy, and then turned and gawked at Murphy. "If this hits the newspapers, Princess Charming will be tarnished for life. I can see the headlines now: *DOPED UP STORYTELLER SEDUCES BODYGUARD!* Lead line: *In a bizarre twist, princess pukes on bodyguard's boots.* What will the parents think? What will the *children* think? I'm supposed to be a role model!"

Murphy suppressed a grin. Her predicament sure as hell wasn't funny, but her whimsical views warmed even the dankest subjects. "They won't think anything because they won't know. Those at the club who asked were told that you had a virus. They have no reason to believe otherwise. Now about the man on the dance floor . . . did he say anything?"

"No." Agitated, she shoved a hand through her wild curls. "He just smiled. He was coming toward me, at least I think he was. He could have been heading past me."

"Can you describe him?"

"Not clearly. It was crowded and dark, and I wasn't exactly coherent."

"Tall? Short? Fat? Thin?"

"Average."

"Young? Old?"

"Middle-aged."

"Short or long hair? Dark or Light?"

"Short. Dark. Brown, no black." She shook her head. "I'm not very good at remembering people. In my line of work I meet so many. I have to see someone a few times, have a discussion, although . . ."

Murphy inched forward. "What?"

"I did feel as though I'd seen him before."

"Can you place him?"

"No. It might come to me later, but just now, no." She massaged her temples. "I'm sorry. I have a lot on my mind."

He smoothed her windblown curls from her tortured face. "I know."

She swallowed hard, backed away from his touch and resumed her pacing. "Besides, my reaction makes no sense. He didn't do anything. Didn't say anything. He just *smiled*. Maybe I was just, you know, whacking out because of the drug."

Murphy angled his head. "It's possible. Paranoia is a side effect. But I'm not convinced. There's a lot to be said for gut feelings. I think you sensed the guy was bad news."

She paced, chewing on a thumbnail. After a few seconds she turned to face him. "Okay. I'll buy that I was drugged. It's not easy, but it does explain my . . ." she rolled her eyes, "unusual behavior. It was unfortunate, and I feel really stupid and angry, but that's what I get for ignoring something every five-year-old should know. That other part though, the part about the obsessed admirer, I just don't believe it. Why should I?" She swept her arms wide. "Look at me!"

"I'm looking." And he sure as hell liked what he saw. She didn't flaunt her figure, but it didn't take much to imagine her in the raw. He'd laid hands on those plentiful curves when they'd danced. And, whereas today her clothes bagged, last night's T-shirt and jeans had hugged in all the right places. *Oh, yeah.* He liked what he saw. *Sexy hair. Bountiful breasts.*

Great ass. But the attraction went beyond the physical. *That*, he decided, was the scary part for him, and, more than likely, the strongest appeal for the stalker.

He dragged a hand over his face.

Ticking off a list of her admirable qualities seemed like a dumb-ass thing to do, so he simply said, "Charismatic fireballs tend to light fires. I'm sure this isn't the first guy who's been hot for you, Princess."

She snorted, tossed up a hand. "Yeah, right. But thanks for trying."

Murphy bristled. This wasn't modesty. She honestly didn't get it. What did this woman see when she looked in the mirror? "Uh-huh. Well, like it or not, you're the girl of this man's dreams. He sent you a specifically orchestrated gift. Pearls in a seashell. Last night I cranked up that music box. It played a song from that movie we watched."

She blinked at him, retreated a step.

Miss Goody Two-shoes was backing away from the obvious, so Murphy got in her face. "Your first party yesterday. What did you appear as?"

"A mermaid. But that could be coincidental." She paused, sighed. "Or not. Okay. So maybe one of the men at the party—one of the catering staff, or a relative or friend of the Ditellis—has a secret fetish for mermaids. Maybe he sent me a gift, an inappropriate gift, but that doesn't mean he's *unsavory*. And how in the world does that tie into my being drugged at Oz?"

"You said the man on the dance floor looked familiar. Is it possible that you saw him earlier yesterday at the Ditelli party?"

She moistened her lips and swallowed hard as recognition flittered across her face.

"There's your connection." It also meant that Bogie had

been at that party. Ten to one the Ditellis were mob connected. "Did this guy approach you at the party? Did you get a name?"

Clearly overwhelmed, she shook her head. "No. He was standing with a group of men, cheering the kids on as we did the crabwalk race. They caught my attention because they were so loud. Actually, he wasn't cheering. He was just watching. Me." She palmed her brow. "I didn't think anything of it. People watch me all the time. I'm an entertainer. Although . . ."

"What?"

"Nothing."

She was holding something back. He wanted to pry, but sensed it wouldn't get him anywhere. He could almost see her erecting protective, fairy-tale castle walls. Everything ugly and evil relegated to the moat.

She moved back to the railing and gazed out at the sea. "This is crazy. Things like this don't happen to people like me."

Murphy thought about his upstanding parents. "Unfortunately, yes, they do."

She turned slowly, her nut-brown eyes swirling with suspicion. "How do you figure into this?"

He wondered when she'd get around to asking. Wondered if the truth would cause her to lower her defenses and let him in, or to shut him out completely. This wisp of a woman challenged him simply by being. His antithesis, she represented the beauty of the soul. His senses vibrated with the need to conquer and possess.

Bogie wasn't the only one in deep.

"Yesterday, I received a tip that you're in danger. That tip came from a trusted friend. Given my friend's line of work, I have good reason to believe your admirer is mob connected."

"I see." Her lips twisted into a skeptical smirk. "What does your friend do?"

"He's a special agent with the FBI. Organized Crime Program." Murphy tore his gaze from her luscious mouth, willed himself to check his raging testosterone. *What the hell?* He wasn't a puberty-cursed teen. He was thirty-nine. *Two months from forty. Two months from middle-freaking-age.* "He's undercover just now, so it makes things tricky. I can't seek him out, can't enlist the aide of authorities. Not without compromising his case and, more importantly, his safety. So, until he can provide me with more information, we'll have to operate on the side of caution."

Brow raised, she perched her fists on her hips. "An FBI agent and a mobster. Jeez, this is better than one of my loonytales."

He ignored her sarcasm and plowed on. "We have two choices. The easiest solution entails canceling your upcoming performances until further notice. I can protect you more effectively if you're out of the public eye."

"Are you nuts?" she shrieked. "I have responsibilities, obligations. Children are counting on me. Forget it, Murphy."

He figured as much.

She hugged herself against a brisk wind. "Even if I did put stock in this madness, I'm not going into hiding just because some idiot schmuck thinks I'm his ideal!"

It occurred to him that he'd misinterpreted Sofie's take on her sister. When faced with unpleasant situations, Lulu didn't fall apart. She fought back. It was a hell of a turn-on. Murphy glanced inland. They had the full attention of Flora and Fluffy and the hedge-trimming guy. He also noticed a familiar blue Lincoln recently parked a block from Lulu's house. Was Sam Marlin sitting in that car? Hiding behind a tree? Lurking near the boardwalk? What did Sofie call him?

A *watcher*. The possibility that the creep was spying on Lulu reinforced Murphy's intention.

"Okay. Plan B." He took off his jacket, wrapped it around her shoulders, and tugged her close. "You're going off the market. As of now you are unavailable and unattainable. You are going to tell everyone who will listen about your new boyfriend."

She blinked up at him, her voice a strangled whisper. "But, I don't have a boyfriend."

"You do now." He had his hands in her hair, his mouth on her lips before she could utter *don't*, or *help*, or whatever was on her fascinating mind. She tasted of bubblegum, oranges, and sunshine. He nipped and suckled her lush lips until she sighed and opened to him. He was ruthless in the invasion. He claimed her sweet tongue and feasted, tasting victory when she moaned into his mouth.

She clung to him. She retaliated. She cold-cocked him by slipping eager fingers beneath his shirt, and digging her nails into his back muscles. She moved in for the kill, hooking a leg around his own, and grinding against his erection. She wanted more and he wanted to give it. Right here, right now, on the damned public boardwalk.

Blood surged to his groin, urging him to spirit her beyond the privacy of the dunes. His analytical mind advised retreat.

Hands framing her face, he eased back and dropped his forehead to hers. Controlling his breathing and other traitorous body parts took keen concentration. Regardless, he was tuned into her stillness.

Charged air. Eerie quiet. The calm before the storm.

* * *

"Do me a favor, Princess," he said softly. "Don't slap me, curse me, or knee me in the nuts. I'd like for Flora and the rest of the enraptured audience to believe we're lovers."

So that kiss had been a strategic *ploy*? Heart thundering in her ears, Lulu feigned a calm she didn't feel. "Lucky for you, I'm a talented actress." She hadn't realized how talented until this moment. Molten lava flowed through her veins. Her private parts throbbed and tingled. The only thing that would have made that torrid kiss hotter was if they'd been rolling around in the surf like Burt Lancaster and Deborah Kerr in *From Here To Eternity*. Yet her tone was even, her expression placid. Somehow, she even managed to conceal her trembling. After all, her dignity was at stake.

Murphy's mouth hitched into a lopsided grin.

She wanted to smack him. Ever the diplomat, she balled her fists at her sides. "I find it hard to believe that I'm in real danger, but I seem to be in the minority. So, for now, I'll go along with this stupid boyfriend ruse." She glanced inland, grimacing when loose-lipped Flora waved. In less than an hour, the whole neighborhood would know of their public display. Jaw set, she looked back to Murphy. "But you're not moving in."

"The threat level necessitates coverage twenty-four/seven."

"I'm really beginning to despise that term. Whatever happened to 'around-the-clock'?"

His grin widened as he pushed her arms through the sleeves of his jacket and ushered her back down onto the street. "If you're worried about your reputation . . ."

"Of course, I'm worried about my reputation," she gritted out as she breathed in the manly scent of leather and spicy aftershave. She felt oddly sexy wearing Murphy's jacket, the lining still warm from his body heat. What would it feel like to wrap herself in his bed sheets? "Children look up to me," she said, refusing to let her imagination take flight. "I'm supposed to set a good example. I can't openly live in sin."

"Isn't that a little old-fashioned?"

"If having standards and morals is old-fashioned, then, yes, hellooo, meet a dinosaur. Go ahead and laugh. Most people do."

He squeezed her elbow. "I'm not most people."

"Bad enough that I'm divorced," she blurted, not wanting to ponder his unexpected acceptance of her archaic views.

Murphy glanced down at her and she cringed. She really hadn't meant to say that out loud. He held silent as he whizzed her past her wide-eyed neighbors. Whatever Flora was whispering to Mr. Thorndyke must've been pretty juicy. He didn't even notice Fluffy peeing on his beloved hedges.

Once they were out of earshot, Murphy picked up their discussion. "Did you try to make the marriage work?"

"For all the good it did me." She winced at the bitterness in her voice. What was wrong with her? Usually she kept the disappointment and hurt bottled.

"So *he* left *you*?"

"It wasn't his fault," she said in a backpedaling rush. "I wasn't the woman he thought he married." She read the curiosity in his gaze and knew she'd just made things worse. Anticipating an awkward question, she quickened her pace. "I don't want to talk about it."

He easily kept up. "Then let's talk about my moving in."

"There's nothing to discuss. You'll just have to find another way to protect me. That's *if* I truly need protection." Denial, just now, was the only thing that kept her fried brain from exploding. Sam Marlin's car was parked up ahead. She hoped he hadn't delivered another *gift*. She'd had enough drama for one day. She sailed into her house and up the stairs. She didn't want to face her sister and friends right now, and surely Murphy would understand her need for privacy after all he'd just dumped on her plate. She swept into her bedroom just as her cell phone rang.

She snatched up the receiver, eager for a distraction. "Lulu's Loony—"

"Who's *Chaz*?"

Her nerves jangled at the sound of a man's abnormally quiet voice. "Who is this?"

"Is he the one you danced with last night? The one who drove you home?"

Lulu faltered as the dam of denial broke and stark reality flooded her senses. Panic and anger warred as she grappled to steady her voice. "Did you drug me?"

"I'm sorry you got ill. It was unfortunate."

"Why?" Her brain and temper exploded. "Because it blew your plan to take advantage of me when my inhibitions were down?"

"I enjoyed watching you dance. Your smile . . . has an effect on me."

"Well, *drugs* have an effect on me," she blurted into the phone. "A big, fat negative effect. You want to make me smile? Promise me you'll never pull another stunt like that. Drugs are illegal and immoral and . . . *dangerous*. Promise me—"

"That man," he repeated softly. "The one who drove you home. Who is he?"

His directness, his eerie calm chafed. She heard a soft rap, glanced up and saw Murphy looming on her threshold. She held his gaze, absorbed his strength. "My boyfriend."

The pregnant pause was frightening, but his final words inflicted more horror than a slasher movie. "He's not good enough for you," he ground out. "None of them are."

She sat there frozen, as silence droned in her ear. It rivaled the buzzing in her head.

Murphy walked over, pried the phone from her grasp, and punched buttons.

"What are you doing?"

"Checking the last incoming call." He shook his head. "No number." He powered off and laid the cell on the nightstand.

She didn't know what to think, what to feel. Only one thing was clear, the mystery caller had blown over her concerns about drugs. "He wouldn't listen to reason."

"I doubt he's a reasonable man." Murphy sat down next to her. "What did he say?"

"He said you're not good enough for me. That none of them are. None of *who*?"

He scraped a hand along his jaw.

Her skin prickled. *More creepy suspense.* "What?"

"I'm not sure. What else?"

"He wanted to know if you were Chaz. I thought maybe the call was about Sofie, but then he asked if that's who I was dancing with last night, if that's who took me home. He asked who you were, and I said my boyfriend. And, well, you know the rest." She realized then that she'd grabbed Murphy's hand. She relaxed her grip, sighed. "Sorry."

"Don't be." He squeezed her fingers when she tried to pull away. "You and I are going to be real cozy from here on out, Princess."

At this moment she wanted that more than anything. She wanted to take refuge in Murphy's arms, give herself over to his protection. Evil had officially infiltrated her happy-go-lucky world.

Part of her was numb with disbelief. Another part, scared. But mostly she was angry. How many other women had this man hassled? Was he completely without morals?

"I don't want that creep anywhere near this neighborhood. At least ten children live in this area." She turned baleful eyes on Murphy. "And what about Flora and Mr. Thorndyke? They're both in their seventies. Defenseless as babes."

He smoothed his thumbs over her knuckles. "He's not interested in your neighbors, Luciana."

"What about Sofie? What if he tries to break into the house? What if she's here and tries to take him down with a karate chop or something? What if she only damages his ego? What if he retaliates?"

Murphy angled his head, his lips curved in a soft smile. "That's a lot of *what ifs*."

"And what if someone, like Mr. Thorndyke or Flora, spots him coming out of the house? Wouldn't he feel compelled to dispose of witnesses? Don't mobsters cut off people's body parts?" Her chest ached as the walls of reality closed in. She couldn't breathe.

Murphy drew her into his arms and stroked his hand down her back. "That imagination of yours is downright wicked, babe."

"Things like that happen, don't they?"

"Yeah." He tightened his hold, nuzzled his chin on her head. "But not on my watch."

His reassurance fell on deaf ears. She'd already concocted the worse case scenario. She refused to give it the slimmest chance of playing out. *Alternate scenario . . . Alternate ending . . .* She pushed off Murphy. "Do you live around here?"

"Smithville."

Thirty minutes from the Carnevale. Perfect. She wouldn't have to miss any work. Sofie could move in with Rudy and Jean-Pierre. They'd keep her safe. Meanwhile the bad guy

would have no reason whatsoever for coming into this neighborhood.

Heart pounding, she bounced up off the bed, raced into her
walk-in closet, and tossed out three suitcases.

Murphy stood. "Going somewhere?"

Upcoming loonytales whizzed though her mind as she
snatched costumes from hangers. Brow damp with sweat, she
told herself she wasn't running away, but taking a creative
approach to self-defense. Told herself she wasn't moving in,
just staying over . . . temporarily. She utilized her acting skills
and met Murphy's challenging gaze with a calm, determined
smile. "Plan C."

Chapter Twelve

✳ Jake steered his car into his driveway and cut the engine. He sat there clutching the wheel, staring at the Victorian money-pit he and Afia had been slowly refurbishing, and pondered the Princess Charming calamity. He wanted to clear his head before he faced his beautiful, intuitive, and highly inquisitive wife. The last thing he wanted was for her to ask, "What's troubling you, Jake?" Because "Nothing, baby," would be his response—a bald-faced lie.

Plenty troubled him.

He'd tried to shake the nagging sense of foreboding. Had tried to reason things out on the way home. After all, Murphy had spirited Lulu away to his fortress in the woods. No way in hell was anyone going to get to her there. And he doubted the stalker would make a play during her appearances at the Carnevale. Too public. Too well-lit. Even if he did try to grab her, Murphy would be there, and he'd have the bastard for lunch.

Regardless—Jake had a bad feeling that stemmed from troubling facts.

Fact: Joe Bogart worked with the organized crime program.

Fact: Anthony Rivelli, who used to work at the Carnevale and now worked at Oz, had a past connection with the Falcones, New Jersey's slipperiest crime family.

Fact: Rivelli also had a past connection with Jean-Pierre, and as a result both JP and Rudy worked part time at Oz.

Fact: Lulu worked at the Carnevale.

Fact: She was drugged at Oz.

Was Lulu's stalker a Falcone? Were the Falcones being set up by the FBI? Was the investigation somehow connected to Oz? Had Rivelli lied when he'd said he'd broken his engagement to the mob boss's daughter?

He should've discussed these suspicions with Murphy, but he had no hard evidence and, where Anthony Rivelli was concerned, Jake constantly felt like he was walking on egg shells. One of his past investigations had turned up a dirty little secret on Rivelli. A secret Afia felt she and Jake were obligated to guard. He didn't agree, but Afia was adamant, and he'd do just about anything to make her happy.

She wouldn't be happy if Rivelli's job was compromised, yet again, as a result of one of Jake's cases. Only this wasn't really Jake's case, it was Murphy's . . . and Bogart's. He'd give the agent until tomorrow to call Murphy with details. In reality, it had only been twenty-four hours since the fed's initial contact. With any luck he'd point the finger at someone other than a Falcone. If Bogart didn't reestablish contact, Jake would clue Murphy in on his concerns. Later tonight, he'd do some digging via the information highway, see if he could verify, or refute, a connection between the Falcones and Oz.

Just now he wanted to hold his wife in his arms. A few months ago Angela Falcone had aimed a gun at Afia. The memory still shook him.

Jake bolted for the house. He opened the front door and faltered on the threshold, thrown off by the absence of Mouser. The black-and-white cat never failed to greet him.

Don't panic. Just because the old tom's getting up in years doesn't mean anything's wrong.

He whipped off his jacket and ball cap and placed his recovered Glock in the top drawer of the Queen Anne bureau. He swept through the sitting room, the living room—no Mouser. He didn't spot even one of their six cats.

Maybe Afia was serving up kitty treats. She spoiled those fur-balls worse than he did. But his sweet-natured wife wasn't in the kitchen or laundry room. She wasn't anywhere downstairs.

So what? he rationalized as the back of his neck prickled. So she's upstairs sleeping, or showering, or cleaning. But it was impossible to think like a sane man with the certifiable Falcones on his brain.

He took the steps two at a time.

His mouth went dry when he entered their bedroom and spotted Mouser, Rosco, Barney, and Velma sitting side by side, staring into the master bedroom's john. Mouser looked over his furry shoulder as if to say, "Where the hell have *you* been?"

Heart in throat, Jake moved toward the sound of soft weeping.

Holy Christ. His petite wife sat cross-legged on the bathroom's cold tile floor in her underwear and his police academy T-shirt, her face buried in her hands. He had to step over four cats to get to her. The other two, Scamp, the loner who trailed after Afia like a puppy, and Gucci, the kitten she'd rescued from a shelter, sat protectively at her side.

Jake squatted in front of her. "Afia." He smoothed his hand over her glossy, waist-length hair. "Baby, what's wrong?"

She wept harder and mumbled disjointed words into her hands.

Willing his nerves steady, he glanced around the bathroom and saw a familiar box, the same brand as the previous month, lying opened on the sink. Understanding clicked. The home pregnancy test had registered negative. Again.

Though disappointed, his body hummed with relief. *This* kind of hurt he could kiss away and make better. "Sweetheart, please don't cry." She was breaking his freaking heart. Jake sat on the floor and pulled her into his lap. "We'll just keep trying. Trying is fun, right?" he teased.

He tilted her chin up and met her watery gaze. Red nose. Puffy eyes. She'd never been a pretty crier. Then she laughed through her tears, and damn, his relief jumped back to concern, because, Christ, she was really losing it.

Before he could say another word, she held up the pregnancy test strip.

It looked different from the others. It looked . . . He blinked. "Are you . . . are we . . ."

"Pregnant." She planted a wet, salty kiss on his mouth and then threw her arms around his neck and hugged tight.

Shaken, Jake clung to his wife as he felt the world tilt. He glanced toward the cats, swore they were smiling. He chuckled, his throat tight with emotion. "Holy shit. I'm going to be a dad."

Laughing, Afia pushed him back on the tile floor and tugged at his jeans' zipper. "Let's celebrate."

* * *

Confetti exploded out of specifically designed cannons, peppering the casino lobby with scraps of bright colored paper. Facilities despised the mess, as did the slot technicians. Never failed, at least a few pieces of confetti would flutter onto the casino floor, slipping through cracks and mucking up the inner workings of the slot machines.

But the patrons loved the hoopla—the colorful parade of stilt-walkers, magicians, jugglers, unicyclists, and the casino mascot. And most of all, they loved the free metallic bead necklaces the strolling entertainers passed out. Since most regulars gambled away the bulk of their weekly income, Sofie almost understood their bizarre enthusiasm for any-thing *free*.

She watched the chaos, grateful she wasn't on bead duty.

"Hey, sweet cheeks. I got this sweepstakes entry in the mail. What do I do with it?"

Stick it up your ass? Sofie bit back the tart reply. *Definitely not on the casino-approved list of appropriate responses.* Besides it's not as if the old man deserved a bitchy reply. It wasn't his fault that she'd been called in on her day off to cover a job that she hated.

Although, in truth, she'd rather be here than twiddling her thumbs back at Rudy and JP's townhouse. She wasn't thrilled about imposing on the lovebirds—like she needed to be reminded of the bliss she'd lost out on with Chaz— but short of leaving the country it was the only way to insure her sister's well-being. Lulu, the stubborn runt, had refused Murphy's protection unless Sofie accepted equal protection from their friends. She could take care of her-self, but she'd sucked it up and acquiesced, harboring an ulterior motive.

You'd have to be an imbecile not to sense the attraction between Murphy and her sister. She wanted Lulu to move into the man's house. She wanted them to have secluded privacy. Maybe then her straight-laced sister would be more inclined to let nature take its course. She kind of liked the idea of Lulu hooking up with a man so totally her opposite. The dreamer and the realist. There was a certain balance in that, a balance neither sister had ever achieved. Even though Sofie wasn't fond of the male gender just now, she sort of liked Colin Murphy. She especially liked the way he looked at her sister. Like he'd kill anyone who hurt her.

"So what do I do with this entry form?" The old man repeated, jerking Sofie out of her thoughts.

She smiled down at the prune-faced, white-bearded man (because he was like, what, four foot nine?) and swept her hand—à la car trade show model—toward the gigantic Plexiglas drum directly behind her. The one with the huge sign that read: *Vacation of a Lifetime Sweepstakes! Deposit entries here!*

"What?" He squinted at the drum filled with hundreds of other entries. "Stick it in there?"

Or up your ass. Your choice. She was definitely in a mood. "Just drop it in the slot, sir."

"Should I fold it first?"

"Whatever you like." She'd witnessed everything from a single-fold, to a tri-fold, to a crumpled ball. Some customers assumed that if the entry was crumpled it would be easier to grab onto when the winner was being plucked from the drum. Gamblers operated under all kinds of quirks and superstitions. Similar to theater people.

"Would you rub it for luck?"

Coming from a theater family, she didn't balk. "Sure." She reached for the entry.

The cantankerous gnome snatched it back, performed a

pelvis thrust, and cackled. "Wasn't talking about my coupon, honey."

Oh, brother. Maybe if he were a foot taller, forty years younger, and looked like Jude Law. Nope. Not even then. She'd never get past the stained polyester pants and the mingling odors of fried fish and medicinal mouthwash. "Don't make me signal a guard, sir." She nabbed smelly-man's entry form and deposited it in the drum and, because a security camera was trained on the sweepstakes area and she needed this job, dismissed him with her friendliest greeter-girl smile. "Have a lucky day."

"Why should today be any different from the others?" he grumbled, adjusting his ratty fanny pack and shuffling onto the crowded casino floor.

Sofie took stock of his stringy white ponytail, striped shirt, plaid pants, and worn red sneakers, trying to decide if he was fashion or *mentally* challenged. Both, she decided as he plopped down on a blue cushioned stool and started pumping coins into a slot machine. After all, the man had just asked her to stroke his pecker for luck. *As if.* She was damned particular about whose pecker she stroked. Well, not as particular as Lulu. The only pecker she'd ever touched was her husband's, and they'd been separated for over two years.

Two years without sex. Sofie couldn't imagine.

Of course, two months ago she wouldn't have imagined herself strutting around an Atlantic City casino in fishnet stockings and a sequined costume befitting a trapeze artist answering questions like "Which way to the bathroom," "How do I get to the boardwalk," and "Where's the buffet," three hundred freaking times a day. Two months ago she was still living in Manhattan, aggressively pursuing her acting career. Two months ago there'd been hope of landing a star role and an ample amount of money in her bank account. Two months ago she'd been under the illusion that she was in an honest-to-God relationship.

Now she was broke, financially and emotionally, and her sister was being stalked by a nut. Speaking of which, Sofie shifted on her T-strap pumps and surreptitiously scanned the crowd for watchers.

Sam and The Clapper were absent, but Maurice was pestering Wizard the magician, and Photo-Boy was snapping away at Raven the showgirl stilt-walker. The disposable camera creep probably had his walls papered with snapshots of female performers. The thought sickened Sofie, but not as much as the thought that Lulu's stalker had followed her to a children's party. He'd drugged Lulu. Would he harm a child? She wished to hell Murphy's *trusted source* had provided them with a specific ID on the stalker. Why all this cloak-and-dagger stuff?

Irritation hummed through her veins as she continued to scan the Sunday evening crowd. Patrons entered the sweepstakes, their questions grating more than usual as she struggled to pinpoint and study suspicious-looking men. Maybe it was her mood, but everyone with two legs and a dick looked suspicious.

She took her break fifteen minutes ahead of schedule. If she didn't seek solace, and now, she was going to punch someone. She abandoned the sweepstakes bin—if people couldn't read the sign, screw 'em—and weaved her way through the crowd to the door that opened to the back of the house. Luckily, the greeter-girl dressing room was a short walk down the hall. Three seconds later she punched the combo on the lock pad and swung open the door.

Her brain seized as she felt someone move in behind her. It happened so fast. The door shut, and a man, a stranger, had her pinned up against the dressing room wall, his hand covering her mouth. His face was too close to get a clear look, but he reeked of cheap aftershave and spearmint gum.

He angled his mouth close to her ear. "I need you—"

She jerked up her knee, and although she managed to cut off whatever crude request he had in mind, he effectively shielded his balls.

"Jesus, woman. Calm down."

Give in without a fight? *Fuck you.* She bit his hand, raked the edge of her shoe down his shin, and stomped the heel of her pump down hard on his toes.

"God*damn*!" He jerked back, hopping on his good foot.

She took advantage, delivering a front kick to his knee. He blocked her strike, grabbing her ankle and flipping her to the carpeted floor. She forgot to scream. She was too busy trying to get the upper hand on the bastard. In two counts he had her flat on her back, his lean, hard body pressed against the length of her.

"Hold still," he said through clenched teeth. "I'm not going to hurt you. I need you to get a message to Murphy."

She froze, blinked up at her assailant, and tried not to obsess on the fact that her corset had shifted in their struggle. The feel of his silk shirt against her bare breasts sent shock waves throughout her body. "How do you know Murphy?" she asked, surprised that she could form a coherent thought, let alone a sentence.

"He's an old friend."

Her mind raced. "Are you his trusted source?"

He managed a wry grin even though his face was contorted with pain. "Is that what he called me?"

"Get the hell off of me," Sofie demanded.

"So that you can maim me?"

"That's what you get for sneaking in and pinning me against the wall. Was that really necessary?"

He sobered. "I needed privacy. I didn't want you to scream. I don't have much time before they start wondering what's taking so long. A man generally drains his bladder in under five minutes."

"Before *who* starts wondering?"

"Never mind about that." He started to get up.

"Wait! Close your eyes."

"Why?"

"Just do it," she growled, struggling to tug up her skimpy costume as he rolled off her and struggled to stand upright. She figured she'd hurt him a lot more than he was letting on. She refused to feel bad. He'd scared the hell out of her.

He fell back against the door, hands on knees.

She scooted back against the lone arm chair and studied him as he caught his ragged breath. Black lambskin blazer, creased black trousers, cobalt blue silk shirt, unbuttoned and showcasing a bronzed chest. When he raised his head she got a clear look at the gold cross hanging around his neck. The man screamed South Philly Italian.

High forehead beaded with sweat, he dragged back his scraggly, dark, shoulder-length hair and breathed deep. She couldn't help but admire his strong, square jaw and deep set eyes. *Smoldering brown eyes, decadent as aged cognac.* Both of his ears were pierced with small, gold hoops. The moustache and the beatnik patch of dark whiskers beneath his bottom lip completed the sinister, sexy package. He reminded Sofie of a grungy Johnny Depp. Lust shot through her veins shocking her more than his invasion. "Who's after my sister?"

"A very bad man." His gaze caressed her cleavage before making lazy contact with her eyes. "But between me and Murph we'll keep her safe."

Her nipples hardened under his not so subtle appraisal, a

perplexing physical reaction since this man had just attacked her. *Must be the adrenaline.* She mustered sarcasm to cover her jitters. "Someone drugged her last night at Oz. You call that keeping her safe?"

"Stay away from Oz."

His expression was so fierce that she blinked. What was wrong with Oz? She'd gone dancing there on several occasions. It was a favorite watering hole of the cast from Venetian Vogue. It was also where Rudy, JP, and Anthony worked. Surely Lulu's incident was an isolated event. "Why?"

"The less you know, the better. And what I have to say is for Murphy's ears only. *Capito, bella signorina?*"

Oh, she understood all right. More than he knew. The fact that he'd just called her *beautiful lady* only added to her discomfort. "*Capito.*" She smirked, adding under her breath, "*Lei arrogante mucca.*"

He angled his head. "Did you just call me an arrogant cow?"

She'd meant to call him an arrogant pig, but she'd dropped Italian after one semester, losing interest just as she had with ballet and theater history class. Close enough, she decided with a righteous sniff. She tapped her wrist watch. "Time's ticking, piss boy."

His full lips twitched into a hint of a smile. "Most women call me Joey, but whatever floats your boat, babe." His good humor faded as he swiped the back of his hand over his moist brow. "Tell Murph your sister's admirer has a reputation for seducing women he's obsessed with and roughing them up when the thrill is gone."

Sofie's stomach turned. "Great."

"Tell him we need this guy or I'd eliminate him myself."

She swallowed. "Eliminate?"

"Tell him it'll be over within a week max. He'll know what to do."

He started to leave. Sofie scrambled to her three-inch heels. "Why didn't you contact Murphy yourself?"

"Tricky getting private time just now. Phones, including my cell, are being monitored."

"So you drove over here to talk to *me*?" She shoved a hand through her thick, tousled hair. "Wait. I'm not even scheduled for today. I'm filling in for someone. How did you know I'd be here?"

"I didn't. My bad boy associate has a weakness for black-jack and friendly eye candy." His smoldering gaze lazed over her scantily clad body. "The Carnevale offers both. We've been here a few times over the past month."

She couldn't tell if he was judging or admiring her. It rankled that she cared. "So this asshole's been watching Lulu for *weeks*?"

"I didn't know he had a hard-on for her until yesterday," he said, sounding defensive. He glanced at his watch. "Is the inquisition over?"

"How did you know I'm Lulu's sister?"

He grinned, and her breath stalled. The man was frickin' gorgeous.

"I know quite a bit about you, Sofia. And by the way, the knee-to-the-balls tactic? Any man worth his salt would antic-ipate that instinctual strike. You need to pay more attention in class." He turned the knob. "Just give Murph the message. A week."

The fact that he knew she attended martial arts class was disconcerting, yet absurdly intriguing. His gaze dropped to her mouth and her brain glitched. If she moved forward she'd clip him on his cocky chin, or worse, tackle him again for the sheer thrill of getting horizontal. The physical pull was *that* intense. She cursed herself an idiot and stood her ground. She stared into those bedroom eyes and issued a heartfelt threat. "If anything happens to my sister, *Joseph*, I'll track you down and send you to hell."

He limped out the door, serious as death. "Too late, babe. I'm already there."

Chapter Thirteen

Colin Murphy was a man of mystery. Forget the part about being an international protection specialist and all the encompassing intrigue. He lived in a fourteen-room house—alone. Only five of the rooms had furniture. None of those rooms contained anything outside of basics. No wall hangings. No knick-knacks. Nothing to suggest he had any interests or hobbies.

The architectural wonder looked as though it was spanking new, and from the severe lack of furnishings, Lulu had assumed Murphy had only recently moved in. She'd been shocked to learn that he'd had the place built six years ago and had since called it home.

In her opinion there wasn't anything homey about this house, although it had grand possibilities. The master bath alone had caused her eyes to bug. Sofie would kill for that much vanity space, but it was the two-person hot tub that made Lulu drool. If she ever needed a therapeutic soak it was now. She was wound up tighter than a cheap watch.

She eyed the bottle of Chablis that Murphy had just set aside. She'd refused a glass when he'd offered, more out of habit than anything. She'd never been a drinker. But it occurred that a few sips might be the ticket for calming her just enough to get her through this dinner. She'd neatly avoided Murphy for a good four hours after he'd given her the grand tour. Hiding out in the guest bedroom—the only furnished room on the second floor—she'd booted up her laptop computer and had worked diligently on an upcoming loonytale. It had been a fabulous way to escape reality. For two hundred and forty glorious minutes all was right with the world. No stalker. No drugs. No Murphy.

Until he'd knocked on the door to announce that he'd cooked dinner.

She'd envisioned sitting at the ultra-modern, ultra-impersonal luncheonette counter scarfing down a plate of Hamburger Helper. That would have been doable. Just her luck the man was a veritable Bobby Flay. Red Snapper with Sweet Garlic Rice. The finely garnished food smelled more decadent than Jean-Pierre's cinnamon rolls, and looked too pretty to eat. Murphy had gone all out, including setting the kitchen table—which had a magnificent bay window view of the surrounding woods—for two.

Reality check. She was spending the night, all night, alone with a gorgeous, dangerous hunk. "*Do you have a condom?*" sprang to mind.

Supremely self-conscious, Lulu clasped her hands in her lap and cleared her throat. "On second thought, maybe I will have a little wine."

His lips curved slightly as he poured her half a glass. "Sofie called me a half hour ago. The federal agent I told you about made contact with her."

Heart pounding, Lulu reached for her glass. "Why Sofie? Why not you?"

"Circumstances." He left it at that, saying, "The point is,

this should be over within a week."

A week. She could endure this insanity, Murphy's twenty-four/seven *protection* for a measly week, couldn't she? She tore her gaze from his handsome face and tried to dissolve the lump in her throat with a sip of wine. Actually it was quite tasty. Like Murphy. *Don't think about that sinfully delicious kiss.*

"That's not to say that we don't have to take precautions." He scooped up a fork of rice. "I'd like you to reconsider clearing your schedule. It would simplify things."

"For you maybe." She dipped the prongs of her fork into her fish, marveling at the texture and aroma. Big difference between Murphy's delicacy and store-bought fish sticks. "Personally, I can't afford to lose the income. Nor am I willing to disappoint forty-five children and their parents."

Murphy chewed his food, cocked an inquiring brow.

"Friday evening I'm appearing at a Halloween party. I've been asked to create a loonytale for two first grade classes. I'm calling it *The Spookytown Scare.* I racked my brain trying to come up with appropriate games to go with the interactive tale. The eyeball relay should be a hoot." She snickered. *Balancing creepy rubber eyeballs on spoons while they raced toward their partner. A guaranteed hit.* "Anyway, those kids are counting on me. You wouldn't know what that's like but . . ." His icy look stopped her cold. It was fleeting but as brisk as an Arctic wind. She sipped more wine, concentrated on her fish. "Anyway, I'm not canceling." *What was that about?*

He changed the subject before she could ask. "What about the rest of the week?"

"I'm off Thursday. Tomorrow through Wednesday I'm booked at the Carnevale. Six hour shifts. Noon to six." She squirmed under his regard. "If you don't want to drop me off I can always call a cab."

"You don't get this, do you? I'm not letting you out of my sight, Princess."

She got it. She wasn't dense. Just nervous. "What about tonight?"

"What about it?"

"You said you're not letting me out of your sight. Are we sleeping in the same room?"

His dark eyes sparked with amusement. Probably because her voice had warbled. She steeled herself for a Sofie-like comment. She wouldn't blame him for poking fun at her. She did sound like a skittish relic. Oh, God, she thought with sudden clarity, I *am* a skittish relic.

"I hadn't planned on bunking with you," he said, surprising her with his professional tone and expression. "But if it would make you feel safer—"

"It wouldn't." She already felt as if she were dancing on the edge of a cliff. Her heart bumping and fluttering as she openly courted danger. Her face flushed with a rush of heat as she acknowledged ulterior reasons for moving into Murphy's home. This wasn't solely about protecting herself from a stalker—because, really, that aspect was still so totally surreal. This was about getting closer to Colin Murphy. Or as Sofie had put it, sampling life and lust. Lust was something she'd never experienced with Terry. Affection, yes. Love, yes. But never lust.

Murphy tapped into a foreign part of her, a passionate, uninhibited slice of her conservative being. It would have been easy to blame the dirty dancing and the couch kiss on that mood elevating drug, but it was the kiss on the boardwalk that spelled out the truth. She was h-o-t for Colin Murphy who was unbelievably s-e-x-y. When she'd asked about their sleeping arrangements her voice hadn't cracked with dread, it had hitched with hope.

Unfortunately, his response had only reinforced her theory that his interest in her was purely professional. Logically, she knew it was for the best. As a lifetime partner he was all wrong.

Wasn't he?

She pondered his odd reaction to her comment on disappointing children while finishing her meal. What was up with that? Had his parents bailed at a time when he'd really needed them? Or, as an adult, had he let down a nephew? An acquaintance? A *son*?

Murphy, who wasn't much of a talker by her standards, ate in companionable silence, refilling her empty wine glass before he cleared their dinner plates. By the time he served the mixed chicories and apple salad, she had a pretty hefty list of questions and observations. Maybe it was her curiosity, maybe it was the wine, but she could no longer curb her tongue.

"Thank you for making dinner," she said, aiming for a casual segue. "It was delicious. You're an incredible cook."

"You're welcome. And thanks. Both of my mothers loved to cook. Guess it wore off."

Two moms? She jumped on that subtle clue eager to unravel the mystery of Colin Murphy. "Viv does the same thing," she noted, stabbing a leaf of radicchio. "Serves salad after the main course. Very Italian of you."

"I grew up in an Italian household."

"You did?" The plot thickens. "Given your name, I assumed you were Irish."

"I am."

She waited for him to elaborate. Instead he sipped his wine. Jeez. "So you're . . . adopted?"

He nodded.

"But you kept your last name."

Another nod.

For cripes sake. It was like talking to a tree stump. A very attractive tree stump, but nonetheless . . . Intrigued, Lulu pushed aside her salad and concentrated on the secretive man across the table. It felt good to focus on something other than her dilemma. "So what are your adopted parents' names?"

"Manny and Rosa Bogart. And before you ask about brothers and sisters, none by blood, one by choice. Joe Bogart. He's the FBI agent I told you about."

Well, hello. That explained why he took the agent's word as gospel. She could tell by his tone of voice that he was fond of the Bogarts, especially his *brother*. It warmed her heart to know that he had people he cared about, and who undoubtedly cared for him. He seemed like such a loner.

Murphy stood to clear the table. She tried to help, but he relieved her of the plates and shooed her toward the open living area with the vaulted ceiling. She really liked that room. The fireplace. The big screen television. *Furniture*. "It'll take me all of three minutes to load the dishwasher," he said. "You're my guest. Take your wine in and relax."

She had to admit she was bone tired, emotionally drained, and a tad tipsy. That brown leather sofa looked darned enticing.

"I grabbed a few DVDs from your collection," he said as he rinsed the flatware. "Thought we could watch a movie tonight."

"Sounds nice," she mumbled, transfixed by his large, strong hands. She suppressed a sigh as she played back the wondrous feel of those long tapered fingers tunneling into her hair and holding her captive while he kissed the daylights out of her. The man was a champion kisser. Blue-ribbon. And that boardwalk kiss had only been for show. Imagine if his actions were fueled by honest-to-God, heart-felt passion. *Imagine what he'd be like in bed.*

"You all right?"

She started. "What?"

"You're flushed."

"I'm hot. I mean, I'm warm. I mean, it's the wine. I'm fine. Just a relic. I mean a light-weight."

He grinned. "Maybe you should go sit down."

Maybe I should keep my head out of your pants. Forcing a weak smile, she attacked a frying pan with a scouring pad while he dropped the rinsed flatware into the dishwasher's basket. She'd never understood the advantage of a dishwasher if you had to scrub and rinse everything in advance. She preferred washing dishes the old-fashioned way. Then again she'd never *owned* a dishwasher. She wondered if it had come with the house or if Murphy had actually visited an appliance store. On second thought, she couldn't imagine him wrangling with a pushy salesman. More than likely he'd cruised the Internet on that fancy computer rig in his library. One-button shopping. The man didn't own much in the way of furniture, but he sure had a lot of electronic gadgets.

He glanced sideways. "You're still here."

"Can I ask you a question?"

"Another one?"

From the twinkle in his eye she could tell that he was teasing, so she smiled and plowed on. "Why did you buy such a big house?"

"Investment."

That's it? That's all? Investment? Intent on getting to know this man, she ignored the comfy sofa and wiped down the counter. "Ever been married?"

"No."

"Ever *wanted* to get married?"

"No."

So he was either commitment shy or he'd yet to meet the woman of his dreams. Hmm. "Have any children?"

"No."

"Ever want to have children?"

Pause.

Crap. She draped the damp cloth over the edge of the sink and washed her hands.

He closed up the dishwasher and hit the on button. "It's a fuc— sorry, screwed up world," he finally said. "Why would I want to bring a kid into it?"

Despite his vulgar language, his answer should've had her bouncing off the walls with glee. He didn't want to have children. *A gift from above. A sexy, intelligent man minus the powerful drive to procreate.* But it was the weariness in his voice that kept her joy at bay. "Your kid could make a difference in the world."

He picked up their wine glasses and headed for the sofa. "Making a difference entails taking risks."

She trailed after, trying to decode that statement. Settling on the opposite end of the sofa, she untied and toed off her sneakers, and tucked her bare feet beneath her. "So you don't want to have a kid because you're worried he or she might get hurt?" Surely he wasn't *that* flappable. Not the gun-wielding protection specialist.

"It goes a little deeper than chipped teeth and skinned knees, Princess."

"Of course it does." She spouted off fears that must run through every parent's mind. "What if your kid's riding his bike and gets hit by a car? What if he gets snatched up by a kidnapper? Or molested by a pedophile?" Her stomach curdled. As much as she tried not to think about it, those things did happen.

"What if your kid gets caught in a cross fire?" he added,

proving he was just as good, if not better, at the *what if* game. A muscle jumped under his left eye. "What if she gets buried in a mudslide or drowns in flood waters? What if he starves due to political chaos?"

He stopped suddenly, and she realized her eyes were wide with horror. She couldn't help it. His God-awful scenarios had sucked the air from her lungs. She held his troubled gaze while massaging an ache in her chest. "You're not hypothesizing. You've seen those things."

He broke eye contact and took a healthy swallow of wine. "How the hell did we get on this subject?"

"I asked if you wanted to have children."

"I'd make a lousy father." He quirked a self-deprecating smile as he set aside his glass. "I should've left it at that." He reached for the TV remote, thumbed on the power.

She disagreed. He'd make a great dad. Despite the fact that his occupation entailed carrying a gun and no doubt coming to occasional blows, he was intelligent, patient, and caring. Her heart broke for this man. She wanted to know how he'd come to be so cautious and cynical. She wanted to ask how and why he'd witnessed those awful things, but clearly he'd ended the discussion.

She glanced at that screen. That huge mega-sharp, ultra-expensive plasma screen. *The Adventures of Robin Hood.* A classic. She'd invested in the collector's special edition DVD with all the bells and whistles. He'd probably picked it for the adventure, but it was the romance between Robin and Marian that won Lulu's heart. She made it through the opening credits, before risking another glance at her host. "Colin?"

"Yeah?"

"Come here."

He glanced over, wary.

She rolled her eyes. "Fine. I'll come to you." She scooted

over and wrapped her arms around him. "Don't freak out or anything. I just thought you could use a hug."

He let out a breath, pulled her onto his lap. "Hon, if anyone needs comforting it's you. You've got an enamored mobster on your tail."

"I'm not worried. You're really good at your job, right?"

He smiled. "Right." He relaxed against the sofa, stroked her hair, and fell silent as they both seemingly focused on the movie.

She ignored the tingling between her legs, the almighty pull to tilt her face up for one of those blue-ribbon kisses. She told herself that this was about comforting Murphy, not exploring her ever-increasing sexual urges.

She forced her attention to the on-screen action—Robin and Marian, the rebel and the maiden—but her mind whirled with another adventure. Lulu and Murphy—the princess and the bodyguard. Lulled by his warm caress and the lingering Chablis, Lulu closed her eyes, and gave over to her imagination. If nothing else, she could dream.

* * *

"Wake up and smell the espresso, Rudy. You're in love."

Rudy didn't shift. He didn't wince or frown or laugh. He just stared at Sofie as the bomb she'd hurled lobbed him in the chest. His breath seized as he waited for the explosion. Afia had made the same observation months ago, after he'd first acknowledged an attraction to Jean-Pierre. He hadn't argued. It was definitely that giddy, walking-on-air feeling that most people attribute to being "in love." But this was different. This was deeper, darker, and frightening in its intensity.

Sofie's bomb scared the hell out of him.

He wouldn't have confided in her but Afia was off-limits

just now, and his houseguest had walked in while he'd been trying to numb his heightened emotions with a bottle of Merlot and an ear blistering session with ABBA's greatest hits. He'd been obsessing on this afternoon's bizarre blow out. The way he'd felt when Lulu had railed into Jean-Pierre. He'd wanted to get in her face and to hurt her as deeply as she'd hurt his lover. He'd never yelled at a woman. Not once. Not for any reason. Knowing that she was upset was the only thing that had enabled him to keep his anger in check.

Other feelings were an entirely different matter. He'd experienced a sharp pain in his chest, so severe, that for a split second he'd imagined he was having a coronary. It was the first time he'd seen Jean-Pierre genuinely upset, and he'd felt sick. All he wanted to do was make it right. His physical reaction to his partner's emotional pain was so over-the-top it had thrown him for a cataclysmic loop.

He'd been relieved when Jean-Pierre had received a phone call from Ruby Slippers regarding a distraught queen and an emergency wardrobe crisis. He'd thanked his lucky stars when Sofie had been called in to cover a shift at the Carnevale, allowing him total privacy to spaz out.

But then she'd returned home an hour early, catching him two-thirds of the way through the bottle and mid-chorus on "Take A Chance On Me." She'd badgered him until he'd spilled his guts. Now life as he knew it was about to be blown to smithereens. Just as soon as he acknowledged that bomb.

"Denying the truth won't change it," Sofie said, as if reading his mind. "You might as well suck it up, admit it, and get on with life. A life with a sexy, talented partner with a heart of gold, I might add. A devoted partner who's willing to work himself into the ground to make your dream come true. Do you know how lucky you are?"

The question of the week. "Yeah, I know how lucky I am."

That was the problem. Jean-Pierre, their relationship, was too good to be true. After years of playing the field, he'd poured his energy into turning his life around. Six months and a stack of self-help books later and—Ta-dah!—there was Jean-Pierre. It was too flipping simple. It *couldn't* be this easy. And now he'd complicated matters by falling in love with the man.

BOOM!

"Ah, hell."

Sofie huffed an exasperated breath and grabbed the bottle out of his hand. "Why are you so freaking upset?"

"Why are you so freaking angry?" Rudy watched while she poured herself a glass of wine, only too happy to focus on someone else's problems.

"Because my life sucks!" She slammed down the bottle and whirled on him. "I had the bad sense to believe a man when he said he loved me and promised me the world. I'm almost thirty and I'm thousands of miles from Hollywood. Instead of standing on a stage or in front of a camera, I'm standing in front of a frickin' sweepstakes bin. My sweet sister's being stalked by a maniac, and my hands are tied because of an *arrogante mucca* who thinks I'm *eye candy*!"

Rudy pushed out of his recliner. He had his arms around Sofie just as she burst into tears. She'd lost him at *arrogante mucca*, but he heard her other woes loud and clear. His own troubles fell by the wayside as he stroked a comforting palm down her spine. "Nothing's going to happen to Lulu, honey. She's got Murphy and Jake. She's got us. And for the record, you're two years from thirty and one hour from the Philadelphia airport. If you wanted, you could be in Tinseltown by tomorrow morning." He gave her a quick squeeze and then guided her to the couch. "Now, let's talk about the asshole who broke your heart."

* * *

His chest hurt like hell. Murphy told himself it had everything to do with the CNN report he'd just watched on the conflict in the Middle East and nothing to do with the conflict raging within. He'd survived enhanced training programs, Desert Storm, and natural and manmade disasters. He could sure as hell survive Lulu's hugs. He could stand fierce in the face of her good will. He refused to be charmed by her antiquated values. As far as wanting to ball her brains out, well, he continued to wrestle that demon.

He had the boner to prove it. He'd been hot and hard, oh, a good three hours now. The moment she'd curled up on his lap, Russell the love muscle had sprung to life. Fortunately, she'd fallen asleep ten minutes into the movie. It had saved him from trying to explain his *predicament*.

Man, he was an ass. Her intentions had been pure, not sexual. She'd tried to comfort him because, Christ, for a moment he'd put his guts on the table. He still couldn't believe it. He never talked about those humanitarian ops. But Lulu had a strange effect on him. She started talking about marriage and kids, and **his** insides twisted in a new and painful way. Talk about taking **ri**sks. He'd lost a mother and father. He couldn't imagine losing a wife and child. Not when he could so easily imagine one thousand freaking calamities.

But then she'd fallen asleep in his arms and, for one hundred and two minutes, the running time of *The Adventures of Robin Hood*, all was right with the world.

If they awarded medals for superhuman control, he'd be polishing a couple right now. One for carrying her upstairs to the guest room instead of depositing her in *his* bed. Another for enduring the major discomfort of a stubborn erection. Waxing the soldier wasn't an option. The object of his desire was sleeping just upstairs. He'd already tried a cold shower, although another might not—his body tensed at the sound of creaking—hurt.

Strike that. The object of his desire was descending the stairs. *Damn.*

"Colin?"

His heart fluttered at the sound of her shaky voice. "I'm in here," he called out. Worried that she'd suffered a panic attack, he kicked off his sheets, swung out of bed and reached for his boxers. "Hold on. I'll be out in a—" he glanced up at a soft intake of breath "—flash." *Oh, shit.* She was standing on his threshold. She'd changed into a pair of baggy pajama bottoms and an oversized T-shirt. He, on the other hand, was buck naked.

The lights were out, but his nineteen-inch television was on and illuminating him in all his seven-inch glory.

Ooo-kay. Here's the part where Miss Goody Two-shoes runs screaming from the room. Except she just stood there. "I can't sleep."

"That makes two of us." *Okay, bonehead. Step into your shorts. You're holding them in your right hand. All you have to do is bend down and . . .*

"It's too quiet upstairs," she said, shifting her weight, but not her gaze. "And dark. I turned on a light but, well, my imagination . . ."

"Yeah, you've got a whopper." He regained his senses enough to stab one leg into his boxers.

"I changed my mind. I *would* feel safer if we . . ." She glanced at his rumpled bed.

"Slept together?" *Holy Christ.* He yanked his shorts up and over his package, for all the good it did. His pole tented the thin fabric. He'd felt less self-conscious in the raw.

Lulu glanced toward the television, wrung her hands. "Did I come at a bad time?"

He blinked at her word choice, stifled a laugh. Then he realized he'd muted the audio, and she wasn't standing at an angle where she could see the screen. Great, so she thought he was watching porn. "Just catching up on the news." *Snap out of it, Murphy.* He pulled on a fresh T-shirt and snatched up one of four pillows. "Climb in. I'll bunk on the floor."

"I can't let you do that."

"Trust me, I've slept on worse."

"No, I . . . really. I wouldn't feel right putting you out. I . . ." She threw up her hands, sighed. "Okay, here's the deal. Even though your house is minutes from civilization, it's so secluded within the pines, I feel like I'm in the boonies. I'm a little freaked out from that creep's phone call today. I'm sure I'll be fine tomorrow, but tonight, I just . . ." She tugged at the hem of her thigh-grazing shirt. "I don't want to sleep alone. I know it's an imposition."

"It's not an imposition." He climbed back into bed, pulled back the covers and motioned her over. He could do this. *Nuns and puppies. Nuns and puppies.*

She climbed in next to him, right up against him, though she was careful to keep her hands clasped to her chest. "It's been a long time since I've slept with a man. I mean in the same bed. I mean—"

"I know what you mean." *Christ.*

"This is really nice of you."

He rolled his eyes.

"You really *are* watching the news."

Since she was looking at the television, he lazed his head left and looked at her. Her face scrubbed free of makeup, her hair tousled, she looked pure and wild, and man he wanted to kiss her—slow, wet, deep. He wanted to do a hell of a lot more than kiss, but he couldn't go there. Couldn't even think about it. He was *nice*.

Nuns and puppies. Nuns and puppies.

"So men at war turn you on?"

He scrunched his brow. "What?" Then he realized she was finally acknowledging his hard-on. He glanced at the screen, soaked in the replay of a U.S. missile strike. Though it did inspire him to cheer *OohRah!*—once a Marine, always a Marine—it wasn't an aphrodisiac. Two choices here. Admit the truth—*she* turned him on—or change the subject. "Tell me about *The Spookytown Scare*."

Her head lulled right. "Tell me what you did before you were a protection specialist."

He met her gaze and allowed himself to bask in her tender regard, unable, this moment, to deny her anything. "I served in the military. MEU SOC."

"Which stands for . . ."

"Marine Expeditionary Unit. Special Operations Capable."

"Sounds dangerous." When he didn't comment she added, "What does that mean? What did you do?"

The list was long and varied. He chose a few select tasks, purposely excluding things like ground offensive combat and hostage extraction. "Peacekeeping/Enforcement. Humanitarian/Disaster Relief. Security Operations."

"Sounds very noble." She glanced back at the screen. "Did you ever have to shoot your gun?"

"I encountered hostiles, yes."

"And?"

Mentally, he took ten paces back. *Distance is key. Distance equals survival.* "You don't want to know particulars."

"You mean you don't want to talk about it." She winced as the camera zoomed in on the carnage of a roadside bomb.

Murphy reached for the remote and searched for a sitcom. "Tell me about *The Spookytown Scare*. What's an eyeball relay?"

She turned toward him, her hands pillowed beneath her head, a smile curving her full lips. "It's really cool."

She described the relay, and he had to admit if he were a six-year-old kid, "cool" would be his response. "Pass the Skeleton" sounded equally fun. So did "Spider Bowling." Where did she get these ideas? What impressed him most was the loonytale itself. She'd managed to point out the ugliness of prejudice and the beauty of working together within an action-packed interactive story. He turned toward her, transfixed by her imagination and enthusiasm as she narrated the setup.

"Once upon a time there was a wacky, eerie, magical city called Spookytown. Wizards and witches lived in Spookytown. Bats and cats lived in Spookytown. Monsters and mummies and ghouls and ghosts. Creepy creatures, big and small, they *all* lived in Spookytown. And mostly they all got along. *Mostly*.

"There were a few troublemakers," she said, crinkling her brow. "Frankie Frankenstein, Wanda Witch, Gus the Ghost, and Scarlett Skeleton. But mostly everyone ignored them. *Mostly*.

"*One* year these pesky troublemakers stirred up a pesky batch of trouble. *That* year, Wardorf the Whimsical Wizard of Spookytown almost canceled Halloween. *Almost*. It was the scariest time ever in Spookytown. Thus, they called it the Spookytown Scare."

Murphy smiled as she went on to describe how she'd divide the children into four groups—representing the divided town—and how each would have a specific response every time she called their group name. The Freaky Frankensteins *growled*, the Wacky Witches *cackled*, the Ghastly Ghosts *booed*, and the Scary Skeletons *moaned*.

For a few blissful moments he was an innocent, carefree boy totally absorbed in a new-fangled ghost story. He couldn't remember the last time he'd felt this relaxed. This . . . good. As her lids drifted shut and her words dissolved into a halting whisper, Murphy acknowledged the ache in his chest for what it was. Apparently he *did* do women who carried pink poodle purses and lived on Mars. At least this one.

Lulu had fallen asleep in the midst of the Freaky Frankenstein rebellion, leaving him wanting more. Much more. He reached over and gently smoothed golden curls from her sweet face, as sunshine flooded the dark crevices of his heart. No wonder he hadn't recognized that curious ache right off.

This was a first.

He was in love.

Chapter Fourteen

✳ She was in trouble. Tangled in bed sheets and snuggled against something warm, Lulu woke up smiling. She smelled fabric softener and fruit and spice. Heaven, she thought. Then she opened her eyes and realized that heaven was Colin Murphy. And she wasn't just snuggled against this hunky gift to mankind; she was wrapped around him like a ribbon.

Oh, boy.

Her heart pounded against her ribs as she vacillated between euphoria and depression. She'd come to his room last night because she'd been truly spooked, but more than that she'd been aroused. She'd dreamt of getting down and really dirty with Murphy. She'd awakened wet and aching for something between her legs, specifically, Murphy's John Thomas. The remnants of a glass of wine had given her the courage to come knocking. But then she'd walked in and found herself staring at the star of her naughty fantasy and, surprise, *bonus*, Mr. John Thomas himself.

Her dream hadn't done the pair justice.

Murphy had an incredible body. *A hard body. Toned, defined, trim.* What kind of rigors did one have to go through to get that buff? She'd shuddered at the thought of five-mile-runs and weight machines. Then her gaze had landed on JT and her body had pulsed with a different kind of appreciation. No doubt about it, the former soldier/present bodyguard was a work of art. Was it any wonder she'd stood there gawking?

Unfortunately, the heat of the moment had fried her brain. Courage went on holiday, and Lulu went on auto-pilot. Instead of being brazen, she'd waited for him to take the lead. He was naked. He had an erection. They were halfway there. All he had to do was snatch her up, toss her on the bed, and rip off her clothes. Instead, he'd tugged on boxer shorts and a baggy Tee. The message clear: No sex.

A huge disappointment. But then he'd climbed into bed and had invited her to join him. To her credit she'd refrained from doing the happy dance. Barely.

She was truly pathetic. All they'd done was talk—no kissing, no fondling, and yet it had been the most sexually-charged night of her life.

Suppressing a sigh, Lulu contemplated her current situation. Were she Sofie, she'd slip her hands beneath Murphy's underwear and coax him awake. Surely that would arouse—ha!—his interest. But she wasn't Sofie. Her experience with men was limited. Her experience was with Terry. Period. She'd never been the aggressor. She didn't know where to begin.

Confidence shattered, she held her breath and gingerly extracted her limbs from Murphy's. Escaping now was the only way to avoid further embarrassment. If he woke up, how would she explain the fact that she'd practically slept on top of him?

Cursing herself a supreme loser, she eased from his bed and tiptoed from the room. She needed to busy her mind. She

needed to feel feminine and useful. She wanted to do something nice for a man who'd provided humanitarian relief and
encountered hostiles.

To think she'd thought she was making a positive difference via her loonytales. Suddenly her world felt very small
and her contribution woefully insignificant.

Sadly, it occurred to her, maybe it was time for her to grow up.

* * *

Murphy stared up at the ceiling, slightly disoriented. He'd felt
Lulu stir against him and for the first time in his life he'd been
paralyzed. He'd wanted to hold her fast. Midway through the
night she'd tossed an arm over his chest, then a leg over his
thighs. He'd worked an arm under and around her, pulling her
closer. In answer she'd moaned and snuggled her face into the
crook of his shoulder. Her hair tickled his face and her knee
rested a little too close to his nads, but he would've stayed that
way for a week and a day.

He couldn't remember the last time, if ever, he'd slept with
a woman without having sex. Yet he couldn't remember ever
feeling this satisfied. The morning after, and he wanted it to
go on forever.

She wanted to disappear.

He'd let her go without letting on he was awake. Knowing
her, as he was beginning to feel he did, he imagined that, come
the light of day, she'd reverted to her old-fashioned senses. So
she'd saved them the awkwardness of morning breath, bed-hair,
and inane small talk. She'd slipped away. And now, he was
lying here cursing himself for letting her go.

Colin Murphy: paralyzed. His team would never believe
it. Not that he had any intention of sharing. This qualified as
a bona fide kiss-and-don't-tell op.

His cell phone chimed. His brain reconnected to his body. *Halle-freakin-lujah.* He snagged the phone from the night-stand. "Murphy."

"You alone?"

Unfortunately. "Yeah. What's up, Jake?"

"A lot. Listen I've only got a few minutes before Afia climbs out of the shower. I don't want her to walk in on this discussion."

Murphy swung out of bed and headed for the master bath. "I'm listening." He shut the door, turned on the faucet, and nabbed his toothpaste out of the medicine cabinet.

"I did some digging late last night. Major expedition. Came up with some disturbing dirt."

"Hit me." He scrubbed his teeth while listening.

"That renovation on Oz last year, the one where they added on Flying Monkeys? Karl Jackson had a silent backer. Vincent Falcone."

Murphy's shoulder muscles bunched. He'd known they were dealing with the mob. But the Falcones? Christ. He rinsed and spit. "Bogie made contact with Sofie last night. He told her to stay away from Oz. Told her Lulu's admirer is a dangerous man with a reputation for abusing the women he's obsessed with."

"There are rumors that the big guy has a thing for younger woman. Speculation as to more than one unsolved murder linked to the Falcones. The feds have been after this guy for years."

"Yeah, and maybe they've found a way to get to him through Oz. But he's not my mark." Murphy splashed water on his face. "Vincent's gotta be pushin' seventy. The bastard that drugged her, the one she recognized from Ruby Slippers and a birthday party, was younger. She pegged him in his late thirties, early forties. Average height and weight. Short, black hair."

"You've just described any one of a dozen wise guys in the Falcone organization."

"I know." He toweled his face dry, padded back into his bedroom. "Listen, Jake, I appreciate the information and your concern, but we need to pull back. Obviously, the Bureau is coordinating a sting. Bogie needs Lulu's stalker to make the score. He said it'll be over within a week. He wants me to do my job, so he can do his. My job is to keep Lulu safe."

"What about Rudy and Jean-Pierre?"

"What about them?"

"They work at Oz. What if they get caught in the middle of whatever's going down?"

"What if they're essential to whatever's going down?"

Jake lowered his voice to a growl. "Are you saying they're willing participants in a criminal activity?"

"I'm saying they could be playing an unwitting part. If they both pull out it could blow the case, or at the very least, raise suspicions." Bogie was undercover. If he got burned . . . He shut down the vivid consequences springing to mind. "The feds aren't in the habit of endangering innocents."

"Shit happens."

He couldn't argue that point. "Sometimes the payoff is worth the risk." Taking down the Falcone organization—a network of unscrupulous dickheads much like the ones responsible for his parents' deaths—sure as hell qualified. Murphy stabbed his legs into a pair of jeans, his mood darkening.

"I'm not risking Rudy's and Jean-Pierre's safety," Jake said, his gruff tone laced with fire. "And there's something else. Anthony Rivelli, Rudy and JP's immediate boss. He has a past with Vincent Falcone's daughter. I thought he'd broken off. I need to know if he's mixed up in family business. It's . . . personal. I need specifics about that sting, Murphy."

"I don't have specifics."

"Then get them. You've got 'til the end of the day."

Jake disconnected and Murphy tossed the cell on his bed. "Fuck." *Damn Jake and that overprotective streak. If he endangered Bogie in any way, swear to God . . .* He shook his head. Yeah, okay, so he'd just called the kettle black. They were both concerned about friends, but dammit, how was he going to get specifics unless he contacted Bogie—whose cell phone was being monitored.

This morning was off to a freaking amazing start.

He stepped into the hall and experienced sensory overload. His nostrils twitched at an acrid stench. The smoke alarm screeched in unison with a woman's scream. Murphy's feet sprouted wings and he flew like a bat out of hell toward the commotion. When he hit the kitchen, he was smacked with a nightmare out of his past. Eye-tearing smoke, scorching flames, and a wild-eyed woman running for her life. Except it wasn't his Ma, but Lulu, and the fire was contained to a skillet.

"Drop it," he ordered, while grabbing a fire extinguisher from under the sink. But she continued her panicked trek toward the back porch door. The flames licked higher, wider. Blood running cold, he discharged the dry chemical dousing the fire, enshrouding Lulu in a white fog.

She dropped the pan with a yelp.

Murphy dropped the extinguisher with a curse and disengaged the alarm. He pulled the gasping woman into his arms examining her for burns. "Are you all right?"

"Yes, I . . . yes. I guess." She coughed, waved away smoke, and palmed her forehead. "I think I singed my eyebrows."

He inspected her face, her hands, her arms. "No, you're okay." Regardless, his heart drummed against his chest. He glanced down at the smoking pan, remembered a fireman's words, *"Your mother ran back into the inferno."* His boyhood rage exploded. "What the hell were you thinking?"

Lulu swallowed hard, licked her lips. "I was making you breakfast, and I don't know what happened. I turned away from the stove to put bread in the toaster and when I turned back the eggs were on fire. I poured water on them, but the flames shot higher."

Un-fucking-believable. "Smother the flames with a lid or drench them with baking soda, but *never* use water. It only splatters the grease and increases the fire." He squeezed her shoulders, trying to talk over the roar in his ears. "Never, *ever*, try to carry a grease fire outside. The pan will get too hot to carry, and you'll spread the fire throughout the entire area. Not to mention the fact that you could have been seriously *burned*!"

Her eyes filled with tears. "I'm sorry. I . . . It was an accident. You don't have to yell. All I could think about was getting the pan outside before I caught the whole house on fire."

"I don't care about the fucking house! I care about you."

She blinked at him as though he'd gone mad. Which he had. He'd smelled smoke, seen Lulu and the fire, and he'd thought the worst. What if . . . what if . . . *what if!*

His adrenaline spiked. He tangled his fingers in her hair and jerked her body against his. He ravaged her mouth, a frantic, carnal kiss fueled by fear and passion. She clung to his shoulders, accepted his will as he worked his zipper and backed her against the wall. He had his jeans around his ankles, his tongue inside her mouth. His hands slid up and under her shirt, down her pants—a full body assault. No finesse, no foreplay. Just a mindless, primitive need to join.

He hooked a hand under her knee, hiked her leg. Hard and aching, his shaft grazed slick, soft folds. *Home.* The welcoming warmth zapped his brain. Reality punched through the haze of white hot lust and socked him sane. No condom.

Heart pounding, he eased away his lower body and softened the kiss to a whisper. He rested his forehead against hers and groaned his frustration. He realized then that she was trembling. He'd probably scared the hell out of her. "I'm sorry, Luciana." His voice was thick, hoarse. "I'm supposed to be protecting you, not taking advantage. I shouldn't have . . . This was a mistake."

He felt her tense as he tugged down her T-shirt. She nudged him back, and pulled up her pajama bottoms without a word. He yanked up his jeans, mindful that her hands were shaking. Holy hell, what had he done? "Why don't you go upstairs and get ready for work? I'll clean this up. Fix us something else to eat. You like cereal?" He was an idiot. He'd tried to nail her, uninvited, against the wall. Like she was going to want to join him for a bowl of corn flakes.

"Sure." She didn't smile, but she didn't glare. She just hightailed it out of the room and up the stairs.

Murphy dragged a hand down his face, and stared after her. In five minutes the charred eggs would be history, but it was going to take a hell of a lot longer for the smoke to clear.

* * *

Lulu fell to her knees the moment she breeched the privacy of the guest room. Amazing that her rubber legs had carried her this far. She'd barely survived Murphy's crushing assessment of their passionate encounter.

A *mistake*? *How could something that felt so right be wrong?*

Okay, the grease fire was a definite bummer. Murphy's mini-meltdown, perplexing, and yeah, absolutely, a little frightening. But then he'd grabbed her and kissed her and she'd been reborn. *Hello life*!

Sheer excitement had coursed through her veins when he'd pinned her against the wall. The anticipation, the wicked sensations—bliss with a capital B! He'd touched her intimately, her breasts, her hiney, her cootch, but there had been nothing intimate in his touch. He'd groped her like a man out of his mind with need.

For her.

It had been an incredible turn on. A wild, *spontaneous* coupling with no goal other than to achieve sexual satisfaction. His savage kisses alone had nearly sent her over the edge. Then he'd lifted her leg, preparing her for a non-missionary invasion, and she'd felt the beginnings of a mind altering shudder. She'd imploded at the feel of the tip of his penis, a quiet orgasm that had rendered her a trembling idiot. If she'd had a working brain cell left she would have slapped away his hands when he'd tried to readjust her clothing, grabbed JT herself, and slid him home. But she'd been too stunned by her hair-trigger orgasm.

She'd followed Murphy's instructions and escaped upstairs, because she didn't know what to do, what to say. Now she quaked with righteousness and a dozen responses. At the top of the list: "It wasn't a mistake!"

If she believed that, then she'd have to believe herself a twisted slut, because more than anything she wanted an instant replay with an alternate ending. Since she'd only ever been with one man, her ex-husband, and since she'd spent the last two years in celibacy, the slut angle didn't compute. She didn't want to have mindless sex with just any guy; she wanted to get kinky with Murphy. More than that, she wanted to know Murphy.

What kind of a man stopped cold in the heat of the moment?

"I'm supposed to be protecting you, not taking advantage."
A man with morals.

She thunked the heel of her hand to her brow. *"I care about you."* Double thunk. Maybe Murphy *was* relationship material. Her heart swelled as she scrambled to her feet and dug her cell phone out of her poodle purse. She could handle getting to know Murphy, learning what made him tick, but if she was going to get kinky with the man she was going to have to get creative. She punched speed-dial, sighing with relief when Sofie, a notorious late sleeper, actually answered her cell phone.

"You okay, Lu?"

"I'm fine. I just . . ." She swallowed her modesty and reluctance to reach out to her little sister. *Time to grow up.* "I want to screw the bodyguard."

Chapter Fifteen

Jake unplugged the waffle iron and poured a fresh cup of coffee. He'd spent the last fifteen minutes whipping up Afia's favorite breakfast and trying not to obsess on that phone call with Murphy. Guaranteed he'd pissed the man off, not that he cared. What he cared about was his friends' well-being. He wanted to know where and when that sting was going down so that he could make sure Rudy and Jean-Pierre were clear of the fireworks.

He wanted peace of mind so that he could focus solely on Afia and prepare for a child. Their child. *His* child. Man, talk about a mindblower. He was dying to tell the world, but Afia had asked him to hold off until after her doctor's appointment later in the week. She didn't even want to tell Rudy yet, which told him that, even though she'd mostly conquered her superstitious background, she was afraid of jinxing the pregnancy. "*I just want to be extra sure*," she'd said. Jake was already sure, he felt it in his heart, his gut, but hell, if it made her happy, he'd hold quiet. For now. He drank his coffee, the corners of his mouth lifting as he wondered if he'd be shopping for doll houses or Lincoln logs?

Afia stepped into the kitchen and his joy kicked up a notch. He imagined her with a swelled belly and his heart nearly burst. "You are so damned beautiful."

Cheeks flushed, she tossed her poker straight hair over her slight shoulders and glided into the room on designer heels. "This old thing?" she teased, smoothing a hand down her pale blue dress as she beelined for the coffee pot.

He set aside his mug, nabbed her hand, and tugged her into his arms. "I wasn't talking about the dress, although it's nice." A man would have to be blind not to notice the way it hugged her petite curves. "I was talking about you." He soaked in her pixie features, those glittering doe-eyes. Oh, yeah, his wife was fashion-model gorgeous, but it was her inner beauty that brought him to his knees. "Have I told you recently that I love you?"

"I think you mentioned it a dozen or so times between last night and this morning, so, yes." Laughing, she cradled his face in her hands and gazed tenderly into his eyes. "You're going to be a total sap over the next several months, aren't you?"

"Probably. You can also count on me being a total pain in the ass." He'd nagged his sister crazy during her difficult pregnancy. With Afia, a former walking magnet for misfortune, the writing was on the wall. He was going to be a first class worrier. "No caffeine."

"What?" She scrunched her nose, glanced longingly at the freshly brewed coffee. "Oh, right."

"I'll get you some milk." He planted a kiss on her pouting mouth then nudged her toward the kitchen table. "Cheer up, sweetheart. I made waffles."

She let out a delighted squeal, then glanced at her watch and groaned. "Oh, darn. Wait. I can't. I'm late."

He opened the refrigerator door. "For what?"

"I have an appointment with Anthony."

His hand froze on the milk carton. "Rivelli?"

"I'm coordinating another benefit. The charity drag show was such a financial success I figured, why reinvent the wheel? Given Anthony's new job, he not only has access to celebrity drag queens, he can provide the perfect venue, Emerald City."

The dinner theater at Oz. Jaw clenched, Jake snagged the milk container off the shelf, careful not to slam the fridge door. *Be cool, man.*

"I'm supposed to meet him at Oz in a half hour."

"Cancel it."

"I can't."

Jake turned and thrust a full glass of milk into Afia's hand, snagged his cell off the counter. "No problem, babe. I'll do it for you." Okay, not so cool, but no way in freakin' hell was he allowing Afia within ten yards of Oz.

Wide-eyed, she grabbed the phone out of his hand and placed it on the butcher block alongside her milk. "You have got to get over this grudge against Anthony, Jake. It's not his fault that his ex-fiancée is a jealous wacko."

He resisted the urge to massage his shoulder. The injury had long since healed, but he was a long way from forgiveness. "*Ex*-fiancée." He braced his hands on his hips. "You sure about that?"

Afia matched his stance. Normally he loved it when she stood up to him. But not today. Not now. "He broke up with Angela after she went to prison," she said. "You know that."

"I know what he told reporters."

"What are you driving at?"

He couldn't tell her that he suspected the Falcones had hired Rivelli as Oz's entertainment coordinator because he was still involved with Angela—family supporting family.

That road led to the FBI investigation. To Bogart and Lulu. It didn't matter that he had a past beef with Murphy; he'd given the man his word. So he circumvented the question by way of another truth. "I can't separate Rivelli from Angela, Afia. When I think about how that crazy bitch attacked you . . ." He rubbed the back of his neck. "I just can't do it, babe. Not yet."

Her expression softened. She moved into his arms and hugged him tight. "This particular benefit will raise money for the pediatric ward at the hospital. There was this article in the paper about HIV babies, and well, I went over to visit, and . . ." Her voice hitched. "I didn't tell you because I didn't think I could talk about it yet without crying."

Ah, hell. He rested his chin on her head, smoothed a hand down her tense spine.

"It's important, Jake."

"Yeah." He felt sick just thinking about those poor babies. But he still wasn't willing to put his own wife and child at risk. They'd find another liaison, another venue. Breeching the subject just now might heighten her suspicions so he improvised. He kissed the top of her head, and sighed. "Will you do me a favor, Afia? Will you postpone the meeting for a couple of days? Let me get used to the idea of you and Rivelli working together." In two days the investigation, and with any luck, the Falcones, would be history. If it turned out Rivelli was clean, then he'd be the first to champion his alliance with Afia and her cause. He nuzzled her ear. "I'd really like to spend the day with you, all day—celebrating."

Afia tipped her head back, her eyes shimmering. "Using sex to get your way." She sniffed back tears, smiled. "I like that."

Relief blew through him with the force of a cyclone.

She reached back, unzipped her dress and let it pool at her ankles.

Jake's cock hardened as his gaze drifted over her skimpy lace bra and thong and those three-inch heels. "What about your waffles?"

"Later." She unfastened his jeans and slid her cool fingers down his briefs. "Right now I'm hungry for something else."

* * *

"Eggs Florentine. Your specialty." Jean-Pierre wrapped his arms around Rudy's waist and kissed the back of his neck. "What is the occasion, Bunny?"

Rudy turned away from the stove, into his lover's arms and maneuvered him into a lip lock. He poured his heart into the kiss because he couldn't give his heart voice. Not yet. He worried that saying the words aloud would somehow cripple the future. More than anything he wanted a future with Jean-Pierre. He'd slept on his candid conversation with Sofie, waking up with a hangover and a smile. He was one lucky son of a bitch.

When at last he eased away, the younger man gazed up at him with tender regard. "I love you, too, Rudy." Instead of getting heavy, Jean-Pierre smacked him on the ass. "Your sausage is burning, *mon amour*."

Rudy laughed. "That's a new one." But yeah, his dick was on fire for the man in his arms.

Jean-Pierre grinned, nodded toward the stove. "No seriously."

Rudy whirled. "Damn. My sausage is burning."

Jean-Pierre laughed. "That is what I said." He gravitated toward the coffee pot while Rudy salvaged breakfast. "Where is Sofie?"

"I'm right here." She schlepped into the kitchen, waving a hand in front of her tearing eyes. "What's smoking?"

"Rudy's sausage," Jean-Pierre said with an ornery grin.

Sofie snickered and moved in beside the Frenchman. "Lucky you."

"Ah, *oui*."

"Great," Rudy quipped. "Now I'm living with *two* smart asses." He covered the charred low-fat links and looked over at the pair. He smiled as Jean-Pierre passed their gravelly-voiced guest a cup of strong java. Long hair mussed, and clad in a gaping, silk robe that barely concealed her lush curves, Sofie looked like JLo on a very bad day. "You're not a morning person, are you, sweetie?"

She shoved her thick locks off her face and smiled. "No, but I am a happy person."

Rudy's brows shot up. "You are?" Last night she'd been the most miserable woman on earth. Had she taken his advice and started her morning with ten-minutes of creative visualization? *Visualize what you want. See it. Be it.*

She sipped her coffee. "Lulu called me a few minutes ago."

Jean-Pierre frowned. "Is *Chaton* well?"

"Sofie wouldn't be happy if she wasn't," Rudy pointed out.

"She's better than okay. She's hot to trot." Sofie waggled her eyebrows. "She wants to seduce Murphy."

Rudy and Jean-Pierre spoke as one. "No way!"

"Yes, way." She edged over and sniffed at the Eggs Florentine. "Is that low-fat?"

Rudy nodded.

She topped off her cup and headed toward the dining room. "Details over breakfast, boys."

"I can't believe it," Rudy said to Jean-Pierre. "Night before last, I advised Lulu to open her heart. To take a chance." He laid aside the spatula, braced a hand on his hip. "Now this."

"I am not surprised. You are well-versed in matters of trust and affection." Jean-Pierre brushed past him with a gentle smile and a light touch. "If only you could practice what you preach."

Rudy chewed on that statement all through breakfast. He listened to Sofie talk about Lulu's infatuation with Murphy, but his mind was on Jean-Pierre. He owed the man the words. Tonight. He'd treat Jean-Pierre to a romantic evening, dinner, dancing, and when the moment was right, he'd bare his soul. "I can do this."

Sofie looked up from her plate. "Do what?"

Had he said that aloud? *Damn.* "Nothing."

Jean-Pierre excused himself, while Sofie finished her meager serving and Rudy contemplated his sanity. A minute later, Jean-Pierre was back with the mail. He tossed all but one letter on the table and returned to his seat.

Rudy watched with interest as his partner excitedly opened the envelope.

"It is from my friend, Luc. We moved to America at the same time, although we settled on different coasts." He glanced over at Rudy. "I told you about him, no?"

Rudy nodded, a sick feeling swirling in his gut. "The screenwriter." An old lover.

Sofie's ears perked up on that one. "You have a friend in Hollywood?"

"Los Angeles," Jean-Pierre said, skimming the note with a smile.

"Same thing," Sofie said.

"Good news?" Rudy asked as casually as possible.

Jean-Pierre placed a hand over his heart as if to soothe the wild beating. Then he flattened his mouth and folded the letter. "It is nothing. Luc, he is involved with a major film, a musical. He showed the producer some sketches of my work and . . ."

He shrugged, sipped his coffee.

"And what?" Sofie asked, nearly rocketing out of her chair.

"The producer liked his work," Rudy surmised, working his way toward nausea. "As well he should. Jean-Pierre is a genius."

His partner blushed. "I am not a genius." He raked a hand through his shaggy hair. "But *oui*, the producer liked my work. Luc wants me to fly out and . . ." He waved a dismissive hand.

"You should go." Rudy nearly choked on the words.

"Hell, yes, you should go," Sofie said. "Designing costumes for a major Hollywood movie? It's a chance of a lifetime! You'd be crazy not to move out there and . . ." She stumbled as if suddenly aware of the tension. She glanced from Jean-Pierre to Rudy and back. "Well, it's certainly a compliment. It's . . ." She moistened her lips. "Do you mind if I jump in the shower first? I've got an early shift at the Carnevale." She didn't wait for an answer.

Once alone, Rudy balled his clammy fists in his lap and locked gazes with Jean-Pierre. "Sofie's right. It's the chance of a lifetime. I want you to go."

Jean-Pierre swallowed, his expression apprehensive. "Will you go with me?"

And witness first hand your daily interactions with Luc? "LA isn't my thing. Besides, I have responsibilities here."

Jean-Pierre clenched his jaw. "So do I."

"It's not like you'd be gone forever." *Or maybe it would be. His career could take off. He could fall for someone else or reunite with Luc, the artistic, twenty-something bastard.* Rudy resisted the urge to massage the fierce ache in his chest. He told himself he was making the supreme sacrifice. Told himself he was doing this because he loved Jean-Pierre. He'd seen the flicker of excitement in his eyes when he'd first read the letter. Deep down he wanted to grab this chance by the balls. "You owe it to yourself to go, honey."

"Funny," Jean-Pierre said as he pushed out of his chair and stormed from the room. "I thought I owed it to myself to stay."

Chapter Sixteen

✳ "Are you okay?"

Lulu sat down across the table from Murphy. "I'm fine." *I'm a nervous wreck.* But she was also a good actress and a pro at keeping her feelings bottled. Amazing that she'd spilled her guts to her sister. Not so amazing that Sofie had come through with an encouraging smile in her voice and a bold suggestion. She'd been pushing Lulu to get busy with a man, any man, for months. *"There is life after Terry,"* she was fond of saying. At long last, for Lulu those words rang true. Colin Murphy colored her world with vibrant images of chivalry and adventurous lovemaking. He inspired her to chase after the happily-ever-after she'd dreamed of forever-and-always.

Embracing Sofie's fail-proof (at least Sofie assured her it was fail-proof) plan of seduction, Lulu had showered and changed into faded jeans and a fuzzy pink pullover sweater. High on anticipation, she was ready to attack the day and take life by the horns.

Murphy, on the other hand, looked as though he'd been through hell. Clearly Mr. Moral had been at war with his conscience the past hour. His remorseful gaze and clenched jaw were a dead giveaway. The fierce stubble shadowing his cheeks and the streak of charred residue on his forehead accentuated his current dark and dangerous vibe. All he was missing were the battle fatigues. He looked just a little too sexy for her comfort, seeing as she wasn't supposed to jump him until later.

She cleared her throat. "You look like you could use a shower."

"Gee, thanks."

"I mean . . ."

"I know what you mean." His lips curved briefly, and then flattened into a grim line. "I'm sorry about coming down on you so hard."

She poured a bowl of corn flakes. "That's all right. I had it coming." She snorted and rolled her eyes to lighten the tone. "I almost burned down your house."

"My birth parents, Maureen and Charlie Murphy, died in a fire."

Lulu's head snapped up. She gently set aside the cereal box, her appetite gone. No wonder he'd freaked out. "I'm so sorry. That's . . . awful."

"I was ten. Bogie, Joe Bogart, was, *is* my best buddy. We bonded in the first grade. I didn't have any siblings or cousins, no fawning relatives to speak of, so over the years his place became a second home." He scraped a hand over his chin, down his neck. "Anyway, that specific weekend Bogie had invited me along for a family camping trip to the Poconos. Otherwise, I probably wouldn't be here now."

Lulu swallowed, held her voice steady. "What caused the fire?"

He leaned in and rested his forearms on the table and clasped his hands. "A faction of the Mafia infiltrated our neighborhood, offered their *protection*. My Da, an honest, hardworking, and extremely stubborn man, refused to pay. Not only that, he encouraged other area businessmen to resist. The mafia torched my Da's pub in order to set an example. We lived upstairs, a second floor apartment."

Lulu's stomach churned as her imagination ran rampant.

Murphy worked his jaw. "According to neighbors, my Da carried my Ma out of the inferno, and then rushed back in for Freddy."

"Freddy?"

"Our cat." He shook his head, spread his hands. "I know. But Freddy was a part of our family. He was a living creature, and Da considered himself invincible, so I'm sure he thought the rescue would be a cinch." He looked out the bay window, toward the towering pines. "I'm guessing he succumbed to the smoke or got hit by a falling rafter."

After a moment, he turned back to Lulu, met her gaze. Sadness and anger swirled in his eyes causing her gut to clench. "By that time the fire department showed," he said. "Ma was frantic. When Da didn't come back, she got past a fireman."

Her heart pounded with admiration and grief. "She went back in to save your father."

"Pretty dumb, huh?"

"She must've loved him very much."

"Yeah." Stone-faced, he eased back in his chair and folded his arms over his chest. "I just thought I owed you an explanation."

"You don't owe me anything." She wanted to run over and hug him, but his body language screamed *back off*. "But I'm glad you told me." Knowing he was a man of few words, she felt privileged that he'd shared such a painful part of his past. Dare she push her luck? "Colin?"

He got that wary look, the one he adopted every time she called him by his first name. "Yeah?"

She shifted in her seat. "I get that the Bogarts adopted you. What I don't get is why you didn't go into the FBI like Joe. Seems natural that you would want to fight organized crime."

He crooked a wry smile. "You need to be a college graduate to qualify for the Bureau. Manny and Rosa aren't rich. I didn't want to put them out financially. They raised me. That was enough. I joined the Marines when I was eighteen. The Corps provided me with a higher education and invaluable life lessons. My goal was to fight evil in every form, on every front. Mission accomplished."

"About that—"

"I think I'll take that shower now." He stood, gestured to the cereal and milk. "Do you need anything else before I go?"

His reluctance to discuss his stint in the military only heightened her curiosity. She flashed a deceptively innocent smile. "Well, since you asked, yeah. Access to the Internet."

* * *

Murphy's assumption that Lulu had holed herself up in his library to check her email was fast falling by the wayside. She'd been abnormally quiet for the past couple of hours, and every now and then, she cast a furtive glance his way.

He zipped the Jag into the parking garage, making a mental note to check the history on his computer when they got back from the Carnevale. Her brain was buzzing with some sort of data. It made the hairs on the back of his neck stand. Not a good sign. Then again the entire morning had been a clusterfuck. Why should the rest of the day differ?

He rounded the car, helped her out, his palm tingling at the feel of her warm grasp. That same heat registered in her eyes as she gazed up at him with something akin to admiration. Or maybe it was pity. He must've sounded like a sentimental bonehead when he'd choked out his long-winded apology. He'd told her about his parents hoping to appease his conscience. Even though there was no excuse for his sexual misconduct, it was important that she understood where his behavior was rooted. The last thing he wanted was for her to be afraid of him. To properly protect her, he needed her trust.

Unfortunately, providing her with a piece of his past had only served to reinforce his mounting attachment to this woman. Bottom line, she was still in danger. He needed to think with his head, not his heart. He needed to detach.

She looped that damned poodle purse over her shoulder, smiled up at him all sunshine and sweetness, and he thought to himself, *good freaking luck*.

"Are you ready for this?" she asked.

Now there was a loaded question. His answer was a wry quirk of the lips as he escorted her toward the elevator. The moment they hit the bustling casino lobby, he developed eyes in the back of his head. Every dark-haired, olive-skinned man under fifty was suspect. Every sequestered, dimly lit area, a potential hot zone. Unable to perform an advance survey, he did an on-the-spot scan, noting points of entry and exit. Murphy kept his hand at the small of her back, calculating a primary and secondary escape route in the unlikely event that all hell broke loose, while Lulu weaved through the crowded concourse apprising him of her overall schedule.

"This is where we do our first and third show," she said. "The second set involves a meet and greet at the buffet and then the bus lobby—*that's* always an adventure. We close with a parade throughout the main casino, and a show in the hotel lobby."

She navigated a portion of the casino floor, acknowledging the greetings of numerous uniformed employees. Near as he could tell the Princess, or Gemma as she was known here, was as popular with adults as she was with children. He wasn't surprised. He was mentally singing her praises when she pulled up short at an unmarked double-door. "What's wrong?"

She twirled one of her golden curls around her finger and shrugged. "I need to change into my costume."

"Okay."

"The dressing room is through here. Back of house. Employees only," she added when he pushed open the door.

He smiled and gave her a gentle nudge.

"Seriously," she whispered out the side of her mouth, "you're not allowed back here. I assumed you'd wait for me in the concourse."

"You know what they say about assuming. Just lead the way, and stop looking guilty."

"I can't help it," she said as she race-walked toward a door with a push button security pad. "We're breaking the rules. I never break rules."

"Now there's a shocker."

She shot him an exasperated look, then punched in a combo, swung open the door and shoved him inside.

The scene that greeted him was chaotic and fascinating. Women and men coming and going through two separate doors, tugging on various parts of sparkling costumes and feather headpieces while trading sexual-innuendo-laced banter, and everything from run-free fishnets to spare body sparkle.

"Who's the hunk?" This from the man resembling a purple and gold jester, sitting on the make-up counter, and strapping on a pair of stilts.

Lulu tugged Murphy toward the elfish-man and the panel of lit mirrors. "My boyfriend."

Impressive, Murphy thought. She'd told the lie without blushing. He offered a hand in greeting. "Colin Murphy."

"Mortimer." The man shook his hand, and then winked at Lulu. "Nice."

She cleared her throat, tossed her purse on the counter. "I know he's not supposed to be in here, but—"

"Who cares, sweetie?" A bombshell of a woman with big eyes and lush lips, snapped on a curly, blonde hairpiece. "Like we haven't snuck people in here before. Well, *you* haven't. Then again you never do anything wrong." Red lipstick poised to her mouth, she glanced over her shoulder at Murphy. "You corrupting our girl?"

Lulu rolled her eyes and opened a pink tackle box filled with various tubes and pots and brushes. "This is Trixie," she told Murphy, gesturing for him to take a seat on a worn arm chair. "She's a juggler too."

Trixie. Murphy smiled. The name fit. His smile faded when Lulu peeled off her sweater and draped it over the back of her chair. He sat rigid in the armchair, stunned that Miss Goody Two-shoes was sitting in a room full of people, half of which were men, in her tight jeans and teeny bra. *A very sexy, pink satin bra. Holy shit.* He stared at her reflection in the mirror, admiring her perfect 34C breasts, the same breasts he'd pawed this morning. His mouth practically watered. *Okay.* So was he the only pig in this room? Looking around, his mind screamed a resounding yes! Not one of the male performers even glanced in her direction. Maybe they were all gay. Now *there* was a comforting thought.

Lulu dipped into her tackle box and started applying— what the hell did they call it—foundation while making further introductions. "Of course everyone has additional, personalized schtick, but in a nutshell, that's Eugene the unicyclist, Wizard the magician, Raven the stilt-walker, Jingles the acrobat, and

Enri the clown. You've met Mortimer and Trixie. Everyone, this is Murphy the bodyguard."

They rang out a welcome in unison, not paying him, or Lulu's breasts, any heed, as men and women alike spackled on more make-up and rhinestones.

"Dammit," Trixie complained as she wrestled with a false eyelash and glanced up at the clock on the wall. "He'll be here in ten minutes."

The energy-level kicked into high-gear as the team scrambled for shoes and props. In Murphy's eyes the scene resembled that of a regiment scrambling for a surprise training op.

"Who'll be here?" Lulu asked as she lined her eyes with a bright blue pencil. "And why is everyone in a rush? We have forty-five minutes 'til show time."

"No, we don't." Mortimer adjusted his gilded half-mask. "Peterson said the shuttle would leave at 11:15 a.m. on the nose. He called everyone last night, said he needed us in an hour early. Didn't you get the message about the special appearance?"

"No. I . . ." She glanced at Murphy. "I wasn't home last night."

Mortimer and Trixie smiled. *"Reeeeally?"*

Lulu sprang out of her chair and raced for a locker. She flung open the dented metal door and tossed out three juggling clubs, curly-toed shoes, and . . . what the hell were those? Sheer purple bloomers?

Please, Jesus, Murphy thought, don't let her strip down here and now. She disappeared through a door marked with a makeshift sign reading: *Femme Fatales.* Saints be praised. Telling himself to suck it up and get back to business, he turned to Mortimer. "Who's Peterson?"

"The entertainment director. A real stickler for rules."

Eugene slapped on a black derby with a sparkly gold band

and snatched up three rubber chickens. "If Peterson finds you in here, we're screwed." He pointed one of those chickens at Murphy. "Sorry, man, you have to leave, *now*."

Murphy stood, wondering if he was supposed to be intimidated by a novelty product, and more, what exactly was Eugene's schtick. "Can't do that."

Jingles gawked at him. "Do you want Lulu to get written up?"

"Forget Lulu," Raven said. "What about Rupert?"

"Oh, hell!" Trixie pivoted, hands on hips. "That blockhead's late again. That's three times this month. His ass is so outta here."

"Who?" Lulu flew out of the adjoining room lacing up some corset type contraption. Her breasts nearly spilled over the metallic gold cups, and yes, those bloomers were sheer. You didn't have to look too damn hard to make out the French-cut, sequined-gold briefs beneath.

Murphy ran a hand over his buzz cut, hoping his head didn't explode as he took in what little there was of her costume.

"Who are you talking about?" Lulu repeated.

"Rupert." Gloved hands clasped behind his back, head down, Enri paced back and forth, a comedic blur who spoke with an exaggerated, clipped French accent. "I spoke to him last night. I know he knew about the time change. *Ooh*! Said he was going to catch a ride with Jean-Pierre. *Merde*!"

"They must've had a flat or something," Trixie said. "Unlike Rupert, JP's never late."

Lulu shot Murphy a panicked look.

"I'm sure he's fine." Not that it didn't deserve a call. Murphy snagged his cell out of his inner jacket pocket.

Mortimer clapped his hands together, demanding attention. "*Hellooo*, people. Peterson will be here in five minutes."

"Great," Jingles grumbled while adjusting the foam pads inside of her sequined bustier. "We've got an outsider in here and one of our own is missing."

"Rupert can't afford to lose this job," Enri said as he paced by.

"Solutions are us." Trixie snagged the cell out of Murphy's hand, tossed it to Lulu, and nudged Murphy toward a door marked *Juggalos* (as in *Gigolòs*?).

Eugene gave her the thumbs up. "Excellent, Trix."

The team concurred.

"Don't sweat it," Raven said with an ornery twinkle in her spidery-lashed eyes. "No makeup or circus skills required. Rupert's the casino mascot."

Catching their drift, Murphy stood his ground. "Not just no, but *hell*, no."

Wizard, who'd been silent up until now, lifted his sorcerer mask and zapped Murphy with the challenging gaze of a wise elder. "I don't know about you, but we take care of our own."

His Marine mentality swallowed that sentiment whole. "Damn."

Cell phone to her ear, Lulu quirked a not-so-sorry smile as Trixie and Mortimer dragged him toward the men's dressing area. "You should've waited in the concourse."

* * *

Jean-Pierre was home safe, sulking. According to Rudy they'd had a tiff, and though Lulu wasn't happy about that, she was delirious that the cause of his absence wasn't more dire. Rudy made sure Sofie got to the Carnevale safely, and then took off for a run to Freehold to pick up a queen for Oz. After learning his butt was covered, Rupert was more than happy to play hooky.

Murphy . . . *Murphy* was more than a trooper. He was an

amazing human being. In order to cover for their co-worker he'd donned a full-body fat suit made of heavy duty foam rubber, and the grotesque (in an adorable sort of way) head of a troll. Beady gold eyes, long pointy ears, a bulbous nose, and a too-wide, too-fleshy mouth. Decked out in royal blue and gold seventeenth-century finery, Murphy, or rather, Tupilo the Troll, was mega-ugly-cute. A glitzy, Venetian version of Yoda.

Lulu had cringed when she'd learned that they were scheduled to appear at the local hospital's pediatric ward. Apparently the president of the Carnevale had been impressed by a recent article, not that she knew anything about it since she never read the newspaper.

Knowing Murphy had a history with disadvantaged children, and knowing it caused him distress, she worried that he'd have one of those meltdowns when faced with all those sick children, many of whom were terminally ill. As it was, Lulu had had to excuse herself three times to pull it together. *Tupilo* had been the hit of the show, spending equal time with each child, dispersing tickles and hugs.

She still hadn't quite recovered from the heart-wrenching experience. Two hours later and back in the shuttle, she grabbed Murphy's oversized, squishy gloved-hand. "That was . . . You were . . ."

"Man, it's hot in here. The fan system choked twenty-minutes ago." He lifted the oversized troll head, trying to let in some air.

Lulu knocked away his hand so that the top portion of the costume fell back into place effectively shielding his identity. "I'm sorry. Rupert must've forgotten to recharge the battery, but you have to stay covered until we get back to the dressing room. If Peterson finds out about this switch we're all dead meat."

"Sounds like a real hard-ass."

"He's all right. Just strict."

"He's a hard-ass," the rest of the characters chimed.

The shuttle rolled up to the porte cochere. The cast poured out of the shuttle. Forming a protective circle around Murphy, they hustled toward the hotel lobby. If they didn't move fast, they'd be stopped by patron after patron wanting to rub Tupilo the Troll for luck.

As *bad* luck would have it they weren't thwarted by patrons, but Peterson. "While you're here, why don't you go ahead and do a lobby set."

"He's got to be kidding," Murphy mumbled from under his big-eared, beady-eyed head.

"Hard-ass," Trixie said.

Lulu shushed them. "Let's just get this over with." She squeezed Murphy's plush arm. "Trixie and I have to move over there to juggle and pass clubs. Jingles and Raven will keep an eye on you. If you feel overwhelmed give the 'Save Me' signal."

"Which is?"

She smiled at the sarcasm in his voice. "Just catch one of the other characters' attention and tug on your right ear. Not *your* ear, the troll's ear. Oh, and remember Tupilo doesn't speak. Just shake hands with people and let them rub you."

"Rub me *where*?"

"Wherever," she teased. Not that he was in any real danger of being violated. His hunky body was safely shielded under layers of foam and fabric. Good-bye, ripped bodyguard. Hello, fat troll. She snickered. "Makes you think twice about breaking rules, huh?"

* * *

Not really, Murphy thought as he watched Lulu skip off with Trixie. It just made him wonder why in the hell anyone would want to do this for a living. Although he had to admit making those pedi-children squeal with joy had been a definite rush. Every hug had reminded him of the better moments of those humanitarian ops.

Truth be told, aside from the fact that he was sweating his ass off and, because of the design of the troll head, suffering shit peripheral vision, he wasn't all that miserable. Miserable was trudging through a one hundred and ten degree sand pit weighted down with one hundred and twenty-five pounds of body armor, weapons, and ammunition. In comparison, this was a cakewalk. He replayed the last three jam-packed days and smiled. This was one weird-ass assignment. Then he saw Sam Marlin hovering in a corner staring at Lulu and Trixie, and his mood instantly soured.

He breathed a little easier when Eugene cycled in between the two and started juggling those chickens. Ah, his schtick. Still, Murphy wanted closer proximity to Lulu. He shook hands with patrons, nodded his big ugly head in greeting, while trying to shuffle monster-sized, pointy-toed feet closer to Eugene and the girls. Problem was they were putting on a hell of show and had attracted a large crowd. Murphy accidentally bumped a man hard, and forgetting he wasn't supposed to speak, mumbled, "Sorry about that, bro."

"You're fucking kidding me," was the reply.

The man turned full front. *Bogie*. He was dressed like a stereo-typical South Philly boy, though his hair was un-typically long. He had some sort of funky facial hair thing happening, but hallelujah, it was Bogie. Alive and well.

"I knew you were around here somewhere," he said, "but hell."

Murphy nudged him toward the fringe of the crowd, careful to keep Lulu in his sights. Worried that their conversation might be overheard, he switched to Italian. Thanks to their dad, Manny, both he and Bogie were fluent. "You look the worse for wear."

"Look who's talking." Bottom lip caught between teeth, he gave Murphy the once over, laughed low. "Man, this is what I call going above and beyond. I don't even want to know where you hid your piece."

Trying to look as nonchalant as a big-ass troll could look, Murphy angled his fat head closer to his friend. "Is that sick fuck here?"

"Yeah. He's on the floor. Got a hot streak going or he'd be over here right now."

Murphy squelched the urge to confront the bastard. "We need to talk."

"Not here."

"We've got a problem."

Bogie cursed, glanced over his shoulder, and then spoke down at the floor. "All right. I'll come to you."

"When?"

"Tonight. I've gotta go, man."

Murphy turned his head and saw Sam Marlin inching closer to Lulu and Trixie. He touched Bogie's arm. "Wait. See that guy? The one with his hands in his pockets?" Murphy rattled a succinct description.

Bogie snorted. "What's he whacking off over there?"

"Just do me a favor and go put the fear of God into him."

"Done."

The show ended and once again Murphy, or rather *Tupilo*, found himself in demand. He endured the sweat rolling down his face, the grabby shakes and rubs of eager patrons, certain he and the gang would be heading back to the dressing room any minute.

He smiled when he saw Bogie conversing with Marlin, smiled wider when Marlin slinked away. But then he shifted and saw Lulu heading for an olive-skinned, dark-haired man standing near a slot machine. Average height. Average weight. Early forties. *Dammit.*

"On it." Bogie breezed past Murphy. "Be cool."

Wasn't he always? It was Lulu he was worried about. "*In special instances I have been known to wig out.*" Given her purposeful stride this "instance" qualified. *Freaking-A.*

* * *

Lulu apologized to Trixie for losing focus and almost clipping her in the nose with a misdirected club as she breezed by, a fake smile plastered on her face. That creepy sensation of being watched had distracted her, jerking her attention to a man in a suit.

The shark.

Fear and anger proved a lethal combination, robbing her of logic and launching her across the floor like a rocket. Confronting a mobster probably wasn't a bright idea. But hey, they were in a crowded, well lit casino. What was he going to do? Shoot her? If he did he'd be arrested and put in jail— good riddance! All she could think was why the heck should she endure this insanity for another minute if she could end it now? This man had stalked her, *drugged* her! White noise roared in her ears as the red haze thickened.

She gripped her clubs, thinking she could use them as a weapon if absolutely necessary, and pondered the man's startled expression as she neared. He *was* the right guy, wasn't he? She ignored the other four thugs surrounding him and narrowed her eyes. "I saw you at the Ditelli party," she said. "I also saw you night before last at Oz, right?"

He looked at his friends and back to her. He smiled. "Cute, isn't she?" he said to his followers.

She gritted her teeth. "You sent me a pearl thong."

Now his friends smiled.

She wanted to bean each and every one of them, but they were five to her three clubs. Instead she wagged one purple metallic club at her dark-suited stalker. "You should be ashamed."

He grinned again and spread his hands. "Look, Princess. I'm sorry—"

"You should be. First you sent me a highly inappropriate gift, and then you *drugged me!*"

Surprise registered in his eyes.

"Lower your voice," said a portly man with a gold tooth.

"Up yours," she retaliated. "Does your mother know what you do? How do you all sleep at night? That's what I want to know."

The tall, grungy-looking man nudged him. "She's nuts, Paulie. Come on, let's go."

"Yeah, boss," said another. "People are starting to stare."

He shrugged them off, his voice low, his dark gaze intent on Lulu. "I think there's been a misunderstanding. I mean you no harm."

"Apology accepted." She thrust back her shoulders, blew out a breath. "I knew we could settle this reasonably." She noticed then that they weren't looking at her, but over her shoulder.

Gold tooth laughed. "What the fuck is that?"

She whirled and bumped into Tupilo. *Uh-oh.* Murphy didn't know who she was talking to, did he? How could he when she'd given him such a vague description of the man at Oz? Then she started wondering how long he'd been standing there, how much he'd overheard. What if he did know this was her stalker? What if he pulled his gun? What if Paulie and his minions pulled their guns? *What if . . .*

"Oh, my gosh. Is it time for another show? Thanks for the heads up, Tupilo." Lulu grabbed the troll's arm and yanked him toward the lobby. Since people were watching, she smiled and called back to the mobsters, "Have a lucky day!"

"You've got exactly two minutes before this head comes off, Princess."

Murphy's tone was low and tight, and Lulu didn't doubt for a second that he was serious. She didn't blame him for being testy. He'd been in that getup for three hours now, and the internal cooling system was busted. He had to be dying. She whizzed him across the lobby, through a door, and took a shortcut to the dressing room. Her co-workers were still out there mingling, but she knew if Peterson asked, they'd cover her butt. Although she wasn't crazy about this job, the camaraderie was priceless.

A nervous laugh bubbled in her throat as she punched in the code, opened the door, and maneuvered Murphy inside. She'd reasoned with a mobster! *Yes!* Score one for diplomacy! Her joy evaporated when Murphy yanked off Tupilo's head. His expression was so fierce and dark that she stumbled backward and fell into the armchair.

He knew.

"Murphy, I—"

"Don't speak." He wrenched off the fat fingered gloves.

"But—"

"I mean it, Luciana. Not one word." Red-faced and soaked with sweat, he peeled off the body suit. "Change your clothes. You're punching out early."

She didn't argue. She had a valid reason. She was in deep doo.

Chapter Seventeen

Silence is golden? Ha! Try silence is torture. Murphy was evil, Lulu decided, just plain evil.

They showered in their respective dressing areas, changed their clothes, left the property, and drove thirty minutes without exchanging a solitary *word*. Desperate to break the excruciating tension, she'd opened her mouth twice only to be cut off with a glare that could freeze boiling water.

By the time they cleared the threshold of Murphy's house she was ready to jump out of her skin. Talk about creepy suspense. Why didn't he just yell and get it over with? Why was he so angry anyway? Bottom line, she'd diffused the situation. Was that it? Had she stepped on his toes? Was this some kind of macho pride thing?

He punched buttons on his home security system, turned, and leveled her with a look that punched *her* buttons.

Fed up, she tossed her poodle purse on the floor—mainly because there wasn't a stick of furniture in what he referred to as the great room—and planted fists on hips. "Are you ever going to talk to me again?

"I needed to cool down."

Yes! His voice, though strained, was music to her audibly-deprived ears. "So, now that you're speaking does that mean you're no longer angry?"

"It means I've chilled to a point where I won't say or do something I'll regret."

Like *almost* having sex with me, she thought, her skin prickling with annoyance. It really bugged her that he regretted what she cherished. "I don't know why you were so miffed to begin with. It's not like anything was going to happen. Not on a packed casino floor. Not with all the security guards and cameras on site. Besides, you were there." *Albeit it in a troll suit,* she bit back, as he advanced with narrowed eyes.

"Do you have any idea who you were talking to?"

This was cool? He looked mad enough to chew nails and spit metal. She swallowed and took a step . . . two . . . three, back. "Of course, I do. The guy who sent me the thong."

"Yes, but do you know *who* he is?"

"Paulie?"

"Falcone. Paulie Falcone." He backed her into the library while taking off his jacket. "That name mean anything to you?"

"Not really." Angry with herself for retreating, she dug in and balled her fists at her side as he unsnapped his holster. "But I'm sure you're going to tell me."

"The Falcones are one of the most notorious crime families in Jersey." He draped his jacket over the leather high-back and placed his gun—God, that thing gave her the willies—on top of the oak credenza. "Paulie Falcone, the eldest nephew of mob boss Vincent Falcone, is second in command. He's bad news. He plays rough, even with the ladies."

Her stomach turned. "Oh."

He leaned back against the wall and folded his arms over his chest. *"Oh?"*

"I didn't know."

"But you knew he was mafia. And *still* you confronted the man. Not just him but his flippin' entourage!" He glanced at the heavens as though begging divine patience.

"I was a little pumped at the time."

"Yeah, I get that." He blew out a breath and met her gaze. "You scared the hell out of me, Princess. I don't do scared."

She thought back on his morning meltdown. Realization dawned, flooding her senses with sunshine and affection. He was bent out of shape because he *cared*. She smiled. She couldn't help it. Seeing how mad he was, he must care *a lot*. *Talk about an aphrodisiac.*

He scowled. "I'm glad you think this is funny."

She toed off her sneakers, savored his strong, clenched jaw, his earth-brown eyes sparking with passionate frustration. "I don't think it's funny." Her pulse hammered as lust and longing commanded her actions. "I think you're sweet."

"Christ, that's worse than *nice*. You are the worst judge of character I have ever . . ." He blinked as she whipped her sweater over her head and tossed it on the credenza. "What the hell are you doing?"

"I'm hot."

"I'll turn down the heat."

"That won't help." She was on fire for this man. This sexy, strong, *honorable* man. Raw hunger glittered in his eyes even as his features registered panic. Warring with his conscience again, was he? Wanting to tempt the devil in him, she unbuttoned her jeans, tugged down the zipper, and rolled the waistband down over her hips. Sofie had suggested an aggressive seduction later this evening—*no man can say no to a naked and willing lady*—but Lulu was in the mood now.

Knowing that Murphy had feelings for her, that he was *attracted* to her, boosted her confidence to dizzying heights. "I haven't had sex in a really long time." She kicked off her pants.

"Okay." He held out a hand, warding her off. "This is adrenaline talking. You're jacked from that confrontation, from *our* confrontation, and—"

"I'm not jacked, unless that's the same thing as, you know, horny." She advanced in nothing but her matching silk pink undies, her smile widening when he swallowed hard. She felt naughty and powerful. Intimidating a man who'd faced down political chaos was a huge rush. "I like you, Murphy."

"You don't know me."

"I know you well enough." She knew he'd enlisted in the Marines to make the world a better place. He'd advanced humanitarian efforts. Then *and* now he protected the innocent. With her very own eyes she'd witnessed him transform into a troll to cover for one of her friends. And she'd never, not in a bazillion years, forget the way he'd lit up the lives of those children in the pediatric ward.

She knew that she wanted to connect with all that goodness and strength.

"What's more," she said, unhooking her bra and letting it fall to the floor, "you like me."

His gaze fastened on her bare breasts. "No, I don't."

She pressed up against him, palmed the bulge in his jeans. "Liar."

He groaned when she brushed her thumb back and forth over his erection, his gaze burning with a sensual heat that made her elbows sweat. "You have no idea what you're playing at here, Princess."

Pulse tripping, she unfastened his jeans. "Show me."

It was a blatant invitation, as close as she was going to get to *screw me*. When he gripped her wrists, halting her progress on his zipper, her insecurities flared. If he rejected her, she'd not only feel like a slut, she'd feel like a failure as a woman. Again. She almost crumbled, almost scrambled for a way to joke her way out of this potentially mega-embarrassing moment, but then she remembered a slogan she'd run across this morning when researching the Marines. *Fear is not an option.*

In a fierce moment of bravado she laid her cards on the table. "Here's the deal, Murphy. I want to get kinky with you. I want to feel what I felt this morning, that bone-deep, intense rush of lust. I've only ever been with one man, and I . . . well, it was never like that."

He banged his head back against the wall.

"I had the most amazing orgasm and—"

"You what?" He tightened his grip on her wrists, slammed her with a look that nearly knocked her on her keister. "That's why you were trembling. You came."

Her entire body burned with mortification. Apparently being fearless wasn't for the faint of heart or skittish relics. "I know. It's ridiculous. It's not like we, well, you know had actual intercourse."

"You're killing me. You know that, right?"

She stared up at him, her heart in her eyes. "I know you're trying to be a gentleman, but if you're attracted to me at all, I wish you'd stop. I want to sample life and lust, Colin. I'm sorry if I mucked this up, but I'm not very good at being the aggressor."

In one swift move he turned the tables and sandwiched her in between the unyielding wall and his hard body. His mouth curved into a wicked grin. "I am."

Her brain screeched into slow motion. Her body tingled with anticipation as his fingers trailed over her collarbone,

between the valley of her breasts and lower . . . lower.
Breathe, Lulu, breathe.

His thumb skimmed below the waistband of her panties.
His mouth grazed her ear. "Kinky, huh?"

"Here and now would qualify," she choked out. Any
minute her brain and tongue would totally disconnect. The
heat of him, the weight and masculine scent of him drove her
insane. Or maybe it was the way he was suckling her earlobe.
Oh, yeah, she thought as her eyes drifted shut, that was a definite mind-warper. She waited for him to wrench off her
panties, braced herself for a fast and furious coupling—that's
what she wanted, wasn't it?

But Murphy seemed of a mind to torture her. Maybe he
didn't understand the word kinky. Firstly, she was nearly
naked and he was fully clothed. When she tried to rectify the
situation, he maneuvered her hands to his shoulders, distracting
her with one of those blue-ribbon kisses. She clung to him as
her mind spun and her knees weakened.

When he broke away she grappled for a steady breath and
a sane thought. Yeah, right. He swept aside her hair, angled
her head, and pressed a warm kiss to the nape of her neck followed by a velvety flick of his tongue. She held tight as time
slowed to a crawl. Another kiss to the hollow of her throat,
another scandalous lick. He nabbed her hand and, *sweet
misery*, kissed and nibbled his way from the inside of her
wrist to the bend of her elbow. Her heart rate accelerated and
she realized he was attacking her pulse points. *How many
were there?* She couldn't remember. He'd disabled her
memory two licks ago.

"Lemons," he rasped. "You've been torturing me with
your signature scent since day one." He teased her with an
ornery glance, his thumb caressing the soft flesh of her wrist.
"Where else do you apply that fragrance, baby?"

Her voice stuck in her throat as she obsessed on the day one part. He'd been attracted to her since the moment they'd met?

He kissed and tongued her cleavage, palmed a breast and ignited internal fireworks. She bit her lower lip, suppressed a throaty, "*Yes!*" Waves of want and wicked lust rolled over her as he squeezed her hardened buds, nipped the undersides of her breasts, her ribs, her tummy. His tongue flicked over her belly button, not a pulse point she thought hazily, but who cares—and then, oh, *God*, her panties were off and he was on his knees with his head in her crotch.

She moaned and squirmed as he sucked, nibbled, and licked her precious parts with mind-boggling skill and creativity. One strong hand kept her from sliding down the wall, while the other explored and teased her wet folds and crevices.

Okay, he definitely knew kinky.

It was her last coherent thought before her brain and body exploded in an earth-shaking climax.

* * *

Satisfaction and wonder coursed through Murphy as Lulu screamed her release. Man, she was quick on the trigger. He could've feasted for another hour, she'd barely lasted two-minutes. He felt her go limp, hoisted her over his shoulder and carried her to his bedroom. He was hard and aching, and out of his freaking mind with need.

He needed to possess Luciana Ross—body and soul.

Keeping in mind that she wanted bone-deep lust and kinky, God help him, he tossed her in the center of his bed and ordered her to stay put. He pinned her with a hungry gaze, devouring her lush, creamy curves as he shucked his clothes.

Though her lips curved into a timid smile as she blatantly admired his arousal, her tone rang with disappointment. "Why did we have to come in here?"

He opened his nightstand drawer, flashed the condom packet before tearing it open.

Something flickered in her eyes. Remorse? Regret? "You don't have to worry about getting me pregnant."

Okay. So she was on the pill. Did she think he'd think less of her because she took precautions? Murphy felt the moment slipping away. What the hell? He covered himself with the rubber and rolled onto the bed pulling her under him. "There are other reasons to practice safe sex, hon." He nuzzled her neck, suckled her earlobe, and worked his hands over her freaking *amazing* body trying to heat things back to boiling.

"I know. But I've only ever been with one man, and I was faithful, and so was he," she managed between throaty gasps of ecstasy. "I think. I just wanted you to know."

That only-ever-been-with-one-man blew his mind and made him cherish her all the more, but the last thing he wanted to do just now was delve into their sexual history. All right then, *his* history. She didn't have a history. One man, her husband no less, did not constitute a history in his eyes. It damn near made her a virgin.

He didn't know which ached more, his heart or his dick. The only certainty was the primitive need to take this woman now. He ravaged her mouth, hi-jacked her senses by fingering her into another shuddering climax. Christ, she was priceless.

Crazy with need—oh, yeah, here's your bone-deep lust, baby—he spread her legs, groaning as his shaft grazed wet and wild heaven.

She tensed, dug her fingers into his shoulders and cold-cocked him with a panicked gaze. "Not like this, Colin, please. This is how Terry—"

He silenced her with a kiss. The last place he wanted her ex-husband was in his goddamned bed. Whatever that bastard had done, he'd done in the missionary. Murphy obliterated the emotional connection by flipping Lulu onto her stomach. He kissed the nape of her neck, her shoulders, the small of her back. He whispered words, tender, raunchy as he explored neglected pulse points. Reveling in her soft sighs and mews, he soothed his hands over her sexy body and coaxed her onto hands and knees.

Taking her from behind would probably count as kinky in her book, and it would sure as hell rock his world . . . another time. The first time, he wanted to see her face when she came. He wanted slow and meaningful, but just now she needed him to slay dragons. In a compromise, he swept her from the bed and pinned her against the wall. She cried her approval, wrapped her hand around his shaft and guided him home.

He nearly lost it on entry. Christ, she was tight. His world blurred as she grabbed his ass, telegraphing her needs loud and clear. He thought he heard "harder" and "faster," but that could have been his imagination at play. His heart pounded like a mother in his ears, drowning out all but her high-pitched squeals.

He tangled his fingers into her wild curls, steadying her as he savaged her mouth with his teeth, lips, and tongue. His other hand roamed over her beautiful curves as he laid claim to her body.

He wanted to excite, to satisfy, to eliminate that fucking ex from her memory. He wanted to be the first.

He felt her shudder, eased back and watched as she screamed her release, a throaty cry that pushed him over the edge. *Hello, God is that you*? It was better than the first time, surpassed countless pornographic dreams. Making love to the princess was like making love to royalty. A rare privilege.

Spent, he dropped his forehead to hers.

She sighed. "That was . . ."

"Yeah." Apparently, being in love added a new and exciting dimension to physical intimacy.

"OohRah," she whispered.

In that instant he knew exactly how she'd spent her morning on the Internet. He wondered what other information she'd tripped upon aside from the Marine battle cry. But his curiosity maxed out in under a minute. He had other things on his mind. Like getting busy with this woman a second time, and breaking her of her fear of the missionary.

As if reading his mind, Lulu smoothed her hands down his back, nipped along his jaw line. "How would you feel if I gave the aggressor thing another whirl?"

Thank you, Jesus. Problem solved, at least for the present. Smiling, he lifted her in his arms and carried her to the bed. "Let's rock and roll."

* * *

Love sucked. Rudy rolled down his window and winged his book-on-CD outside. The silver disc soared like a Frisbee into the grassy medium as he whizzed the limo west on 195. Let some other poor schmuck listen to Dr. Marvin's advice on dating, mating, and the joy of fidelity. The concept was lost on him. There was no joy in relinquishing your heart and having it trampled.

Cursing, he veered right, taking the exit toward Freehold. If only he hadn't walked in on Jean-Pierre while he was on the phone. He'd heard, "I'll think about it," "I miss you too," and "Luc," and his mind had filled in the blanks. He'd backed out of the room before Jean-Pierre saw him. Like a coward, he'd ducked into the bathroom where he'd swallowed four aspirin in anticipation of a blinding stress headache. Unfortunately, he couldn't find any medicine to annihilate the green-eyed-monster.

Okay, yes, he'd told Jean-Pierre to jump on the opportunity, but he'd been referring to the job, not the chance to rekindle an old flame. "*I miss you too.*" What the hell?

Even now, hours later and miles away from Jean-Pierre, jealousy and resentment coursed through Rudy's veins like poison.

He pounded a fist on the dashboard, damning fate. Two days ago his life had been near perfect. Last night he'd acknowledged, to himself anyway, that he loved Jean-Pierre, and today he was miserable. No, *worse* than miserable. He couldn't even think of a word to describe his severe angst. All he knew was that he'd never felt like this before. It was powerful, painful, and ugly.

He'd never hurt like this in the old days. The King of Quickies. Master of a stiff prick with no conscience. He'd had it made. No emotional entanglements. What the hell had possessed him to turn his life around, investing a fortune in books, meditating, and chanting affirmations? *I am open and ready for a serious, long-term relationship.* Like hell he was!

One of two things was going to happen. Either Jean-Pierre was going to turn down the job, only to regret the decision and resent Rudy later down the line. Or he was going to take the job, and reconnect with an old lover—a *younger* lover. Either way, Jean-Pierre was going to leave him. It was only a matter of when.

Hot tears pricked his eyes. Great, just great. He was crying in his beer over a man, sans the beer. Could this day get any worse? Steering into his appointed pick-up's housing development, Rudy snatched up his cell phone and speed-dialed Afia. He needed someone, *something* to make him feel better.

What he got was her message machine. He sighed heavily. "Hi, honey. So is it better to let go and see if they come back or to hold on and see if they let go?" A bastardized version of a quote or a song lyric, he couldn't remember. Rational thinking had gone out the window the moment he'd heard Jean-Pierre speaking with Luc. His voice hitched. "Uh, call me."

Rudy tossed the cell on the seat, parked the limo, and thumbed back tears. *Shake it off, Gallow.* He straightened his tie, exited the limo, and knocked on the door of an upscale rancher. He'd deliver Perry Davis aka Sucha Tramp to Ruby Slippers and then go somewhere and drink himself blind. All he could think about was numbing the pain.

The door eased open. Perry greeted him in clingy sweat pants and no shirt. Like Rudy, the man had a love affair with free weights. Rudy would have to be dead not to admire the Muscle Mary's buff body and devastating blue eyes. He wasn't dead, just bleeding profusely from his broken heart.

Perry quirked a coy smile as he acknowledged Rudy's not-so-subtle appraisal, and returned the admiration. "You here to pick me up?"

Rudy fidgeted. "I . . . uh . . ." *Yes, Rivelli asked me to deliver you to Oz*, would have been the appropriate answer. Since when had he allowed harmless flirting to rob him of sense and speech?

Since Jean-Pierre had commandeered his heart and soul.

"I'm a little early. I . . ." *Couldn't stomach a confrontation with my lover, so I blew out of the house ahead of schedule.*

Perry reached out and tenderly touched his shoulder. "You look like you could use a friend. Want to come in for a beer?"

Rudy's emotions spun wildly, his future uncertain. *Your life is out of control because you have no control in your life.* Isn't that what he'd told Afia months ago? Love had robbed him of control, and now he hurt like hell. He took comfort in the thinly-veiled interest in Perry's gaze, told himself that his past was safer than his future. He followed the man into his house and kissed Christmas in Vermont good-bye.

Chapter Eighteen

✳ Cheating bastard.

Sofie refused to acknowledge how striking Chaz looked leaning against his luxury Mercedes in his single-breasted, pinstriped Armani suit. So he was classy as hell, and GQ gorgeous. So he had a lot of money. He also had a string of girlfriends. She could forgive many things. But not infidelity.

She willed her nerves steady as she thanked Trixie for the lift, and waved good-bye. Of all days for JP and Rudy to be fighting. The tension pinging off Rudy when he'd driven her to the Carnevale had been excruciating. She'd decided not to spend the night at their townhouse in the hopes that they'd talk things out, kiss, and make up. She'd phoned JP to let him know she was staying over with a friend, a bald lie, but if he knew she planned on spending the night alone at Viv's he would have pitched a fit. Or called Lulu. The lie seemed the easiest solution. She certainly didn't believe she was at risk.

Then again she hadn't expected Chaz.

She summoned a mask of indifference as she walked toward the asshole who'd robbed her of her dreams. "Go away."

He pushed off the car and nabbed her elbow. "We need to talk."

"No, we don't." God, he smelled good—cedar and musk—his cologne, like his clothes, designer chic. But beneath the classy exterior beat the heart of a snake-oil salesman. If she wasn't careful, in less than five minutes, he'd have her believing that those other actresses forced themselves into his bed, and that she was his one-and-only love. He was that smooth.

He grasped her other elbow and pulled her close, his blue eyes serene and as enticing as Caribbean waters. "I've apologized."

She steeled her heart, hardened her voice. "Chocolates and roses. It's like applying a Band-Aid to an amputated limb."

He shook his head as though disappointed by a child. "Dramatic as always."

A jab. *Good.* It hurt. *Even better.*

She smirked. "Me, dramatic? A professional actress? Imagine that."

"I made a mistake, honey."

"So did I." *I believed you when you said you loved me.*

"I miss you."

"You mean you miss the commission you made off my bookings."

He pulled her into a warm embrace, tempted her with a seductive gaze. "Come home."

She swallowed hard as the sky faded to purple and the automatically-timed security lamp flicked on, bathing the yard in romantic, pink light. "I am home." *Okay. That felt weird.* Like she hadn't dreamed of busting out of Jersey since she was old enough to walk.

His gaze flicked toward the house. "Rough neighborhood."

Compared to Manhattan? Was he nuts?

Chaz studied her face, grazed a thumb over her lower lip. "I'm ready to take this to the next level, Sofia."

Her heart pounded. Not in anticipation, she realized, but in dread. He was going to kiss her, he was going to propose, and she was going to forgive everything.

He claimed her lips, his hands sliding to her ass. Chaz had a real thing for her firm, but plentiful booty. He seared her mouth with a ten-alarm kiss. She should've been on fire. *Where was the heat?*

He eased back and smiled, an arrogant tilt of the lips that used to melt her bones. "I can give you what you want, Sofia. Security and countless orgasms. You're a handful." His gaze slid over her body. "But worth it. Come back to the city and move in with me."

Move in? Okay. She felt something *now*. Insulted, betrayed, disappointed, angry. Good enough to be his lover, but not his wife? "Fuck you."

The bastard actually laughed. "I love it when you're pissed." He clasped her right hand, placed it over his bulge. "It means hot sex."

She knew she was rattled, because instead of squeezing his nuts and inflicting much deserved pain, she wrenched away and slapped his face. *Big wussy deal.*

He laughed. "God, you're hot. Let's take this inside, baby."

Tears stung her eyes as he hooked an arm about her waist and maneuvered her toward the house. The sex, it was all about the sex. So what? She gave the best BJ out of his roster of lays, and as an award he was going to make her his live-in mistress? Numb with grief, she stumbled blindly forward. She was such a loser. Why didn't she deck him? Why was she crying?

"Hey, asshole. Mind taking your hands off of my girl?"

Chaz froze, and then slowly swung around.

"Joseph?" Dammit, her voice actually *cracked*.

Murphy's sinister-sexy friend quirked a dark, dangerous smile. "Hi, babe. Sorry I'm late."

Dressed in holey bell-bottom jeans, a bulky black sweater, and a sock cap, he looked like a thirty-something home boy. She didn't know why he was here, but he offered her a means to save face. She swiped away tears, hoping it was dark enough that neither noticed the waterworks. "I only just got home, so . . . your timing's perfect."

Joe nudged Chaz aside. "Do you mind, dude?" He grasped Sofie's hand and gave a gentle tug. She moved into his arms. Willingly. Naturally. He reeked of that horrid aftershave. She wanted to drown in it. He nodded toward Chaz. "Who's the suit?"

Drawing strength from Joe's badass attitude, she shot her ex a deadly look. "A salesman. But what he's offering, I'm not buying."

Joe smoothed his palm up and down her back, a comforting gesture as he eyeballed Chaz, and shrugged. "You heard her, pretty boy. Hit the road."

Chaz smirked, gave Joe the once-over, then glanced at Sofie. "I don't believe it."

"Believe it." She wanted to hurt Chaz Bradley. She wanted him out of her life forever. That's the *only* reason she wrapped her arms around Joe's neck and instigated an open-mouthed kiss. He didn't seem to mind when she stuck her tongue halfway down his throat. In fact, he immersed himself in the ruse, palming and squeezing Chaz's favorite part of her anatomy while kissing her blind.

Chaz cursed, at least she thought he cursed. Add deafness to the list of lost senses, along with smell. Touch and taste, however, ruled. Stone muscles and velvet tongue. Spearmint and licorice. For an instant she forgot this was an act, and gave over to the raw passion attacking every fiber of her pliant body. Joe's kiss was so deep, so *tender*, she wanted to weep in admiration of its beauty.

"Make sure to get your pole smoked before you leave, *Joseph*. No one gives head better than Sofia."

Now *that* she heard.

The kiss ended abruptly. Although Joe didn't just stand there staring after Chaz as he sulked toward his Mercedes. Unlike her, he hadn't been stunned stupid by the vicious taunt. He clamped a hand on Chaz's shoulder, jerked him around, and socked him in the jaw.

The designer suited man staggered back, touched his manicured fingertips to his mouth, and spat blood. "Crazy hoodlum!"

"You're half right, *Chaz*."

Sofie blinked as Joe advanced on her ex-lover, *a man he knew by name*. He reached back, pulled something out from under his sweater. A gun? Jesus, was that a gun? It was dark now, and they'd moved out of the wash of the yard lamp. Next thing she knew a door slammed and the Mercedes squealed away from the curb. She palmed her forehead as the red taillights faded quickly from view.

Joe stalked toward her readjusting his sweater. She didn't see a gun, but she was certain he had one. Relatively certain. Whatever he'd done or said, he'd put the fear of God into Chaz-I-could-charm-a-snake-into-buying-shoes-Bradley. "You're crazy," she whispered.

"That's the half your ex got right." He grasped her arm and steered her toward the house. His touch was gentle, unlike his tone. The man was pissed. "Why didn't you clip him in the balls or shin rake the bastard when he took liberties?

I know you have it in you. I have the bruises to prove it. What the hell was with the girly slap?"

Her stomach rollercoastered as she tried to reconcile this volatile man with the one who'd kissed her into a blind stupor. "Just how much did you witness?"

"Enough to know you weren't happy about him being here. I wasn't going to interfere, but you disappointed me, babe."

She jerked out of his grasp. "Don't call me that. And screw you." She was more angry with herself than Joe. He was right. She should've defended herself better. She practiced martial arts, for chrissake. But where Chaz was concerned it wasn't that simple. A part of her, a desperate part, she thought with disgust, still clung to a dream. "What are you doing here?"

"I came to talk with Murphy."

"He's not here."

"I gathered. Otherwise he would've been the one chasing off pretty boy."

Sofie chafed. "I can take care of myself." She *could*.

"What the hell's that?"

She moved forward and squinted at the gooey mess on the porch steps. "Someone smashed in Lulu's jack-o-lantern. Damn, I thought the kids in this area were better behaved."

Joe plucked a penlight from his pocket, shined it at the door. The culprit had used pumpkin pulp to finger paint a message on the window. "Any chance this is pretty boy's handiwork?"

Sofie blinked at the word "TRAMP" and moistened her lips. So this is what Chaz meant by rough neighborhood. He must've approached the house before he knew she wasn't home. She shook her head. "It would've meant getting his hands dirty."

"Wishful thinking on my part," Joe said. "Preferable to the alternative."

Sofie shivered. "Lulu's stalker?"

"Doesn't make sense," he muttered while gesturing to her to hand over her keys.

She turned the knob, pushed open the door. "Lock's busted."

He shot her an exasperated look and then stepped in ahead of her.

"Be careful," she warned, even though he was being a jerk. "There's stuff everywhere."

"I'll say."

She shimmied past a stack of boxes, peeked around his shoulder, and gaped at a gigantic teddy bear and an array of floral bouquets blocking the main entrance. Her stomach churned with dread. Outside destruction. Inside *seduction*.

"Where's your sister?" Joe asked, after stooping and reading a gift card.

"Murphy's house." Before he could argue otherwise she latched onto his arm. "I'm coming with you."

* * *

Fear is not an option. Weak from her creative stint as aggressor, Lulu collapsed on top of Murphy, adopting the Marine motto as her own. She was also fond of "OohRah" and "Let's rock and roll," both of which she now equated with mind-blowing sex.

Slick with exertion, she pressed a kiss to Murphy's neck, tasted salt. Sweat was never so sexy. She sighed. "I saw stars. No, I saw another galaxy!" She didn't care if he thought she was daft, she wanted him to know how she was affected by their lovemaking. When he didn't respond, she noted his controlled breathing, lifted her head and saw that his eyes were closed. "Are you sleeping?"

"No, just having a quiet heart attack."

She smiled. "Is that similar to seeing stars?"

He grinned.

Her stomach did a funny flip. How had she ever thought him quietly handsome? He was heart-stopping gorgeous. He lazed open his eyes and peered up at her with such intense affection, her breath caught in her throat.

He framed her face in his hands. "You are so fucking beautiful."

Her pulse raced as he stared up at her for what seemed an eternity. *Okay.* Her turn to have heart palpitations. No one, not even the man she'd been married to for ten years, had ever called her beautiful. Cute. Perky. A living doll. But never *beautiful.* And not just beautiful, but *f---ing* beautiful! How was it that a vulgar word could sound so tender? Overwhelmed, she blinked back tears and summoned an ornery smile. Wiggling against his amazing body, she purred, "I like being on top."

Smiling, he smoothed his hands down her back sending a delicious chill up her spine. "I got that distinct impression, tiger."

Tiger. She liked that. She also liked the way he brushed his fingertips over her backside, eliciting sensual shivers. Desire knotted her belly, even as she second-guessed her love-making skills. "Was I too loud?"

"I like loud."

"Too wild?"

He studied her a moment. Again, she caught that flicker of affection, as one of his hands came up to smooth her curls out of her face. "You were perfect, honey." In the next instant, he finessed her onto her back. Stretched out alongside her, he propped himself on one elbow, using his free hand to caress her curves. "Lulu, when this is over, I don't want *this*," he interlaced his fingers with hers, "us, to end."

"Wow," she croaked past the lump in her throat. "So I was that good, huh? Who knew?" If she didn't joke about it, she'd cry. All those years of trying to nudge Terry into trying something slightly exotic, just for the physical thrill. But Terry wasn't interested in exotic. He was interested in making babies. Sex with Terry had been a means to an end. In the end she'd felt like a failure as a woman. Barren. Undesirable.

Murphy squeezed her hand. "It's not about the sex, although—"

"I need it to be about the sex," she blurted. She palmed her brow. What a stupid thing to say.

"Okay."

She glanced sideways. "Okay?"

"For now." He leaned over, banished her worries with a deep kiss, and then eased back with a devilish smile. "Hungry?"

She waggled her eyebrows, shifted, and walked her fingers down his amazing abs.

Laughing, he rolled out of bed before she got her hands on JT. "I need some chow and a break if we're going to go another round. Or two," he added with a gleam in his eye.

Grateful for the levity, she scrambled to her feet, dragging a sheet with her. "Where the heck are my clothes?"

"The library." Crossing the room in all his naked glory—an image she'd carry to her grave—Murphy snagged a blue oxford shirt from his drawer and tossed it to her. "Put this on." He cocked a sexy brow when she dropped the sheet. "No panties."

She shrugged into his shirt, smiling when he snatched up a pair of boxer shorts. "No shirt."

Grinning, he crossed to the bathroom. "I'll meet you in the kitchen."

* * *

Murphy showered in record time. He'd never been so intrigued or perplexed by a woman in his life. He'd been so sure that her ex had done something to turn her off to sex, and yet she was enthusiastic and insatiable . . . as long as they didn't slam missionary style. That restriction bothered the hell out of him. He wouldn't push her into anything she didn't want, but he'd help her get over that inhibition if it killed him. A distinct possibility given her staying power. The woman was tireless and prone to multiple orgasms. In short, she was every man's dream girl.

Girl of My Dreams.

Murphy's blood ran cold when he thought back on the way Lulu had approached Paulie Falcone. There was a fine line between bravery and stupidity, and she'd crossed it. Did she really think the man would back off simply because she'd told him to? Just the opposite. He'd probably take her rebuff as a challenge. If Bogie didn't take Paulie down in that sting, Murphy would have to take the situation into his own hands. Whatever the cost, he aimed to hand back the Princess her fairy-tale world.

He glanced at the clock on his desk as he passed through the library. Bogie had promised to connect tonight. They hadn't discussed a time. Come to think of it, they hadn't discussed location. *Shit.* Bogie would assume that he'd secured the principal's house. *Well, hell.* Rather than risk calling his friend's cell, he maintained he'd figure it out. He better figure it out. If Jake didn't get the answers he wanted tonight, the possibility loomed that he'd warn Rudy and Jean-Pierre away from Oz, potentially putting the sting, and Bogie, at risk.

His mood teetered on edgy, when suddenly the house rocked with a Motown classic. Apparently Lulu had located his CD player. He padded into the kitchen. The lighthearted scene bumped him back up to euphoric. Tousled curls bouncing, she danced back and forth between the fridge and counter, juggling food products and singing wrong lyrics to "I Heard it Through the Grapevine." He forgave the way she butchered one of his favorite songs, because she looked so damned sexy doing it. *Oh, yeah.* His shirt and no panties had been a brilliant call. "What are you making, tiger?"

"Turkey sandwiches." She held up a loaf of rye bread and a package of sliced deli meat. "*This* I can handle."

"Good." He moved in behind her and slid his hands up the back of her thighs and over her bare ass. "Because my hands are busy."

She giggled and elbowed him back. "I thought you needed a break."

"I was wrong."

She looked over her shoulder and flashed an ornery grin. "You need to eat. You're going to need lots of energy."

"That so?"

Her eyes twinkled with mischief and—oh, yeah, that's what he'd been waiting for—affection. She cleared her throat. "Um, do you like it spicy?"

He leaned back in, pressed his erection against her backside. "That's a loaded question."

She looked at him with a flash of heat, then rolled her eyes. "I was referring to your sandwich. Yellow mustard or brown?" She gestured to two jars. "You had both."

He slid the brown mustard within her reach and brushed a kiss over her temple. "I could get used to this."

She blushed, concentrating on opening the mustard jar. "Me too."

That's all he wanted to know. Smiling, he gave her backside a light slap, and moved to the refrigerator. "Beer?"

"No, thank you. But I'll take spring water if you have it." She started singing again, the wrong lyrics again, while smearing mustard on slices of bread.

Murphy placed a cold bottle of water next to where she worked, and then hopped up and sat on the center luncheonette counter. Bare legs dangling, he swigged from the longneck bottle, and watched her hack up a beautiful beefsteak tomato. The woman was a menace in the kitchen, God love her.

She turned and handed him the sloppiest turkey sandwich ever made. At least she hadn't cranked up the stove. She stopped singing long enough to say, "I like this song."

"Remind me to teach you the words someday," he teased, then bit into the sandwich. *Sloppy, but good.*

She leaned back against the opposing counter, nibbled on her sandwich. "I figured out a few things about you."

He thought about another kind of hacking, Internet style. Wondered how good she was tracking down data. Bracing himself, he took another pull on the longneck. "Like?"

"Well, for one, you listen to oldies. I peeked at your CD collection. Really limited, Murphy."

"No more limited than your DVD and video collection."

She scrunched up her nose. "I have tons of movies."

"Yeah, and all of them have a happy ending."

"Do you have something against happy endings?"

He considered her crestfallen expression, realizing suddenly that she looked adorable whether she was laughing, frowning, or screwing her face up in disgust. He imagined himself waking up next to "adorable" every morning for the rest of his life, and grinned. "No. As a matter of fact, I'm hoping for one of my own."

"Really?"

"Really."

Her face burned red under his pointed regard. She abandoned her half-eaten sandwich and twisted the cap off her water. "I also know why you haven't furnished this house properly. No collectables. Essentials only." She sipped from the bottle before continuing. "What's here today could be gone tomorrow, right?"

"Something like that."

"Just because you lost everything once, doesn't mean it will happen again."

"You're telling me not to live in the past." Murphy tossed back another swallow of beer, nailed her with a meaningful look. "Good advice, Princess."

She twisted her lips into a pout. "I like Tiger better."

"Why?"

"Because princess makes me sound like a Goody Two-shoes."

"You are a Goody Two-shoes, hon. That's what I love about you."

Whoa.

The devastated look in her eyes suggested he'd said something wrong. *Shit.* Was it the L word? It's not like he'd said *I love you,* which he did, but figured it was way too soon to admit. *Well, damn.*

"I thought you saw something different in me."

He set his beer aside, but held his place. "You lost me."

She swallowed hard, shrugged. "If you think of me as sweet or pure, you know, like a Madonna type, then you won't want to, you know . . ."

"Ball your brains out for the carnal thrill of it?"

She blushed. "I wouldn't have put it quite like that, but," she took up her sandwich, picked at the crust, "yeah."

Okay. He was getting a bead on good old Terry now. Missionary only. Conservative or staunchly religious. Sex for a reason, not sex for fun. Or maybe he just couldn't get it up unless she was flat on her back, the good, submissive wife. What he didn't get was why she was too embarrassed to talk about it. He thought back on something she'd said, Christ, was it just yesterday? Something about not being the woman her ex thought he married. "So, correct me if I'm wrong, because I'm guessing here, I assume your husband didn't like it when you got too loud or too wild."

"Ex-husband, and something like that."

"If that's why he left you, the guy's a moron."

"He left me because I'm flawed."

Murphy curled his fingers into the counter, checked his temper . . . to a degree. "What the hell does that mean?"

She glanced away. "Can we not talk about this?"

Flawed? Murphy rubbed the back of his neck. He wasn't sure how to handle this. He wished to hell she'd be more specific. *Flawed?* "I've never known anyone like you, Luciana. You're vibrant, caring, sweet, sexy . . ." *I want to grow old with you.*

She raked her teeth over her lower lip, met his gaze. "You think I'm sexy?"

The music track changed over to Marvin Gaye's "Let's Get it On." *Ooh, baby.* "Angel, imp. Princess, tigress. I get hard just looking at you."

"Really?" She grinned, and his heart swelled in recognition of her vulnerability.

"And you're talented." He winked. "In more ways than one." Digging that she was smiling now, not just smiling, but *beaming*, he reached into the ceramic bowl to his left and tossed her one, two, three oranges. She caught them, just the way she'd caught the clubs Trixie had flung her way, and smoothly juggled them into a continuous arc. "Great hands," he said.

"Thanks," she said, with a lopsided grin.

"Guess you've heard that one, huh?"

"If I had a nickel." She reversed the pattern. "You know the eyes factor in too. Eye and hand coordination and lots of practice."

He swigged the rest of his beer, truly entertained. "I could never do that."

"Sure you could. It's a simple three-ball cascade. You teach me the words to Grapevine, and I'll teach you to juggle."

He laughed. "Deal."

She squealed, a freaking shrill shriek, and launched the oranges—one, two, three—past his head. A blur of fast flying fruit. What the—

"Fuck!"

He turned in time to see Bogie dodge the second and third orange. Between the pained curse and the way he was palming his eye, Murphy was relatively sure the first ball of Florida sunshine hit its mark.

"It's Paulie's goon!" she cried to Murphy. "Take cover!"

Murphy sprang from the counter and snatched up Lulu before she lobbed the bottle of spring water. He tried not to laugh, she thought she was protecting him after all, but it was damn difficult. Especially since Bogie looked stunned. A rarity. He glanced away from his injured brother, spoke low in Lulu's ear. "Assaulting a federal agent is against the law, hon. You might want to think twice about hurling that bottle."

She pressed a hand to her chest, gasped for a steady breath. "*That's* Joe Bogart?"

"Man," Bogie complained, snatching a cold beer from the fridge and pressing it to his cheek. "What is it with you Marino sisters?"

Sofie skidded into the room, took one look at Murphy and Lulu in their state of undress, and glared at Bogie. "I told you we should've knocked. But, no, *you* knew the security code." She cursed, mumbling, "*Asino arrogante*," under her breath.

That was it. The last straw. Murphy burst out laughing, even as Bogie scowled, and the sisters traded bemused looks. To think three days ago he'd been bored and depressed. Life was damn good.

Chapter Nineteen

✳ "Glad one of us is having fun," Bogie complained, rolling that cool beer bottle over what was sure to be a shiner. "We need to talk and I'm crunched for time. Think you can pull it together?"

"Sorry, bro." Murphy couldn't remember when he'd last laughed this hard. Ribs aching, he braced one hand on the counter and tried to catch his breath.

Blushing head to toe, Lulu tugged down the hem of her, his, shirt, and edged in behind him for additional cover. "I'm so sorry, Agent Bogart."

"Call me Joe, and don't worry about it," he said. "My fault." He ignored Sofie's mumbled agreement, cracked open the beer, and chugged.

Murphy winked over his shoulder at Lulu, and then looked back at Bogie. "Why don't you show Sofie into the living area? Offer her a beer or something. Where the hell are your manners?"

Sofie smirked. "What manners?" Her gaze bounced from her sister to Murphy, her lips curving into a wry smile. "Interrupt something, did we?"

Bogie steered the smart-assed, mocha-skinned beauty toward the living room. "You might want to put on some clothes before you join us."

Murphy noted with amusement that the surly comment was directed at him, not Lulu. *Curious.* It's not like Sofie had been visibly offended or intrigued by the sight of him in his skivvies. Even if that were the case, what the hell did Bogie care? *Unless . . . Now wouldn't that be interesting?*

As soon as their unexpected guests were out of sight, Lulu scooted toward the library and picked up her jeans and sweater. "I don't understand what's so funny," she whispered.

"You mean other than the part where you torpedoed a fed with fruit?" He copped her bra and panties, fondling the cool silk. "You know I'm growing kind of fond of pink."

"Oh, for goodness . . ." She snatched back her underwear. "This is serious, Murphy. You don't think he'll press charges, do you?"

"And reveal the details of the assault?" Oh, yeah. The boys at the Bureau would have a field day with that one. "I think he'll let it slide."

He ushered her into his bedroom, pondering Bogie's foul mood. Normally he would've seen the humor in being clocked by an orange. Especially an orange lobbed by a cute-as-hell, half-naked, half-pint. Instead he'd barked that he was rushed while practically shoving Sofie from the room. The friction between those two was tangible. Interesting. But not as interesting as whatever details Bogie had to offer on Paulie Falcone.

"I can't believe how rude my sister was to your brother. Then again she hasn't been herself lately." She pulled on her panties and shed his shirt. "What did she call him anyway?"

His mouth watered at the site of her jiggling breasts as she wrangled with her bra. He had to squeeze his freaking package into his jeans. *Nuns and puppies. Nuns and puppies.* "You don't speak Italian?"

"Grandpa used to mutter some phrases, but, no, I never picked it up."

"It was slang, and she was mumbling, but I'm pretty sure she called him an arrogant donkey. Probably meant *ass*."

She swept up her jeans, shook out the wrinkles. "I don't think they like each other."

"I don't think they like that they like each other."

She scrunched her brow.

"Never mind." A thought occurred and he moved in before she could finish dressing. He hugged her, nuzzled her neck, her hair. "You smell good, tiger," he whispered in her ear. "Like sex."

She stiffened in his arms. "I do?"

He smiled, nipped her earlobe. "Turns me on." He pressed her hand over his arousal to prove the point.

She pushed off him, eyes wide, cheeks red. "Well, stop it! I mean save it. I mean . . . I have to take a shower." She flung her jeans on the bed and streaked toward the master bathroom. "Can I use your shampoo?"

"Help yourself."

"Don't discuss anything important without me," she said, and slammed shut the bathroom door.

That's exactly what he planned to do. Murphy bolted, pulling a T-shirt over his head as he strode toward the living area. He heard the shower blast and grinned. He hadn't meant to embarrass Lulu . . . well, yeah, he had. Telling her she smelled like sex had been a sure fire way to buy a few private minutes with Bogie. Given the intensity of her mortification, she'd probably shampoo and soap up her body three times before risking a confrontation with their company. Too bad he couldn't witness the festivities.

He adjusted himself—damned boner—and paused in the archway separating the library from the living area. Bogie had killed the music. He and Sofie sat at opposite ends of his couch, drinking beers and trading glares. *Okay.* He strode in and settled in the opposing recliner. He didn't bother asking Sofie to leave. He knew she wouldn't budge. Besides, if Bogie didn't want her privy to info, she wouldn't be here. "Talk to me."

Bogie leaned forward, the beer bottle dangling from his fingertips. "You've probably guessed, but we're setting up the Falcones. This has been a long time coming. The government's been after these bastards for years. I've been undercover for three months. I only recently gained Paulie's trust enough to be included on a few outings with him and his flunkies."

"How'd you get in and how did you know about Paulie's interest in Lulu?"

Bogie picked at the beer label. Peeled, picked. Peeled, picked. He glanced up at Murphy, his eyes raging with guilt. "I hooked up with Paulie's niece, Julietta Marcella. We're . . . living together."

Sofie stirred, her voice a strangled rasp. "You're sleeping with the enemy?" It sounded more like an accusation than a question.

Bogie directed his answer at Murphy. "It's business."

"She know that?" he asked, cringing at the conflict in his brother's eyes.

"She thinks I'm a legit wannabe club manager. The Bureau set me up as a bartender at one of her favorite hangs. A few drinks on the house and I was in."

Sofie snorted. "So to speak."

"Julietta has a weakness for alcohol, drugs, and attentive men," he went on. "She's young, jaded, and needy as hell."

Sofie shook her head in awe. "You're using an innocent girl to get to a bunch of thugs. How does that make you any better than them?"

"She's not so innocent," Bogie said, without making eye contact. No comment on his ethics. "Julietta's taken me to a few family functions. The Princess appeared at one of them on Saturday."

"The Ditelli party," Murphy offered.

"Yeah. I'd seen her before at the Carnevale."

"Paulie has a weakness for blackjack and friendly eye-candy," Sofie said with a smirk.

Again, Bogie ignored her. "I didn't realize how serious his fascination was until I overheard him talking to his brother, Sal. Paulie talked Louis Ditelli, his second cousin, into firing the clown he'd hired for his daughter's party in favor of Princess Charming. Said his daughter would get a kick out of the Princess, which she did. Everyone did. She charmed the entire family, from age three to eighty-three, the moment she entered the room. A bundle of energy with a thousand-watt smile."

"That's Lulu," Sofie said, and Murphy silently agreed.

"Paulie was mesmerized. At one point, he nudged Sal, who always looks like he's in a fucking daze, and said, *She's the one*." That's when I knew Lulu was in trouble. His rumored pattern is obsession, seduction, and destruction."

"Jesus." Sofie paled two shades, bolted out of her seat and started pacing.

Bogie started to rise, and then changed his mind. He closed his eyes and pressed fingertips to his lids as if stemming a blinding migraine.

Murphy reached out and caught the woman's hand as she walked by. Her skin was ice cold. "Bogie and I can take this to another room, Sofie. You don't need to hear this."

"Yes, I do. I need to know what Lu's up against. I'm fine." She forced a smile, squeezed his hand. "Really." She pulled free, and reclaimed her seat. "It's just so twisted. I think of a man like that getting a hold of her and . . ."

Bogie cut her off. "Don't go there."

"It's not going to happen," Murphy added. The thought of that sick bastard laying hands on Lulu filled him with disgust and a rage he rarely experienced. The kind of rage that blurred a man's thinking. *Distance yourself. Distance is key.* He rolled back his shoulders, focused. "Why didn't you report this to the SAC? He could've assigned one of your own to watch her back."

"Robinson's obsessed with this case. He'll do whatever it takes to bring down the Falcones."

"Sounds contagious," Sofie mumbled.

Bogie nailed her with a sidelong glare. "If he thought he could've somehow used your sister as bait, he would have."

"And you figured one sacrificial lamb was enough," she bit off.

Ouch. Yeah, the fact that Bogie was banging an unsuspecting woman to get close with the Falcones sucked. But Sofie didn't know Bogie the way Murphy did. The guilt was eating his brother alive.

Bogie slammed back the rest of his beer.

Murphy cocked a brow at Sofie, silently warning her to back off. "All right. I get why you called me in. I get that the feds are setting up a sting and that somehow Oz is involved. I get that you need, *want*, Paulie Falcone." He dipped his chin. "By the way, bro, off the record? You better handle Paulie, or I will."

Bogie's answer was an almost imperceptible nod.

"I'd ix-na the illing-ka talk before Lulu gets in here," Sofie whispered.

"Your Pig Latin sucks almost as bad as your Italian," Bogie said, though his mouth was curved in what almost resembled a smile. "And who said anything about killing?"

She rolled her eyes. "I wasn't born yesterday. Lulu, however, is a throw back to the Victorian age."

"The Princess is a peacekeeper," Murphy told him. "Just say no to guns."

Now Bogie did smile. "Presents a bit of a problem for you, doesn't it, Murph?" He glanced toward the bedroom. "That's if I'm reading this right."

"I'll handle it." *Somehow.* "It's you who has a problem. I needed backup. I called Jake Leeds."

"Man," Bogie said, stroking that beatnik patch of hair beneath his mouth. "You must've been up shit's creek. Is he still carrying that grudge?"

" 'Til the day he dies, no doubt."

"Or until you get married."

Murphy noticed Sofie glancing back and forth between the two of them trying to make sense of the conversation. He wasn't about to fill her in. His affair with Joni was ancient history.

She crossed her arms over her chest. "You have something against marriage, Murphy?"

He thought about Lulu, smiled. "Nope."

"You don't?" Wide-eyed, Bogie swept off his sock cap and dragged his hand through his too-long hair. "Well, damn. This got complicated, didn't it?"

"Actually, the complication comes in the form of two guys who work at Oz. Rudy Gallow and Jean-Pierre Legrand."

Bogie nodded. "The chauffeur and that flaming costume dude. They're a couple, right?"

"Yes," Sofie snapped. "And Jean-Pierre is not a flamer. He's just a little flamboyant."

"Yeah, whatever, so what about them?"

"Lulu and Sofie know them well. And so does Jake. They don't just know them," Murphy said, "they're friends. The topper? Rudy's best friend is Jake's wife."

"Jake got married? Where the hell have I been?"

"Screwing the sacrificial lamb," Sofie grumbled.

Murphy was about to ask Sofie-I've-got-a-burr-up-my-ass-Marino to wait outside when a barefoot Lulu blew into the room. Wet curls slicked back into a messy ponytail, she wore her curve-hugging jeans and had helped herself to one of his T-shirts. She looked damn cute and perfectly at home.

"What did I miss?"

Sofie jerked a thumb at Bogie. "Special Agent Bogart is screwing someone for God and country."

"At least I'm not screwing someone to advance my career."

Sofie blanched then came back with an eye-blackening, "You sure about that?"

Murphy blinked at the backbiting pair. What the hell? Lulu looked just as perplexed, and significantly more upset. She eyed the canyon-wide space on the couch that separated Hatfield and McCoy. Murphy snagged her hand and pulled her onto his lap. He didn't know what was brewing between Bogie and Sofie, but he didn't want her in the middle of the bizarre feud. Also, discussing her stalker made him edgy, and he wanted her close. *Real* close. That she didn't resist warmed his heart. In fact, she settled on his lap and reached for his hand as if it were the most natural thing in the world. *Weird.* One sexual encounter, okay, two, and they were in relationship sync. He waited for Sofie to make a snide comment, but she seemed to be saving those for Bogie.

"We were discussing Rudy and Jean-Pierre," Murphy said. *Time to cut to the chase.* "Bro, I need you to guarantee that those two won't get caught up in whatever's going down."

"Can't do that." Bogie held out his palm to silence them. "Legrand is probably clear. But Gallow's in the thick of it."

"Are you saying Rudy's a criminal?" Lulu snapped, balling her free hand in her lap

"I'm saying there's a 99% chance that he'll play a key role in the transaction."

Sofie gripped the arm of the couch. "What transaction?"

Murphy wrapped his hand around Lulu's clenched fist and gave a comforting squeeze. "Jake threatened to warn Rudy and Jean-Pierre away from Oz if I couldn't guarantee their safety, Joe." Murphy kept his tone calm to counteract the rising tension. "If I can't do that, I need to qualify the risk. I know Jake. He'll do what he deems necessary to protect his own. That includes compromising your investigation."

Bogie glanced at his watch, stroked his moustache. "If this gets out—"

"It won't," Sofie and Lulu said as one.

He nodded. "All right. The Falcones are involved in an international Ecstasy smuggling ring. The actual investigation, Operation Candy Jar, has been underway for over a year. They're importing millions of dollars worth of tablets from a source in Paris using exotic dancers and cocktail waitresses as couriers. Paulie compensates the couriers with a paid vacation to France and a hefty cash bonus to fly back into the United States with a load of Ecstasy."

"What's Ecstasy?" Lulu asked.

"It's a street name for MDMA," Bogie said. "An illegal stimulant that—"

"I know what it does," Lulu said, her cheeks burning red.

Murphy soothed a hand up and down her rigid spine. What she didn't know was that MDMA was the drug of choice at teenage raves. When she learned kids twelve and up experimented with the "love drug," she was going to, as she called it, wig out. "So the Falcones are dealing through Ruby Slippers?"

"The entire Oz complex operates as a base. We're attempting to nail the Falcones and various accomplices for illegal importation, trafficking, and use of Ecstasy. Vincent's the ringleader, but we can't seem to hook the slippery bastard. We can get Sal, not the brightest stick in the candelabrum, and we can get to Paulie. He pays an unsuspecting decoy, usually in the form of a flamboyant cross-dresser, to travel with the courier hoping that he'll command the attention of the customs agents, allowing the courier to slip by undetected. All of the pieces are in place." Bogie leaned forward. "We know that another shipment is scheduled to arrive this week. We just don't know the specific date."

Sofie palmed her forehead. "Anthony said something about his boss hiring a European drag artist. He was pissed because he'd never heard of this performer and couldn't scare up any credentials. He didn't even have the flight information yet, and that really irked him because he didn't know when to schedule rehearsals or the actual performance."

"There's your decoy," Murphy said to Bogie. "He'll probably send the company chauffeur to pick up this so-called drag artist and the courier, which makes Gallow a freaking accessory."

"Tell Jake if Gallow's clean, he won't get burned. He has my word. Tell him not to rock the boat. We're days away from putting a serious dent in the accessibility of an increasingly dangerous narcotic. I think that qualifies the risk."

"It does," Lulu said, surprising Murphy as well as her sister. "Well, it *does*. Rudy would agree. Can't we let him in on it though? I mean wouldn't he be safer if he knew details?" She asked Bogie.

Bogie was too busy glaring at Sofie to answer. "You're tight with Rivelli? Are you *insane*? His fiancée is a freaking nutcase! Angela's almost as possessive and vindictive as her cousin Paulie! If she finds out you're screwing—"

"It's not like that!" Sofie's cheeks bloomed with two fire-red blotches.

Murphy watched in amazement as her eyes filled with tears. Sofie who'd threatened his nads with a pair of scissors. Sofie with the smart-ass, kick-ass attitude.

She rose stiffly, her purse tucked beneath her arm. "Excuse me. I need to go to the bathroom." She glanced around, looking lost in more ways than one.

Murphy pointed. "Through there. Down the hall, second door on the right."

Lulu scowled at Bogie, then called to her sister who was already halfway across the room. "Do you want me to come with you?"

Sofie shook her head, no, and then she was gone. A door slammed. Presumably the bathroom door.

"If I advocated violence," Lulu said to Bogie. "I'd come over there and smack you."

"He deserves a hell of a lot more than a smack," Murphy said. He'd never known his brother to be so cruel. That was twice now that he'd made a judgmental crack about Sofie's sexual conduct. "Why did you yell at her?"

"Because she doesn't use the brain she was born with."

"We all know Anthony," Lulu said, coming to her sister's defense. "He used to be a VP at the Carnevale."

Murphy squeezed her hand, showing his support. "According to the newspapers, Rivelli broke off with Angela Falcone."

"He lied. With Angela's blessing. Thought it would save his executive casino position. It bought him some time, but eventually he was booted. So she asked Paulie to set him up with a job and to keep an eye on him while she's in prison. Even though she doesn't trust Rivelli, and he *knows* she doesn't trust him, they have plans to elope when she gets out. A real weird-ass love match. Anyway, Paulie gave Rivelli a job, but he told Angela he wasn't a fu—" He glanced at Lulu. "Sorry. A freaking babysitter. That doesn't mean Sal wouldn't tip off Angela if he saw Rivelli cheating. Unlike Paulie, Sal has strict ideas on fidelity."

Murphy shook his head. "How do you know all this?"

Bogie worked his jaw. "Julietta."

"Who's Julietta?" Lulu asked.

"Never mind. Christ," Murphy said, scraping his hand over his chin. "Could this get anymore complicated?"

"Actually, yeah." Bogie stood, reached into his pocket, and passed Murphy a gift card. "Lulu has rival admirers."

His blood heated as he read the fancy script aloud. "Hope this makes up for the inappropriate gift and our cross words. *Love*, Paulie." *Freaking-A.* Jaw clenched, he glanced at Bogie. "Where'd you get this?"

"The girls' house. The screened porch to be exact. Along with a gigantic pink teddy bear and six different flower arrangements." Bogie looked at Lulu. "Guess he hasn't learned your fave flower yet. But color he knows. Roses, carnations, other varieties I didn't recognize. All pink."

Lulu snatched the card from Murphy's hands, stood, and paced. "I don't believe this! I told him I wasn't interested, didn't I?" She stopped, thunked her forehead. "I didn't." She thunked her head again. "Darn! I scolded him for sending me an inappropriate gift and drugging me. I didn't specifically tell him to bug off."

"Bug off," Bogie said, with a quirk of the lips. "You sure you and Sofia are sisters?"

"Same dad, different mom," she said, looking half-dazed.

Murphy grinned.

Bogie blew out a breath. "Okay, Princess. A: You don't scold a wise-guy. B: Fighting him only heightens the rush of the chase."

"I can't believe this," she croaked. "I can't . . . think." She massaged her temples. "My head is killing me."

Murphy reached for her. "Come here, honey."

"No, I need an aspirin. I need . . ." She drifted toward the stairs. "I'll be back in a minute."

"Seems rattled," Bogie said.

"She'll be okay." Murphy fought the urge to follow. "She's tougher than she looks." Once she was out of earshot, he leaned forward and braced his forearms on his knees. "You mentioned rival admirers."

Bogie dropped back down on the couch, raked both of his hands through his hair, then copied Murphy's stance. "Someone smashed in her jack-o-lantern. Smeared the word 'tramp' on the porch door window. Paulie didn't do it. He's in the seduction phase."

"You're thinking she has another admirer. Someone who doesn't appreciate that she's getting gifts from another man. Someone who's maybe seen her with me and assumes we're an item."

"Are you?"

Murphy raised a brow.

"Man, when you fall, you fall fast."

"And hard." Murphy blew out a breath, told himself to focus on the stalker, not the fact that Lulu was being stalked. "Sam Marlin."

"Who?"

"The creep I asked you to scare off earlier today at the Carnevale. Sofie calls him a watcher. He follows the female performers around, lurks, leers. He's taken a specific liking to Sofie and Lulu. And guess what? He lives in their neighborhood."

"That's gotta suck."

"So what did you say to him today?"

"That if I caught him staring at my girlfriend again, I'd cut off his balls and serve them to the sharks."

Murphy suppressed a grin. Typical Bogie. And, hey now, reminiscent of the tougher Sofie. "Yesterday, I'm pretty sure Marlin witnessed me kissing *your* girlfriend on the boardwalk."

"Hmm. I guess that pretty much makes her tramp material. Is Marlin pumpkin-smashing material?"

"Oh, yeah. He's a whiney-ass weasel."

"Well, at least we know what we're dealing with. As for Jake, tell him to chill. And do *not* brief Gallow. It might make him nervous. I just need him to drive the car, transport the couriers to Oz. That's *if* he's even the one sent to do the job." Bogie glanced at his watch. "I've really got to go, Murph. Julietta's going to start wondering where I am, and if she starts making calls, I'm fucked."

They both rose. "About this girl," Murphy said.

"I'm not going to desert her when this is over." Bogie tucked his hair behind his ears, pulled on the knit cap. "She needs help, Murph. I'll see she gets it. She'll be okay."

Sofie poked her head in the door. She looked dry-eyed, but harried. "I need to go," she said to Bogie. "Can you give me a lift? Thanks." And then she was gone.

Bogie stared after her, frustration and—was that freaking longing swirling in his eyes? "What about you?" Murphy asked. "Are you going to be okay?"

Bogie forced a smile. "Aren't I always?"

Chapter Twenty

❋ "Baby, will you please stop pacing and come back to bed?"

"I can't help it, Jake. I'm nervous." Afia continued her back and forth trek, from the bed to the bureau, cell phone clutched in her right hand. "Rudy sounded so upset. You heard the message. He sounded upset, right?"

He sounded close to tears, but Jake didn't figure that was the best thing to say if he wanted Afia to settle down. He wished they hadn't crawled out of bed to raid the refrigerator. Wished he hadn't checked the message machine, but he'd been expecting a call from Murphy with an update on the Oz situation. No Murphy, just a cryptic sad sack message from an obviously down-in-the-mouth Rudy. "He's a big boy, Afia. Yes, he sounded upset. He'll get over it."

"He told me to call him. He's *expecting* my call. So why isn't he answering his phone?"

"He's probably in a place with low or zip signal."

"I left three messages on his cell and one at home, and what do I get?" she lamented as though Jake hadn't spoken. "A phone call back from Jean-Pierre saying that they had a fight and that he hasn't seen Rudy since this morning."

Jake threw back the covers and swung his legs over the edge of the bed. He'd allow her two more minutes of pacing then he was going to sweep her off those frantic feet. All that agitation couldn't be good for the baby. He knew it wasn't good for Afia. *This* is why he'd wanted an assurance from Murphy that Bogart's sting wouldn't put Rudy and Jean-Pierre in harm's way. Afia loved Rudy with a fierceness that should have made him jealous. At one time it did. Before he knew the man was gay. Before he learned that his shrimp-sized wife had a heart the size of a whale, and was capable of loving deeply on several different levels. A quality he wholly admired. But it was also a quality that made her extremely vulnerable to hurt.

"Jean-Pierre said Rudy was slated to deliver a drag queen from Freehold to Ruby Slippers, but other than that he didn't know his schedule. What if he had an accident?" Her eyes filled with tears. "What if he's not answering his phone because he *can't?*"

That did it. Jake moved swiftly, scooping her off her feet and depositing her in bed. "Take a breath and calm down." He pressed a hand to her shoulder when she tried to bounce back up. "I mean it, Afia. You're overreacting. Rudy and JP had a fight. Rudy's upset. He's also proud and stubborn. Ten to one he's not answering his phone because, despite the message he left hours ago, he's not in the mood to talk. He's probably off somewhere poring over some damned relationship book on 'how to fight fair.' Or maybe he dropped off the queen at Ruby Slippers and decided to stick around and brood over a few beers."

"You think?" She swiped away tears and blinked up at him with a hopeful smile. "Maybe we should go over there and check up on him. See if he needs some company."

"Maybe you should give the man some breathing room." No freaking way was he taking her to Oz. He brushed aside her bangs and kissed her crinkled brow. "If he needs you, Afia, he knows where to find you."

She sighed. "You're right. I'm sorry. I just . . . I have a feeling something bad is going to happen."

She clasped her wrist, and he knew she was mentally stroking the charm bracelet she no longer wore. Her good luck talisman. It was an old habit, one that wrenched his heart, because it meant she was feeling insecure and vulnerable to a crisis or tragedy. "Nothing bad is going to happen, sweetheart." He intended to kiss away her pout, but his phone rang. He reached over and snagged his cell from the nightstand.

Afia bolted upright. "Is it Rudy?"

He glanced at the incoming number. "No." It was Murphy. He tried to roll out of bed, but Afia groaned and clung. Okay. She didn't want to be alone. He got that. He'd just have to deal. He kissed the top of her head, relaxed against the pillows then hit the answer button. "Yeah?"

"It's Murphy."

"I know."

"You alone?"

"No."

"So you can't talk freely."

"Not at the moment." Jake smoothed his hand down Afia's back as she snuggled in against him. Earlier they'd burned up the mattress, the couch, and had even gone a round in the shower. With any luck, she'd conk out from exhaustion and stop worrying about Gallow.

"Good," Murphy said. "Means you can't give me shit."

Jake fought to keep his expression neutral and his body relaxed as Murphy laid out what he'd learned from Bogart. He wasn't thrilled to know that Rudy and Jean-Pierre were smack dab in the middle of a drug-smuggling investigation, but he did relish the thought of decimating the Falcones. Bogart's assurance that Rudy would be shielded from prosecution was a bonus, but he didn't agree that Rudy should be left in the dark. He knew the man. Bogart didn't. "I'm cool with everything except the last part. Forewarned is forearmed."

"Let's cross that road if we come to it," Murphy said. "Maybe they won't even send Gallow."

"Maybe." Or maybe Rudy would be too busy sulking or mending bridges with JP to take the assignment. One could hope.

"Oh, and Jake. About Rivelli? I don't think he's tangled in the family business, but he's sure as hell tied to the family. He still plans on marrying the mob boss's daughter."

The fact that Rivelli *wanted* to marry that jealous bitch blew his mind. He was also surprised that Angela was willing to accept Rivelli's quirky lifestyle. "Life is full of surprises," Jake mumbled.

"I'll say. Aside from a couple of glowing moments, this day has been cursed with one calamity after another."

Cursed. Jinxed. Jake blinked at the ceiling, his brain zinging with illogical thoughts.

"Let's keep in touch," Murphy said.

"Yeah." Jake signed off and tossed aside his cell phone. Afia had freaked when she'd thought Angela had cursed her with the Evil Eye, dooming her to "dry up." *"I'll never have children,"* she'd cried one night. He'd blasted the ancient belief as bullshit, and, over the weeks, as she'd shed her superstitious ways, she'd shed her fear.

"I have a feeling something bad is going to happen."
Holy shit.

"What's wrong, Jake?"

He shifted, cocooning his wife and their unborn child in his arms. "Nothing, honey."

Positive thoughts over negative. Isn't that what he'd told her once?

Nothing bad is going to happen.

* * *

Could this night get any worse? Lulu descended the stairs in a daze, her cell phone in hand. She found Murphy in the library signing off from his own call. "Where's Sofie?" she rasped.

"She had to be somewhere. Bogie gave her a lift." He glanced at the phone in her hand and immediately stood. "Was it Paulie?"

"What?" She blinked, shook her head. "Oh. No. It was Viv."

"Is she okay?"

"Yes. No. I just can't believe it." She started to pace. If she didn't walk off this nervous energy she'd explode. "I was feeling overwhelmed, and scared, and I know this sounds childish, but I wanted my *Nonna*. I wanted her to make everything better. Viv has a way of doing that, you know. She's this incredible ball of positive energy. She could make a stone laugh."

"Sounds a lot like you."

She chewed on a thumbnail and quickened her pace. "Comparing me to Viv is an incredibly kind compliment. She's the nicest person I've ever known." She snorted. "Even though she is a little nutty."

"I can say the same about you."

She glanced over and saw that he was smiling. An affectionate smile that made her insides gooey. Her knees weakened, and she tripped over her own two feet. He caught her before she fell flat out, relieved her of the cell phone, and kissed away her harried thoughts. *Oh, to spend a lifetime in this man's arms.*

She sighed when he eased away, trying to remember why she'd been so upset.

"So what did your nutty grandmother say or do that's got you so riled, tiger?"

"She eloped." That was it. The staggering news that had sent her into a deeper tailspin. "My seventy-two-year-old grandmother is in Las Vegas on her *honeymoon*."

He chuckled. "And this is bad because . . ."

Because now she'll probably move to Florida. Because Sofie's hurting and I don't know why and it's only a matter of time before she moves on to wherever.

Because everyone I've ever loved leaves me, and I'm terrified that I'm falling in love with you.

She swiped a stray curl off her face, and took a calming breath. She *would not* wig out. "It's not bad. I mean I like Franklin. He and Viv met years ago when they worked on a cartoon feature together. He was the animator and she did a voice-over. Anyway, he's funny and nice, and well, grandpa has been gone a long time. It's just unexpected. Like everything else in my life lately."

He stroked his thumb over her cheek. "Like us, for instance."

Us. The concept struck her with simultaneous joy and panic. Her throat tightened as she put her heart on the line. "I couldn't tell Viv about Paulie. I didn't want to upset her. But I told her about you. I told her I'd met a kind and brave man who's wonderful with children, but whose job entails carrying a gun. I told her that, in the space of three days, you changed the way I look at the world and that terrifies me. I told her I'm afraid you're too good to be true."

She realized suddenly that she'd inched away from Murphy with every admission, and now her back was against the wall, literally. He advanced and her entire body tingled with awareness. She nearly shot out of her skin when he grasped her hand and placed it over his heart.

"I'm real. I'm flawed. And you're not the only one who's looking at the world differently. Just because we bonded fast, doesn't make what we feel any less real. I'm in this for the long haul, Luciana."

His eyes sparked with sincerity and strength. She believed him. Unlike Terry, she couldn't imagine Murphy giving up when the going got tough. He'd dig in and fight harder. Like a Marine. Her heart thumped in rhythm with his. Deep down, they really weren't that different. They both wanted to make the world a better place.

Going on what little he'd revealed about his military stint, and after doing some calculations and surfing the Internet, she'd come to the conclusion that he'd participated in Operation Sea Angel and Operation Restore Hope, the latter being a humanitarian effort in Somalia. As she'd spent her life shunning the news, she was ashamed to admit that she didn't know much about these events. The more she'd read, the more she'd been tempted to fall back on old ways and shut it all out. So much pain and destruction. The only thing that made her eager to learn more was knowing that Murphy and countless others had witnessed these horrible things first hand. *Making a difference entails taking risks.*

She'd spent her life casting mental stones at men, good and bad, who carried guns, focusing on the violence and not the peacekeeping. She'd lived her life in a bubble, playing it safe and never achieving true happiness or satisfaction. Never making a big enough difference.

"Do you know what Viv said?" She swallowed hard, her voice a nervous whisper. "Life's short. Live large. No regrets."

He smiled. "OohRah."

"We attack life differently, Colin. We'll drive each other crazy. You do realize that, don't you?"

He framed her face in his hands, hands that had fed starving children, hands that had dug people free of mudslides. "I'm ready to fill this house with memories."

Her lips curved as toe-curling joy banished the last of her doubts. "What about furniture?"

He laughed. "That too." He gazed into her eyes, and the earth moved. "So what do you think?"

That the zing could fizzle in six months. That he could be caught in a cross fire in two weeks. That she could bite it tomorrow in a car accident like her dad and Sofie's mom. *Life's short. Live large. No regrets.* "I think Viv's a genius." Smiling, she stood on her tiptoes and brushed a kiss across his mouth. "Let's rock and roll."

* * *

Muffled disco music charged the brisk night air. Sofie glanced at her watch. One o'clock in the morning. She glanced at the entrance to Ruby Slippers. Special Agent Joseph Bogart's voice rang in her ear. "*Stay away from Oz.*"

If she had any respect for the fed, she might've had second thoughts. Loathing was all she could dredge up for a man who'd saved and seduced her only to make snide cracks about her sexual conduct. Like he had room to talk. He'd used sugar words and a stiff prick to advance an investigation.

Joe's behavior only reinforced her conclusion that men were pigs and not to be trusted. The episode with Chaz still cramped her stomach, and her sister's plight with the stalker made her sick with worry and rage. Life in general was the pits right now and to top things off, Rudy was missing.

Jaw clenched, she pushed through the glittering red doors of the gay nightclub, intent on doing something worthwhile and obliterating the awful feeling of helplessness. Intent on finding the selfish ass who was putting poor Jean-Pierre through hell just because he was jealous. JP was certain Rudy had overheard him speaking with Luc. The conversation was harmless, but how could he explain that if Rudy wasn't willing to listen? *"Why is he pushing me to go to California and yet refuses to come along? Are we not a couple? Are we not working toward a united goal?"*

Sofie didn't have the answers. She sucked at relationships. Misery loved company, so she'd joined JP in a bitch and moan session while attempting to drown their sorrows in a bottle and a half of wine. Jean-Pierre had passed out on the couch. Sofie wasn't sure she'd ever sleep again. Her body and brain surged with morbid thoughts and raw emotions.

She elbowed her way through the packed house, searching faces, asking questions. No Rudy. A Donna Summers song blared over the speakers. The audience whistled and cheered. Sofie glanced toward the stage and saw a buff drag queen dancing in five-inch acrylic platforms while lip-syncing into the microphone. Okay. At least she knew Rudy had followed through and transported the scheduled performer to the club. Maybe he'd checked in with Anthony.

She made her way to the bar and signaled a bartender. "Where's Anthony Rivelli?"

"Flying Monkeys," he shouted over the music. "Problem with a cage dancer."

She nodded and then squeezed and shimmied her way through the shoulder-to-shoulder crush of men. She pressed a hand to her moist brow, breathing easier when she reached the

Over the Rainbow skywalk. No crowds here. Just a few adventurous women crossing over to Ruby Slippers. One of them eyed her and smiled. Sofie smiled back, wondering for a scant moment if she'd have better luck in a same sex relationship. Then she thought about Rudy and JP who had their own set of problems. A relationship was a relationship was a relationship. Besides it would be kind of hard to pursue a gay affair when she was hard core straight.

She hurried past the women, her spiked heels sinking into the plush carpet as she made her way toward the hetero dance club. When she finally crossed over into Flying Monkeys, a suffocating wave of heat and hedonism greeted her. Trance music blasted from high tech speakers. Bright colored, man-sized birdcages were strategically placed throughout the cavernous room. Inside: male and female dancers wore outrageous, skimpy costumes so obviously designed by Jean-Pierre. The man truly was a genius. Sofie grabbed the gold railing of the upper tier and scanned the club for Anthony.

Hordes of sweaty, half-naked people undulated on the dance floor below, most of them with drinks in hand. The erotic atmosphere sent a shiver up her spine. Strange. She'd partied here on several occasions. She'd danced seductively. She'd drunk too much. She'd even experimented with Ecstasy, though she'd die before ever admitting that to Lulu. But once had been enough. Knowing what she knew now about the Falcones and the drug-smuggling ring put a new and ugly slant on the whole party scene. Her heart pounded with repulsion and dread. *Stay away from Oz.*

She was ready to take flight when she spied Anthony on the lower level talking with one of the dancers. Swallowing her trepidation, she hurried down the spiral staircase and elbowed her way through another crush of patrons.

Anthony turned just as she got to him. He smiled. "Sofia.

A pleasure as always."

"I need to talk to you."

His brow furrowed with concern. Probably thought she was going to burst into another crying jag over Chaz. He tenderly grasped her elbow and led her to a more private corner. "What's wrong?"

"It's Rudy."

"What about him?"

"I'm wondering if you might know where he is."

Anthony slid his hands into his designer trouser pockets and shook his head, no. "I wish I did. He dropped off Sucha Tramp earlier this evening and left before I got a chance to talk to him. I need to book him for a short notice transport." He frowned. "Remember when I told you about that European drag artist?"

Sofie's senses tingled. "The one that your boss hired? The one with no credentials?"

"That's the one. Apparently he's flying in tomorrow with a small entourage. Must be a bona fide diva."

She tucked her hands into the pockets of her suede jacket to conceal their trembling. This was what Joe had been waiting for. The information to instigate the sting. The shipment of drugs would arrive tomorrow. But what time? What airport?

"I've left two messages for Rudy. If I don't hear back from him by tomorrow morning, I'm going to have to hire an outside source or make the drive myself, which means canceling a few meetings. Damned inconvenient."

"I'll do it."

"Do what?"

Sofie moistened her lips, and affected a casual demeanor. "Pick up the queen and his entourage. I have the day free tomorrow. I don't mind." She smiled. "It's the least I can do for a guy who let me blubber on his shoulder twice this week."

He angled his head, and she swore her lungs were going to explode if he didn't answer, yes. "Hopefully, I'll hear back from Rudy, but if I don't, why not?" He smiled, grasped her shoulders. "Thank you. You're a good friend, Sofia."

Guilt fluttered in her stomach as she moved into his arms for a hug. "And you're the only man currently not on my shit list," she teased. Anthony had been nothing but kind to her, and now she was manipulating him. She didn't think he knew about the Ecstasy shipment. Then again he *was* connected to the Falcones. She could only pray he was innocent of any dirty dealings and that he escaped prosecution. "So when and where," she asked past the lump in her throat.

"Philadelphia International Airport," he said in her ear. "It's a 5:00 p.m. arrival from Paris on Delta. The diva's name is Emile Loren. Let's touch base tomorrow morning. If I can connect with Rudy, you won't have to bother."

"No bother," she said, pushing back to arm's length. "Until tomorrow then."

Her pulse raced as she moved back into the crowd. She had to get out of here, had to call Murphy. They had to get this information to Joe. The sooner Paulie Falcone was off the street, the sooner her sister would be safe. Her brain buzzed, her adrenaline pumping so hard she weaved with dizziness.

And suddenly there he was. Special Agent Joseph Bogart standing in front of her, brandishing a glass of liquor, and looking ticked and sexy as hell in his undercover get up. He'd changed into black trousers and a red, open-collar shirt. He almost looked stylish. He definitely looked handsome.

She hated that she noticed.

"You're drunk," he said.

"I'm perfectly sober."

He moved in against her, wrapped his free arm about her waist. "You're falling down drunk and two-seconds from puking," he growled into her ear. "Use those acting skills now, goddammit, and don't argue."

She sensed the urgency in his tone, his touch. Her knees gave way as she sagged against him and groaned.

He simultaneously dumped his drink, soaking his shoes in the process. He disposed of the glass, before dragging her past a dark-suited man with a fleshy mouth and vacant eyes. "The plastered bitch puked on my shoes," Joe said to the man with an annoyed laugh. "I'm going to toss her in a cab before she passes out and causes a scene. Be right back."

"Oh, my God," she rasped when they cleared the main entrance. "Was that Paulie?"

"Sal," he barked quietly. He hauled her around the corner, into a dark alley before she could respond. His body vibrated with anger, and she actually squealed when he shoved her into a rank secluded corner. "Jesus, Sofia. Do you have a death wish?"

"What? *No.*"

"I told you to stay away from Oz. I told you Rivelli's fiancée has her cousins keeping an eye on him. Yet here you are hanging all over the guy."

"I wasn't hanging," she shoved at his shoulders, anxious for breathing room, but the bastard wouldn't budge. "Rudy's missing. I thought he might be here. I thought Anthony might know . . ." She fought to catch an even breath. None of that mattered right now. "I got the information, Joe. Tomorrow. The shipment's coming in tomorrow. Delta flight from Paris. 5:00 p.m. Emile Loren. That's the decoy's name."

He raked back his hair, exposing those killer cheekbones. "I'll be damned."

"Anthony left messages for Rudy, who's off sulking because of a fight with JP. But don't worry. If Rudy doesn't step up to the plate, I'm going in his place. I volunteered, and Anthony agreed."

He narrowed those intoxicating whiskey-colored eyes. "Like hell you are."

"I'm trying to help."

He slammed his palm against the brick wall, making her jump. "I don't want your fucking help."

"I'm not doing it for you. I'm doing it for Lulu, and you can't stop me."

"Wanna bet?"

He snatched her into his arms and punished her with a savage, soul-searing kiss. A kiss she'd never forget if she lived to be a hundred. A kiss that rendered her weak. Or was that his hands? Fingertips. Gentle pressing.

By the time she realized he was manipulating a pressure point it was too late.

The world went black.

* * *

Rudy sat in his darkened limo staring at Afia and Jake's house. It was two in the morning. They were sound asleep. He had no business knocking on their door. No right dumping his misery in their laps in the middle of the night. But he couldn't go home. Couldn't face Jean-Pierre. He'd been driving around for hours in a daze. He couldn't even remember where he'd been. He'd mindfucked his dilemma until his brain threatened to explode.

He was exhausted. He didn't even have the energy to start up the limo and drive away. So he just sat there in the dark, staring at the dark house, thinking dark thoughts.

He swallowed hard when the front door swung open and Jake stepped out onto the porch. "Golden-boy" crossed the moonlit yard in sweatpants and a T-shirt, his feet bare. Rudy drummed up the energy to roll down his window. "Chilly night," he said when Jake palmed his car roof and leaned in. "You're going to catch cold, Leeds."

"*You're* going to catch hell. Afia's worried sick about you. I'm worried sick over her worrying. And let's not forget about your other half. Did you at least call and let him know you're okay?"

"No." Guilt knotted Rudy's stomach. "Consideration for Jean-Pierre's feelings flew out the window earlier this afternoon. I've been struggling with the consequences of my actions ever since."

Jake groaned. "This can't be good." He stepped back and motioned Rudy to get out of the limo. "Let's take this inside."

Rudy shook his head. "I don't want to bother you and Afia."

"Too late. Come on, Gallow. I'm freezing my nuts off."

Heart heavy, Rudy dragged himself out of the car and followed his friend into the cozy Victorian house. A house he and Afia were remodeling together. A house filled with love and the promise of a bright and happy future. He felt sick to his stomach.

Afia hit the bottom landing of the stairs just as he and Jake cleared the foyer. She looked rumpled and cute as hell in her satin cheetah pajamas. With a squeal she bounced off the last step and flew into his arms. "You're okay!"

Far from it. Rudy clung to his best friend as the tears he'd been holding back all day burst forth. Jake averted his gaze, but he didn't leave.

Afia hugged his shaking body tight and smoothed a loving hand over the back of his head. "Shh," she cooed gently. "Whatever it is, it can't be that bad."

"It's unforgivable." The admission scraped his throat and heart raw. "I betrayed Jean-Pierre."

Chapter Twenty-One

✱ Murphy groped in the dark for his chiming cell phone. He squinted at the illuminated alarm clock. 03:00. Three o'clock in the freaking morning. He thumbed the answer button knowing it couldn't be good. "Yeah?"

"You alone?"

"No."

"Rectify that. Meanwhile listen."

Phone pressed to his ear, Murphy tried to extricate himself from a tangle of arms and legs without waking Lulu, while Bogie related a run-in with Sofie.

Lulu reached for him. "Don't leave me," she whimpered, at the same time Bogie said something about putting Sofie into protective custody.

His head spun. "Hold on, bro." He clasped Lulu's small hand, and pressed a kiss to her palm. "I'm just getting a drink of water, hon."

She mumbled an indecipherable response, and he realized then she was still asleep. He'd like to think that she was dreaming about their latest sex-capade, an imaginative toss in the hot tub that rivaled positions in the *Kama Sutra*. But what if she was dreaming about mermaids and sharks? Paulie? What if she woke up alone and panicked? He hesitated a moment—*those damned what ifs*—then crept from the bedroom, prodding Bogie to continue. He wanted this case over and done. He wanted Lulu safe.

"I admire Sofia for having the presence of mind to get essential details, but dammit Murph, she was ready to put herself in the mix."

"So you did what you had to do to keep her safe. I would've done the same thing."

"Would you have slept with Julietta?"

The question was swift and laced with angst. Murphy could envision Bogie cursing himself for letting it slip. The conflict in his tone was worrisome. He'd never known the man to doubt his actions. "I don't know," he answered honestly. "I'm not in your shoes." Is this why he'd really called? To discuss morals? Bogie had to be pretty tortured to even broach the subject. "Wanna talk about it?"

"No."

A thought occurred. "Isn't your cell being monitored?"

"Say hi to the boys."

The Bureau. No doubt the agents operating out of the covert surveillance van he'd mentioned. The agents he'd entrusted with Sofie. Apparently, Bogie didn't care if his SAC learned about Lulu at this point. The sting was only hours away. "You know even though I don't blame you for taking control, Sofie's going to be pissed as hell when she wakes up."

"Better pissed than dead. Listen, we're set on this end," he said, switching back to official mode. "If Gallow doesn't surface, Rivelli will probably pull transport duty. All that matters is that the couriers and drugs get from point A to B. I only called because I didn't want Lulu to worry if she tried and couldn't get a hold of her sister."

"I appreciate that." Murphy snagged a bottle of water from the fridge. "I want in, Bogie."

"I'm not surprised."

"I want to see that son of a bitch taken down with my own eyes." He also wanted to watch his brother's back. Not that he didn't trust the Bureau. He didn't trust whatever was going down personally with Bogie. Worried it would somehow compromise his performance, and put him at risk.

"What about Lulu? I know your house is a fortress, but that Marlin character's still floating around. Who knows what he's capable of?"

"I'll get Jake to cover."

"I'll have to get clearance."

"Do it."

"I'll be in touch," Bogie said, and signed off.

Murphy chugged a quarter of the bottled water, his body pulsing with anticipation. Actively thwarting the bad guy held a rush and a level of satisfaction he couldn't dismiss. It had factored heavily into his decision to become a protection specialist after retiring from the Marines. Lulu was right. They attacked life differently. They were definitely in for some major head butting sessions. Cross-eyed in love with her, all he could think was *bring them on*.

The phone chimed. It better be a go, or he and Bogie were in for a verbal tussle. "Yeah?"

"The shipment's coming in tomorrow," Jake said, surprising Murphy with the night owl phone call. "Philadelphia airport. 5:00 p.m."

"I know."

"How?"

"Bogie via Sofie. Long story. You?"

"Rudy via one of fifteen voice mails. Complicated story."

He blew out a breath. "Let's just say it involves a life crisis and poor judgment."

Murphy sympathized. He'd certainly endured his share of personal crises and fuck ups. "We all make mistakes."

"That's what I told him, but he didn't want to hear it. Christ, it's not like he actually ended up in the sack with the guy."

"Too much information," Murphy said, eager to get back to his own love interest.

"He's pretty messed up over this," Jake went on, making it clear that he was equally shaken. "Afia's trying to talk him out of spilling his guts to Jean-Pierre. Why hurt JP's feelings over a stupid weak-ass moment? Nothing of consequence happened."

So even though Gallow hadn't actually cheated, he'd come close. "That's pretty open-minded of Afia."

"She's the most tolerant and caring woman I've ever known. Just two of the hundred things I love about her."

"Speaking of special women, I need you to watch over Lulu tomorrow. I want in on that crackdown, and I don't want to leave her alone."

"Done," Jake said. "In return you can watch Rudy's back."

"Given Gallow's state of mind just now, are you sure he's up for this?"

"You won't be able to hold him back once he knows specifics."

"Bogie doesn't want him to know specifics," Murphy said.

"Tough shit. I'm not sending him in blind. You'll have to trust me on this, Murphy. Think you can handle that?"

"If I didn't trust you, Jake, I wouldn't have called you when this first started."

"This conversation's getting way too sappy for me," the

P.I. quipped. "Call me tomorrow with an exact time for babysitting duty. Hey, wait. That thing about Lulu being a special woman—"

"I'm going to ask her to marry me."

"You've known her what, three, four days?"

Murphy's heart pounded with joy and affection. His gut said all systems go. "When it's right, it's right."

After a significant pause, Jake said, "No argument there. In fact, the more I think about it, the more I like the idea of you being tied to that woman. Lulu's an unpredictable fireball. She'll probably make your life hell."

Murphy's lips twitched. "So much for sappy." He signed off while padding back into his bedroom.

He slipped beneath the sheets and the woman he loved rolled into his arms. She threw her leg over his thighs, clipped his chin as she wrapped an arm around his shoulders. A restless sleeper, he'd probably seen the last of his peaceful nights. She grumbled something about resilient balls, and he stifled a laugh. He hoped to hell she was talking about juggling.

His heart flooded with contentment as he contemplated life with an artistic fireball.

Four days ago he'd battled a month-long depression. He recognized it now for what it was. A midlife crisis. Almost forty and alone. No wife, no kids. No future beyond his job and investments. And all because he'd been clinging to the past.

He couldn't lose what he didn't have.

Lulu had nailed his hang-up dead on. Amazing that one person could make such a positive difference. Luciana Ross was a one-of-a-kind superhero, capable of nurturing decency and saving troubled souls. He'd basked in her sunshine. He'd soaked in her goodness. Tonight, instead of having nightmares about death and destruction, he'd dream about new beginnings and the power of hope, love, and laughter.

He'd dream about Lulu.

* * *

Sunbeams streamed in through the gauzy curtains signifying a new day. Murphy slept soundly beside Lulu signifying a new life. A life filled with challenging discussions and adventurous lovemaking. He'd mentioned being in this relationship for the long haul, so that meant forever, right? He'd said he was ready to fill *this* house with memories, which was a round-about way of asking her to move in, yes? Yes. She couldn't possibly be that naïve. What surprised her was that she was ready to dive in. Living in sin no longer seemed sinful. How could it be wrong when it felt so right?

Yet something niggled at her. Instead of daydreaming about how she was going to breathe life into this house, she was obsessing on nightmares of death and desertion. Sad images of those she loved abandoning her, intermingled with disturbing visions of an international drug-smuggling ring. Was her fairy-tale bubble about to burst? Was she having a premonition? Maintaining Viv's "live large" credo proved more difficult in the light of day. What if she was setting herself up for another fall? What if Murphy lost interest after the FBI felled the Falcones?

Why was she entertaining such negative thoughts?

Rudy would have a fit. He'd tell her to have faith. To visualize a positive future. *See it. Be it.*

She closed her eyes and visualized life with a man who loved children, but didn't want children. A man who wouldn't care that she's barren. A man who believed in taking risks and making a difference. Her perfect match.

She opened her eyes and found Murphy studying her. Her body vibrated under his blatant regard. Intense to the bone, this man oozed sex appeal. She squeezed her tingling thighs together, shocked that he'd rendered her wet and ready with a soulful gaze.

His lips curved into a tantalizing smile. "What are you thinking about, Princess?"

"You. Us."

"I'd like that, except you're frowning."

"I can't cook," she blurted, when she'd really meant *I can't have children*. Even though he didn't want to bring kids into this world, he needed to know her biggest flaw. What if he changed his mind? *What if?* Maybe that was her biggest flaw. Her ability to *what if* any situation into a catastrophe. For the first time ever, she cursed her imagination.

He smoothed her hair out of her face, traced his finger along her jaw. "I don't see that as a problem, hon." He gazed into her eyes as he skimmed his fingers down her throat and then drew lazy, feather-light circles around her bare breasts. "I'm more concerned with the issue of restrictions."

Her stomach tightened and fluttered with anticipation. "Restrictions?" Last night's romp in the hot tub had been thrillingly erotic. What would he think of next?

"Do you trust me?"

She looked into his eyes, his soul. "I do." The words tumbled without thought.

He grabbed a condom from the nightstand. She watched, entranced as he covered his mouthwatering erection, her imagination painting a dozen fantasies. What did he have in mind? Then he rolled on top of her and her brain overloaded. The feel of his naked body pinning her down summoned images of fruitless, joyless coupling. But then he plied her mouth with a deep kiss, his fingers working magic on her body, teasing, tempting, loving, and her worries ebbed leaving her with a solitary thought: *"You're the one."*

He stilled, capturing her heart for now and always with a look that ignited her soul. "You and no other."

She realized suddenly that she'd spoken her thought aloud, and he'd responded with an ancient pledge. Her heart burst with mind altering rapture when he sank deep inside. She clung to his shoulders, breathless, as he made love to her, slow and tender with an intensity that had her seeing rainbows. Colin Murphy colored her future with vibrant images of a fairy-tale happy ending.

Time blurred as they soared higher and higher . . . over the rainbow. Utopia. He groaned his release as her body shuddered with the fiercest climax of her life. She cried. She couldn't help it. Her prince had given her a glimpse of Camelot.

"Please tell me those are tears of joy," he rasped, his features strained with guilt.

Smiling, she smoothed her hands over the hard planes of his beautiful face. "You're really stuck with me now."

* * *

"Where are you going?"

"LA."

Heart in throat, Rudy stared as Jean-Pierre snatched clothes from his dresser and crammed them into a suitcase. After a few hours restless sleep at Jake and Afia's, he'd tired of putting off the inevitable. He'd driven home. He hadn't even bared his soul and Jean-Pierre was already packing. It only served to reinforce his fear that their relationship was truly fragile.

Jean-Pierre turned to face him, hands on hips. "It is what you wanted, is it not?"

Rudy swallowed hard. His lover looked hung over and angry as hell. Unshaven, dark circles beneath his normally luminous eyes. His shirt was actually wrinkled and clashed with his pants. He'd never seen this side of good-natured, fashion-conscious Jean-Pierre. He feared no matter what he said or did, he'd only make matters worse. Somehow he managed to force words past the gigantic lump in his throat. "I want you to take advantage of a phenomenal opportunity. I want you to win the recognition you deserve. I don't want you to pass up a chance to design costumes for a Hollywood film, only to resent me months from now."

"Your lack of faith in my judgment is astonishing, Bunny."

The nickname that used to irk Rudy, and then later warmed his heart, now sent a shiver down his spine. "I just . . . I want you to be happy."

"Yet you did not come home last night. You did not return my calls, did not bother to let me know that you had not crashed and burned on the highway. No. I had to learn from Jake that you were safe. At three in the morning no less."

"I behaved badly."

"Ah, *oui*." He returned to his packing.

"No, I mean . . ." Both Afia and Jake had warned him against confessing his indiscretion. Suggested he'd be better off addressing his insecurities, strengthening instead of sabotaging the relationship. He supposed it didn't matter now. He had a reputation. He hadn't come home. No doubt Jean-Pierre already assumed the worst.

Address your insecurities.

"I heard you talking to Luc. I was consumed with jealousy, convinced that you were going to pick up with your old lover." When Jean-Pierre didn't comment, he tossed up his hands in frustration. "The two of you have so much more in common. You're young and artistic. *French*. I don't know what happened. I lost it. I . . . I . . ." Ah, Christ, he couldn't say it.

"You sought solace in another man's arms."

"It wasn't . . . We didn't . . ."

"It does not matter." Jean-Pierre snapped shut two suitcases, curled his long fingers around the handles. "I will advise Anthony of my decision tomorrow. I already gave my notice at the Carnevale. I will be staying at a motel for the next few days."

At last, Rudy moved forward and risked contact. He placed his hand over Jean-Pierre's, the only hand whose touch he truly craved. Renewed guilt flooded his being, causing his voice to sound flat and detached. "You don't have to do that. Stay here. I can move into the guest room."

Jean-Pierre's eyes brimmed with tears as he broke free and moved toward the door. "Ah, Bunny. If only you had asked me to stay, period."

* * *

"I'm not leaving you."

"Don't be ridiculous, Jake. If you don't watch over Lulu, Murphy won't leave her, meaning he won't be able to watch over Rudy. You have to go. I'm fine, really. Just tired."

Jake watched as Afia spooned canned gourmet food into their cats' double serving dish. She looked pale and exhausted. The exhausted part he understood. She'd tossed and turned with worry most of the night, only to spend the wee hours into dawn comforting Rudy. Even her attempt at an afternoon nap had been a bust.

But it was her trembling hands that caused him real concern. The scene with Rudy had stressed her out. Even worse, she'd walked in at the end of his red-eye phone call with Murphy.

He'd had two choices: come clean or straight out lie. The latter was not an option. So now she was not only worried about JP and Rudy, but Rudy and Lulu pitted against those crazy Falcones.

"I have a feeling something bad is going to happen."

Shit. Shaking off his own sense of foreboding, he moved in from behind and wrapped his arms around Afia's waist, his palms against her flat belly. Knowing that Joni had almost lost her baby in the early stages of pregnancy tweaked his concern to an excruciating level. "Baby, why don't I drop you off at Joni's. I'd feel a helluva lot better if you weren't alone just now."

Afia dropped her head back against his shoulder and sighed. "If I don't go, you're going to be distracted, aren't you?'

"Probably."

"In that case, I'll go. If you're distracted, Lulu won't be the only one at risk. I have enough on my mind without having to worry about you." She nudged him away and carried the dish toward the laundry room. "I'll feed the cats. You run up and get my purse." She looked over her shoulder and winked. "Chop, chop, baby."

He'd once used that phrase when trying to coax her into dumpster diving for a case. The Angela Falcone case to be exact. Her attempt to lighten his mood failed. He forced a smile then headed for the stairs. In addition to her purse, he was tempted to dig her charm bracelet out of the top dresser drawer and to clasp it around her wrist for good luck.

Though it went against his logical nature, at this moment Jake welcomed any and all protection from misfortune and evil, even the magical kind.

* * *

Sofie was in protective custody. Rudy was on his way to Philadelphia. As soon as Jake arrived, Murphy would be off to meet Bogie. Their objective: to crack down on an international smuggling ring and to incapacitate the upper echelon of a notorious crime family.

Murphy, Lulu knew, had a special eye on her stalker, Paulie Falcone.

Her Disney life had become a Hollywood thriller. And it was only getting worse.

Lulu stared at the computer screen, disbelieving. An estimated 2.8 million teenagers had tried Ecstasy at least once and many went on to become regular users despite the dangerous cognitive, physical, and psychological effects. Children as young as twelve years old experimented with the increasingly popular *love drug*.

Twelve years old!

She hadn't argued when Murphy had asked her to call in sick to work. Hadn't panicked when he'd relayed an update on Operation Candy Jar. She knew her impulsive sister was in safe hands and that Rudy could take care of himself. But nervous energy had demanded she rein in her imagination before she *what if'd* Murphy and his brother into a deadly shoot-out with the Falcones. That meant occupying her mind.

Murphy had suggested she work on a loonytale while he prepared for the sting. Wanting to better understand the significance of this particular FBI investigation, she'd ended up surfing the Net. Knowledge, she'd recently decided, was power.

Knowledge was also dangerous.

The red haze intensified as she skimmed more statistics and scientific reviews. Pumped up and armed with disturbing facts, she catapulted out of her chair, and into the bedroom.

"Did you know that MDMA is a popular club drug for teens?"

Murphy pulled a black mock turtleneck shirt over his head. "I thought you were going to work on a loonytale."

"We're talking *millions* of kids," she vented, as she paced the length of the room. "It's not addictive, but they begin to crave the effects. Chronic users of MDMA experience cognitive or memory loss. In high doses, MDMA can lead to hyperthermia, resulting in liver, kidney, and cardiovascular system failure. It's not just a harmless *mood-altering* drug, Murphy!"

He tucked in his shirt, regarded her with a somber expression. "I know, honey."

"Did you know that one tablet costs about twenty-five dollars? Joe said the Falcones are importing millions of dollars worth of Ecstasy! How many tablets is that? How many children and teenagers will be affected? Those mobsters are greedy, treacherous scum!" She spied his gun on the bed and, without any hesitation whatsoever, picked it up and thrust it at him. "You're going to need this."

"Whoa." Murphy relieved her of the weapon, redirecting the business end. "Watch where you point that thing, tiger."

"Make sure you have lots of bullets. If one of them shoots at you, shoot back. Just try not to kill anyone. I'd hate for you to have that on your conscience."

He grinned while holstering his firearm. "I think I can handle it."

Lulu sank down on the bed with an exasperated sigh. "Why do people use drugs? Drugs that can damage your brain and other vital parts? I just don't get it. Aren't kids listening? Say no to drugs!"

Murphy moved toward the bed, reached out, and tucked a curl behind her ear. "Apparently, that catchy slogan isn't enough, Princess. So what are you going to do about it?"

"Me?"

"If anyone can sway the hearts and minds of young kids, I suspect it's you. Determine where you can do the most good and attack with a vengeance."

She blinked up at him, absorbing the confidence in his tender, heart-tripping gaze. Her mind whirled. "I could create specific loonytales geared toward drug education. Maybe I could submit them to schools as special programs. I think they have grants for things like that."

He smiled. "I'm sure they do."

"It would take a lot of time and dedication. To do it right, I'd probably have to give up my job at the Carnevale."

"So do it."

"And kiss my health benefits good-bye?"

"You don't have to worry about that."

"Of course, I do. Then again making a difference entails taking risks, right?"

His eyes twinkled with pride. "Right."

A man of action. A man of honor. A warrior. Lulu's heart pounded with an epiphany. She'd been so worried about falling for the man, that she'd missed the obvious. She'd been a goner at "hello." She loved Colin Murphy. This love was fierce and all-consuming and on an entirely different level than what she'd felt for Terry. The enormity of the realization struck her speechless.

The doorbell rang.

"That's Jake." Murphy's smile faded as he urged her to her feet and into his arms. "When I get home this battle with the Falcones will be over and we'll be free to begin. As clichéd as it is, you've inspired me to look on the bright side, Lulu. You're right. My kid could make a difference. I'd be happy with four or five." He stroked a thumb over her flaming cheek, smiled into her burning eyes. "How about you?"

Her stomach rolled with nausea. "I'd be happy with one," she choked out.

"Well, that's certainly a start." He brushed a kiss across her mouth, then stepped back and ruffled her hair with a cocky grin. "Don't look so glum, tiger. The Falcones are nothing compared to enemy forces." He strode for the door, winked over his shoulder. "OohRah."

She stared after him, dizzy with grief, as her happily-ever-after died a bitter death.

Chapter Twenty-Two

✳ Jake glanced over at Lulu just to make sure she was still breathing. She hadn't moved or said a word in forty minutes. Granted they were watching a movie, but her focus seemed to be somewhere else. The chick-flick was fairly amusing, and she'd yet to crack a smile. In fact, at times, she'd looked on the verge of tears. A far cry from the firecracker who'd given him hell days before.

He supposed she was worried about Murphy. He would ask, but that would mean conversation. He didn't feel like talking. He had worries of his own. He focused on the big-ass plasma screen—Murphy had an obvious boner for state-of-the-art electronics—but all he saw was a blur of flapping lips. All he heard was blah, blah, blah and a ringing phone. *His* phone.

He glanced at the incoming number. Joni. His gut clenched as he rose from the recliner, distanced himself from the television and Lulu, and hit the answer button. "Hey, sis. Everything okay?"

"Don't panic, Jake."

Nice. "Freaking hell, Joni."

"Afia's spotting."

His stomach dropped. "What?"

"Vaginal bleeding. She told me that she's only a few weeks along, and that she had a very upsetting night. It's probably nothing. Probably stress. I'm betting the doctor simply advises bed rest."

Jake palmed his forehead certain his brain was going to shoot through his skull. "Don't sugarcoat, Joni. Is Afia having a miscarriage?"

Lulu's head snapped up, and he realized then that he was shouting.

"I don't know." She sighed, lowered her voice. "I hope not."

"Where are you? Where's Afia?"

"We're on our way to the hospital. Carson's driving. Afia's sitting in between Kylie and me. She didn't want to call you. Said you're on an important case. But I knew you'd want to know."

"Put her on the phone."

"She's upset, Jake."

"Put her on the *fucking* phone." His body vibrated with the urge to ram his fist through a wall. He just wanted to hear her voice. He felt a gentle squeeze on his arm, glanced down and saw Lulu gazing up at him with tender support.

"Jake?"

"Baby." He struggled to keep his voice calm. "Are you in pain?"

"No. I'm just . . ." Her voice cracked. "I'm scared."

A thousand knives stabbed at his heart. "I know, honey. But you're with Joni and Carson. And I'll meet you at the hospital."

"You can't. You have to stay with Lulu." She sniffed back tears. "Like you said, I have Joni and Carson."

"I'll bring Lulu with me." Lulu shook her head no, but he ignored her.

"I love you, Jake."

"I love you, too, baby. Remember positive thoughts over negative." He slipped the phone into his inner jean jacket pocket, conscious that his hands were shaking. He leveled Lulu with a deadly glare. "You're going to the hospital with me if I have to knock you out and carry you."

The golden-haired pain-in-his-backside inched away, eyes brimming with tears. "I can't, Jake."

He wanted to throttle her. "My wife might be losing our baby."

The tears overflowed. "I know. I heard. That's why I can't go. I can't handle anything having to do with babies just now."

The pain in her voice intensified the crack in his heart. "I can't leave you here alone, Lulu. I can't call Murphy or Bogie or Rudy—"

"Jean-Pierre!" She was already across the room, rooting through that ridiculous poodle purse for her cell. She punched in numbers as she shooed him toward the door. "Go on, Jake. Afia needs you. I'll lock the door behind you, and I won't let anyone in but Jean-Pierre."

It sounded like a safe alternative. Or maybe he just wanted it to sound safe. He should've been five minutes down the road already. "Goddammit, woman."

"Hello? Jean-Pierre? Yeah, it's me. Fine, but I need you. Now." She rattled off directions, hurried over and physically shoved Jake toward the front door. "Fifteen minutes? Great. See you then." She signed off, disengaged the security system by punching in a code, and swung open the door.

All Jake could think about was getting to Afia. "Lock this

door behind me. Set the security system. Do *not* leave this house under any circumstances."

"Positive thoughts over negative," she said, before nudging him outside and firmly shutting the door.

* * *

The waiting was painful. Waiting to learn whether or not Murphy was safe. If his brother and Rudy were safe. Waiting to learn whether Paulie Falcone was out of her life and if a huge amount of drugs was off the street. And lastly, waiting to hear that Afia and her baby were okay. She'd only met the woman once, but she was kind and generous, and deserving of a child with the man she loved.

Positive thoughts over negative.

Lulu paced the spacious living room, trying to put a positive spin on Murphy's bombshell. *He wanted kids. Four or five no less.* She couldn't even give him one. She could suggest adoption, but she'd done that with Terry and he'd balked. He didn't even want to discuss the option. *"It's not the same."* Personally, she didn't see the difference. She didn't love Sofie any less because she was only her *half* sister. But men, apparently, were cut from a different cloth. In researching infertility, she'd also examined sociobiological studies, hoping to pinpoint Terry's increasing disinterest in sex. Time and again she'd read man's natural tendency was to pursue and procreate. The role being primal and important to his sexual drive.

Terry lost interest in her because she couldn't reproduce. Even if Murphy was open to adoption, she feared she'd eventually suffer the same fate with him. Just the thought of him shying away from her physically left her feeling undesirable, inadequate, and thoroughly sick to her stomach.

Her cell phone rang and she sagged with relief. She didn't

care who it was as long as they had good news, anything to lift her self-pitying spirits. "Lulu's Loonytales."

"Thank goodness," came a woman's voice. "I was afraid I wouldn't get you. This is Martha Hudson. I'm Jessie Hudson's aunt. You performed at Jessie's birthday party two years in a row and also at a family reunion a few months back. Do you remember?"

"Yes, I remember." Only because she'd dealt with the Hudsons on three occasions now. She didn't remember Martha per se, although her voice sounded familiar, but little Jessie's face was firmly in her mind. "How can I help you?"

"Jessie was involved in a car accident." The woman's voice quavered. "They don't know if she's going to make it through the night. Her mother thought, we all thought . . ." she paused, sniffled.

Lulu sank down on the couch, knees weak. This was one of those scenarios she'd discussed with Murphy. A parent's worst nightmare. She felt sick for Jessie and her family.

"Jessie treasures her personalized storybooks," the woman continued. "She calls you her very own fairy-tale princess. We were hoping that you'd be willing to pay her a visit at the hospital as Princess Charming."

"Of course." Jake's warning not to leave the house flashed through her head, but surely this counted as an extraordinary circumstance. Surely he'd understand, and besides, even now, Murphy and Bogie were in the process of capturing Paulie Falcone, so where was the danger?

The doorbell rang. *Jean-Pierre.* Lulu rose, grabbed her poodle purse and bolted. "I have to pick up my princess gown and change, Martha. I'll be there as quickly as possible."

"Bless you, Princess Charming."

Lulu signed off, keyed the security pad and flung open the door, her thoughts on a dying little girl.

"Bon soir, Chaton. I am glad you called. I need to talk and—"

"Later." She slammed the door behind her and prodded Jean-Pierre back toward his car. "We're on a mission."

* * *

"You're a fucking dead man." Paulie Falcone spat on Bogie's shoes.

Murphy itched to step in, but a squad of special agents stood between him and his brother.

Expression staid, Bogie pulled a pack of Wrigley's Spearmint gum from his leather jacket pocket. "Good luck."

To Murphy it sounded like a challenge. He couldn't decide if the comment was typical, cocky Bogie, or a thinly-veiled death wish. One thing was certain. His brother was in deep shit. Someone had blown his cover during the crackdown.

Other than that unfortunate glitch, and Murphy's near miss with a wise guy's bullet, Operation Candy Jar was a success. Rudy had come through with flying colors, delivering the couriers and drugs straight to Oz. A specialized team of federal agents had descended on Paulie Falcone and his accomplices, trading minimal gunfire and making fourteen arrests. By the end of the day that total would double. And although Rudy was being detained for questioning, Murphy had been assured he'd be released by tomorrow at the latest.

The only good guy to suffer was Bogie.

"Columbo's going into retirement," said the SAC, utilizing Bogie's undercover name.

"I don't care if he's going to the moon." Paulie leveled Bogie with a sinister glare as another agent slapped his wrists in cuffs. "When Vinnie learns that you screwed this family, and one of its members *literally*, there won't be a place you can hide."

Nonplussed, Bogie folded a stick of gum into his mouth. "Small price to pay in order to get a woman beater and millions of dollars of drugs off the street."

"Woman beater?" Paulie barked a sarcastic laugh. "I'm a lover, not a fighter."

"Stalker," Murphy corrected. He couldn't hold back. The longer he listened to this jerk, the more he wanted to annihilate his ass.

"Seducer," Paulie said with a slow, perverted smile.

Murphy's stomach burned with rage. "Since when does drugging a woman to lower her inhibitions count as seduction?"

"You're the second person in two days to accuse me of that." Paulie shook his head. "Not my style. My obsessions come to me willingly."

Murphy traded a look with Bogie. The man who'd called Lulu, the one who'd threatened her, had accepted responsibility for her drug-induced state.

"On the inside and still clueless." Paulie laughed as the SAC prodded him toward the door. "You're a fucking idiot, Columbo."

* * *

"Are you sure you do not want me to come inside with you, Chaton?"

Lulu unfastened her seatbelt. "I'm sure. Honestly, Jean-Pierre, I'm going to run in, change into my costume, and run out. Just keep the engine running. They said Jessie might not even make it through the night." She choked back frantic tears, feeling ultra-sensitive due to the night's multiple disasters.

On top of everything else, Jean-Pierre was leaving Rudy to move to LA. *Death and desertion.* Her nightmare come to life.

Spooked, she scrambled from the car. "I'll be right back."

She ran across the lawn and up the steps, nearly breaking her neck when she slipped on shattered remnants of her jack-o-lantern. Darned mischievous kids. Swearing, she pushed open the outer door, and squeezed past boxes and bicycles to get to the front door. Luckily, she'd already dug her keys out of her purse because it was pitch black. The porch light must've burned out. She was certain Murphy had left it on.

Racing against the clock, she pushed through the door and flicked on the foyer light. Nothing. "Gosh darn it!" It wasn't the first time they'd tripped a breaker, but she'd be hanged if she was going to venture into the basement to fuss with the breaker box. Jessie Hudson's face haunted her, blinding her with purpose. She had to get to that girl and fast. *Six years old*! How could fate be so cruel?

Snatching a flashlight from the hutch, she flew up the darkened stairs and down the hall. She had her sweater over her head and her jeans unzipped by the time she hit her bedroom. Her heart pounded in her ears, echoing like a monstrous clock.

Tick-tock. Tick-tock.

Wielding the flashlight, she tossed her poodle purse on the bed, kicked off her pants, and wrenched open her closet door.

Her princess gown floated toward her like a pink, sparkly ghost.

Stunned, she staggered backward, a scream welling in her throat.

The gown lowered. A man's face appeared, the flashlight casting eerie shadows and causing Lulu's heart to jackhammer. Dark hair, beady eyes. A flash of teeth in a predatory smile.

Shark!

* * *

"What do you mean you're not with her?" Concern and anger warred within Murphy as he paced outside the entrance of Emerald City. Though the actual sting had taken place inside the vacant dinner theater, early bird patrons of Flying Monkeys and Ruby Slippers now crowded the street along with local camera crews. Operation Candy Jar was fast escalating into a media frenzy.

"I'm sorry, Murphy. Something happened to Afia. I'm at the hospital and . . ."

Jake's voice faltered, stopping Murphy in his tracks. "Is she all right?"

"I think so. She's resting now." He cleared his throat. "Scared the hell out of me."

Murphy commiserated. He was worried about his own loved one. "Why didn't you take Lulu with you?"

"She said she couldn't be around babies."

"What the hell does that mean, and what's it got to do with—"

"Afia's pregnant."

"Well, hell." Murphy hitched back his jacket and slid a hand in his pocket, unclear on why she was hospitalized, unsure what to say. He opted for optimism. "Congratulations, Jake."

"Thanks." He cleared his throat again. "Listen, I'm sorry I deserted Lulu, Murphy, but she's not alone. JP's with her."

The tension in his shoulders eased a bit. "That's something I guess. Where did they go? His place?"

"What do you mean? I told her not to leave your house under any circumstance."

"I called home. No one answered."

"Did you try Lulu's cell?"

Murphy dipped his chin, rocked on his heels. *Hold it together, man.* "No answer."

"Dammit." Jake blew out a breath, relayed Jean-Pierre's cell number. "Do me a favor, after you speak with JP, call back and let me know what's up. How's Rudy?"

"Fine. He did great, and he's safe."

Murphy signed off with a curse. It was more than he could say for Lulu.

* * *

Lulu awoke feeling groggy and disoriented. Why was she in bed? Why was she wearing her princess gown? She pushed herself up on her elbows. What was with all the candles? Oh, right. Tripped breakers. She palmed her forehead and groaned. She remembered a flashlight, not candles. She remembered . . .

"Don't scream."

Not likely. The strangled feeling in her throat summoned those nightmares where you try to scream for help, but can't. She now knew the true meaning of *paralyzed with fear.* She stared at the man who'd issued the order, trying to bring him into focus. Had she fainted? Had he knocked her out? "Paulie?" she croaked.

"Paulie's brother." He moved closer. "Sal."

He looked so much like Paulie. His voice though . . . softer, huskier. *Oh, no.* "You're the one who had me drugged. The one who called."

"I'm the one, period. Paulie, your ex-husband, the others who leer at you at the Carnevale . . . none of them are good enough for you. You don't ask for it like the others."

Her stomach turned. "What others?"

"Paulie's others. The ones he bought with presents. Promiscuous girls who needed to be purified. You're not promiscuous. You've been waiting a long time for the right person."

What did he mean, *purified*? "I have a boyfriend," she blurted. Hadn't she told him that before? But this time she meant it. Maybe if he knew she was committed . . .

"No, you don't!" The flash of fury was brief, frightening. But not as frightening as the controlled, calm smile that followed. "He was a mistake." His cold gaze wandered slowly down her body, making her skin crawl. "I am willing to forgive one lapse." He reached into his pocket and pulled out a tape recorder. He hit a button, set the little black box on her dresser.

She recognized the tune immediately. "Someday My Prince Will Come" from the Disney classic Snow White.

"The waiting is over, Princess. I'm here." He held out his arms. "Dance with me."

Was he nuts? He'd broken into her home for God's sake! Seen her in her underwear. *Dressed her*. Her anger surged as she remembered why she'd come here in the first place. Jessie Hudson's sweet little face flashed in her clearing mind and propelled her to her feet.

He nodded his approval. "Make my dreams come true and this story can have a happy ending."

She absorbed the romantic setting, the candles, the music, her costume. The man was certifiable. He reached for her, and she slapped away his hands. "Stop it and get out of my way. There's a sick little girl—"

"Jessie?" The side of his mouth hitched up as he toyed with his pinkie ring.

Her mouth went dry. "How do you know about Jessie?"

"You keep excellent files, Princess. I chose a child I knew

you'd feel a connection with, someone you'd met several times. I knew you wouldn't be able to refuse a dying kid. I looked through your closet, chose a costume you'd have to come home for." He fingered the lace on her puffy sleeve. "Personally, this is my favorite. It personifies the real you." His eyes flickered with repulsive longing. "The innocent you."

Again, she shoved aside his hand, her mind reeling. "But Martha—"

"You mean Dara. A cohort of mine. The same woman who gave you the Ecstasy. I asked her to make a call, and she did." He angled his head, raised a brow. "I am not without my own loyal following."

The reminder that this man dealt drugs, to kids no less, sparked red haze fury. "You mean she only pretended to be Jessie's aunt? It was all a setup? Jessie's safe?" Relief and outrage poured through her like a tidal wave, powerful and overwhelming.

He smiled. "You are so naïve. Truly, it is your most endearing quality."

She disagreed. Her naïveté was her biggest fault. She inched back, bumping into her nightstand, freezing as he crept slowly forward. The music swelled. The candles flickered. She looked at this man through Murphy's eyes and knew there would be no reasoning, no diplomatic solution. Sal Falcone was a crazy mobster with a fairy-tale fixation. He'd drugged her. Stalked her. Now that she wasn't looking through rose-colored glasses, his intentions were nauseatingly clear. Rape or murder.

She curled her fists in the folds of her gown. *Fear is not an option*. She'd fight to the death. It was a startling realization. "When Murphy gets hold of you—"

"*Murphy's* out of the picture, along with his friend, and Paulie."

Her lungs seized. "What?"

The music stopped. Amazingly, Sal backed away from her to rewind the tape. It was her chance to make a mad dash, but his cryptic statement about Colin had her rooted.

"I've been watching you, Princess. The moment I saw Columbo going into Murphy's house, I knew we had a snitch in the family. Probably an undercover fed. I never trusted that long-haired prick."

Her already frantic pulse raced. He had to be talking about Bogie.

"I knew of the scheduled shipment. Assumed we were being set up. If my brother wasn't so damned arrogant, he would've smelled it too. Why do you think I'm not at Oz? It's perfect. With Paulie in prison, I'll finally get the responsibilities and respect I deserve. My uncle will see that Columbo gets his due. As for Murphy, let's just say that mistake has been erased."

Erased? As in eliminated? As in *killed*? Lulu's stomach cramped with nausea, her vision blurred.

A distant door creaked. Downstairs, footsteps. *Jean-Pierre*! He must've tired of waiting in the car.

Sal pulled a gun.

White noise roared in her ears. She couldn't protect Murphy, but she could save Jean-Pierre. She grappled behind her for a weapon. Her fingers curled around metal. Swallowing bile, she winged the makeshift weapon with the ferocity of a well directed club.

Sal dropped the gun and stumbled back with a guttural yowl. The sewing shears Sofie had threatened Murphy with days before were grossly implanted in his shoulder. He yanked the scissors free and stumbled again, knocking over a collection of candles.

Lulu watched in horror as her floor length curtains and bedspread ignited in flames.

Cursing, Sal grappled for his gun.

She whirled and ran from the room colliding in the dark with Jean-Pierre. "Run!" She shoved him toward the stairs. In the mayhem, the toe of her shoe caught in the hem of her gown. She tripped, falling forward and plowing into Jean-Pierre as a shot rang out.

Jean-Pierre tumbled down the stairs, a series of thumps that ended with a heavy thud.

"*Noooo*!" She didn't know if he'd fallen because of her or the bullet. She didn't know if he was dead or alive. Frantic, she scrambled to her feet, but Sal snatched her wrist, reeled her in.

Smoke plumed into the hall, searing her throat. But it was the thought of Murphy and Jean-Pierre, dead—gone from her life forever—that had her sobbing.

Sal sang "Someday My Prince Will Come" in her ear as the spreading flames burned orange and red in the background. He kissed her wet cheeks. "And they rode off into the sunset."

Somewhere through the haze of panic, she heard Sofie's voice in her head. Lulu stomped down hard on her attacker's foot with the spiked heel of her glass slipper, jerking free when he flinched in pain. "Over my dead body."

* * *

Murphy dinged the bumper of a vacant car as he squealed the Jag into Lulu's driveway, his attention on the flames shooting from a second-story window. Bogie was on the phone with the fire department as they cleared the car in tandem and raced for the burning house.

Murphy flashed on the past. He instantly connected with his mother, and at last he understood. She'd braved the inferno to save the man she loved. No thought. No choice. True love struck a person blind, deaf, and fearless. How could he have blocked such a simple concept for all these years? *She'd had no choice*.

He stormed up the front steps, focusing on the present, the future. Lulu. Praying that she'd made her way downstairs. Praying that she wasn't at someone's mercy.

They blew through the porch, the front door. Murphy spotted the body first. "Jean-Pierre. Dammit, I told him to wait in the car."

Bogie squatted, checked his pulse. "Banged up, but breathing."

Jean-Pierre stirred. "Upstairs."

"Get him out," Murphy said, foot on the landing.

The Frenchman shoved off help. "I'll get myself out. Get Lulu."

Gun drawn, Murphy topped the stairs, stunned to find his fairytale princess in a face off with an armed man, flames licking at the netting of her full skirt. The man limped toward her even as she removed her tiara. What the hell was she doing? Murphy aimed at the bastard, but thick smoke and her position compromised a clear shot. Bogie tapped his shoulder, signaling intent.

The man caught sight of Murphy, raised his gun at Lulu. "If I can't have her no one can."

She hurled her pointy-diamond-tipped tiara at the bastard's face, causing him to dodge the hit.

Murphy lunged.

Bogie fired.

Lulu landed with an *oomph* beneath Murphy's shielding body. He didn't stop to ask if she was hurt. He hauled her into his arms, and rushed down the stairs, frantic to get her out of the burning house. Bogie was on his heels, dragging along

Lulu's felled assailant. Murphy would have left the fucker to his fate.

Sirens whirred in the distance.

"Jean-Pierre," Lulu rasped in Murphy's ear.

"He got out." He spied the Frenchman sitting on the ground, propped up against his car, cell phone pressed to his ear. The man gave him the thumb's up. "He's all right." In more ways than one, Murphy thought. Even though they were unsure as to whether or not Lulu was in danger, he'd told Jean-Pierre to stay in the car until they arrived. The man not only had a mind of his own, he had balls.

Murphy dropped to his knees, settled Lulu on the grass. Neighbors had turned on their porch lights and flooded onto the sidewalks. Fire trucks and squad cars pulled to the curb. Chaos surrounded them, but Murphy only had eyes and ears for Lulu. His throat closed when he spied the blood staining her bodice and chest. "You're hurt." His hands roamed her body, gently prodding. "Where the hell are you hit?"

"Not my blood. His." She spoke in raspy, fractured sentences, her eyes glazed. "He had a gun. Jean-Pierre was coming. Had to do it."

Murphy cradled her in his arms, smoothed her disheveled hair off her sweaty, ash-covered face. She was in shock.

"I stabbed him. The scissors were there and I . . ." Her wide eyes overflowed with tears.

His heart broke, knowing how much that violent act had cost her. "It's okay, honey. You saved Jean-Pierre. You protected yourself." He was damned proud and relieved. "Your actions were justified." He hoped to hell she'd be able to accept the notion.

She focused on his face, threw her arms around his neck, and sobbed. "I thought you were dead."

His heart flooded with optimism and joy, even as firefighters battled destructive flames and paramedics struggled to save a psychotic mobster's life. The woman in his arms personified strength and goodness, and she was his. He brushed a kiss across her trembling lips. "I've never felt more alive."

Chapter Twenty-Three

✳ "What the hell were you thinking?"

Jean-Pierre winced as the nurse applied antiseptic to a gash on his forehead, one of three abrasions on his face. "That Lulu was in trouble. I know Murphy said to wait. But I couldn't." He glanced sideways at Jake. "Would you have waited?"

"No. But I'm a trained professional." Jake folded his arms over his chest and regarded his gentle friend with new found admiration. Guilt also flowed in abundance. "I'm sorry, JP. If I would've dragged Lulu along with me like my gut advised, this wouldn't have happened."

"Do not fret," the man said with a shaky smile. "Everything happens for a reason."

Jake's mouth curved. "You sound like Rudy."

Jean-Pierre broke eye contact and thanked the nurse when she stepped away.

"He sustained some nasty bruises on his arms and legs. He'll be sore for a few days," she told Jake. "But he's fine. You're free to go Mr. Legrand," she said, while backing out of the partitioned area, "although you do need to handle some paperwork at the administrative desk."

"I'll come with you," Jake said, when Jean-Pierre slid off the table. "I'm getting ready to sign out Afia. Can we give you a lift home?"

"I am not going home. But *oui*, a ride would be appreciated." He crinkled his brow, winced, and touched the bandage above his right eye. "What do you mean sign out Afia?"

Jake frowned. "What do you mean, you're not going home?"

Just then the curtain parted and Rudy stepped in. He took one look at Jean-Pierre and paled.

"I am fine, Rudy."

Rudy? Not, Bunny? Jake noted the strain in Jean-Pierre's voice. He also noted that Rudy, the caretaker, kept his distance. No emotional hug, no tender caress. He eyed the tense pair, his stomach sinking.

"Murphy told me what you did," Rudy said.

"Ah, *oui*, and he told me what you did." Jean-Pierre avoided eye contact, while buttoning his shirt. "Superhero fairies." He laughed without mirth. "Who knew?"

"At the risk of sticking my nose in where it doesn't belong," Jake said. "What the hell is going on?"

Rudy stroked his goatee and sighed. "Jean-Pierre is moving to LA."

Jake regarded the couple with shock. "You're breaking up?"

Rudy glanced at his partner with a pitiful look that made Jake extremely uncomfortable. What the hell had he confessed?

Jean-Pierre met Rudy's gaze, his voice gentle yet firm. "We are taking a break."

"Ah, Christ." Jake jammed his hand through his hair. "You can't tell Afia."

They turned to him in tandem. "Why?"

"She's pregnant."

Rudy palmed his forehead and smiled. "Wow. That's . . . wonderful."

Jean-Pierre nodded, smiled. "Congratulations, Jake. Is that why she is in the hospital?"

Rudy frowned, shifted his weight. "What's wrong?"

"She almost miscarried," Jake said, voice gruff. "Stress." He met Rudy's gaze, telegraphing the reason, without verbally laying blame.

Rudy licked his lips, glanced at Jean-Pierre. "We can't tell her."

"We are going to lie?"

"Damn straight," Jake said. With any luck they'd work things out. Maybe they just needed a shove. "At least until she's out of danger."

Jean-Pierre raked his hand through his shaggy hair. "I already committed to Luc." He winced. "I mean to the film."

Jake tried to fit pieces of the puzzle together while Rudy and Jean-Pierre faced off in a silent battle. He was sorry for their troubles, he *was*, but Afia and their baby came first. He pointed to Jean-Pierre. "You're moving to LA *temporarily* to work on a film. A once-in-a-lifetime opportunity," he said, using Rudy's words from earlier this morning. He turned to Rudy. "You are going to fly out there to spend quality time whenever your schedule allows." In his heart, Jake was convinced that these two were meant to be. Like he and Afia. Like Murphy and Lulu. "You are not *taking a break*. You're . . . maintaining a long-distance relationship."

The boys traded an uncomfortable look. "Agreed."

"Good." He whipped aside the curtain, desperate for a breath of non-charged air. "Afia's waiting downstairs. She'll sleep better if she sees you two are safe and . . . together." He glanced over to make sure they were following, frustrated when he noted their awkward body language. "For chrissakes, could you at least hold hands?" He shook his head, punched the elevator button. "I can't believe I just said that."

* * *

To say that he was baffled was an understatement. Somewhere between their emotional reunion, the hospital, and the police station, Murphy's relationship with Lulu unraveled.

"What do you mean, you can't do this?"

"Us," she'd squeaked through a new flood of tears. *"I can't go home with you. I can't move in."*

"Talk to me, Luciana. What's the problem?"

"Me."

That was four days ago.

Every minute seemed like a year.

Murphy sat at Charlie's Pub nursing a drink. Better than sitting at home feeling sorry for himself. He couldn't walk into his kitchen without having visions of Lulu juggling food products. Couldn't listen to his Motown collection without hearing her butchered lyrics. Forget about sleeping in his bed. He'd opted for the couch three nights running.

His back ached. His head ached. His heart was fucking roadkill.

"Hey." Bogie slid in on the stool next to him.

Murphy noted his brother's appearance with a raised brow. He'd chucked his South Philly duds the day after the sting in favor of a dark suit and tie—stereotypical special agent attire. Today he wore Levis and a long-sleeved flannel shirt. His standard autumn fare . . . when he was off duty. The ponytail was an interesting look. If you were a rock star or one of those Fabio dudes. "When are you going to lose the cheesy moustache and whatever's growing under your lip?"

Bogie scratched his jaw. "Actually, I'm thinking of growing a full beard."

"That'll go down well with your people."

"They don't give a shit what I look like when I'm on vacation."

"You're taking a vacation?" He was relatively sure his brother's name was listed in the dictionary under workaholic.

Bogie shrugged. "Sounds better than mandatory leave." He signaled the bartender for a drink. "Whiskey, neat."

"Psych evaluation didn't go so well, huh?"

"Damned shrink."

Murphy waved off Bogie's money when Thomas, his most valued employee, served the drink. "On the house."

"You'll be sorry you said that, bro." Bogie downed the whiskey and slid the glass back to Thomas. "Keep 'em coming."

Operation Candy Jar had been a success. Given the FBI's extensive evidence, Paulie and his minions would be serving serious prison time. Sal, the psychotic woman-beater, hadn't survived his gunshot wound. Bogie, aka Columbo, had rid the streets of a dangerous stalker and millions of dollars worth of Ecstasy. Along with the rest of his team, he'd effectively crippled the Falcone organization.

Still, his brother mourned the one thing he couldn't fix. Julietta Marcella. Learning of his deception, she'd sought solace in Vincent Falcone's home, no doubt drowning her misery in drugs and alcohol. Bogie couldn't help her if he wanted too, which he did. "Maybe this . . . *vacation* is a good thing," Murphy said, acknowledging the waves of pent-up frustration rolling off his brother. "A person can only dwell in the underworld so long before he starts to lose himself."

"Like you don't dwell."

"Not lately," Murphy said. "I've been sleeping pretty

well." He massaged a stiff neck muscle. "Or at least I was when Lulu was in my life."

"So what's up with the Princess?"

"Hell if I know."

"Have you tried to talk to her?"

Murphy smirked. "What do you think?" He traced his finger along the rim of his glass. "I know she's busy with the house restoration. The damage was pretty much contained to her bedroom and Sofie's. She asked her grandmother to let her handle the preliminaries. Didn't want to interrupt her honeymoon. Can you believe that? According to Sofie, Viv wasn't crazy about the idea. Wanted to be there for her girls. But Lulu wouldn't hear of it."

Bogie grinned. "Stubborn little cuss."

Murphy grunted. "She won't take my calls. Any info I've gotten has come from Sofie. I asked her if she knew why Lulu had pulled away. She said, 'yes.' "

"But she didn't feel right betraying her sister's confidence."

"You got it."

Bogie slid his glass away, signaling for a refill. "Do you even have a clue?"

"I think that showdown with Sal Falcone freaked her out."

"Understandable. That guy was whacked. The best-kept secret in the Falcone family. His brother and uncle have been covering up his *purifications* for years. I still can't believe I didn't catch on."

Murphy squeezed his brother's shoulder. "You gotta let that go, man. You're good, but you're not a mind reader." He shook his head, his thoughts on Lulu. "I'm pretty sure her troubles run deeper than the stalker angle. She's a peace activist and she stabbed a man. Then you killed the bastard in front of her eyes."

"He deserved it."

"Am I arguing? The point is, I don't think she can deal with my world. The intrigue. The ugliness."

Bogie stroked his moustache. "What would you give up for this woman?"

Murphy's chest ached with longing. What wouldn't he give up?

"You've got a nest egg. You've got Charlie's Pub." He glanced around the crowded bar. "This place is turning a profit, right?"

"Steady and climbing." Another investment. If Murphy had learned anything from his birth father, it was to invest in his future. It had seemed only fitting to name the pub after his Da.

Bogie spread his hands. "So walk away from the team. Look for your adrenaline highs somewhere else."

"I don't have to look. I know what rocks my world." A curly-haired sprite who skipped through life sporting pink high-top sneakers and a poodle purse. Sadly, both of those belongings had gone up in smoke.

"Then why the hell are you sitting here nursing that watered down scotch? Since when do you avoid confrontation? Who are you, and what have you done with my brother?"

He wasn't avoiding confrontation. He was giving her time to come around. Although he had to admit his patience had run its course. Murphy cracked his first smile in days. "Did you come in here for a specific reason? Or just to drink my liquor and bust my balls?"

"Although I did enjoy the whisky and ball-busting, there is an additional reason for this visit." He downed his third drink, angled his body toward Murphy. "I came to say good-bye. I'll fly back when the trial kicks in, but until then I'll be communing with nature."

"The cabin in the Pocono Mountains?" The Bogart family retreat. Bogie dug the seclusion, always had.

"Actually, I made an investment of my own. A home in the Superstition Mountains."

"You're moving to Arizona?" He was stunned and concerned. Bogie was tight with their parents, and Arizona was a freaking long haul from Pennsylvania. True, the Bureau had temporarily relocated Manny and Rosa under assumed names as a precautionary measure. And he understood Bogie separating himself from family until the Falcone fervor died down, but this sounded permanent.

"Time for a change," he said, while rising. "Listen, I'm driving to Philly to tie up some loose ends. I'm flying out tomorrow. Sofia and Legrand are flying out today. From Atlantic City International on a 4:00 p.m. flight. Seems I'm not the only one in need of change."

Murphy knew of Sofie's plans to move to Los Angeles with Jean-Pierre. He didn't know they were scheduled to leave today. He stood and walked his brother to the door. "How is it you know Sofie's itinerary?"

"The Bureau needed to know the whereabouts of all those connected to the case in the event they're needed for the trial."

Murphy lifted a brow. "So, it's not like you have a personal interest."

Bogie paused on the threshold, dipped his chin. "Let's not go there."

"Whatever you say." They'd make an interesting pair to say the least. Although, both struck him as being in a dark place just now. Probably not the best time to explore an infatuation.

"Safe to assume Lulu will be at the airport saying her good-byes to her sister and close friend." Bogie rolled a stick of gum into his mouth, slid on his sunglasses. "Might be nice if someone was there to ease the sting."

Murphy smiled. "Subtle." He caught his brother up in a hug, holding the embrace a little longer than usual. "I hope you find what you're looking for, bro."

Bogie gave him a quick squeeze, slapped his back. "Ditto."

Murphy watched him slide into his car and drive off, told himself to check in with the man at least once a week. He wasn't entirely convinced that seclusion was the answer to Bogie's problems. Then again every man conquered his demons in his own way.

Murphy had his own battle to fight. And he didn't intend to lose. He glanced at his watch. It was 1400 hours. Perfect. He had some shopping to do.

* * *

Rudy slid his hands into his pants' pockets to conceal their trembling. Watching Jean-Pierre check his baggage was harder than he'd anticipated. He'd spent three days preparing for this moment. Three days convincing himself that he'd be making a disastrous mistake if he succumbed to his own selfish needs and asked Jean-Pierre to stay. He needed to work on himself before he could work on the relationship. He wanted to come to Jean-Pierre whole. Confident. No reservations. He wanted Christmas in Vermont. *See it. Be it.*

Until then, Jean-Pierre would have his shot at success and Rudy would have to dig deep and have faith that Luc, or any other man, wouldn't step in and muck things up while Rudy was getting his act together.

"Are you okay?"

This from Afia who was standing to his right. Jake was standing to her right and glaring over her head at Rudy.

"I'm fine, honey. Just nervous for Jean-Pierre. LA's a big place."

"Yes, but he has a friend there, right?"

Rudy swallowed his jealousy. "Right."

"And Sofie's going with him. She seems very . . . capable. He'll be fine." She reached over and squeezed his arm. "I think it's wonderful of you to be so supportive of this opportunity. I mean, what if he won an Oscar for costume design? Wouldn't that be awesome?" She looked over at Jake. "If he does get nominated, we're all flying out." She palmed her stomach. "It could be our baby's first trip to the West Coast."

Jake placed his hand over his wife's and winked down at her. "You just want an excuse to see me in my tux."

"Please," Rudy said, grateful for the levity. "If I have to hear that story about car sex one more time . . ."

"Christ, Afia," Jake admonished with a twinkle in his eye. "Just because he's your best friend doesn't mean you have to tell him everything."

"I didn't tell him *everything*. Just . . . parts." She blushed and flipped her long hair over her shoulder. "Besides Rudy and I don't keep secrets."

Hell. Rudy fingered the collar of his blue oxford, loosened his tie. "Do you mind if I say good-bye to Jean-Pierre in private."

Jake jumped on the diversion. He nabbed Afia's hand and tugged her toward an ice cream vendor. "Come on, baby. I have a craving for Rocky Road."

Rudy smiled at Afia's befuddled expression, tamped down the guilt. This charade was for her benefit. And selfishly, he preferred Jake's "long-distance relationship" over Jean-Pierre's "we're taking a break."

He blew out a nervous breath and joined Jean-Pierre near the line of passengers waiting to pass through the metal detector.

He looked fiercely edible in his thigh-hugging jeans, black-and-white striped shirt, and blazing orange jacket. Like a sixth member of the Fab Five. He'd fit right into the West Coast scene. Rudy covered his anxiety with a forced smile. "All set?"

Jean-Pierre nodded, hiked his carry-on higher on his shoulder. Tears welled in his long-lashed eyes. "This is not easy."

Rudy's throat constricted. "Frankly, it sucks." An awkward moment passed before he got the nerve to ask what he'd been dying to know for days. "Can you ever forgive me?"

Jean-Pierre grasped his shoulder, his gaze wise beyond his years. "You were forgiven the moment you walked into my room and looked at me with those tortured eyes, Bunny. This is not about infidelity. This is about trust and respect for one another's feelings."

Rudy nodded. "You don't trust me. I understand."

Jean-Pierre quirked a sad smile. "How is it that you are so attuned to other relationships and not your own? It is *you* who lacks trust. Trust in me, in our love. *You* who chose to avoid confrontation rather than placing a simple phone call to let me know you weren't dead on the highway." He softened his voice, his gaze. "It is *you* who lacks the courage to embrace what you fear most. Perhaps you should stop looking to books for the answers, and look into your heart."

Rudy stared at Jean-Pierre, his throat clogged with the words he longed to say, but couldn't. Tears burned his eyes as he damned his crippling insecurities.

"Should you attain enlightenment, you know where to find me." Jean-Pierre glanced over at Afia, smiled, waved, then kissed both of Rudy's cheeks, squeezed his hand. "*Au revoir,* Bunny."

He died a thousand deaths as he watched Jean-Pierre pass

through security and beyond to the gate. "No, not good-bye," he whispered. "Until we meet again."

* * *

"Are you sure you don't want me to postpone this trip?"

Lulu smiled at her sister. "I'm sure." Why postpone the inevitable? She'd known it was only a matter of time before Sofie got the itch to leave town. She knew she craved validation and fame. Where better to pursue stardom than Hollywood? "If you have to go to Los Angeles, I feel better knowing you'll be rooming with Jean-Pierre. Maybe his friend can introduce you to the right people. You know what they say."

"It's all in who you know."

Lulu shrugged. "Sad but true. The bonus is that you are young, beautiful, and talented."

Sofie laughed. "You just described three-quarters of the women who frequent Hollywood casting calls."

"Yes, but you're special." And she hoped Sof found happiness and peace of mind soon.

"You're my sister. You're prejudiced, but thank you." She reached out and tugged on one of Lulu's pigtails. "Speaking of special, what about you? Promise me you're not going to continue to fret over that stalker freak."

Lulu rolled her eyes, trying to make light of the difficult subject. "Which one?"

Sofie smirked. "You know which one. The one you stabbed. The one who gives you nightmares."

Her cheeks burned. "It's a struggle, but I think I'm coming to terms."

"Anthony said the same thing." Sofie shifted on her spiked heels. "He's kicking himself for being a blind fool. Personally, I'm over the moon that he had no knowledge of the smuggling ring. The good news is, he broke off with his wacky fiancée for good." She angled her head, "Speaking of break-ups, please tell me you're going to work things out with Murphy. If someone looked at me the way he looks at you—"

"What about Joe?" She couldn't bear to think about Murphy. Not now. Not when she was saying good-bye to another loved one. Sofie and Jean-Pierre were relocating to California, Viv to Florida. The sadness was almost unbearable.

Sofie arched a brow. "What about him?"

"Well, I sensed, I thought maybe—"

"Forget it. If I never see that arrogant prick again, it will be too soon."

"If you say so," Lulu said, unconvinced.

Sofie glanced across the airport, moistened her lips. "Let's not drag this out, Lu. I hate mushy good-byes." She hugged Lulu tight, then kissed her cheek and hurried toward the security line. "I'll call you when I get there."

Eyes swimming with tears, Lulu lifted her hand and waved as Sofie disappeared. "Love you."

"I love you, too, tiger."

His voice flowed over her like warm honey and sunshine. Her skin prickled with anticipation. She turned and faced Murphy, her heart missing several beats before racing uncontrollably. She'd only been away from him for four days. It felt like eternity.

"I just thought I should say it aloud, get it out there, in case 'you and no other' was too subtle."

She clasped a hand over her throat, speechless. The sights and sounds of the bustling airport dissolved into a quiet blur. She saw Rudy, Jake, and Afia in the distance. They waved, then, as a tight trio, exited through the main doors, leaving her alone with Prince Charming and her fractured fairy-tale romance.

He held out a package, a big square box wrapped in pink and white polka-dot wrapping paper, and topped with a curly pink and purple bow. "I bought you something."

She stood there like an idiot, tongue-tied and staring, her emotions spinning like a tornado.

He grasped her elbow and led her toward a row of empty seats.

She plopped her butt in a chair before her knees gave way.

He sat next to her, placed the gift on her lap, and smiled as she fumbled with the wrapping.

Her hands trembled as she lifted the lid. She stared down at the contents, disbelieving. "A poodle purse."

"I had a hard time finding one. Sofie suggested a toy store."

She glanced sideways, furrowed her brow. Sofie knew he was coming?

"I needed to ask her your shoe size."

She pushed aside more tissue paper. *Pink high-tops.*

"A much easier find."

Other men might've bought her chocolates or roses. A former Marine, a fearless bodyguard, had cruised the mall for a poodle purse and pink sneakers. His thoughtfulness turned her brain to mush. She couldn't form a coherent sentence. Thank you would be a start, but even that lodged in her throat.

He took her hand and rubbed his thumb across her knuckles. "I love you, Luciana. I'll never get over you. I'll never love anyone as completely and genuinely as I love you."

Humbled and overwhelmed, her emotions continued to spin, fast and furious. "Oh, Colin."

"If it's my job, all you have to do is say the word. I don't have to work as a protection specialist. I have investments, income. Say the word and I'll walk away."

She snapped out of her daze, deeply affected by his proposition. "I don't want you to walk away. I admire what you do. You protect people from harm. You fight evil. That's important, and I know now that battles can't always be won with words."

"Wow. Okay. So it's not my job." He blew out a breath, rubbed his forehead. "Ah, hell. Is it because I said I wanted four or five kids? Jake said you had a problem with being around babies. Is it that you don't want children? You're so wonderful with kids. I just assumed—"

"Sometimes what you want and what you can have are two different things." Her eyes overflowed.

He thumbed away her tears and regarded her with tenderness and confusion. "You're talking to a man, honey. We're not as sensitive and attuned as women. You're going to have to spell it out."

"I'm infertile." The words scraped past her throat, but now that they were out she felt incredibly relieved. "I don't know why. Ten percent of infertile women never know the cause. I just know that Terry and I tried for years, and even with the help of medication, nothing ever happened."

He scraped a hand along his jaw. "Maybe it was him."

She cocked a weepy smile. "His girlfriend's pregnant."

He nodded, processed. "I don't want to minimize your . . ."

"Flaw."

"You're not flawed, goddammit." He tempered his frustration, kissed her hand. "You're perfect. Stubborn, impetuous, and sometimes infuriatingly naïve, but otherwise perfect."

She laughed. "Gee, thanks." She marveled that he'd taken her news so well. Then he blew her mind completely.

"Haven't you ever thought about adopting? Surely you don't love Sofie any less because she's your half sister. Bogie and I aren't blood, but tell us we're not brothers and we'd have to fight you."

She swiped away tears, her heart full. "You'd consider adoption?"

He stood and nailed her with a look that brooked no argument. "Don't move."

She sat there for five minutes, staring at her purse and shoes, wondering how she could have had so little faith in herself, in Colin. She felt strangely disconnected. Euphoric. And without the aid of Ecstasy. Joy bubbled within her as she contemplated forever with Colin Murphy.

"Hell, yes, I'll consider adoption," he said, picking up the conversation and startling her out of her thoughts. He reached for her hand and tugged her to her feet. "There are countless children around the world who need a loving home. Trust me, I know. I've seen them. And for the record, I don't give a damn about age or race."

"Oh, Colin . . . I . . . I . . ."

"Not one for small talk, are you?" he teased with a smile.

"I'm overwhelmed," she said in a rush. "I've never felt this way, and I know I'll never feel this way again. I was afraid . . ." *Fear is not an option.* "I love you, Colin. I love you so much, it's disorienting."

"Good to know." His eyes twinkled with relief and mischief. "Means the odds are in my favor." He held up two boarding passes. "We can be in Vegas in a few hours. Viv's already there. Sofie can hop a puddle jumper."

She blinked up at him, her heart tripping in her constricted chest. "What are you saying?"

"That I don't want to live apart for the next six months to a year while I court you with the intension of asking you to marry me. When it's right, it's right. I'm asking now." He smiled down at her, his heart and soul in his eyes. "Will you marry me, Luciana?"

She framed his face in her hands, kissed him with all the love in her heart, then eased away and wrapped her hand around the boarding passes. "Life's short. Live large. No regrets."

He smiled. "OohRah."

Jinxed

Beth Ciotta

Since the day beautiful socialite Afia St. John was born, her life has been plagued with bad luck. After losing her father and two older husbands in "freak" accidents, Afia now discovers her business manager has absconded with her fortune. Vowing not to rely on another man to guide her life, Afia refuses her godfather's help, and jumps at an unexpected job with Leeds Investigations.

With a pregnant, broke, sister, and an investigation agency in the red, control-freak Jake Leeds can't turn down the hefty but secret retainer offered by Afia's godfather for hiring her. Quickly seeing beyond her poor business skills, wacky superstitions, and sensationalized personal history, he realizes Afia is as generous in the heart as she is misunderstood.

But life is never easy for the woman born on Friday the 13th. Will the sexy PI be the good luck charm that puts her on a winning streak, or like everything else in her life, will their relationship wind up *Jinxed*?

ISBN# 0-9743639-4-4
Contemporary Romance
Available Now

www.bethciotta.com
www.medallionpress.com

Seduced

Beth Ciotta

A blazing hot action star?

Sofia Marino is a kick-ass heroine. Her role on the cheesy TV sitcom 'Spy Girl' has garnered her a male cult following, fan sites, and a hefty bank account. Okay. So it's not Scorsese or Spielberg, but at least she's in front of the camera doing what she was born to do. Faster than a director yells, "Action", her life goes from Hollywood to Hollyweird when she wakes up in Arizona, disoriented and caked with blood. With several hours of her life unaccounted for, Sofia finds herself on the run and under the protection of a man who once broke her heart with a single kiss.

A burned out FBI Agent?

On his last undercover case, Special Agent Joe Bogart crossed his personal line of honor to bust a crime family and their million-dollar drug ring. Afterwards, he retreated to an isolated home in Arizona to make peace with his past and to rid himself of his fascination with his sister-in-law's badass sister. The last thing he wants is more intrigue. The last thing he needs is Sofia Marino. Now the woman he can't get out of his mind is back in his life. He's smack dab in the middle of a murder mystery and in danger of losing his heart.

Hit Men, Hi-Jinx and Hot Sex . . .

Sofie and Joe embark on a mission to save not only themselves, but also their friends and family. If they succeed in staying alive, will these two jaded souls' then risk their hearts on each other, or will they forever remain . . . Seduced?

ISBN# 1-932815-23-6
Contemporary Romance
Ruby release from the Jewel Imprint
Coming 2005

Saddle up and brace yourself for a hilarious ride . . .

LASSO THE MOON
BETH CIOTTA

A Wild West adventure that will rope your heart!

Motivated by a childhood promise, Paris Garrett travels to the wilds of Arizona Territory (1877) to seek fame as a stage actress. Never mind that she doesn't possess a lick of experience or that her true passion is songwriting. Before he died, her beloved papa encouraged her to reach for the stars. She promised to lasso the moon! She's already slipped free of her over-protective brothers. Nothing and no one, especially some badge-wearing Romeo, is going to rein her in or stand in her way.

Joshua Grant's life went from diamonds to dirt in less time than a rattler strikes. His uncle was killed, leaving him with an opera house he doesn't want, and forcing him to quit the law enforcement job he loved. The topper: In order to keep his sidewinder snake of a cousin from inheriting, he has to honor his uncle's will and marry within two weeks. Life can't get much worse, and then he falls for an eccentric, spitfire songwriter with a mysterious past and a passel of troublesome admirers. Marrying Paris is about as smart as kissing a coyote, but that's exactly what he intends to do—whether she likes it or not.

Together they could realize their dreams.
That's if they don't drive each other crazy first!

ISBN# 1-932815-28-7
Historical Romance
Sapphire release from the Jewel Imprint
Coming 2006

All Keyed Up

by Mary Stella

A MAN WITH A PLAN …
At home in the Florida Keys on medical leave, undercover agent Jack Benton is on a mission to save his beloved aunt's failing dolphin facility. He's sure he can close a seven-figure deal, until his sassy Aunt Ruby accepts the proposal of a world renowned marine mammal scientist, Dr. Vic Sheffield. Against his better judgment, Jack must cooperate with the project, or break Ruby's heart.

A WOMAN WITH A DREAM …
More than the temperature in the Florida Keys heats up when Dr. Victoria Sheffield finesses her way into the facility under the guise of her famous father's name, hoping to finally establish herself as a top notch researcher. A lifetime of behavioral observation hasn't prepared her, however, for a suspicious, sexy *homo-sapien* like Jack Benton. She'll need every last point of her elevated I.Q. to outwit this wily alpha male. He knows she's hiding something, and sooner or later he'll figure it out. And to complicate matters, it's not only his suspicions Victoria is arousing.

When things begin to heat up between the scientist and the undercover agent, a Category Five attraction may cause the biggest storm of the season.

ISBN# 1-932815-08-2
Contemporary Romance
Available Now

www.mary-stella.com
www.medallionpress.com